Dragon's Claw

Dragon's Claw

Peter O'Donnell

THE MYSTERIOUS PRESS • New York

The Mysterious Press, 129 West 56th Street, New York, N.Y. 10019

Printed in the United States of America
First Printing: November 1985
10 9 8 7 6 5 4 3 2 1

Library of Congress Cataloging in Publication Data

O'Donnell, Peter.
    Dragon's claw.

    I. Title.
PR6029.D55D7   1985   823'.914   84-60561
ISBN 0-89296-105-8

*This book was originally published in Great Britain
by Souvenir Press.*

1

They brought Barboza to the place of execution at a few minutes before nine in the morning, loaded his own revolver with a single cartridge, showed him that it was in the correct chamber, and placed the gun in the holster at his hip. He stood blinking in the sunlight, trying to control his fear.

Barboza had deserted from the Cuban forces in Angola more than two years ago, but it was not for this that he was about to die on a small island in the Tasman Sea. He was to die because he had omitted to bar a door, and had fallen asleep.

Condori, the big Mexican in charge of the permanent guards, had said Barboza could die by the noose or the gun, and he had chosen the gun, but not because he thought it a better way to die, for he was a dull-witted man of stunted imagination. His choice sprang from the sullen resentment he felt towards the people who had ordered his death, the people who lived in the white house on the hill. With the gun, he thought, it was possible ... well, just barely possible, that he might manage to take his executioner with him. To do so would be very satisfying, for Barboza hated priests.

The gun at his hip was a Smith & Wesson .41 Magnum. Hit a man almost anywhere with a bullet from that six-inch barrel, and the large flat soft-point nose would knock him down as surely as a blow from a sledge-hammer. The thought brought a measure of comfort to Barboza in the last minutes

5

of his life, and helped to channel his fear into a taut readiness that was strangely clear-headed and far beyond his normal capacity.

Unshaven, still wearing the rumpled shirt and trousers he had been wearing when his fellow guards had bundled him into a cell two days earlier, he stood facing across the big patio to steps which zig-zagged in several flights up the green hill to the white walls of *Dragon's Heart*. Squinting against the sun, he could make out three figures on the long balcony. They would be the red-haired girl with big breasts, the China-man, and the tall man with a halo of tight golden curls, who moved and spoke like a fairy but who made your stomach twist with quick fear when he looked at you in a particular way.

In the two years that Barboza had been on the island, he had barely exchanged a word with any of the people who lived in the white house. They came and went, occasionally using the yacht which lay in the natural harbour on the far side of the hill, but more often using the twin jet Grumman Gulfstream. When they were away, Condori was in charge of the island with his seventeen guards. At this moment five were on duty, one each on the switchboard, the radio station, and airstrip control, and two at the harbour. The rest were spread along the strip of coarse grass edging the patio on Barboza's right, with the new excavation for the sunken garden behind them.

He turned his head a little to watch them, some standing, some sprawled on the grass, and he hated them because in an hour's time they would still be alive. Barboza had no enemies among them, and no friends. His natural surliness had made him an outsider, a position in which he had taken vague pride. His execution today would cause no grief among his recent colleagues. For them it would perhaps be a stimulating event in their rather tedious lives.

Regan, the Irishman, sat astride his motorcycle smoking absently. The narrow lightweight trailer was hooked behind, ready to carry Barboza's body down to East Point to be weighted and sunk. Chater, the Australian, and Li Gomm, the chigro from Macau, were still taking bets on the outcome; not on the simple issue of whether Barboza would die, for nobody doubted that, but on finer points such as whether he would succeed in drawing his gun, or actually getting a shot off.

Barboza remembered the execution of the Italian woman six months before, when bets had been laid on how she would react when the time came. She had made no attempt even to lift the gun which had been put in her plump hand, but had thrown it aside, folded her arms, turned her back, and waited a full four minutes for the vituperative obsequies to end with the shot that pierced her head. It had been disappointing, except for Tan Sin, the shrewd Malayan, who had won a month's money on her that day.

From a few paces behind Barboza, and a little to one side, Condori said, "He comes." Barboza's muscles twitched and his heart hammered suddenly as fresh adrenalin was pumped into his bloodstream. He lifted his head, and saw the figure moving down the steps from the white house. The guards on the grass fell silent. Those who had been sitting got to their feet.

The Reverend Uriah Crisp was dressed completely in black except for his white collar. His spidery legs, enclosed in drainpipe trousers, moved rhythmically as he descended step after step, turning at the end of each zig-zag, never needing to glance at the open Prayer Book in his hands as he began to

7

recite in a high, piercing voice which carried easily to those watching from the balcony above.

"I will take heed to my ways, that I offend not in my tongue. I will keep my mouth as it were with a bridle, while the ungodly is in my sight."

The voice rose and fell, but there was nothing unctuous in the manner of delivery, only a controlled yet ever increasing fury. *"Forget not the voice of thine enemies, O Lord! Thou smotest the heads of Leviathan in pieces, and gavest him to be meat for the people in the wilderness."* The voice quivered with terrible passion. *"Lift up thy feet that thou mayest destroy every enemy!"*

The Reverend Uriah Crisp's face was thin and hollow-cheeked. As he lifted his head to cry to the heavens the men below could see the fringe of gingery hair protruding from beneath the round black low-crowned hat he wore. *"For now is the axe put unto the root of the tree, so that every tree that bringeth not forth good fruit is hewn down and cast into the fire ..."*

Barboza drew in a deep breath and released it slowly. Now that it had begun, he felt almost calm. He knew that when the priest came down the last of the steps on to the patio he would halt there, facing Barboza and about ten paces away. Holding the Prayer Book in his left hand, he would take off his hat with his right, and hold it over his chest, almost as if offering a target. The harangue against sinners would continue for several minutes ... unless Barboza tried to draw his gun.

It was not a matter of deciding whether to take the initiative; only a fool would throw away such a substantial advantage. It was a matter of deciding the precise moment to act, to make the utmost of that advantage.

"Make thine enemies as stubble before the wind, O Lord,

like as the fire that burneth up the wood, and as the flame that consumeth the mountains. Persecute them with thy tempest and make them afraid with thy storm. Let them be put to shame, and perish." The last word was a spluttering shriek of fury, then the voice dropped to a low fierce tone and began slowly to rise again.

The Reverend Uriah Crisp came down the last twelve steps to the patio, still reciting, and slowly took off his hat. Pale grey eyes, red-rimmed, stared fixedly at Barboza over the top of the Prayer Book. "*Man that is born of woman hath but a short time to live, and is full of misery. He cometh up and is cut down like a flower ...*"

Barboza screwed up his eyes in concentration, taking great care not to let his right hand make any unintentional movement. Some of his recent colleagues were good with a handgun. In the small cinema attached to the guards' quarters, blue films came first in popularity but Westerns came a close second, and among the guards there was keen interest in target shooting, varieties of holster, and quick draws, no doubt stimulated by the remarkable demonstrations of the Reverend Uriah Crisp. Barboza was not among the enthusiasts. His training enabled him to shoot reasonably accurately with a handgun, and for him the rest of it seemed childish, like playing at cowboys.

His lack of interest in such diversions was to be regretted now. He could never get the .41 Magnum out really fast, there was no hope of that. But if he could just manage to get it out fast *enough ...*

"*Forasmuch as it hath pleased Almighty God of his great mercy to be about to take unto Himself the soul of our dear brother, here about to depart, let us remember the anger and judgments of the Most High. For the living God shall pour down rain upon the sinner; snares, fire and brimstone, storm*

9

and tempest. He will burn the chaff with the unquenchable fire. Up, Lord, and cast them down!" Again the hard, penetrating voice rose to a peak of frenzy before dropping to a lower pitch, grieving and regretful. *"So shall the sorrows of death encompass him ..."*

With an effort Barboza broke from the almost hypnotic effect of the braying voice and made the move he had planned during a long sleepless night. Slowly, using his left hand, he took the denim cap from his head. With a sudden flick of the wrist he sent it spinning through the air towards the face of the Reverend Uriah Crisp. Then his right hand darted to the gun butt at his hip.

"... So shall the pains of hell come upon him ..." The man in black made no move until Barboza touched the butt of the revolver. Then the flat round hat dropped from where the Reverend Uriah Crisp's right hand held it in front of his chest. The hand blurred. A shot clipped the peak of the spinning cap and continued on its way into Barboza's brain, on through the back of the skull, a flattened slug of lead now, to drop at last some way short of where the ground fell away sheer to the sea in a low cliff. Barboza's half-drawn gun slid back into its holster and he fell, his shoulders hitting the white paving stones of the patio with a solid thump.

"... for the Lord shall thunder out of heaven with hailstones and coals of fire," continued the Reverend Uriah Crisp, *"sending forth his arrows to scatter them, and casting forth lightnings to destroy them."* His voice had flowed on without pause or falter during the brief moment of action. The open Prayer Book was still held in front of him, level with his chin. Beneath it, his right hand now held an automatic, a Colt Commander with a lightweight alloy steel frame and chequered walnut grips.

"Amen," said the Reverend Uriah Crisp. He closed the

Prayer Book and put it into the pocket of his jacket, applied the safety catch on the automatic and pushed it back into the armpit holster, a modified Berns–Martin transverse holster with a friction screw, strapped beneath the left breast of the jacket. Bending to pick up his hat, he dusted it with a large yet strangely elegant hand, and set it carefully on his head.

"I am the Hammer of the Lord," he said humbly, "an unworthy instrument of His hand. By His will has the sinner died, and of His mercy have I been spared this day." He turned away and began to mount the first flight of steps.

The guards stirred. Chater said resentfully, "I never reckoned Barboza had the bloody sense to try a trick. All right, I'm paying threes on that, and evens on the half-draw. All other bets lose."

Condori moved to look down at the dead man, lit a thin cigar, then raised his eyes to follow the Hammer of the Lord. Condori could not remember being afraid of any man, but that one made him feel uneasy. If he ever had to kill the crazy priest, Condori thought, he would go about it by night and by stealth rather than by any sort of confrontation. He exhaled smoke and called, "You two. Riza and Fuzuli. Get this on Regan's trailer." He touched the body with his toe. "Check the gun into the armoury, and bring his personal effects to my office."

On the long balcony of the white house two men and a girl watched the spidery black figure mounting the steps. Beauregard Browne shook his golden head and laughed. "Isn't he superb? I mean, really. Isn't he?"

Dr. Feng Hsi-shan considered the question. He was a psychiatrist, specialising in mind-bending, who had left the People's Liberation Army of the People's Republic of China because he had diagnosed a political condition in which it seemed probable that his own mind might be severely bent. He had been here on Dragon's Claw island with his new employers for only four weeks, and would have found them as incomprehensible as aliens from another galaxy if he had not spent three years dealing with American prisoners during the Korean War, and another two in New York keeping a psychiatric eye on the Chinese delegation to the United Nations. He spoke perfect if rather stilted English.

Now he said, "Superb? Yes. Mr. Crisp is certainly very efficient at his job, which I assume to be that of killing undesirable persons. He is also, of course, a schizophrenic paranoid, and quite incurable. Naturally I have not said this to him."

"But my dear old prudent medico, he wouldn't be in the least perturbed," said Beauregard Browne, flapping a hand vaguely in the direction of the man climbing the steps. "He really wouldn't. Clarissa will tell you."

Dr. Feng looked at the striking red-haired girl in the white dress, and waited inquiringly for her to speak. She was gazing absently down the hill, very gently touching her breasts with her palms, the fine large eyes a little glazed. Dr. Feng had discovered that Clarissa de Courtney-Scott, who held the position of Beauregard Browne's secretary, was a young woman of great administrative ability who virtually ran the island in matters of everyday organisation. He had also discovered that she was a nymphomaniac who served all males in *Dragon's Heart* with immense enthusiasm, including The Patron when he was in residence, but excluding the guards.

Dr. Feng said, "Do you agree, Miss de Courtney-Scott?"

She came out of her daydream and gave him a smile showing large white teeth. "About Uriah? Oh God, yes, you can't possibly offend him, in fact it's sometimes frightfully funny with him, isn't it, Beau?"

"Delirious." Beauregard Browne turned his gaze on Dr. Feng, who wished he wouldn't. Perhaps it was the very slight cast in the deep violet eyes which made this young man's stare so chilling, for the effect was the same whether he was in an angry or light-hearted mood.

"I remember saying a dreadful thing to him one night," Clarissa went on. She gave a smile of self-deprecation. "It really was rather unkind of me, but he'd been rambling on for ages about the holiness of the gun as an instrument of God's judgment. Then he went into a long sort of hypothesis that he might actually have saved Jesus if only he'd been there at Calvary with his Colt. It really was too much, even for Uriah, because he was screwing me at the time, and he kept stopping at just the wrong moment to rave about how he would have destroyed all the sinners."

Beauregard Browne said, "Darling, you're putting us on."

"No, honestly, Beau. I was thinking that if he didn't get me over the hump soon I'd go out of my mind, but completely. So I absolutely screeched at him: 'I know you can't help being a raving lunatic,' I yelled, 'but if you don't stop acting like one and get moving, Uriah, I'll bloody *ruin* you before you get off this bed!'" She gave a half-laugh and looked slightly ashamed.

"What happened?" asked Dr. Feng, fascinated.

"Oh, he just heaved up a bit and looked down at me with a sad smile and said something like: 'I am Uriah, which means Fire of the Lord. I am the Hammer of God. It was prophesied that His servants should be mocked and reviled, but I glory in it, for the Lord is with me.' Then he set his teeth in my shoulder and went at it hammer and tongs." Clarissa sighed and ran a hand sensuously over a scroll topping the wrought iron balustrade. "It was rather good," she added wistfully.

Beauregard Browne giggled. "He won't be rather good for

the next few days, poppet. Dispatching a sinner always quietens him down for a while."

"There's no need to laugh about it, Beau," said Miss de Courtney-Scott plaintively. "It's jolly rotten for me, being a man short. I mean, it's not awfully funny to be insatiable, you know. People don't understand. Gosh, I remember when I was young how Daddy used to fly into a simply colossal temper when I tried to explain."

Beauregard Browne rolled up his eyes. "Your Daddy. Now there was a pain in the arse. You should have let me attend to him."

"Well ... it would have seemed a bit mouldy, Beau. After all, he wasn't *too* bad, and anyway it would have looked frightfully suspicious so soon after what happened to your parents."

Dr. Feng made a mental note. He had started a dossier on each of his colleagues out of long habit, and was slowly adding little pieces of information as they came his way. He knew, not in detail but in vague outline, that years ago Beauregard Browne and Clarissa de Courtney-Scott had lived next door to each other in detached houses in Buckinghamshire. He knew that Browne's father had been a prosperous solicitor, his mother French and alcoholic. Clarissa's father had been a top surgeon who had died of a massive heart attack while in harness, in fact while operating on a patient for hernia. In his collapse he had made a large, accidental and fatal incision, an event which was still a standing joke between his daughter and Beauregard Browne.

Dr. Feng was almost sure that Beauregard Browne, while in his late teens, had arranged the death of his parents in some way, but had yet to pick up confirmation of this. The red-haired girl's last remark added a little weight to the theory but was hardly conclusive. Still, as a psychiatrist he was used to working with tenuous evidence.

14

There were more gaps and speculation than substance in Dr. Feng's notes. He would dearly like to have known when Beauregard Browne and Clarissa de Courtney-Scott had first become a criminal team, and when the Reverend Uriah Crisp had joined them. He had been told by The Patron that these three had been operating together for a number of years, but precise data on them was annoyingly scanty.

Clarissa called, "Well done, Uriah. Jolly good." The man in black had reached the garden immediately below the balcony, walking at a solemn pace, his usually intense face relaxed and almost sleepy. He glanced up and shook his head pityingly. "Lay no merit upon me, dear friend. Had the man been without sin, he would have prevailed. It is ever the Lord's finger on the trigger, not mine."

He made a sign of blessing and moved on into the house. Beauregard Browne turned and went through the open windows into the big living room. Clarissa and Dr. Feng followed. The furnishing was simple but pleasant, canework chairs and settees, folk-weave cushions, thick rugs scattered on a cool terrazzo floor, a few oriental pictures, and some Polynesian wood-carvings on the walls.

Beauregard Browne sprawled on a settee, carefully hitched up a leg of his pale lilac trousers before crossing that leg over the other, and said, "Drinkies, Clarissa."

Dr. Feng said, "Our friend, Uriah. May one ask how he selects sinners for execution?"

"For trial," Beauregard Browne amended, and stared fixedly at Dr. Feng for several seconds. "Yes, one may ask, Doctor, and the answer is that he doesn't select them. They are selected by the Almighty, who informs me, and I inform Uriah. Uriah may be the Hammer of God, but I am, as it were, His earthly Mouthpiece."

Dr. Feng chuckled. "Most convenient."

"So we have found, even in more complex circumstances."

"More complex?"

"When we have no leisure for the delicious trial-by-combat system. When we are operational, Doctor. I might, for example, post Uriah outside a door and tell him that *anyone* who comes along is a sinner. The mere act of coming along is definitive."

Clarissa put a tall iced drink in Beauregard Browne's hand and laughed. Dr. Feng watched the bouncing of her fine and unfettered bosom with interest. "Honestly Beau," she said, "you're sometimes so frightfully crude with Uriah. I mean, you practically say it as plainly as you said it just now, hardly wrapping it up at all. Last time, in Milan, well, I really wondered how he could go on believing you about sinners and all that. Doctor?"

"A fruit juice, please. I think you will find, Miss de Courtney-Scott, that on one level Mr. Crisp has never believed it. On another level he persuades himself to do so by his own rhetoric, because it is necessary if he is to use a gun. That is his over-riding need, to use a gun." He looked at Beauregard Browne. "May one ask if he is a genuine clergyman?"

The violet eyes fixed disconcertingly on Dr. Feng's left ear. "Well now, beloved physician, one may not ask *too* many questions. It's a bad principle, don't you think? However, just this one. Yes, Uriah was duly ordained. One glimpse of his father and you realised that the poor sod was ordained from birth to be ordained. John Knox, fire and brimstone— or do I mean Calvin? Clarissa, do I mean Calvin?"

"Golly, I don't know, Beau. I remember we spent about a month at that ghastly place in Berkshire as paying guests at the vicarage, while you were sizing up the job at Homerton Hall."

"Clarissa opened new doors for Uriah," said Beauregard

Browne, and grinned. "We were supposed to be a married couple, of course, but I'm hardly enough for her, even at my most hetero."

"Uriah showed me his secret," said Clarissa. "Ten years of a magazine called *Guns & Ammo* in a chest under his bed, plus a dozen different model handguns, perfectly carved in hardwood and accurately weighted, and a variety of home-made holsters." She carried a glass to where Dr. Feng sat, and gave him a stimulating view of her cleavage as she bent to put the drink beside him. "How much later was it when we found him in California, Beau?"

"About two years, sweetie. But it turned out that he vanished from the vicarage only a month after we left, and got himself equipped for real shooting as soon as he reached the States." Beauregard Browne looked at Dr. Feng. "Would you know what a dude ranch is?"

"Yes. I have not seen one, but I understand the term."

"He was doing shooting exhibitions there, dressed as a cowboy. He's a natural genius with a gun, of course, but unfortunately he's terrified of horses, cows, or anything on four legs bigger than he is, and this rather marred his Junior John Wayne image." One elegant hand flickered in a languid gesture. "So we took him away and began training him for more suitable work. And found a new name for him—just to keep the record straight in your little dossier, Doctor."

Dr. Feng nodded slowly, noting his own unease with professional interest. "Yes, I have a case-book on him," he said. "After all, I am a psychiatrist, Mr. Browne."

"True, duckie. And at this moment I have a passionate interest in your psychiatric opinion, but not of Uriah, thank you very much. It's the escapee whose condition engages me, as it does Our Patron, who spoke somewhat tersely to me on the radio link yesterday."

17

Dr. Feng stared. "I hope you do not suggest that I am to blame for the fact that Mr. Lucian Fletcher escaped from custody and from the island?"

Beauregard Browne smiled wearily. "Don't be touchy, my little cabbage. You're supposed to be inscrutable, aren't you? Barboza went to sleep on duty and left the door unbarred. Lucian Fletcher must have been sufficiently *compos mentis* to do a bunk. No blame to you. Barboza was immediately responsible, and he won't do it again. Condori was second-arily responsible, and I've kicked his arse and stopped his pay." He smoothed an eyebrow. "I myself am ultimately responsible, but I shan't depart *à la* Barboza, possibly because Our Glorious Patron knows that my mental anguish will be suffering enough, but more probably because I should be extremely difficult to replace and even more difficult to kill, and I'll have another little drinkie, Clarissa, *ma belle*."

She emerged, rather heavy-eyed, from an erotic reverie, said "Righty-ho," and rose to take his glass.

Beauregard Browne said, "Now let us consider the alter-natives for the boring Mr. Fletcher. He took a small inflatable with enough fuel for about twenty-four hours, and since he got away soon after dusk he had a nice long start. With the radar being on the blink I rather doubt if we'd have spotted him even if I could have taken up the Teal, but that was stripped down for maintenance in the hangar, and our mad scudding around in the powerboat got us nowhere."

"The sea's jolly big," said Clarissa, handing him his replenished glass.

"Profoundly true, sweetie. And that's rather good for us. Outside the shipping lanes you can go on practically for ever without seeeing a damn thing except lots of water. So what's most likely to happen is that within the next few days the tedious Mr. Fletcher will die of thirst, since he had no water as far as we know. If he did, it will take longer, that's all. And eventually, if the boat isn't sunk by a tropical storm or a petulant whale, he might be found years hence, anywhere on the seven seas, a drifting skeleton, yet another mystery of the unfathomable briny. Have you arranged for the technician to fly in and put the radar right?"

"Tomorrow, Beau."

"A vigorous chap. He might also serve you while he's here, my pretty." Beauregard Browne stretched out a leg and admired the lilac toenails revealed by the open sandals. "The only other alternative for our Mr. Fletcher is that he just might be picked up. Highly improbable, like winning a football pool, but then people do win football pools, don't they?" He looked at Dr. Feng again. "Now, if that happens, what we want to know is this, O Flower of the East. Are you *quite* sure your brain-washing will hold?"

Dr. Feng took out a packet of cigarettes and lit one. He knew Beauregard Browne did not like him smoking, but felt this was a suitable moment to show a measure of self-assertion. "You know I cannot guarantee that, Mr. Browne," he said casually. "I had Mr. Fletcher under treatment for sixteen days, and would have continued for perhaps another seven before making him available to you for testing. However, it is my opinion that the memory blocks I created will resist penetration either by Mr. Fletcher himself or by any person other than myself."

Clarissa was paying attention now. She said briskly, "But he escaped, Doctor. Surely he can't fail to remember what he escaped from. I mean—his cell, you, the guards, this island, everything and everyone he saw here."

"One must realise, Miss de Courtney-Scott, that I had reached the preliminary testing stage with Mr. Fletcher. I was opening and shutting various boxes in his mind, both by

19

immediate suggestion and by post-hypnotic suggestion. This is essential in order to establish total control, and you may remember my instructions were that I should not destroy his memory or personality, but simply erase selected memories." Dr. Feng shrugged. "One must operate the keys to make sure they work, you understand."

Beauregard Browne said, "Do I take it, dear friend, that the ghastly Fletcher was able to conceive the very idea of escape because you had temporarily opened a few boxes in his napper?"

"Napper?"

"His head, sweetie-pie. You had allowed a little memory to seep out."

"Yes. For a time he knew where he was and knew what was happening to him. But there was at all times an overriding command which limited the period of his awareness. The boxes, as we have called them, would be firmly sealed from nightfall on the day following his escape."

"You can be as precise as that?"

"Yes."

"But not quite so certain that sometime, somewhere, a box might not just accidentally pop open?"

"It would require a massive shock, and even this would be unlikely to break down the blocks."

Beauregard Browne drained his glass and stood up. "Then we shall have to see, shan't we?" he said lightly. "We shall also have to keep our ear to the ground, I fancy. And if the dreary Fletcher *should* be spared a watery grave, then we shall have to be rather spry. But for the moment I shall go and spend an hour on Paradise Peak with my little friends."

Clarissa had resignedly expected this, knowing that the Reverend Uriah Crisp was not the only one whose interest in her body was somewhat assuaged by a killing. In the days before radar had been installed, Paradise Peak had served as a lookout point. Now it was Beau's special preserve, with the long glass-houses and all the equipment for tending his little friends, the variety of rare orchids he grew with such immense delight and pride. He would go to the chair-lift now, and be carried up to the peak, there to perform his green-fingered mysteries. Clarissa remembered his white fury when a freak storm had broken a few panes of glass, killing some of his specimens at the time of their blooming. After that, workmen had been brought in to build a small chalet up there, a hut where Beauregard Browne would sleep if very severe weather was forecast, ready to improvise repairs with polythene sheets.

Clarissa sighed inwardly. It was very beautiful on the wide sunken crest of Paradise Peak, and the thought of Beau delicately cross-pollinating his little friends up there, or whatever he did with them, was very frustrating. She could have found much more enjoyable things for him to do.

Dr. Feng carried his cigarette to the window to flick ash from it. "What is my situation here, now that I no longer have a subject for treatment?" he said.

Clarissa squeezed her hands palm to palm between her substantial thighs, and her eyes became a little dreamy. Beauregard Browne said, "Oh, you'll have another in due course, Doctor dear. Our Illustrious Patron remains greatly attached to his new idea of preserving secrecy by adjusting the *memory* of his distinguished guests rather than by adjusting their life-span. Meantime you must simply enjoy yourself here in whatever way you please. The facilities are reasonably comprehensive, as you have seen, and I've decided that they now include Miss de Courtney-Scott—if she so wishes, of course."

"Of that you may be sure," said Clarissa, and laughed with

relief. "Honestly, I'm in an awful state. It always turns me on frightfully, watching Uriah deal with a sinner." She stood up, moved across the room and stood very close to Dr. Feng, a tall meaty girl, her eyes level with his, her large breasts almost touching him. "Oh, Dr. Feng," she said earnestly, "I do hope you find me sexually desirable."

Dr. Feng was undergoing a release of tension, for certain logical fears as to his immediate future had apparently proved groundless. Until this moment the girl had aroused no particular emotion in him, but quite suddenly the female animal potency of her, urgent and demanding, caught him by the throat and sent desire surging through his loins. He thought of his cool, air-conditioned bedroom, and the girl's big naked body writhing with his on the bed. A prickle of sweat touched his brow, and he forced a smile. "Of that you may be sure, Miss de Courtney-Scott," he said.

Beauregard Browne ran a hand through his tight golden curls, picked up a telephone, and spoke into it. "Radio room." After a pause he said, "I want a twenty-four hour listening watch set up on emergency frequencies, with regular sweeps on the amateur bands. Arrange it, will you." He put the instrument down, waggled his fingers vaguely in the direction of his companions, and said to Clarissa, "I'll need you for a couple of hours dreary old workies in the office after lunch, poppet. Do make sure our matchless mind-bender doesn't spare himself with you this morning, because your work does become a teensy bit sub-marvellous when you're not entirely slaked, doesn't it? I mean, doesn't it?"

2

The Treadmill stood in three acres of ground on the Thames, an old and rather rambling pub with a good class of customer. It was two hours since the last drinks had been served, and a quarter of an hour less since the last car had pulled out of the car park into the Berkshire lanes.

In a large attic room Willie Garvin sat at a long table against the wall, wearing a dark blue bathrobe. With the earphones covering his ears, and his eyes on the vernier control as he turned it slowly, he was aware of no movement behind him until two hands came to rest gently on his shoulders. He slipped the earphones down round his neck and turned to look up at Janet Gillam with a smile of apology.

"Sorry, Jan. I didn't mean to wake you."

"You didn't. My leg itched, and I woke up and you weren't there, so I came on the prowl." The light shone from her chestnut hair as she nodded at the radio. "Are you talking to Modesty?"

"I've been trying for the last four days, but no luck. Can't pick 'er up." He yawned, switched off the set, and stood up. "Come on, let's get back to bed."

She put a hand on his chest. "No, you go on trying for a wee while. You would if I hadn't stayed the night, wouldn't you?"

He cocked an eye at the ceiling. "M'mm. I suppose so. But it's not polite with you 'ere."

Lady Janet Gillam laughed. She had been Willie Garvin's regular girl for a long time now, and still liked him better than any man she had ever known, even though well aware that he was exclusive to her only within a limited radius. You took Willie on his own terms, and he took you on yours; but only if it suited you both. If not, there were no negotiations and no hard feelings.

She said, "How would you like me to go and make a cup of tea?"

"Now you're 'eaping coals of fire."

"That's right. I'll teach you to seduce a female member of the gentry and then sneak out of bed in the night to call another bird." Her face changed. "She's not in danger is she, Willie?"

"No, no, nothing like that, Jan. She's just taking a sloop down from Brisbane to Wellington for a friend."

Lady Janet shrugged and managed not to stare. "But isn't everybody these days?"

"You can't move for sloops in the Tasman Sea."

"How many crew?"

"It's just a thirty-four foot job. She's on 'er own."

"Ah. There are some who might think there was a smidgen of danger in it, despite your airy 'No, no.'"

"I meant nobody's gunning for 'er. It's not like it was at Chateau Lancieux."

"Well that's something." A shudder touched her at the memory of that long day and night in a remote part of Ariège, when she had been caught up with Modesty and Willie in their attempt to save a man named Tarrant, a secret service chief, from torture and death. They had come within a hair's breadth of defeat, and in those endless hours of disaster she had known captivity, humiliation, and the pulsing terror of being hunted by armed men out to kill. In those hours, too, she had been purged of any lingering resentment or jealousy of the bonds which linked Willie Garvin with the strange dark girl he had served for so long.

Now she pulled Willie's head down and kissed him. "Go on. Try giving her another call. I'll make some tea."

He watched her as she went out of the room, limping a little. From just below the knee, her left leg was artificial. She had lost it before he had known her, in the same car crash in which her drunken husband had killed himself. She now ran a successful farm a few miles from *The Treadmill*, working hard and getting her hands dirty, but the fact of her being the daughter of an earl, with a noble Scottish lineage reaching back six hundred years, showed in the bones of her face, in her eyes, her voice, and the turn of her head. Willie still marvelled sometimes that she was content to be his girl.

He sat down at the FT101 multiband transceiver, picked up the mike, and said, "G3QRO stroke maritime mobile, here is G3QRM calling. How copy?" The set was vox-operated, and switched automatically to receive when he stopped speaking. A faint background of mush came through the headphones, but nothing more. Ten minutes later, when Janet returned with a tray of tea, he took off the headphones, switched on the loudspeaker, and brought a chair up beside the table for her. "You're a kind lady, Jan."

"I was thinking the same thing myself, down in the kitchen, waiting for the kettle to boil. Any luck, Willie?"

"Not yet." He shrugged and looked at the clock on the wall above the radio. "And you need a bit of luck to get through from the other side of the world, conditions 'ave to be just right. But it works more often than you'd think. You never know what you'll get with radio. She might pick me up loud and clear, but not be able to get Brisbane or Sydney."

Janet passed him a cup of tea and said, "Are you calling on a schedule?"

He nodded. "She rang me from Brisbane before she left,

and we thought we'd give it a try at noon and midnight GMT. We're ten or eleven hours be'ind local time at longitude one-sixty, so it'll be about 'alf past ten in the morning where the Princess is now."

"What is it she's really up to, Willie?"

"Only what I said. She went out there to go to the wedding of an Abo friend—"

"Och, she has Aborigine friends?"

"We both 'ave, but that's another story."

"All right, go on."

"Well, then she went on to see old Ben Hollinson. Ben used to be in charge of our boat section during *The Network* days. Now he builds small boats in Brisbane."

She knew about *The Network*. It was the criminal organisation, based in the Mediterranean, which Modesty Blaise had set up when she was in her teens, after wandering the Middle East from childhood. She had found a man called Willie Garvin in a squalid Far East gaol two or three years later, secured his release, and re-made him completely by giving him first trust and then responsibility. In return, the new Willie Garvin had given her his total loyalty once and for all, and had become her right arm.

Looking at Willie now, as he sipped his tea and slowly turned the dial of the vernier control, Janet found it impossible to imagine that he could ever have been a sullen, friendless creature, filled with hate for himself and for all men. But he had assured her soberly that this was true.

"... So Modesty went up to Brisbane to look in on Ben," he was saying, "and there was this boat to be delivered to a bloke in Wellington. Thirty-four foot glass-fibre sloop with a diesel and a self-steering rig. Roller-furling gear for the jib, to make for easier 'andling solo. Ben was going to sail the boat down to Wellington 'imself, because he reckoned by doing that he'd open up a nice market in New Zealand for this new design. Then he broke 'is arm, so the Princess said she'd deliver the boat for 'im."

"Surely that's a wee bit reckless, Willie? She always says she's awful cautious. So do you, for that matter."

"She is. We both are, Jan. Oh, I suppose there's a bit of risk from tropical storms and all the usual cruel-sea stuff, but the boat's 'ad a shakedown cruise and she said it 'andles beautifully. Makes a fair speed in a decent breeze, and can look after 'erself in a forty knot gale without turning somersaults. Anyway, Ben Hollinson's a friend, and you know what she's like."

"Aye, Willie, I know. I take it she's a good sailor?"

"Sure. And a first-class navigator."

"Sometimes you make me sick, the two of you. You're good at too many things, Willie."

He said seriously, "Not really, but I suppose we're lucky 'aving loads of time to spend on whatever it is. Modesty's always setting 'erself something new to learn, and I picked it up from 'er. Hire the best teacher and then go at it pretty well full time for a month, or two months, or a year, or 'owever long it takes, whether it's sailing or gliding or scubadiving, or maybe learning a new language—"

He broke off and his hand froze on the dial as the mush was suddenly deadened by a barely audible hum, and a voice said clearly: "... and I've jiggered around with the aerial now, but maybe we have one-way communication only. On the other hand you might have gone back to bed by now, in which case I'm wasting my time, but let's try once more. G3QRM, G3QRM, here is G3QRO stroke maritime mobile calling on sked. How copy?"

Lady Janet started and blinked at the set, unable quite to take in that the voice could be coming from a girl in a boat on the Tasman Sea, half a world away. Willie picked up the mike, smiling, and said: "G3QRO stroke maritime mobile, here is G3QRM replying. You're coming in clear as a bell, Princess. Haven't picked up a whisper from you on any sked since you left Brisbane, but you suddenly seem to have knocked a hole in the wall. How copy?"

She came through so strongly that he turned down the volume. "You're like next door, Willie, and it's lovely to hear your voice. I always kid myself I'm the quiet sort, but after being on my own for five days I find I'm basically garrulous. I've been talking to some dolphins quite a bit today. I squeak at them and they squeak back. What's your QTH, Willie?"

"*The Treadmill*, and as it 'appens I've got Janet beside me."

"It must be ... what? Gone one o'clock summer time? I bet she made you some tea."

Willie looked surprised. "As a matter of fact, she did. How d'you guess, Princess?"

"I'm psychic. Give her my best and tell her not to spoil you."

Janet mouthed words. Willie nodded and said into the mike, "Done. And hers to you. What's the trip like?"

"Very comfortable so far, except for a hell of a squall a couple of days ago. It only lasted an hour, but I thought *The Wasp* was going to start turning cartwheels with me."

"She didn't, though?"

"No, she's a very good boat, and we had no real trouble. Apart from that, the weather's been fine and the sea calm to moderate. Enough wind to keep me going nicely most of the time, except for a couple of hours dead calm yesterday afternoon. I didn't use the engine, though, I went over the side on a lifeline and had a swim with Bubble and Squeak, who seem to be head prefects of the school."

28

"The dolphins?"

"Yes. Oh, they're gorgeous, Willie. I'm sure it's the same lot that turn up every afternoon. My fellow-traveller in the morning is a shark, a whitetip. He seems to be a loner, and he pushes off when the dolphins arrive."

"Is he with you now?"

"Yes, I can see him a couple of hundred yards astern. He tends to lag behind, then comes spurting up and swims round the boat. I think he fancies me with a bit of egg and breadcrumb."

"Hang on a sec, Jan's saying something. Oh yes, she wonders 'ow you keep yourself occupied when the going's good."

"You can answer that one, Willie. Time never hangs heavy, there's always some cleaning or maintenance to do, and I often spend hours just trimming the sails, trying to get an extra half knot out of her. You know how you can fool around indefinitely on a boat. After dark I usually spend a few hours with the tape recorder and a Teach Yourself Russian course I'm working on."

"Does the self-steering rig work okay?"

"It's pretty good. A swivel sheared through last night and *The Wasp* came round to the north-east, but I woke up."

Willie made a mental note to explain that to Janet later. Modesty had a quite inexplicable gift of orientation. Put her down blindfold in any part of the world, and after a little contemplation she could give you her position plus or minus five degrees north or south, east or west, and could also give you local time to within a few minutes. That she should be roused from sleep by the boat turning off course was quite unsurprising to him.

"I take my hat off to these intrepid round-the-world sailors," she was saying. "I don't think I'd sleep at all if I was anywhere near a shipping route. Even on this bit of watery desert I get the wind up at night. I lie tucked up in the bunk with my ears pricked, imagining some mile-long oil tanker about to tread on me. It's stupid, of course. The chances of seeing anything at all before I sight North Island are pretty remote, so ..." Her voice trailed away. Willie lifted an eyebrow, drew breath to speak, then hesitated. As he did so there came the hum of her transmission and her voice saying, "Well I'm damned. I can see something out of the portlight. Looks like a small inflatable, and only about half a mile away to starboard. Hang on while I go on deck and take a look, Willie love."

Lady Janet took Willie's cup and poured more tea. "I'm glad I came up," she said. "I'd not have believed what an exciting thing it is to talk to somebody on the other side of the world. By radio, I mean, like this. It's an awful lot different from the telephone."

"M'mm." Willie tugged at his ear absently. "It's rum about this dinghy, though. Or whatever it is."

"I suppose there's all sorts of things floating about on the sea."

"Sure. But seeing something like that would be about the same as spotting a split pea on Loch Lomond, in proportion."

Janet shook her head firmly, the chestnut hair glinting. "Not when it's Her Highness there, Willie. She makes things happen like ... like a poltergeist. No, I mean she attracts happenings to take place near wherever she happens to be. Lord, but that was a poor gawky sentence."

Willie grinned and patted her hand. "You're beautiful and you're sexy. I don't care about you talking funny and not being literate."

"Cockney sod," said Lady Janet amiably.

Five minutes passed before Modesty came on the air again. She was breathing a little heavily, as if she had been busy.

"Sorry to keep you but I've been getting all the canvas down and changing course. Using the engine now. I've had a look through binoculars, and it's a small inflatable all right, a yacht's tender. There's someone in it. I can see him when a wave tilts the thing, which isn't too well inflated. I think it's a man. It's not a skeleton, anyway, I could see that much. He's just sprawled in the bottom, not moving. The trouble is, my camp-follower is taking an interest. Seamus the Shark. Every now and then he butts at the dinghy, and sooner or later he'll either turn it over or bite a chunk out. So if the man's alive, I'd better get him aboard *The Wasp* as fast as I can."

Janet felt a chill of apprehension touch her stomach. She glanced quickly at Willie, and saw that his face was impassive.

"Quite apart from the shark," Modesty was saying, "we have a weather problem coming up. In the last few minutes the sky in the north-east has turned almost black, so I imagine this morning's forecast is going to be right. Bad weather for two or three days, we're promised." Urgency touched her voice. "I have to go now, we're getting pretty close. I'll call you back as soon as I can, but we might lose the conditions, so don't worry if you hear nothing. I'll come through on sked when—oh God, the bastard's turned it over. Off and clear with eighty-eight."

The mush closed in as the hum of her transmission ceased. Willie gazed at the set without expression, eyes half closed. Janet felt a sudden sweat break out upon her body. She slid an arm through Willie's, and said in a low voice, "What will she do?"

"Dunno, Jan." His tone was as expressionless as his face. "Depends on a lot of things. But if we don't 'ear in a couple of minutes it'll mean she's 'ad to go in the water to get 'im."

31

"Oh, dear God."

He picked up a pencil and pulled a pad towards him. "All we can do is wait."

*   *   *

The Wasp had been no more than fifty yards from the dinghy when a butt from the shark had combined with the lift of a wave to capsize the little inflatable. She cut the engine and held her course, steering to interpose the boat between the dinghy and the dorsal fin which had moved smoothly away and was now circling back.

She was quite sure that in the moment of capsizing she had seen the man move of his own volition, as if roused from stupor and trying feebly to cling to the side of the dinghy. Bringing the boat round with the last of its momentum, she let the tiller go and stood up. A seventy-foot nylon lifeline was already secured about her waist. She wore very short denim shorts, much salt-stained, with a nylon bikini top. Her feet were bare, her black hair drawn back and tied in a club at the nape of her neck. Once the sun was well up she usually spent most of the day naked, but for a whim she had decided to dress up for the call to England. In her hand was the small deck mop.

She slipped the three-foot handle under her belt now, so that it lay along her flank, unhooked a section of the guard-wire, and dropped overside the short rope ladder she used for bathing. The half-naked, blue-trousered body came to the surface, rolling over, arms moving feebly. Pulling on her scuba mask, she slipped quietly over the side and swam to-wards the man, who was slowly sinking again.

Sharks favoured easy prey. The irregular sound of a feeble or disabled creature, fish or mammal, was a sure attraction, and so she swam with a firm and measured leg-beat. Forty feet from the drifting boat she drew up her legs, dived, caught the man under his arms from behind, and brought him to the surface. Lying on her back, one arm hooked under his chin to hold his head high on her breast, she continued to kick steadily with her legs as she drew in an arm's length of the nylon lifeline, twisted her head to grip it with her teeth, then reached out to haul in some more, dragging herself and her burden a little nearer the boat with each pull.

The waves were not yet high, but had become steeper with an increase in the wind. Sometimes as she twisted her head to bite on the line she could see only the mast above the waves, sometimes the whole boat sliding over a crest. She felt the man try to kick with his legs, and paused before biting on the rope again to say, "Lie still, lie still, please. It's very important." Her voice was breathless with exertion, but she tried to keep it steady and emphatic, hoping to reach through his stupor and that he understood English. For whatever reason, he stopped moving. She kept her own strong leg-beat going and began to haul in again with hand and teeth.

The whitetip was not a big shark, perhaps twelve feet long, but it was a man-eater. It would be circling now within sight distance, moving cautiously, and slowly drawing closer, its tiny and unpredictable brain occupied in primitive assessment. In time it would bump the possible prey with its snout, presumably to test reaction before moving in again for the first great rending, head-shaking bite. That was the usual feeding pattern with a lone shark. If there had been others, then a bloody and competitive attack would in all likelihood have been launched as soon as the man was tipped into the sea.

All this she knew, but her awareness of the shark, and any imaginings of what it might do in the next two minutes or two seconds, were sealed off in a tiny compartment of her being, dark and remote, the closure held fast by a huge and continuing act of will. For this moment her whole world had narrowed to the simplicity of hauling and holding, hauling and holding. She was strong, very strong, but this was gruelling work, and the hardest part was yet to come.

An endless minute brought her alongside the boat, and she held the rope in her teeth for the last time as she reached up to grasp the rope ladder. Above the sound of water slapping against the hull she heard the man say something in a croaking voice. Thirty feet away she saw the fin of the white-tip show fleetingly on the surface. Still beating rhythmically with her legs she said quietly, close to his ear, "Are you strong enough to hang on?"

To her enormous relief, he understood. His arm moved, and she saw that the skin was blistered with sunburn as he reached slowly up and hooked a hand over a rung of the ladder, turning to face her as he did so. She glimpsed a stubble of beard, puffy eyes, and a very high sunburned forehead half hidden by a tangle of dark brown hair. Then she was turning her head, seeking the shark, fighting the urge to stop beating with her legs and draw them up tightly.

The boat leaned away from them as it slid down into a trough, then masked part of the sky as it swung over them the other way. The small deck mop was in her hand. She saw the fin reappear, moving more slowly now, and closer. Sucking in air, she forced herself to wait while she summoned her strength for the next move, certain there would be no second chance.

She pressed the back of her hand to her mouth, then looked at it. No blood. Her lips were sore from the rope, but not bleeding, thank God. A trace of blood would trigger a swift and frenzied attack. Breath rasping, she said, "Listen.

34

When the boat leans over and helps lift us, I'm going to heave you aboard. Give it everything you've got when I say the word. Do you understand?"

His face bumped against her arm, and she heard him croak the word, "Yes." Across the crests of three waves she saw the fin appear, angling towards the boat. Then it vanished. She snapped "Wait!" and ducked her head below the surface, the scuba mask giving her clear vision. The whitetip was gliding towards her. She pushed gently away from the boat, holding the lifeline with one hand, and presented herself head-on to the shark, extending the mop, pushing firmly down on the flat forepart of the head just above the nose, turning the creature aside.

The great body curved smoothly away and began to cruise back and forth at a distance of some thirty or forty feet, turning with a flick of the white-tipped tail. She watched it as she dragged herself back to the boat in two easy hauls, then lifted her head from the water, gripped the highest rung of the ladder she could reach, and said in a taut voice, "Get ready, we haven't much time." The shark had been deterred by encountering a non-passive reaction, but it would soon come back.

A wave lifted *The Wasp*. Modesty tossed the mop aboard, reached down, slid an arm between the legs of the man facing her, and said, "Now *go*!" As the boat leaned away she pressed her body against it and let all the held-down terrors explode within her. Adrenalin surged through her blood, bringing added strength as she poured the total power of her body and will into lifting the man with the roll of the boat ... up, up, muscles protesting, mouth wide in a silent scream to give yet more power, *now, now, now*! and his weight was gone. She heard a gasping cry as he tumbled into the cockpit.

The boat tilted above her and she clawed her way up to grip the top rung of the ladder, then waited through long seconds of shuddering fear for the boat to mount the next crest, for she was helpless under the curving hull. As it lay over again she rose to grasp the lifting gunwale, chinning herself, then pressing up. The man had dragged himself to his knees and was pawing feebly at her, trying to help. She leaned forward, caught at a backstay, and snatched her legs from the water in a final spasm of terror before swivelling round and rolling over on to the cockpit grating deck.

Slowly she pulled off the mask, and for a long time she knelt there on all fours, head bowed, teeth chattering, chest heaving, letting the fear repossess her in retrospect so that it might run its course. The man lay sprawled half out of the cockpit, close to her, a blistered forearm resting across his swollen eyelids. After a moment his cracked lips moved and he said hoarsely but distinctly, "Thank you ... very much."

She gave a shaky laugh and lifted her head to look down at him. "Don't mention it."

He took his arm from his face and made a grimace that might have been a smile. The slitted eyes became fixed, staring up at her intently. Slowly he lifted a hand to her chin and pressed gently to turn her head a little, then his hand fell away, but his absorbed scrutiny continued. "Please ... who ...?"

"Modesty Blaise," she said, and squatted on her heels. "Where on earth did you come from?"

"Luke ... Lucian Fletcher. I'm staying at ... at *The Dragonara*. Can't quite recall ... what happened." The eyes closed and the head slumped.

She stared down at him for a full half minute, studying his features, mentally replaying what he had just said, and trying to collect her wits so that she could put fragmentary memories together. At last she stirred, and unfastened the lifeline from her waist. It was a considerable effort to heave him into the cabin out of the sun, but once she had driven her weary body to hoist him on to the bunk she left him sprawled there and went to the radio.

The man who called himself Lucian Fletcher, and who could not possibly be who he claimed, would come to no further harm by waiting until Willie Garvin's mind had been set at rest.

*   *   *

It was quiet in the attic room. The only sound was the faint mush and crackle from the radio. Willie Garvin sat lost in concentration as he carefully sketched what looked to Lady Janet a very complex circuit diagram.

She was thinking, *Over five minutes since she signed off. Surely to God it's finished one way or another now. Either she pulled him out or the shark got him, poor devil, and whatever happened she'd let us know ... except Willie said she might go into the sea for him ... but then how could she ever get him out? And herself ...?*

She stubbed out her cigarette and glanced at Willie. He had known from the start what might be demanded of Modesty out there, and had switched off his imagination. Janet wished she had the same ability. Vivid memories of Cousteau films and of *Jaws* tumbled through her mind, and she felt her stomach contract with shivering horror. Trying to sound natural, she said, "What will Modesty do when she gets him safe aboard?"

Willie added a condenser to the circuit diagram. "It depends," he said. "If it's life or death, she'll put out a call on 2182 kiloHertz. That's the international distress frequency."

37

He looked up and indicated the FT101 transceiver. "She's got one of these for working on the amateur frequencies, like just now, when we were on the twenty-metre band. But she's got ship's radio too, and that distress frequency's monitored by coast radio stations, fishing boats over twelve metres, ships above three 'undred tons, ocean weather ships, warships, and Coastguard. So someone's bound to pick 'er up, 'specially in the silent period."

"What's that?"

"Well, for three minutes after the hour and 'alf-hour you're not allowed to broadcast anything that's not concerned with distress, urgency, or safety on the distress channels. If this bloke in the dinghy isn't too bad, then she'll probably just call Sydney on emergency and leave them to fix whatever's best. They might divert a ship if there's one near enough—"

He stopped short. An emptiness pushed through the mush from the loudspeaker, then Modesty's voice, breathy and uneven, said, "Willie? How copy?"

He put down his pencil and picked up the mike, moving without haste, but Janet saw that his knuckles whitened for a moment as he gripped the instrument. He said briskly, "Still receiving you, Princess. What 'appened?"

"He's safe aboard, Willie. But I had to go in after him." They heard her drag in a long wavering breath. "I don't know how some of these sub-aqua boys can play around with sharks. I'm scared spitless. And I'm surprised you can still hear me okay. It's getting pretty black around here with a storm coming down from the north. Over."

Willie smiled at Janet, blew out his cheeks in open relief, and said into the mike, "You're coming and going a bit, Princess. We're glad you're safe. Anything I can do for you this end?"

The background crackle was distinctly louder, but her voice was still audible through it as she said, "Yes, please, and I'll make it quick. This man's suffering from exposure and sunburn. I think he's also in shock. I'll try to radio Sydney or Wellington, hoping they can organise a pick-up for him if there's a ship anywhere about, or maybe get an amphibian to me. But in case I don't get through, will you phone Ben Hollinson and tell him to start things moving? I got a fix on my position a couple of hours ago—wait, I'll give it to you. Thirty-eight twelve south, one-sixty-one twenty-seven east. Check, please."

Willie checked the figures back and said, "Over."

"Right. I don't know where we'll be after the storm, but I'm just going to ride it out rather than try to make any distance. I hope they can pick him up for his sake, but if not I'll just carry on to Wellington with him. That's all the important stuff, and now stand by to be made agog, if we can stay in touch for another couple of minutes. You remember the picture I bought at the Mailer Gallery last year? How copy and over."

Willie said, "Still okay. You mean *Estaminet*? The one you hung in the dining room at Benildon?"

Janet had seen it there in the Wiltshire cottage, *Ashlea*, that was Modesty's country home, a picture in oils of a French workman in his blues, sitting at a rickety table outside a café with half a carafe of red wine. It was a typical Fletcher, with its tumult of fine brush strokes producing an extraordinary feeling of detail. She did not know what it had cost. She did know that her father had bought a Fletcher still life for his mansion in the Highlands three years ago for something above eight thousand pounds.

Modesty was saying, "Yes. The Fletcher. Dredge up your total recall and give me a quick run-down on him, Willie."

39

He looked at Janet with amused puzzlement and said, "Lucian Fletcher. Signed 'is stuff Luke Fletcher. About thirty-seven or eight. I'm quoting from a piece in a colour supplement a while back, Princess, so I expect it's fairly accurate. Let's see ... Fletcher married young, when 'e was still at art school. Wife's name was Bridget, a fellow student. Seems like a love-match, because they stayed together. Early struggles for Fletcher, then 'e got an exhibition in Paris about twelve years ago, and never looked back. In the top ten of the century, they reckon. Quiet man by all accounts. Always ducked publicity. Wife was killed in an air-crash about two years ago, and Fletcher didn't produce any work after that. He died last month. You getting me, Princess?"

"Yes. He was drowned, wasn't he?"

"Off Malta. Went in for a swim one evening about dusk, and never came back. It was in all the papers, with suggestions it might 'ave been suicide."

"It made the papers in Brisbane, too. But Willie, this man I've just pulled out of the sea, before he passed out he mumbled that he was Luke Fletcher. I know it's crazy, but behind the stubble and sunburn he really does look like photographs I've seen of Fletcher. And anyway, he's much too far gone to have been conning me. Over."

"You're fading, Princess, but I 'eard that all right. Either he's a very good swimmer or it's another bloke with the same name. Over."

"You're fading, too. The thing is, he said he was staying at *The Dragonara*, and the hotel of that name that first comes to mind is in Malta by Dragonara Point. It was as if I'd picked him up out of the Med, and he was telling me where he'd come from. It's pretty weird ..."

A crash of static blotted out her words. For a few moments they could hear her fragmented voice dwindling behind increasing mush, and then she was gone. Willie lifted his mike and said, "We've lost you, Princess. Good luck with the weather, and give us a call when you get a chance. I'll set the alarm this end. Off and clear." He put down the mike, plugged a small box into the radio, then sat back and exhaled loudly, running fingers through his tousled hair.

Janet said, "That must have been a scary, lonely thing to do. I mean, going into the sea for that man, with the shark there, and nobody to help." Willie nodded, and she saw a gleam of sweat on his forehead now. When he did not speak she said, "I'm awful glad she's all right, Willie. What did you mean about an alarm?"

"She can key a signal to set off an alarm this end, if the signal gets through. It's wired all through the pub, so I'll know if she calls."

"What about this Luke Fletcher thing? It surely can't be so?"

He stood up and gave a brief laugh. "Like you said, if it was anyone but the Princess, it couldn't be so. But once she's in the picture I wouldn't bet either way."

"Aye, things do seem to happen around her." Lady Janet rose to face him, watching him with interest as he stretched hard and long. Then she reached up to link her hands behind his neck and said, "You're all wound up."

He grinned down at her, holding her gently. "You're not supposed to notice. You're supposed to think I've got nerves of steel."

"I was thinking, Willie, if we go back to bed and to sleep, just, it'll be too domestic for words."

"Unromantic?"

"Exactly that. And what's worse than an unromantic mistress? Besides, you need urgent treatment for shock, and I know a sovereign remedy."

"Does it 'urt, Jan?"

She pursed her lips and shook her head, green eyes looking up at him solemnly. "Not if it's done right. All you need is to be cupped firmly between the thighs of a warm-hearted lady."

"A lady? Blimey, what a bit of luck you 'appened to be 'ere, Jan. And that's all there is to it?"

"Well, not quite all, but it's a good start."

He laughed and bent to pick her up easily, though she was not a small girl. Resting her cheek against his as he carried her down the stairs to the bedroom, she was happy to feel the almost exuberant relief in him. Her blood stirred suddenly, hotly, with the thought that it was with her and no other girl that he would find release tonight from the tensions of the last half-hour.

Over several years past, her feelings towards Modesty Blaise had moved from restrained hostility to grudging respect, and then, after the horror of the Chateau Lancieux affair, to ungrudging respect and even liking. She accepted now, without resentment, that Modesty had virtually created Willie Garvin, or at least re-created him, and that their years together had made him a part of her. Yet they did not sleep together. This had once baffled Janet, and she had only gradually come to understand that to do so would have changed the whole equation between them. It was not a matter of denying themselves. She suspected that they simply could not envisage a possibility which would alter a relationship they both found so entirely satisfying.

"Hey," she murmured in Willie's ear as he pushed open the bedroom door with his foot, "I'm glad your crazy Princess came out of it all right." Then she made a soft snarling sound in her throat, and sank her teeth gently into his neck.

3

Modesty Blaise fastened a broad retaining strap across the man in the bunk, then paused to get her breath. It had not been easy, in the lurching boat, to strip him and wrap his dehydrated body in a wet sheet. For a minute or two he had half recovered consciousness, and she had taken the chance to hold him propped up while she trickled water down his throat from the spout of a plastic beaker. She was glad he was unconscious again now, for his face and body were cruelly sunburned.

A glance through the portlight showed a darkening sky above ever steeper waves, and she went quickly out of the cabin, buckling on her safety harness. Two big dolphins broke the surface very close to the boat. That meant the whitetip would be gone. Dolphins did not seek trouble, but one could kill a shark with a thirty-knot butt behind the gill. "And where were you when I needed you?" she called, then began to wind in the roller-furling gear before tackling the mainsail. It would have to be severely reefed. When the dirty weather struck, and that would be very soon now, she could risk no more than a few square feet of sail.

Long before she had finished, the wind was whipping the tops from the waves, and she was soaked with spray. Moving aft, she paid out twenty fathoms of line for the boat to tow. This would act as a warp to hold her steady. By the time she had made all secure on deck and returned to the cabin, *The*

Wasp was butting into thirty-foot seas, climbing and falling as if on a switch-back, so that she could make no move without a firm hand-hold.

Her muscles were aching as she stripped off her wet clothes, threw them into the wash-basin and began to make secure everything movable in the cabin. When she had finished her body was dry. She pulled on fresh shorts and fastened a dry swimsuit top in place, every move a problem under the constant pitching of the little sloop. Kneeling beside the bunk with a tube of Caladryl from the first-aid box, she began to spread it gently on the man's burnt brow, lips, and cheekbones, steadying herself with a hand on the grab-rail alongside the bunk, timing her moves as his head rolled with the plunging of the boat, her eyes thoughtful, a little abstracted.

If the weather forecast was right, the storm would last for at least two days, and *The Wasp* was scarcely geared for nursing a sick man. He was dehydrated, and she would have to get more water down him. His body was that of an average fit man but no athlete. There was a hint of wasting, from which she judged that he had not eaten for several days. He would need nourishment as soon as she could manage it, and vitamins. Another worry was the problem of securing him so that his burnt body would not be constantly chafed by movement if the full force of the storm engulfed *The Wasp*.

She unfastened the strap, pulled the wet sheet down, and began to cream his chest, arms, and the tops of his shoulders. His temperature was down, she decided, and it would be safe to get him into dry bedding. She would also have to make up a bed for herself on the other bunk, for she would be spending most of the next two days in the cabin. There was nothing useful to be done outside unless some emergency forced her out.

She braced herself as the boat skimmed down into a trough, then prepared for the task of turning him over so that she could attend to his back. Suddenly she was still, leaning closer to look at his forearm. With the next lurch of the boat she reached above the man's head to snap on the cabin light, then peered again.

Punctures. Hypodermic punctures on the inner part of the forearm. She switched the light off and squatted back on her heels, swaying to the erratic plunging of the boat. Speaking aloud, but softly, she said, "My word, we've got a funny one here, Willie." The noise of the wind grew suddenly shrill, and green water showed through the portlight as the boat rolled. The man's blistered eyelids flickered, and he gave a groan of pain.

Crouched on the cabin deck, lower lip caught between her teeth, eyes narrowed, she drained her mind of all questions and mysteries, and set herself to devising how best to succour the half-dead man the sea had given into her charge.

*   *   *

In the velvet darkness of his mind, movement was colour, and pain was colour, and the easement when she came to him was colour. Cool hands, strong. Steady voice, low-toned, reassuring.

Time was out of joint, and there was no sense of order in the dream or reality he was living through.

"Bridie?" he said, but perhaps he spoke only in his mind.

He was in the sea, going down. She lifted him into air. Head on firm breast. He glimpsed the dreadful fin. Heard her voice. Memory blurred.

Boat. Bucking, rearing, plunging. Hurting badly. Back and shoulders on fire. Then a little respite.

45

"Bridie?"

"I'm here. Try to swallow this."

A spout in the corner of his mouth. Soup flavour. Luke-warm. Small pills. "Please try to swallow."

Time passing. Howling wind, like a great scream. The colour of pain flaring through his brain. Lurching to this side, to that. Held by something, but still the constant small movements setting fire to the skin. Never still. Hurting, hurting.

Cool flesh. The length of her body pressed hard against his. Her arm across his chest, strong, friendly, comforting. Stillness now, though the plunging continues. His body locked and cushioned by hers. Smell of salt and good flesh. The pain-colour fading, allowing a moment of coherent thought; she can only hold me so while her strength lasts.

Bridie?

Not Bridie. Another voice. Another body. Bridie is dead ...

Memory blurs once more. Water. Food. A kind of sleep as her body holds him again. There is the colour of compassion in her hands and her voice and her body. Once she is gone from him for a long time, and he cries out for her in terror as the giant shakes the little place in which he is imprisoned like a beetle in a matchbox.

Memory. The sea, the moving fin. Her voice, her arms holding him. The boat. The sudden strength as she lifts him. Then her face above him, framed by wet black hair. Yes, yes, the face. Dear God, he must see the profile. He puts up a hand to turn her head. It is etched upon his mind before the long darkness comes.

And now it is there again, looking down at him. The lips move. *"Hallo, you've woken up at last."* Lurching, rising, falling. Crash of sea on hull. *"With any luck we'll have better weather in a few hours."* A dirty plaster across her brow, rough bandage round hand and upper arm. Eyes deep dark blue, hollow with weariness, totally serene. *"It doesn't matter, don't try to talk yet."* A smile, a lighting up from within. A smile to live or die for. Then gone.

Snapshots of sight and sound, of touch, taste, and smell. She is in the cockpit, framed by the companionway, struggling with a mass of canvas and ... a broken mast? Wind claws at the wet hair, presses sodden shirt against the fine contours of the body. Hours or minutes later the companionway curtain is secured and she crouches in the cabin in the dim light, bracing herself, winding a bandage round her hand. Her head lifts to look at him. A grin. A companionable urchin grin.

Another memory snapshot. She strips off wet clothes and dries herself before coming to him. Then the blessed relief from strain as again her body cushions his from the remorseless battering. His senses reach out to know her, untinged by desire. There is the good feel of flesh against flesh, comforting beyond measure. His head turns into the warmth of her shoulder and he savours the fine fresh smell of the sea-scoured body. Cautiously his cracked lips part a little and his mouth presses against her with the roll of the boat, presses a hand's span below the collarbone, where the swell of breast begins. Unobtrusively he tastes her.

The touch and smell and taste of her are colours in his mind, moving, blending, taking shape. Quietly he slides down into sleep, but the colours are with him still.

*   *   *

The mast had snapped on the second morning, at the height of the storm. She heard it go, even above the shrieking wind. The man secured by her body moaned in his sleep, trying feebly to hold her as she rolled from the bunk to pull on

47

shorts, shirt, and safety harness. It took all her strength to force one of the cockpit doors open against the power of the wind, then she was out in the howling gloom, foam lashing at her as she clipped herself to the lifeline.

The mast hung across the cabin, held by shrouds and stays. When it slipped into the sea, the sloop would be pulled broadside-on to the waves, and turn turtle. Instinct outpaced thought, and she was already moving as she narrowed her mind to the sequence of tasks for survival.

Bolt-cutters. Shearing through the backstays and the topping lift. Every movement calling for an effort of will. Wind tearing at her viciously as she dragged herself forward to cut the shrouds ... starboard side, port side. Only the forestay now. A moment of relief as the mast slid into the water and the boat was freed from its murderous drag.

More to be done. Body flogged by the wind, battered by the endless lurching and plunging. Muscles burning with the monstrous task of hauling the boom into a fore-and-aft position, then lashing the sail with ties against the storm's attempts to tear it away.

At last. The comparative peace of the little cabin again. Numb with effort, summoning strength to dry herself, bandage her hurts, and reassure the man in the bunk as he called fretfully, "Bridie ...? Please, Bridie ..."

*　　*　　*

A new day, and another world. *The Wasp* almost unmoving on a calm sea.

Working patiently, she stripped the sail from the boom. The sliders which had held the mainsail to the mast also fitted the track on the boom, and when she found this was so she laughed in pleased surprise, then began to sing as she worked,

48

very softly and in a voice she knew with resignation to be almost comically tuneless.

Much later she sat in the sternsheets eyeing the results of her many improvisations with a critical eye. The boom was now stepped as a jurymast in the stump of the old mast, prevented from rocking by wedges cut from the grabrail of the unused forecabin. She had fashioned new stays and shrouds from Terylene rope. The spinnaker pole was now serving as a replacement boom. With blowlamp and hammer she had bent one end to make a rough fit around the gooseneck fitting of the old mast, and the other end to take the mainsheet. A light breeze had sprung up in the last hour, and *The Wasp* was sailing again. She listened to the gurgle of water under the bows with deep pleasure and whispered, "How about that, Willie?"

Suddenly she was ravenous. Checking her course, she took a last look at the sea and the sky, then went into the cabin. Ten minutes later she had heated two tins of steak and was crouched feeding the man from the sea, her mouth watering with the smell, trying not to feel impatient for her own turn.

*   *   *

"It lasted just over three days," said Willie Garvin. "She came through on the radio early this morning."

"Good." The bespectacled man Willie was talking to looked with disgust at the stick of pink candyfloss he held, then peered up at the Big Wheel which towered above the sprawl of the funfair. "I'm glad she's all right," he added. "We can do with conserving her sort, which is more than I can say for little Malcolm." He blinked at Willie hopefully. "You don't think Lady Janet might give him a quick shove while they're up there?"

49

"No chance, Jack. She quite likes kids."

"Malcolm will soon straighten her out on that."

Jack Fraser was slightly built with a timid and ingratiating manner which had deceived many men, some at the cost of their lives. He now worked behind a desk, but for fifteen years he had been a field agent operating for a secret department of the Foreign Office headed by Sir Gerald Tarrant. Very few people knew that the department existed or that Tarrant ran it. Modesty Blaise and Willie Garvin were among the few. So, by chance, was Lady Janet Gillam, who had been a prisoner with Tarrant in Ariège.

The meeting with Fraser today had not been planned. It was a Sunday, and early that morning Willie had rung Janet at her farm with the news that Modesty had made contact. Later he had picked her up and driven to town for lunch at a riverside pub in the City. There they had seen a poster advertising the funfair at Blackheath, and Janet had at once wanted to go there, confessing that she had never in her life attended such an event. In the shadow of the Helter Skelter they had found themselves confronted by Fraser and a plump, too neatly dressed schoolboy of about twelve. This was Malcolm, son of Fraser's married sister, and Willie had been fascinated to meet him at last, for Malcolm figured often and luridly as a hideous comparative in Fraser's conversation; though only when Fraser was speaking as himself rather than as the humble character he affected among all but the closest of his professional contacts.

"Twice a year," Fraser was saying morosely. "A pantomime just after Christmas, and this bloody mad-house one day during his half-term holiday. I try every trick I know to get out of it, Willie, but my sister takes not a scrap of notice. Last time I said I'd got a heart condition, and this time I told her my latest medical check-up revealed I was a suppressed pervert, and the psychiatrist said I might turn dangerous any moment. I don't think she even *hears* me, Willie. Just sends me off with her unspeakable progeny without a thought for his safety. She never did like me, mind you."

Willie grinned. Before Fraser became desk-bound as assistant to Tarrant he had achieved a record few agents could match. His penetration and destruction of the Prague Syndicate was a classic operation, even in the flat dry words of the operations file which Tarrant had once allowed Modesty and Willie to study for a special purpose. It was amusing to find such a man bewailing his sister's dominance.

"I've been trying to make the little bugger sick," said Fraser absently, gazing at the wheel and giving a cringing smile as Lady Janet and Malcolm swept by at the bottom of the down-swing. "A good dose of the heaves, and I can whip him smartly off home to his ghastly mum and dad, but he just wraps himself around all the goodies I give him without batting an eyelid. I hope you called Tarrant about Modesty being safe, he's been fidgety since you first phoned. Does this shipwrecked mariner of hers still claim he's Luke Fletcher?"

"Sort of," said Willie, "except that 'claim' puts it a bit strong. He's been pretty groggy and I don't think there's been much chat between 'em. The mast broke off during the second night, so as soon as the storm was over she 'ad to get busy stepping the boom as a mast."

Fraser screwed up his eyes and grimaced. "Sooner her than me. I'm no sailor. What's happening now?"

"They've been trying to raise 'er from Sydney ever since the weather cleared, and they got through about 'alf an hour before she called me. She managed to get a fix soon after dusk, so they've got 'er position now and they're sending out a flying-boat to pick up Luke Fletcher, or whoever it is."

51

"Just him?"

"She says the boat's still seaworthy."

"Even so."

"She'd only abandon the boat if it was stupid to go on. It's important to Ben Hollinson."

"Ah." Fraser nodded his understanding. After a moment or two he said, "How the hell can it be Luke Fletcher?"

"I don't suppose it is, Jack, but according to Modesty he's not pretending. I mean there's nothing phoney about 'im being nearly dead from exposure when she found 'im."

"So *he* must think he's Fletcher." Fraser shrugged. "Some people think they're Napoleon."

"So did Napoleon."

Fraser turned to stare at Willie. "You really think it might be him?"

"I can't see 'ow it could be, but that doesn't mean it's not. I've grown a bit cautious about things that aren't possible. Besides ..."

"Well?"

"I think the Princess is 'alf convinced. Nothing concrete, just little nuances. When 'e was delirious, this bloke kept calling 'er Bridie. That's what Fletcher used to call 'is wife, Bridget."

Fraser rubbed his chin, then laughed. "A man vanishes in the Mediterranean and turns up in a dinghy on the other side of the world. Even the most lunatic press agent of the most idiot film star would baulk at such totally phoney publicity. With Luke Fletcher it's inconceivable. My Fleet Street sources tell me he never agreed to be interviewed in his life. Hated publicity."

Willie said, "You've been looking into it, then?"

"Tarrant's greatly intrigued, partly because he's a Fletcher fan and partly because he's a Modesty Blaise fan."

"I 'ope you didn't tell the press boys anything. The last thing she wants is a big hoo-ha in the papers."

"Of course I didn't, you silly sod." Fraser glared, then grinned suddenly. "But Willie boy, if it turns out that this man she picked up in the Tasman Sea *is* Luke Fletcher, then there's going to be one hell of a hoo-ha, whether she likes it or not."

"Oh, sure." Willie responded to a wave from Lady Janet and Malcolm at the top of the wheel. "But she's on *The Wasp* under one of 'er other names, because she didn't want any Lone Sailoress write-ups under 'er own name anyway. Sydney radio thinks she's Lucienne Bouchier, and she 'asn't mentioned Fletcher's name at all. They can sort that out for themselves. And when we talked this morning we used Arabic, so it's long odds against being understood by anyone roaming the amateur frequencies."

"If they take the man to Sydney and identify him as Fletcher, she's going to find a reception committee waiting for her in Wellington."

"I doubt if they'll identify 'im that quick. Anyway, Ben Hollinson is fixing for a switch off New Plymouth, a hundred miles north of Wellington. When *The Wasp* comes in there'll be a man sailing 'er. A non English-speaking Chinese."

Fraser chuckled maliciously. "I like it. Fearless journalists eat pencils and notebooks. What about the man himself, Fletcher or pseudo-Fletcher? Can he finger her?"

"She reckons she didn't give 'im any name at all, so that should be all right. And she'll make sure the flying-boat party don't get any shots of 'er."

"It seems ages since I saw that girl," said Fraser regretfully, squinting a little as he polished his spectacles. "Why don't you invite her and me out to dinner one evening when she gets back?"

"Me? What's wrong with you inviting us out?"

"What's wrong with it is that I'm a badly paid civil servant and you're stinking rich on ill-gotten gains. Make it somewhere exclusive and expensive, Willie, I don't want to waste my time."

"You're irresistible you are, Jack. All right."

Lady Janet and Malcolm were released from their swing seat on the Big Wheel. The hard sour look vanished from Fraser's eyes and he became a meek, harassed little man in his Sunday casual wear of sports jacket and flannels of unfashionable cut. He had looked much the same sort of character ten years before, when he had lured the top KGB assassin of that day to West Berlin and strangled him in five seconds in a subway.

"Most kind, most kind, Lady Janet," he declared obsequiously. "Such a treat for the little chap. I have no head for heights myself, I fear. Most grateful, I assure you."

Janet gave him a rather cool smile. "Not at all, Mr. Fraser. I hope Malcolm enjoyed it."

"Oh, he did, he did, Lady Janet. Have you said thank you to the kind lady, Malcolm?'

The boy nodded, his plump face expressionless, and reached out to take the stick of candyfloss from his uncle's hand. 'Can I go on the bumper cars again?" he asked in a voice just beginning to break.

Fraser smiled nervously. "Eh? Well, yes, I don't see why not. You wouldn't like some cream buns and cherryade first, and perhaps a spin on The Octopus?"

The boy shook his head. "No, it might make me feel sick."

"Oh, well—er—we'll go along then." Fraser began to nod vaguely. "Great pleasure to have met you, Lady Janet. Ah ... goodbye, Willie. We'll—um—be in touch sometime ..."

"See you, Jack."

When they had vanished into the crowd, Janet let out a long breath and said, "You have the oddest friends, Willie. I must say I preferred Malcolm to your Mr. Fraser. At least the boy was motivated."

"Motivated?"

"He had a hand clamped on my left boob before we'd been round once, and after that it was a busy trip."

"Eh?" Willie's eyebrows shot up in astonishment.

"Och, at least he was being positive, not like that awful wee drip of an uncle."

Willie took her arm and they began to stroll. "Sorry about the junior rapist bit, Jan, but thanks for picking up the cue and getting 'im out of the way. I was glad of a word with Jack."

She shook her head, puzzled. "Who is he, Willie?"

"Tarrant's assistant."

"Oh!" She turned to look at him, round-eyed. "So ...?"

"So I wouldn't take too much notice of the impression 'e likes to give."

*   *   *

Soon after nine in the morning local time, and a little before eleven p.m. Greenwich Mean Time, Modesty said into the mike, 'He's asleep at the moment, but I'll have to wake him soon. Sydney radio tell me the flying-boat's only a few miles north of my position."

"You got a link with it through Sydney, then?"

"Not a direct link, but I figured that even knowing my position they might have a job spotting us, so I've been sending out a signal and Sydney have been directing the flying-boat straight down it. They say it's a Shin Meiwa PS-1, by the way, so we're getting VIP treatment."

55

"Somebody there must like you, Princess."

"Somebody there likes the story, I think. It's an Aussie tycoon who's sort of taken over the operation, and he owns some newspapers among many other things. Greek extraction, self-made, rags to riches, does it ring a bell, Willie? Name of Sam Solon." She switched to Arabic. "He was on our list of possibles back in *The Network* days, remember? But then I decided I liked his style, and anyway he didn't go in for owning the sort of things we were interested in stealing."

Willie said, "I was once in a poker school with Sam Solon. That was in Athens, when you put me in to size him up. Danny Chavasse worked the introduction, and I was supposed to be a rich dumb Englishman spending my way through a fortune I'd been left. I always had a nasty feeling I didn't fool Solon." He switched to English. "How's the patient, Princess? Over."

'I think he's in a lot better nick physically than when I hauled him aboard, but conversation still hasn't progressed much beyond the one-way stage. He watches me a lot. I don't mean leering, just looking very intently." She laughed. "Maybe the way an artist looks at people? Oh, and he keeps thanking me when he does speak, and still seems to think he's you-know-who. That's about all. It's as if his mind's a blank, and maybe it is, if he's suffering from amnesia. Over."

"Did you tell 'im where you are, Princess? In the Tasman Sea?"

"I think I got through with that, but he just looked embarrassed, as if he knew I must be wrong but was too polite to tell me. One thing, Willie. I've seen him with his guard right down over a long period, and he's no crook. He's very ... well, it sounds silly, but the word innocent comes to mind." Her voice faded for a moment or two, then became strong again. "I've just spotted the PS-1 so I'll be busy for a while. Let's try for contact same time tomorrow if you're going to be around."

She waited for him to acknowledge, then quickly signed off and switched to the Sydney frequency to report the aircraft's arrival. Two minutes later she was out on deck, shading her eyes to stare up at the growing shape of the four turboprop flying-boat approaching on a line half a mile to port. Even as she watched, the aircraft banked round, passing in a great circle south of her and losing height. She waved a towel, went into the cabin, and gently shook the sleeping man. He stirred, then his still swollen eyelids opened suddenly. After staring for a moment, he smiled. "Thank you. You're very kind." His voice was a hoarse whisper.

"An aircraft has come to take you to hospital. You'll be properly looked after there. Do you understand?"

After several seconds he nodded slowly, but she saw uncertainty and fear creeping into his eyes. She said, "There's nothing to be afraid of. Now just lie quietly and try to wake up a little. I should think we'll be ready to transfer you in about ten minutes." She rested a hand against his cheek for a few moments, then gave a reassuring smile and went out into the cockpit.

By the time the Shin Meiwa had landed on a glassy calm sea she had taken in all canvas and started the motor. Sitting with one bare foot on the tiller, she watched the aircraft taxi slowly towards *The Wasp* and come to a halt a stone's-throw away. The roar of the engines died. The door on the port side of the rear fuselage opened. A big inflatable, bright orange in colour, splashed down. Two men lowered themselves into it. A stretcher and an outboard motor were passed down to them, then a third man descended. After a short pause the motor was started and the inflatable began to move slowly towards *The Wasp*, which was hove-to now. The first two men were both tall, deeply tanned, wearing cotton shirts and slacks. The other was older, wearing a battered yachting cap on a head of tight-curled iron grey hair.

As the gap closed she saw that the third man's grey hair belied his age by perhaps ten years. The blue eyes in the weatherbeaten brown face, and the firm skin of the neck, told of a man who had still to reach his middle fifties. The face was square, with a wide mouth, somewhat flattened nose, and jutting ears. It was a face hardened by experience yet softened by humour, and perhaps a little arrogant from long-held authority.

As the inflatable came alongside *The Wasp* the older man cut the motor, gave her an approving nod, and said, "Hallo, girl. Did you tell Sydney we've found you?" His Australian accent was slight, and overlaid an even slighter tinge of Continental accent in his English.

"Yes, I've just called them," she said. "Thanks for coming."

"I'm Sam Solon. How's this feller you picked up?"

"Not too bad."

"Good." He nodded to the two men. "Charlie, Jack, you hop aboard, get him on the stretcher and lower him into the dinghy. I'll ferry him across to the Doc, then come back for you."

"No, wait," she said, a little sharply. "He's still in shock, and I don't want him upset, so we'll do this my way. You pass me the stretcher and wait till I've got him on it. I can manage that myself. I'll call you when I'm ready for you to carry him out."

The two men looked at Sam Solon, who eyed her with head on one side for a moment, then said, "All right, beautiful. Go ahead."

She manoeuvred the stretcher into the cabin and opened it out on the deck there. The man on the bunk watched her, and began to shiver. She said, "It's all right. Just a little boat-ride, then a nice comfortable trip to a hospital full of beautiful nurses."

He caught her hand as she knelt beside him, and croaked urgently, "No. Please. Don't let them take me."

"There's nothing to be afraid of."

He reached up and clung to her, almost sobbing with the fear and weakness that possessed him. "I'm safe with you. Please let me stay with you. Please.'

She rested her head on his chest and put a hand on his brow. Somehow she had sensed what his reaction might be, and it was for this that she had told the men to keep out until she was ready, not wanting them, in their rude health and confidence, to see him in the indignity of his sickness and his fantasy fears.

"Luke," she said softly, using the name for the first time, "I promise that you'll be quite safe and nobody will hurt you. I've done all I can for you, but I'm very tired, and I have a long way to go. They're waiting to take you aboard the aircraft now, so I want you to say goodbye to me and then go along quietly, without any fuss, just the way you've been all along. Will you do that for me? Please?"

She felt the shaking of his body gradually cease. His hand patted her back slowly, and she heard him sigh. For a moment he craned his head forward and touched blistered lips to her cheek at the corner of her eye, then he fell limply back on the pillow. When she straightened up he was looking at her with that strange, intent gaze of his. He whispered, "Goodbye. And thank you. I'm ready now." His eyes closed.

She said, "Right, I'll ease your legs down first, then lift your top half down. Ready? Fine. Can you ease up to let me get a hand under here? That's it. Gently now. Ahh ... that's great."

She called, "All right, two of you can come aboard now.

59

One can keep out of the way forward, and the other can take the companionway end of the stretcher."

Two minutes later, wrapped in a blanket and strapped on the stretcher, eyes tightly closed, the man who called himself Luke Fletcher was lowered into the inflatable. Modesty said to Sam Solon, "Can you manage getting him into the flying-boat?"

Solon started the motor. "Easy. I got a full crew and two spare hands, on top of a doctor and nurse. I'll be back in five minutes."

She watched him steer to the aircraft and begin to organise the lifting of the sick man aboard. Charlie and Jack had settled down one on each side of the cabin housing and were smoking, studying her with open interest. Charlie, with a powerful Australian accent, said, "You're a Frenchie, then? Lucienne something, the bloke at Sydney radio said." He offered a packet of cigarettes.

"Bouchier." She shook her head. "No thanks."

Jack laughed. "Speaks English as good as we do, Charlie." He ran his eyes over her, noting the odd strip of plaster and bandage. "Got a few lumps in the storm, eh?"

"One or two little things." She injected a hint of accent into her voice. "But I heal quickly. You were very quick in finding me."

Jack shrugged. "The official blokes are probably still thinking about diverting a ship or wondering where to find a sea-plane. But old Sam don't sit around on his backside."

"How did he know?"

Charlie studied her bare legs with idle lust and said, "There's a standing arrangement for Sydney radio to pass on anything interesting to Sam's news agency. He was there, having a nose around, when the radio bloke came through about you." Charlie jerked a thumb towards the Shin Meiwa. "Funny thing was, he'd hired that plane only three days ago for some sort of coastal survey project he's cooking up, so it was right there."

"He's made things easy for me. I appreciate that. He didn't have to get involved."

Jack was squinting at the curve of the shirt over her breasts. "It's a hell of a good story, sweetheart. Solo sailor-girl finds a bloke from nowhere adrift a thousand miles from anywhere. Sam's editors are going to be licking their lips. Did you find out the bloke's name?"

Unhurriedly, but without hesitation, she shook her head. "There hasn't been much time for talk, and he's still pretty much blanked out."

Sam Solon was returning with the inflatable, and she reflected that though he may have been extremely rich for most of his adult life, he was still a very physical man, who was now maintaining the callouses on his hands by doing something he could easily have ordered his men to do. As he came alongside and reached out to grasp the gunwale he smiled at her, showing white but uneven teeth with a flash of gold to one side. "Want a job, Lucy?"

"Job?"

"Been looking for a girl like you to marry all my life."

She responded to his smile with an effort. "I'll think about it."

"Doc says you've done a pretty good job with the bloke."

"Good. The sooner you get him to hospital the better."

"Too right. Okay, hop in. Give her a hand, Jack."

She stiffened where she sat by the tiller. "What do you mean?"

"I mean let's all go home for Christ's sake. You just said to hurry."

"You've got it wrong. I'm taking this boat to Wellington."

"You're what?" He ran a cold gaze over the little sloop. The boom had been wedged in the hollow base of the broken

61

aluminium mast and was stayed by Terylene rope shrouds. The mainsail was ready to hoist as a jury rig. "No chance," said Sam Solon.

Modesty held down her irritation. "The boat's fully seaworthy," she said patiently, "the forecast is good, and I won't have to sail to windward, which would be a problem. There's a breeze building up, it's a prevailing wind, and I can make a steady four or five knots with this rig, to bring me to Wellington in about six days. I've plenty of food and water, and I've got enough fuel to use the motor for up to forty-eight hours." She turned her cheek to the steadily freshening breeze, then looked at the two men aboard and gave a pleasant nod. "Thanks for your help, and have a good trip home."

Still gripping the gunwale, Sam Solon pushed back his cap and glared across at her from under hooked black eyebrows. "Do as you're told, girl," he said in a low hard voice.

"Goodbye, Mr. Solon."

He looked away from her. "Charlie. Jack. Put her aboard. Hog-tie her first, if you have to. This dinghy's no place for a rumpus."

The two men stared at each other, then at the black-haired brown-skinned long-legged girl who sat relaxed in the stern. They were too late to see a moment of fury in the midnight-blue eyes, and her face was impassive as she gazed thoughtfully up at the makeshift mast. Jack said, "Right, boss," and gave a laugh tinged with embarrassment as he moved from where he leant against the cabin housing. "How about coming quietly, sweetheart? It's just for your own good."

The Wasp provided no stable base for a text-book throw, and she knew she would have to improvise. With a resigned shrug she stretched out a hand. As he reached to take it she leaned forward, gripped his wrist, jerked, twisted, then went down on one knee to hook a hand behind his leg, converting his forward movement to a sideways roll which took him clear over the starboard quarter. His hoarse shout of unbelieving wrath was cut short by the splash.

Solon stopped the dinghy's motor and said, "Bloody hell. Grab her, Charlie."

Charlie stared blankly for a moment, then lunged forward, keeping low for balance, mouth tight with anger. She turned to face him, her back to the companionway now. As he closed, she offered him her right foot, and he snatched at the ankle. At once she snapped knee to chin, jerking him forward. Supported by elbows on the top of the cabin, she brought her free foot up to hook behind his neck and start swinging him sideways, to port. He released her ankle to save himself. Instantly her right leg straightened, the flat of her foot against his chest, and he was sent reeling back.

Solon had swung a leg over the gunwale when Charlie cannoned into him, and both went sprawling back over the side into the inflatable. It lurched with the impact and began to drift away. *The Wasp* came slowly round a few degrees. She saw Jack treading water astern, coughing and spluttering. He shook wet hair from his eyes, looked about him, then started swimming with a clumsy breast stroke towards the inflatable. She started the motor, brought *The Wasp* to a southerly heading, then settled beside the tiller, resentfully rubbing a bruised elbow. It was only one more hurt for an already aching body, but it was the unnecessary one too many. She drew a deep breath, realised that it was shaky, and muttered, "Oh shut up, you snivelling bitch."

When she looked back two minutes later she saw Jack being helped into the inflatable, legs waving in the air. Sam Solon was kneeling in the bow, looking towards her, a hand lifted to shade his eyes. *"Do as you're told, girl?"* she repeated to herself wonderingly. Solon's arm moved. She saw him take off his cap, wave it back and forth twice, then hold it quite still at arm's length above his head in a long salute. She decided it was a no-hard-feelings signal, and that he expected her to wave in acknowledgment.

She said, "Patronising bastard." Then, making a circle round her mouth with finger and thumb, she blew a long raspberry. She knew he could not hear, and might not even be able to see the gesture, but it made her laugh at herself, and she felt sudden elation dissolving the tensions of the last few days, the last few minutes.

It was a huge relief to be free of responsibility for the sick man, to be alone again. She looked about her, consciously revelling in the joy of her situation. Fine weather, a bunk to sleep in alone, no more sick nursing. Tonight she would cook herself a meal and open a bottle of red wine. It was scarcely possible to get any closer to perfection, she decided.

Twenty minutes later, with the engine stopped and the mainsail hoisted on the boom jurymast, *The Wasp* was running smoothly before a pleasant breeze. Modesty lay face down on a lounging mat spread on the foredeck, letting the sun and air do its healing work on her naked body, half asleep in the growing warmth of the day. The flying-boat came in low, banking as it swept over the little sloop. When she opened an eye and half lifted her head she could see the spray suppression strakes along the nose, the suppressor slots in the fuselage undersides. The aircraft flattened out, wings waggling. An Aldis lamp flashed. Dah-dit-dah-dit, dit-dit-dah.

C.U. See you. A statement for the moment or a promise for the future? She shrugged mentally, and settled down again to doze. Two minutes later the aircraft made another pass low over *The Wasp*, but this time she did not stir, and soon there was silence again except for the familiar sounds of the sea and the little boat.

4

The man who stood on the pavement in a residential street west of Sloterpark was decked out as if for a carnival or a fancy dress ball, though it was hard to imagine where either might be imminent at noon on a weekday in Amsterdam.

He wore a white Stetson, a check shirt, cowboy boots, and a drooping black moustache which was obviously false. His face was long, with puffy cheeks. A fringe of black hair showed beneath the brim of the Stetson. A revolver hung low on his right hip from a gunbelt. His appearance drew amused glances from passing cyclists and pedestrians, but their attention was brief, the Dutch being good at minding their own business.

The patrolman who eventually approached the Amsterdam cowboy considered that it was part of his business to look into the matter. He assumed the stranger to be American, and said in English, "Good morning. Please show me the gun you are wearing. I must be sure it is not a real one."

The cowboy stared for a moment with wild eyes. His hand moved and suddenly the gun was there, spinning on his middle finger. The patrolman watched uncertainly, wondering for a moment if he had stumbled upon a film unit making one of those crazy American comedies. The cowboy moved slowly back. Behind him was a terrace of houses, four steps leading up to each front door. The gun flashed from his right hand to his left, still spinning, then back again. People were stopping to watch now, and a mass twitch of startled reaction passed through the spectators as the cowboy fired into the air. It would be a blank, no doubt, but ...

The patrolman took a step forward and said, "Stop!" Even as he did so, the gun cracked again. A street lamp shattered. There were cries of alarm and protest, and a sudden drawing back. The gun spun, and fired once more. A youth straddling a Honda fell sideways with it as his front tyre burst. The patrolman called a warning to the crowd to keep back, and reached for the flap holster at his hip. The cowboy's gun stopped spinning and was fired again in the same instant. The patrolman fell limply back, his head striking the pavement with a dreadful sound.

There was a moment of unbelieving silence, then a girl began to scream and there came a babble of voices, frightened, angry, shocked, exhorting. The cowboy turned, mounted the steps to the front door behind him, pushed it open, and passed into the house. The door closed after him. The babble of the crowd almost ceased for a moment, then rose again more loudly. People clustered round the patrolman. A girl knelt beside him, saying she was a nurse, urging some of the men to keep the crowd back and to find a telephone. After thirty seconds or so, two young men tried the door of the house, found it locked, and began to hammer on it.

Four minutes later a police car and ambulance arrived. At the same time a man in clerical attire emerged from a sidestreet. He was a thin, cadaverous young man with hollow cheeks, dressed all in black except for his white collar, a fringe of gingery hair showing beneath the flat round hat he wore. He carried a street map, and a small haversack hung from his shoulder.

One policeman went running past him to reach the back

of the house, another was speaking urgently to a woman in the doorway of the house next door, a third was jemmying open the door through which the cowboy had disappeared. The clergyman spoke to a bystander in English and was told briefly what had happened. At once he pushed through the crowd to kneel beside the shot patrolman. The girl who was a nurse, kneeling on the other side, saw his collar and spoke in Dutch.

The man said, "I'm sorry, I don't understand. I'm English. Can I help?"

The girl said, "He's dead, father." She bit her lip and tears came to her eyes. She gestured to the patrolman's chest, where she had loosened the clothing about the ruin of the bullet's entry. A silver cross hung on a chain at his neck. She said, "He was a Catholic, I think."

The Reverend Uriah Crisp bowed his head. "We have the same shepherd, though we be of different flocks," he said in a loud, plangent voice. "I will pray for his soul."

He was still kneeling over the dead man, large hands clasped in prayer, eyes tightly closed, when the police broke down the door and entered the house. It proved to be untenanted, as the woman next door had told them, the furniture covered with dust sheets, for the owner had gone to Jakarta for six months. The back door was unlocked. On the kitchen floor lay a check shirt, cowboy pants and boots, a gunbelt, a drooping false moustache, and a Stetson with a fringe of black hair attached to the inside of the brim. There was no sign of any gun.

Four hundred yards away, in the small private Bor Museum which housed the collection of oriental furniture accumulated by Hendrik Bor in the nineteenth century, two men in overalls were carrying a chair along a corridor. A cloth was draped over their burden, a carved red-lacquer

67

chair made five hundred years before in the Hsuan-te period of the Ming dynasty. There were no visitors in the museum, which was closed between twelve and two. A guard and two attendants had been chloroformed and lay bound in different parts of the building.

The two men in overalls carried the draped chair out to the yard at the back of the museum. There, a third man was waiting. He opened the door of a plain brown van and helped lift the chair carefully into the back. The three men climbed in with it, and one of them spoke a word to the driver. The van pulled out of the yard and moved off. At the next road junction a police motorcyclist and two police cars flashed by in the opposite direction with sirens blaring.

*　　*　　*

In the Hotel Okura Inter-Continental, sitting in bed with a breakfast tray on his knees, Beauregard Browne looked up from the newspaper and called, "Come." Clarissa de Courtney-Scott entered wearing a low-cut Thai silk dress with a coat thrown round her shoulders. She looked bright-eyed and cheerful.

"Ah, there you are, poppet." Beauregard Browne put aside De Telegraaf and gave her an appraising smile. "Where did you spend the night?"

"Oh, with two awfully friendly Dutch journalists, Beau. Well, I spent the evening with one and the night with the other."

"Good. What's the score on Uriah's performance? I've been trying to read this Dutch stuff by sheer will-power."

"Well, Hugo said the police said they were following up clues, but that was official, and unofficially they hadn't got one. A clue, I mean." She slipped off the coat and came forward to sit on the bed. "Then later Wilhelm said much the same thing. He actually telephoned some police contact at about three this morning, to see if there were any developments. Is it all right about the chair?"

"I saw it carefully loaded into the container yesterday evening with the rest of the furniture we bought. It had been very nicely framed and upholstered to make a pair for that huge armchair in green uncut moquette."

"Super. The container will be aboard ship by now. I say, the Bor Museum losing that chair hardly made any space in last night's papers, did it?"

"As expected, chèrie. When a cop's been shot, people concentrate on that. Especially other cops, and especially when he's been shot by a mad disappearing cowboy. It was a nice diversion. Our friends could have walked out of the Bor with the thing in plain view, and I doubt if anyone would have noticed. Take this tray, my angel. I'm about to rise."

She carried the tray to a table and said pensively, "Are you quite happy about our friends, Beau?"

"You mean the local lads?" He stripped off cerise pyjamas and began to run through some limbering-up exercises, the well-proportioned muscles moving beautifully. "Well, the museum team have no idea who we are, they simply followed precise instructions and they'll be paid by Weber, who put the package together for us under my direction."

"It's Weber I'm just a spot worried about really, Beau. I've studied his file pretty closely, and there's nothing to put your finger on, but I just have a feeling he might talk one day. Either under pressure or if he needs to bargain. I know he's a hard man, very tough, but I think we should be careful."

"The potentially naughty Weber has been much on my mind, and for the same reason. So we shall indeed be very careful, sweetie."

"We're to meet him at the houseboat this morning at eleven."

"Thank you, my little secretary bird. That's when we must persuade the devious Weber to be utterly reliable." He completed a series of press-ups and looked over his shoulder at her. "Utterly reliable for ever."

Her eyebrows lifted, then she gave a nod. "Ah. Jolly good, Beau. We wouldn't use him again, and there's nothing like a complete cut-out." She glanced towards the door which led to an adjoining bedroom. "How's Uriah?"

"Sleeping the sleep of the just after yesterday's effort. He's always a trifle post-orgasmic after dispatching one of the ungodly."

"Gosh, yes, I know. Will you take him with you to see Weber this morning?"

"No, treasure. We mustn't be monotonous." He spoke from the floor, sitting up and lying back with hands behind his head, his voice giving little evidence of exertion. "It's really not wise to feed Uriah too much raw meat. Besides, you and I must keep our hands in. The cautious Weber will have that permanent bodyguard gorilla with him, of course, so we'll pop along together, you and I, shall we?" The violet eyes smiled up at her invitingly, and Clarissa de Courtney-Scott felt the sinews of her loins go taut with desire. She let nothing show in her face, for she knew it amused Beau to tease her, and the more she reacted the more he would prolong it.

"Yes, lovely," she said with enthusiasm, then picked up the newspaper and began to glance at it idly. "I must say Uriah was absolutely terrific yesterday. I was all set to move in and run an interference if anyone went after him too quickly, but he had them totally stunned. Did you have any trouble briefing him?"

"Not the tiniest." Beauregard Browne examined a cerise toenail which had chipped slightly, then rose smoothly to his feet and walked into the bathroom, leaving the door open. "I simply told him to wait till the copper came along, then do a few tricks and blast him, since he was an enemy of the Almighty. There were no questions. I really don't think one needs to bother any longer about finding reasons for the Hammer of God to operate. As the perceptive Dr. Feng says, Uriah's need is to use a gun. Give him a target and he'll concoct his own sufficient reasons. Come here and talk to me, *querida*."

Clarissa moved to the bathroom and leaned in the doorway, watching Beau take a shower. She and Dr. Feng were staying at the Carlton, as part of general security to avoid being identified as a group of four. Her Chinese colleague had proved something of a disappointment of late. On the island, during the six weeks following Lucian Fletcher's escape, Dr. Feng had been an inventive and attentive bed-mate whenever his turn came, but she now suspected that part of his interest stemmed from a wish to study her as a psychiatric case. Since coming to Amsterdam he had tended to neglect her in favour of the variety of girls the city had to offer.

Watching Beau turn off the shower and lather himself with fragrant soap, Clarissa said, "Did you see in the English papers yesterday that Fletcher flew home from Sydney?"

"I did indeed, but you had to look for it. He no longer presents an on-going story for the press, of course, so naturally he wouldn't stay in the headlines. They've exhausted both fact and speculation, and they managed to get sweet bugger-all out of dear Luke himself, except that the last thing he remembers is sitting on that little beach in Malta. I don't know which paper you read, but *The Times* suggests he was smitten by amnesia, and while wandering around in a daze he got caught up in a charter flight to Australia, and so on."

Clarissa laughed. "It's a bit thin. The *Mail* hinted that it was a publicity thing, not that Fletcher would go in for anything like that off his own bat, of course. They suggest it was all organised by some cunning press agent, who shall be nameless, and that Luke Fletcher went through with it in a kind of daze, still broken up by the death of his wife. He hasn't painted anything since then, and this unknown chap thought a big news splash might sort of get him going, you see."

"Oh dear. One sighs for a touch of logic in their invention."

"Yes. I was just thinking ... I haven't had a shower yet myself, so would it be all right if I popped in there with you, Beau? Then I'd only have to nip into the Carlton for a quick change on the way to do the Weber job."

"What a splendidly expert time-and-motion concept, Clarissa. Yes, do."

She sighed inwardly with relief, slipped the straps from her shoulders and let the dress fall. When she stood in the shower with him he soaped her body between embraces, then entered her.

"Ohhh ... doesn't it take you back, Beau? Remember how you used to sneak over the fence and in the back door when our people had gone out?"

"And you'd put away your homework and we'd end up like this in the bathroom, so we wouldn't leave any clues in your bedroom? Of course I remember, angel."

"M'mmm ... ah, that's good."

"Steady now. Time-and-motion is all very well, poppet, but since Daddy won't be bursting in there's plenty of time, so go easy with the motion, there's a good girl. I adore to linger."

72

"Gosh, sorry. I forgot."

"There. Now stay like that and keep still while I do your back."

"Beau, it ... it's frightfully difficult for me to keep still when I'm being screwed."

"Then chat, my precious. Converse. Distract that hot little mind from your erogenous zones."

She drew a deep breath and held the grabrail to brace herself. "Well ... the other day I asked Dr. Feng if he thought the chance of Luke Fletcher remembering anything had completely gone now, but he said there was still no guarantee."

"Of course there's no guarantee, sweetie-pie. Our Esteemed Patron knows that, so naturally we're having a close eye kept on the amnesiac Fletcher." Beauregard Browne laughed, and Clarissa caught her breath. "But wasn't it exciting for us all, my little honeypot? I mean, wasn't it? Picking up that transmission between such as the formidable Modesty Blaise and Willie Garvin, and monitoring her calls to Sydney later. Oh yes, and wondering if the blocks Feng had welded into the noble St. Luke's mind would really hold, or if he would talk, and tell Blaise all. It really was fantastically enlivening, I thought."

"Are they ... are they quite formidable?"

"Your conversation is becoming a trifle clipped, my little jewel. Blaise and Garvin? Oh yes, they're formidable all right. They put down Sexton, among others, which suggests major talent."

Clarissa made an effort to concentrate, to move her mind away from the area where Beau had now commenced a slow and delightful activity. Recalling what had occurred was as good a distraction as any, and she focused on that. At the time of Fletcher's rescue, Modesty Blaise had been sailing under the name of Lucienne Bouchier, but the conversation

73

on the amateur radio link had been immediately revealing to anyone who knew anything about the team of Blaise and Garvin. On Dragon's Claw island, she and Beau had listened-in to the rescue. Then had come the storm, and when it was over Blaise and Garvin had talked mainly in Arabic. This had seemed ominous, but when Fouad, one of Condori's guards, had been called in to translate the tape recording, it became clear that Dr. Feng's memory blocks had held firm, and Luke Fletcher had told her no more than that he was Luke Fletcher. The only reason for secrecy in the transmission was Modesty Blaise's wish to avoid publicity.

Clarissa de Courtney-Scott had never suffered from anxiety. It was an emotion virtually outside her concepts, as were several allied emotions. She had not worried that Fletcher might talk when he was picked up and taken to hospital in Sydney. If he did, then Beau or The Patron would do something about him. For a while the story had been splashed in all the newspapers, but then it died on them. The Patron had not lost interest, though. He had flown from Hobart to Sydney as soon as he was alerted by Beau over the island radio, in cipher, that Fletcher had escaped, and he had remained on red alert there for action until Fletcher had flown home. There had been no problems ...

"Beau ... can I ... move now?"

"Wait."

"Ohhh, you bastard."

The Patron had an ear planted in the hospital by the time Fletcher was brought in. Nursing staff, perhaps. And Fletcher had remembered nothing. The doctors had tried narco-hypnosis, but without result, and he had refused any further probing. By then Beau had flown down there on standby, ready to put Fletcher down if need be, but ...

Clarissa drew in a shuddering breath and clutched the

grabrail harder. He would be furious, and might not touch her for weeks, if she did not wait. Through clenched teeth she said, "I know we're having an eye kept on him, Beau, but that can't go on for ever. I think it ... it would be much safer to knock him off, honestly."

"That's up to Our Illustrious Patron to decide. It's a gamble, of course, but he's a gambler, like us." Beauregard Browne's voice was not quite controlled now. "And isn't it a superbly *stimulating* gamble, poppet? I mean, isn't it?"

"M'mmm."

"Isn't it? You agree?"

"M'mmm. Beau!"

"All right. Now *go*! Come on you luscious bitch! *Go, go, go!*"

*　　*　　*

At one minute to eleven Beauregard Browne and Clarissa de Courtney-Scott approached a houseboat on a canal near Ooster Park. He wore a black wig and a small moustache. From the left sleeve of his dark blue suit the corner of a white silk handkerchief protruded. The girl's hair was hidden under a headscarf. She wore jeans, a shapeless grey sweater, and dark glasses. In her hand she carried a rolled-up news-paper. She had no handbag.

When they walked up the short gangway and tapped on the door it was opened by a man with a big square face and big square shoulders, wearing a dark suit, a white shirt, and a tie in grey-and-white check. He stood back, jerked his head to instruct them to enter, then closed the door after them, leaned back against it, and slipped a hand under his jacket. Weber sat at a table smoking a brown cigarette and making notes on a pad. There was a bottle and some glasses on the table. With his fresh smooth complexion and jolly smile, Weber always looked avuncular.

"My friends," he said, and waved an inviting hand. "Come, sit and let us drink to a good success."

Beauregard Browne glanced at the big man with the hidden hand and said, "You are suspicious, meneer Weber. That's good. I like working with suspicious people. I feel safer."

Weber chuckled. "You have good security with me, Mr. Smith. Come. You and Miss Smith will join me in a schnapps, yes?"

They moved to the table, shook hands, accepted the drinks, and smiled polite acknowledgment when Weber raised his glass to "A very clever Englishman." Beaming, he went on, "You are the architect, Mr. Smith, and I am the contractor. You design, and I organise the execution of the work."

Beauregard Browne nodded. In dealing with Weber he had presented a brisk, pleasant personality, with no hint of his usual camp manner. "You have paid all the contracting parties, meneer Weber?" he asked.

"Yes. They are well satisfied."

"And you are well satisfied with your own fee?"

Weber spread his hands. "To be frank, I hope you will suggest a modest increase, in view of the manner in which the work was carried out."

"I prefer to keep to the agreement."

"Then let us say no more." Weber chuckled again. "Next time I must negotiate better terms for myself, yes?"

"That will be perfectly in order. It was part of our agreement that none of the contracting parties you employed should know of my existence. They were to understand that you were the principal and originator of the affair. Have I your assurance that this has been the case?"

"Most certainly, my dear friend." Weber tapped his nose. "Even if I were not an honest man, I would not give away a piece of information so valuable. I hope we shall have occasion to do more business together. The Rijksmuseum holds many fine treasures."

Beauregard Browne stroked his cheek musingly. "The Rembrandt self-portrait might interest me ... and it could well be sound strategy to act again very quickly, since that is the last thing the police would expect." He gave a little nod. "Yes. You may well hear from me in the course of the next few days, meneer Weber."

"Excellent! Another schnapps?"

"Thank you, no. We have to meet a friend at Schiphol."

"Then I will not detain you." Weber passed a pink document across the table. "This is the receipt for the consignment of furniture, in case you should need it."

"Thank you."

The container had been consigned to Athens. Before it arrived, Beauregard Browne would have arranged for it to be reconsigned to Sydney. He did not believe in letting his contractors know more than was necessary. The original purpose of today's visit had been to collect the receipt, since it would have been unwise to leave it in Weber's hands. Now, with the decision to put Weber down, it had been vital to ensure that the receipt should not be found in his possession.

Beauregard Browne and Clarissa stood up. Weber came round the table to shake hands. The bodyguard stood away from the door. Clarissa took two steps, then staggered, a hand to her head. She muttered, "Sorry. I feel a little dizzy."

Beauregard Browne caught her arm. "Surely not on one glass of schnapps? Sit down by the window for a moment." He helped her to the bench seat and glanced at Weber. "Could we have a little air?"

"Of course." Weber gestured to his minder and said, "*Open het raam.*"

The man moved forward and reached for the handle of

the window to one side of Clarissa's head. Beauregard Browne straightened up and turned towards Weber. "Sorry about this. She'll be all right in a minute."

The rolled-up newspaper was still clutched in Clarissa's hand. It was a thin roll, consisting of only a few pages. As the bodyguard reached out beside her, she presented one end of the roll to a point just below his breast-bone, and pushed hard upwards. The roll of newspaper crumpled. Within it, gripped in her hand, was a short wooden handle in which was sunk one end of a twelve-inch length of bicycle spoke. The other end of the tempered steel wire had been filed to a sharp point which slid easily into the bodyguard's heart.

Weber was startled to see the man slump suddenly to his knees, head and shoulders resting on the bench seat beside the girl. She gave a sudden toothy smile, then took off her dark glasses. Weber saw that she was gazing at him with what seemed intense fascination. Fear struck suddenly into him, and he looked quickly at the Englishman. Mr. Smith wore an absent-minded smile. His hands, held in front of him, were empty. Then they moved. The right hand took the corner of the silk handkerchief which protruded from the left sleeve. With a smooth swift movement the silk was drawn out; too long and narrow to be a handkerchief.

Clarissa held her breath. It was several months now since she had seen Beau do what he called his Handkerchief Trick. This was the way the Thugs of India had claimed a million victims through centuries past in their worship of the goddess Kali, the Dark Mother. The silk was a modification of the *rumal* used by the Thugs for their ritual killing.

The small weight in the free end brought the silk round in a flowing curve about Weber's neck and into Beauregard Browne's waiting left hand, all so fast that Weber had not even begun to react. Clarissa saw the sharp forward jerk, saw the powerful wrists turn down and in, snapping across so that the fists came up against the side of Weber's neck, beneath the ear. The man's head jerked sideways, and there came a muffled sound as the neck broke.

Beauregard Browne let the dead man fall and put the *rumal* away. Clarissa said, "Gosh, that was terrific, Beau. So absolutely smooth."

"You were rather neat yourself, my little honeypot." He moved to the table and carefully wiped the glasses they had used. Clarissa pushed the bodyguard over so that he fell to the floor on his back, pulled out the slender spoke, and wiped it on the newspaper. There was virtually no bleeding.

She said, "Should we take the spoke or leave it, Beau?"

"Leave it. But hang on a second, duckie." He pressed Weber's fingers to one of the glasses he had wiped, and the bodyguard's to the other, then put them both back on the table. "Right, let's have it." He wiped the hilt of the weapon, which was simply four inches of broom-handle, then wrapped Weber's fingers round it before letting it drop to the floor. "Did you touch anything else?"

"No, I was terribly careful all the time, Beau."

The violet eyes rested approvingly on her. "Right, sweetie, let's go." He took her arm, then paused to survey the scene. "Weber stabbed the gorilla, who broke Weber's neck before expiring. It won't stand up to close scrutiny, but one must always offer an overworked police force a simple answer of some sort, even if they rather doubt that it's the right one. After all, they're only human, aren't they, treasure? I mean, aren't they?"

5

"If there's one thing I cannot stand," said Judith Rigby, glancing towards the refreshment stall, "it's a woman going with a man old enough to be her father, like that Blaise creature."

It was not true that this was the one thing the attractive and energetic Mrs. Rigby could not stand. There was an almost unlimited number of vexations she found insupportable, such as abstract art, amateur psychologists, association football, and Australian cricketers, to name only the first few alphabetically, but when she declared her inability to tolerate these affronts, she invariably described them as unique in this respect.

George Rigby, her husband, sold an old Superman comic to a Cub Scout for two pence and looked across to the present cause of his wife's suffering. The girl had black hair tied in two bunches behind her ears, and wore a fine check shirt with a denim skirt. She was drinking from a bottle of lemonade through a straw, and had her hand through the arm of a rather good-looking man in his early sixties, with upright carriage and greying hair.

George Rigby had seen the girl on several occasions and met her briefly once. Her name was Modesty Blaise, and two or three years ago she had bought and renovated *Ashlea*, the rambling cottage which stood in several acres of land a mile or so outside the village of Benildon. Here she had since spent a total of two or three months in each year. There was no pattern to her visits. She might be at the cottage winter or summer, for a week-end, a week, or a month.

It was understood in the village that she was rich, lived mainly in a penthouse overlooking Hyde Park, but travelled abroad frequently. She did not attach herself to any social circle in the area, but was friendly enough and often attended village functions, which she seemed to enjoy. Watching her now as she strolled with her companion across the centre of the small field where the fête was being held, George Rigby said, "Perhaps he *is* her father."

"Oh, rubbish," his wife said impatiently. "His name's Sir Gerald Tarrant, and he's something or other in the Foreign Office. Margaret Dee told me."

"Who told her?"

"Roger, of course."

"Ah, yes. Roger was a Whitehall Warrior until he retired. But perhaps," continued George Rigby, who was far better informed than his wife but enjoyed annoying her, "perhaps he's her uncle."

"Oh, don't talk like an idiot, George. You know very well she has all sorts of men staying with her at *Ashlea*. There's that young Chinese."

"Weng."

"What?"

"Weng. His name is Weng, and he's a sort of houseboy cum chauffeur cum groom cum whatever."

"How do *you* know?"

"Old Arnold the blacksmith told me. Arnold looks after her horses and says she's a very pleasant young lady."

"Of course. You men always go for the flashy type."

George Rigby re-stacked a pile of *British Medical Journals* from 1948 to 1953 left over from the last three fêtes. "She's got looks all right, but I wouldn't go along with flashy. Look at her. No jewellery and hardly a scrap of make-up. Just very good, very expensive, but unflashy clothes."

"If there's one thing I cannot stand," said Judith Rigby, "it's the sort of husband who always leaps to the defence of other women."

"I'm not defending her, my dear. Just saying she's not flashy."

"*Don't* call me my dear."

"Sorry." George glowed inwardly. That always got under her skin.

Judith said, "Then there's that extraordinary Cockney man with the stupid name. He often stays with her."

"Willie Garvin. He has his own room at *Ashlea*."

"What? How do you know?"

"The girl who works for the Hammonds also works at *Ashlea* when it's occupied. Bob Hammond told me."

"You men have obviously discussed her very thoroughly."

"So have you women, but that's not surprising, either. She's a pretty intriguing character. Old Harry used to be on *The Standard*, and he said she's a bit of a mystery, but in Fleet Street it's generally agreed that she's done one or two quite spectacular things."

"I'm sure she's capable of that."

"No, he meant hush-hush stuff."

Judith Rigby sniffed. "If there's one thing I cannot stand it's journalists who put out idiotic rumours. George, you'd do much better to have all the paperbacks at the front of the stall and those silly bound volumes of the *Sunday Circle* at the back. I'm just going across to see if the Scouts have killed anybody with their Throwing the Wellie-boot competition. Such an absurd game."

"All right, darling." George let her turn her back before

launching his kidney punch. "Oh Judy, when you pass the refreshment stall, you might remind Geoffrey to be ready to announce the hang-gliding demo."

She stopped short and turned to stare. "The what?"

George waved his arm in a vague gesture out across the broad valley to the hills beyond. "Your Cockney man, he's giving a hang-gliding demonstration at three o'clock."

"He's *what*?"

"Giving a demonstration of—"

"Yes, I *heard*, George. I was simply expressing amazement. What happened? Who arranged it? How do you know? Why wasn't I told? After all, I am a member of the committee."

"Well, Willie Garvin and the Blaise girl both do a bit of hang-gliding over at Barnwell." George nodded towards the hills across the valley and a distant spire. "Mary Forester happened to see them there yesterday, and thought it would be a bit interesting, especially for the young folk, so this morning she phoned the cottage and spoke to Modesty Blaise, and one way or another it was agreed that Willie Garvin would fly across from Barnwell and do some zooming about over the valley—if the weather's okay and he can find a thermal."

"That Mary Forester takes *far* too much upon herself."

"Oh, I don't know. It was all on the spur of the moment, and it seemed a pretty good idea to me. Nigel told me about it when I was setting up the stall. I thought you knew," George lied earnestly.

"Then you thought wrong, George, as usual. And what's the *point*, anyway? It won't make any money for us."

"Ah, well, he's going to land in Draper's Meadow next door, so Nigel and Mary have set up a table there selling markers for twenty pence each. You go and stick your

83

marker in the ground, and whoever owns the one closest to where Willie Garvin lands after the demo wins the prize."

"What prize?"

"Well, the usual bloody awful sort of prize, I suppose. A bottle of elderberry wine, or something. But when I popped across to look at the meadow just now I saw lots of people there shoving in markers."

"If there's one thing I cannot stand, George, it's people like Mary Forester who—*Ma-a-ary*, why there you are, dear! George was just telling me about this marvellous idea of yours ..."

* * *

Modesty Blaise squinted along the straw and sucked the last of the lemonade from the bottle with a long, unmannerly gurgle. Tarrant said, "I'm glad you enjoyed that."

"I enjoy it all." She looked about her, at the stalls and bunting, the scuffed grass, the little amateurish sideshows, the strolling villagers, the scattering of those who had once been termed the gentry, and the blue sky above the line of great elms planted by order of a squire who had died with the Light Brigade at Balaclava. "I enjoy having lucky dips and getting sticky with hot sausages and ice cream, and watching the whole scene, and hearing bits of conversation."

"The rural English are a risible people, I agree. I'm one of them myself, by birth."

"For goodness' sake, I'm not laughing at them." She dropped the empty bottle in a litter bin, and wiped her hands and mouth on a tissue. "I savour the stability of it. Deep roots. Long traditions. A sense of continuity. When you've lived the weird and wicked life I have, you become a sucker for the quiet pleasures of normality. Coming to watch me throw a bale of straw?"

"Is that your idea of normality?"

"I've done it at the last two fêtes, so it's almost a tradition."

They moved to where a group of countrymen stood by two vertical poles with a long bamboo cane strung between them on halliards, so that it could be raised or lowered. Several tightly compressed wire-bound bales of straw lay nearby. Pitchforks were stuck in two of the bales. On another sat a little old man with a wrinkled face, brown as a nutmeg, wearing a smock. A placard said cryptically: *Beat Old Davey For A Prize.*

Modesty's approach was greeted with the slightly forced jollity of men not quite at ease. It was hardly surprising, thought Tarrant. She was a young woman of striking beauty, almost a stranger, and one who fitted into no niche that they could easily imagine.

"Afternoon, Miss. I 'ope you been practising."

"Going to give Ol' Davey a good 'iding, eh, Miss?"

"We been waiting for you to come an' stir 'im up a bit."

She said a general hallo, exchanged a few smiling words, then indicated Tarrant. "This gentleman is going to back me today, and he's very rich, so let's make it five pounds."

"Ooh, my word. Come on, Ol' Davey. There's a fiver in the kitty if you can beat the young lady."

Old Davey got creakingly to his feet, plunged one of the pitchforks into a bale of straw, then with an easy turn of his body tossed it over the cane strung nine feet from the ground. Modesty smiled at Tarrant. "You want to try it?"

He took a pitchfork, drove it carefully into a bale, and tested the weight, judging it to be about half a hundredweight. "I think not, my dear."

"All right. Hold my bag." She lifted the bale on the fork, balanced herself, swung with the same movement as Old

85

Davey, and the bale flew easily over the cane. The little old man grinned, showing three teeth, and nodded at his companions. "Up three 'ands, then," he said in a high throaty voice.

The cane was raised. Old Davey tossed the bale again, then Modesty. After two more raises, Modesty's effort failed to clear. Old Davey pronged her own bale on his fork and tossed it over, then sat down again and lit a half-smoked cigarette taken from behind his ear. She said, "Thank you, Davey," and received an amiable nod of acknowledgment. "That's five pounds then, Mr. Hobbs."

"Well, 'at's what you said, Miss."

Tarrant handed over a note, and there was a chorus of polite thank-you's and goodbyes from the countrymen as he moved away with Modesty on his arm. When they were out of earshot he said, "Could you have beaten Old Davey?"

She turned a startled gaze on him. "No, of course not. I wouldn't patronise him like that, and I wouldn't take a dive on your money."

"Yes. A stupid question. What a remarkable old chap."

"He's over seventy, and there's nobody can beat him at that, not even men twice as strong. I could watch him for hours. It's a marvellous example of what you can do with perfect timing and coordination."

"I've seen you demonstrate that yourself, in somewhat more exacting circumstances."

She shot him a quick, rather troubled glance and said, "Oh dear, do I remind you of that time?"

He thought for a few moments. "Whenever I see you, I remember very vividly those minutes in the caves when you were fighting the invincible Sexton."

"I mean before that, when he was trying to break you."

"No," he said a little shortly. "I rarely think of that."

86

"I'm not prying, but you've seemed a little sad since you came down, and I just wondered what's wrong. When I spoke to you on the phone last week you sounded on top of the world, and looking forward to your retirement in a couple of months. But then, just now, I thought perhaps I make you depressed because I remind you of that bad time."

"Oh God, no, Modesty," he said softly. "You remind me of nothing I want to forget. I'm sorry if I haven't been very good company. I didn't think I was letting it show."

"Letting what show?"

He sighed and glanced about him. "It's true I look forward to retirement. I'm tired of putting my people into situations which kill them. Oh, I know it has to be done, but I've been doing it long enough, and I'll be glad to have someone else carry the load."

They halted a little way from the Punch and Judy booth, and she said, "So?"

"So I believed I'd done it for the last time, but three days ago I found I was wrong. Remember John Ryan?"

She thought, then shook her head. "No. One of your agents?"

"You had dealings with him when I was buying some I.E. stuff from you during the days of *The Network*. He met you in Marseilles to negotiate."

"That was Alan Ritchie."

"No, it was Ryan using his cover name. He was one of my best."

"I found him impressive. You say 'was'?"

"He got blown in Sofia, and I understand he's now in Lubyanka Prison about to be sucked dry."

"Will they get anything important?"

Tarrant shrugged. "A few insights, perhaps. Nothing startling. I've grown old and soft, I suppose, but the thought that he's now about to be broken by experts depresses me. I'm truly sorry I've failed to conceal it from you."

"It's time you retired." She stood gazing absently towards the Punch and Judy booth. "I have a cover identity that allows me to operate in East Germany, so does Willie. We might be able to get hold of somebody important enough to offer as a swap—"

"No!" he said sharply. "They wouldn't play. And in any case I want your unqualified promise that you won't act on anything I've just said."

Punch had just persuaded the policeman to demonstrate how to put one's head in the noose, and was now busy hanging him to delighted laughter from the children watching. Modesty opened a bag of home-made coconut ice she had bought earlier. "All right," she said. "But if we're not going to do anything about it, then let's forget it."

"Yes. Again I'm sorry."

"Is this anything to do with why you're being watched?" She offered him the bag.

"Watched?" He lifted a hand in refusal.

"There's a girl with red hair. Rather strapping and horsey but no less attractive for that. Fits in very well with this scene." She put a piece of the coconut ice in her mouth.

Tarrant kept his eyes on her and said, "How do you know she's watching?"

"I just know. I suppose it could be me, though. One or both of us, anyway."

Tarrant believed her, and smiled as if she had made a joke. "Shall we stroll on a bit? Ah, you mean the girl by the white elephant stall? Yes, very county. Have you any idea why either of us should be under surveillance?"

"No. But there are plenty of reasons rooted in the present for you and the past for me."

"Action?"

"Not unless she starts something. My guess is she's just doing a routine job on you. After all, you're a natural subject for regular surveillance."

The loudspeaker said, "May I have your attention, please, ladies and gentlemen? Very shortly we hope to see a demonstration of hang-gliding over the valley. If you stand with your backs towards the church and look west, you should soon be able to see—ah, one moment, please. We have some binoculars here. Yes, there he is, high over Furze Hill, after taking off on the far side into the wind. He must have found some up-currents to gain height. The flyer is Mr. Garvin, by the way. I think some of you know him, he stays here in Benildon from time to time. I must thank Mr. and Mrs. Forester for arranging this, and as you know there's a splendid prize for whoever has marked the spot which is closest to where the hang-glider lands . . ."

The voice droned on. Tarrant shaded his eyes and stared out across the valley. Modesty said, "There. At about a thousand feet, a couple of degrees south of Barnwell church spire."

"Ah, I've got him." Tarrant watched the red wing swell and foreshorten as the glider banked first to one side then the other. "Is it very dangerous?" he said.

"I think less so than driving a couple of hundred miles on the M1. That's always providing you're cautious about your equipment, the weather, and staying within your limits. We've been doing it for about three years now, and I don't think we've had any truly hairy moments. Just a few minor bumps and scrapes on landing."

Willie was nearer now, turning in a wide circle on one wing-tip. Tarrant saw that he wore a crash helmet and what looked like motorbike leathers. His hands gripped the triangular frame beneath the wing, and he was extended in a horizontal position in his harness. There was something magical in the lazy way the glider lolled about above the valley. Tarrant said, "Is it as exhilarating as it looks?"

Her voice beside him said, "Every bit. No engines, no power. It's as near to true flying as we'll ever get. I'll take you for a little glide next time you're here, if the weather's right."

"Is that possible, a passenger?"

"Yes, with sufficient wing area. We can make a short straight flight down from the hill-top, sitting side by side. Enough to give you something of how it feels."

"I shall look forward to that," said Tarrant, and meant it. The glider levelled out at a hundred feet, turning into the wind for the approach to Draper's Meadow. The loudspeaker squawked metallically, warning everybody to keep clear. The red wing swept down, surprisingly fast, Tarrant thought. Then it tilted back, slowing abruptly. Willie's legs swung down, his feet touched the ground and he trotted forward two or three paces before coming to a halt.

A man went running out to mark the touchdown point. Modesty said, "Willie was going to do a belly-landing. It looks dramatic, but it's pretty painless on grass." She giggled. "I was encouraging him like mad, hoping for a laugh, but he must have caught on."

"Caught on to what?"

"There were cows in that meadow all morning. Nice healthy unconstipated cows. I had visions of Willie doing a belly-skid right through a cow-pack. He's a hoot when things turn slapstick."

Tarrant laughed, and wondered if he would ever fully understand these two. Their affection, never spoken, was measureless, yet it had dawned on him only of late that each

90

took occasional delight in disconcerting the other. As if echoing his thoughts, Modesty said, "Incidentally, that Willie Garvin is up to something. He asked if he could bring a friend to tea."

"Unnamed?"

"Yes. And I didn't want to spoil it for him by asking, so we'll wait and see." She patted Tarrant's arm. "Look, I think he needs help. Will you go and keep the children from trampling all over his glider while he folds it up? I'll fetch the Land-Rover."

"Wait a minute," he said anxiously as she turned to go. "How do you keep children from doing something these days? It's not my line at all."

"Just keep hitting them with your stick. Oh, go *on*, don't be such a coward." She moved away, then looked back. "And don't forget the cows."

*   *   *

An hour had gone by. Tarrant sat on a high stool in the kitchen, holding a tankard of ale, watching Modesty make a salad. He had put on a fresh pair of socks and spare trousers.

"The horrible Garvin was convulsed, of course," he said. "And I must say it distracted the children."

She gave a snuffle of laughter. "It was certainly impressive, going right in up to mid-calf. I warned you they were healthy cows."

"Very true. And thank you for the cleansing operations."

"We women know our place. They'll be dry by morning." She examined a tomato and began to slice it. "I'm sorry you have to go back to town tomorrow, but at least you and Willie can go together. He's cutting down two dead elms for Janet."

91

"So he was saying." Tarrant drank some ale. "Modesty, was he joking when he said he was watched in Barnwell today?"

"No. He was a bit amused, but he meant it."

"A vicar, though?"

"A man in clerical garb, he said. And at Benildon we had the squire's red-haired daughter type. It seems as if Willie and I are the subjects, rather than you."

Tarrant watched the movement of her body, the play of hands and arms as she moved from worktop to sink to wash a head of celery. He remembered the moments deep under the earth's skin, in the great Lancieux Caves, when that same flesh and blood and bone, together with the will that animated them, had held back death itself from him by destroying a killer who was accounted undefeatable.

"What will you do?" he said. "I mean about being watched?"

"Oh ... nothing yet. It's rather like hearing a faint noise from your car. If it's anything bad, it'll get worse and become more obvious, but often it just disappears. Not worth taking the whole thing apart to see what's wrong. Besides, we might have been mistaken."

Tarrant thought this unlikely, but did not pursue the matter. "What about this friend Willie's gone to meet at the station, the one who's coming to tea?"

"He modified it to 'acquaintance', didn't he? But no sex was specified. I know our Willie, though. He's inwardly smug because he knows I'm going to be taken aback."

"And you can't begin to guess?"

She laughed. "I haven't really tried. As a matter of fact I've realised I quite like being taken aback. It's an antidote for complacency. Will you push the trolley or carry the tray?"

He drained his tankard. "Carry, please."

"All right, there it is. I wonder if we can manage the salad just with forks? Well, if we can't it'll be good practice." She took off her pinafore and hung it on a hook. "Let's take up our positions."

They had not been in the long drawing room with its dark beams for more than five minutes when Tarrant, by the window, turned his head to say, "Here's Willie."

She came and stood beside him, watching the car move steadily up the long drive from the road. It halted on the apron near the big double garage, and two men got out. One was Willie Garvin, a bland smile on his rough-hewn face. The other was two or three inches shorter than Willie, and of slighter build. His untidy brown hair looked as if it had been lopped by his own hand. He was clean shaven, his face rather pale and hollow, the eyes deepset. His hands kept moving in and out of the pockets of the shabby green corduroy jacket he wore over a thin rollneck shirt. Every movement seemed effortful, as if he were fighting some heavy tension, and when he turned at last, with Willie beside him, to look towards the cottage, it was as if he had to brace himself to do so.

Modesty said softly, "My God, I'll kill Willie for this. It's Luke Fletcher."

They moved from the window, and after a few moments heard the sound of the front door being opened and Willie's voice saying cheerfully, "Honest, Mr. Fletcher, she won't eat you." The two men appeared in the doorway of the drawing room, Fletcher chewing his lip, Willie urging him gently forward. "There we are, Mr. Fletcher. This is the young lady you wanted to meet again, eh? Princess, this is Luke Fletcher."

Modesty smiled. "Who needs no introduction." She put out her hand. "This is a welcome surprise, Mr. Fletcher."

"Surprise?" Still holding her hand, he glanced round

93

anxiously at Willie, then looked at her again. "I understood Mr. Garvin had ...?"

"Ah, well, no, I don't think I actually said it was you," Willie broke in, eyes half closed in an effort of memory. "You came an' saw me at *The Treadmill*, asking if I thought it would be all right for you to look up Miss Blaise, and I said I thought she'd be very 'appy to see you, and maybe you could come down today. But I don't think I actually mentioned your name to 'er."

Willie stopped, disconcerted, for it was clear that Luke Fletcher was no longer listening. He had released Modesty's hand and moved closer, staring with enormous intensity, his hand moving lightly to touch her face, to lift her chin a little, to adjust a wisp of hair. He nodded, breathing hard through his nose as if from exertion, and gently ran fingers and thumbs down the open neck of her shirt, parting it a little.

She did not move, but said with a touch of amusement, "We're not on the boat now, with you half delirious, Mr. Fletcher."

He jumped as if stung, and stepped back, pressing fists to his temples. "Oh God, I'm sorry. So sorry. It was just seeing you, and wondering how I could best capture ... I used to do it with Bridie all the time, and I forgot ... I really do beg your pardon."

"That's quite all right. Let me introduce you to Sir Gerald Tarrant."

"Oh. How—how do you do? You must be ..." He looked at Modesty again. "No, the name's different, so this gentleman isn't your father?"

"Well, no. But I suppose he's the nearest I have to one. Now come and sit down, Mr. Fletcher. We're going to have tea on our knees, and we can leave Willie to pass things round and look after us. Do you mind if I ask you some questions?"

"No. No, of course not. Er—could I thank you first? I mean, for what you did. I remember everything, right from when that shark tipped me in the water." He began to shiver. "I don't know how you did it. And then afterwards, you . . ." He lifted his head to stare at her. "I think you must be the kindest person I've ever known."

Greatly entertained, Tarrant saw her direct a baleful glare at Willie as he held the salad bowl for her. "Everyone says the same thing, Mr. Fletcher," Willie agreed soberly.

"Er . . . I'd be glad if you'd call me Luke." He looked embarrassed. "Miss Blaise did, on the boat, just before they took me away."

"So I did, even though I didn't entirely believe it then. How is it you knew who I was, Luke? I was travelling under another name."

"Yes, but just after you got me away from the shark you said who you were, and I remembered the name later."

She grimaced. "That wasn't very clever of me."

"I didn't mention it to anybody," he said hastily. "In the hospital in Sydney they thought you were Lucienne Bouchier, so I realised you didn't want people to know. Then I came back to England, and I wanted to find you and say thank you, and I mentioned you to a chap I know who works in Fleet Street—oh, not about you being the girl on the boat. Anyway, he said, 'Christ, Luke, she's a mystery, that one, what d'you want to see her for?' But I didn't tell him, and then he went on to say you had a special friend, and where he lived, so I went to see Willie Garvin first." Fletcher sucked in a long breath, then drank his cup of tea in two gulps.

Modesty said, "Why see Willie first?"

"Oh, to ask if he thought you'd mind. I mean, I realised

95

you didn't want people to know it was you on that boat, and I understand, because I feel the same way. I'm a painter, you see, and I've always hated it when people wanted to ask questions and take photographs and so on."

Tarrant stared at the man wonderingly. It was hard to credit that Luke Fletcher felt it necessary to tell anybody that Luke Fletcher was a painter, but his honesty was patent. Modesty said gravely, "Yes, we know you're a painter, Luke. I have *Estaminet* hanging in the dining room here. I bought it last year."

His face lit up. "That's marvellous! I'm so glad you like it. Oh God, you *must* like it, Berenson sticks such enormous prices on them. Look, Mr. Garvin said you wouldn't mind if I came, so I did what he suggested, but if it's not convenient, then please say so."

She shook her head. "Willie didn't put it strongly enough. I admire your work immensely and I'm very glad to have you visit me. Now Willie's going to pour you another cup of tea, then he'll fetch a cloth to sponge that tomato and French dressing off your trousers, then we'll stop being polite and worried and apologetic, and just relax. How does that strike you?"

Fletcher looked in surprise at the plate in his hand, at the small spillage from it, at Willie, Tarrant, and finally at Modesty. Tension seemed suddenly to drain out of him, and he gave a smiling sigh of relief. "Yes, I'd like that," he said. "Um ... would you mind if I popped to the loo first? I forgot to go on the train, I was busy looking out of the window."

"I'm afraid our manners have slipped with the surprise. I might have thought to offer you the bathroom when you arrived. Willie?"

"Sure, Princess."

When they were on their way upstairs, Tarrant said softly, "What an extraordinary man."

She nodded. "Not a shred of harm, guile, or vanity in him. I don't wonder his wife had to shelter him from the world, he's far too vulnerable. And no wonder he doted on her. He kept thinking I was Bridie the first day or two on the boat."

"I have a feeling that he's composed almost entirely of talent," said Tarrant slowly, "and that perhaps there's not much else."

"Well at least he has admirable talents, not nasty ones like us."

"My dear, you're being defensive on his behalf."

"Why not? I pulled him out of the sea and nursed him for several days, so naturally I have a proprietary interest."

Willie came into the room chuckling to himself. "He's just been telling me how you'd bring 'im a bucket on the boat every time he wanted to go. Said I'd no idea 'ow marvellous you were. I think you've got a fan there, Princess."

She laughed and shook her head. "You're a wicked bastard, Willie love."

He raised his eyebrows and looked vaguely hurt. "Not really. Luke Fletcher wasn't going to stop till 'e found you, so it was no use putting 'im off. All I did was make it a surprise."

"Did he say anything about himself when he came to *The Treadmill*? About being adrift in that dinghy?"

"Only that he's still got no idea what 'appened. I mentioned those hypodermic marks on 'is arm, but he didn't know where they came from. It's funny, he doesn't seem all that interested."

Modesty nodded. "Then let's leave it out of the conversation. I'm relying on you two to carry the chat. When he's talking to me, his eyes start glazing and he begins to go into that painter-trance, seeing me as a subject."

Willie cocked an ear, rolled up his eyes in mock despair,

97

then went out of the room again, calling, "Turn *left* out of the bathroom, Luke. Left, then right."

Modesty watched the door pensively. She murmured, "So all Willie did was make it a surprise? Well, I'll tell you this. Our Willie is lying his head off. There's something else."

During the next hour Luke Fletcher spoke little, listening contentedly to an easy conversation in which there were openings for him to join in if he wished, and ate his way hungrily through two large plates of chicken salad, several pieces of brown bread and butter, and some fruit cake. After tea he eagerly accepted Modesty's invitation to walk with her while Willie Garvin and Sir Gerald Tarrant washed up.

He enjoyed the stables, the walk across the small meadow and back through the copse, and the bright colours of the untidy flower beds. He did not react at all to the workshop in the converted barn, and looked uneasily at the clay pigeon layout. It was as they returned to the cottage that he clapped a hand to his brow and said, "I forgot. I brought something for you to see." He ran to where Willie had parked the car, and was opening the rear door when Willie called from the cottage doorway. "In 'ere, Luke. I brought them in."

"Oh. Oh, thanks, Willie. I forgot." He took Modesty's arm, his eyes anxious once more. "I was going to throw them away, but I showed Willie, and he said I ought to bring them down. Well, actually he said he'd cut my arms and legs off if I didn't."

At the door she gave Willie a wary, questioning look and received a puzzled smile in return. When she entered the drawing room, Tarrant was contemplating a large thin package of rumpled brown paper tied with string and resting on the sofa. Luke Fletcher picked it up, tried to undo the knot, then gave up and pulled the string carelessly over one corner. Willie Garvin caught his breath and said, "Careful, you dozy burke!"

Fletcher grinned. "You worry too much, Willie," he said surprisingly. "Try to relax."

The wrapping fell away, and he moved to set three oblongs of hardboard on the back of the sofa so that they were propped against the wall. Each was about thirty inches wide by twenty deep. Modesty moved to stand beside Tarrant, and there began a silence in the room which was to last for several minutes.

In the natural light which came obliquely from the windows the colours were bold and powerful, typical of a Fletcher painting. His handling of light and texture seemed to spring from careless virtuosity. His attack was that of one who had total mastery of technique. Above all, the paintings held an aching intensity of emotion, a matrix from which emerged a simple statement of desperate need.

The first showed a dark-haired girl crouching as she came through the companionway of a small boat. The patch of sky visible beyond her was black and red, menacing as a spiked mace. She wore shorts and a shirt open to the waist, both soaked and clinging to her. The moulding of the thin material over the curves of her body was breath-taking. The background detail, as in any Fletcher painting, was immaculately suggested. Somehow, in the lines of body, neck, and head, he had conveyed an overwhelming sense of struggle, yet rising even above this was the conviction that though she was alone in the struggle she was not in fact alone; she was coming to one who was with her, depending upon her, needing her.

Tarrant gave a tiny start as he saw in the foreground the seed of that powerful conviction—part of a rumpled blanket lying not quite flat on the bunk because a fold of it rose to cover one foot of whoever lay there in the cabin.

The second picture showed part of her face, her temple, ear, eye, and line of jaw; then the shoulder and the long line

of naked back and spine reaching away to the rise of buttocks. A strangely beautiful picture. This was what a man
would see if she were lying partly on top of him, head low,
an arm and a leg spread across him, holding him. It did not
suggest sexual union, but there was no doubting the presence
of the unseen man, and again came that sense of his need, of
his clinging to sanity or survival in the person of the dark-
haired girl.

The third picture showed Modesty almost full face. She
was sitting on the deck of the cabin, her legs braced across
it, leaning to the pitch of the boat. She wore the same shirt
and shorts, but dry now. Her tangled hair was tied back in
a club. In her hands she held an open can of food and a
spoon. There were hollows under her eyes, a bandage about
one arm and one hand, a grubby plaster across her brow; but
the gaze, the posture, the whole aura captured by Luke
Fletcher's fierce brush, spoke of a contemplative calm as she
ate from the can. And for the third time there came that
certainty of another presence, quietly depicted here by an
empty can with a spoon in it, wedged against the bunk rail
at the extreme edge of the picture.

Willie Garvin had seen the pictures before, but he stood
drinking them in with dreamy pleasure. Tarrant was feeling
excitement throb in his veins as the impact kept coming at
him; almost painfully, for the paintings caught the very
essence of her in that aspect in which he had himself seen
her and needed her, at a time when he had suffered long and
brutally, and awaited a hard death.

It was Luke Fletcher himself who spoke first. "They're
from memory, of course," he said regretfully. "I suppose they
catch a bit of what I wanted, but they don't really say it." He
scratched his cheek unhappily, and looked at Modesty. "Even
if I was pleased with them, I'd never have shown them

publicly. I mean, they're too personal. Anyway, Willie insisted on me showing them to you before I got rid of them."

Tarrant muttered, "For God's sake."

Modesty said slowly, "They're beautiful, Luke."

He looked relieved. "Well, if you really like them I'd be very happy for you to have them."

Modesty stood with arms crossed, holding her elbows, eyes on the paintings. She said, "Luke, I know they're very personal to you. They're also Fletcher originals, the first you've done for a long time, and you simply cannot give them to me. At a guess, Sir Gerald, what would they fetch?"

For the first time in his life Tarrant longed to be rich. He said wistfully, "Not less than thirty thousand for the three. Perhaps very much more, especially in America. They're very keen on Fletchers just now. I can't imagine what your friend John Dall would be prepared to pay." John Dall was a multi-millionaire with whom Modesty had a close and amiable relationship.

"He'd bleed to death," said Willie, "rather than let anyone else 'ave them."

Luke Fletcher was looking from one to the other, bewildered. "I don't need money," he said. "Berenson tells me I've got heaps of it, and I don't spend much. Anyway I didn't paint them to sell, I just hammered them out because I had to, but they're not good enough. I told you, I was going to get rid of them."

Modesty rubbed her eyes hard, then stood in front of Fletcher and took his hands. "Please understand. I can't accept a gift worth a fortune. And I couldn't hang them in my own home, not pictures of me."

He smiled. "It doesn't matter. I didn't intend them for you or anybody."

Willie said quietly, "I'd like to buy one, Luke. Market price."

Tarrant said quickly, "Could I take an option on one, just while I look at my finances?"

Eyes on Modesty, the painter shook his head in distress. "I can't sell them. I can't do that."

"All right, now listen, Luke." She felt his hands begin to shake, and held them tightly. "May I take your paintings and give them to my closest friends? *I* don't want to look at me, but sometimes they might."

"Yes, yes of course!" He grinned with relief. "Well, that solves that." He stood gazing at her, and gradually his eyes became distant. He lifted a hand and smoothed it down her neck and along her shoulder. "Wish she'd sit for me," he muttered. "There ... that line. Not a nude, maybe ... something off the shoulder ...?"

"Luke, you're thinking out loud."

"What? Oh God, I'm sorry." He stepped back, embarrassed.

"That's all right. I'm not a sitter by nature, but anything for an old friend."

"Old friend?" He flushed with pleasure. "That's nice."

"What else, after the hours we've spent in a bunk together? Just give me a little notice about the sitting." She turned to look at Willie and Tarrant. "I'll send the bare-back one to Johnny Dall. You can sort out the other two between you while I take Luke to look at his *Estaminet*."

Holding his arm, she led him from the room. The two men stood gazing at the pictures in silence for a while, then Tarrant said, "The despised narrative picture, and aren't they tremendous?"

Willie nodded. "You choose, Sir G, but leave it to me in your will."

"Ha. You'll go before I do. I'll have the contemplative one, please."

"Right."

After a while Tarrant gave a bemused sigh and said, "I'm still finding it hard to believe. My God, to own a Fletcher. And that particular Fletcher above all."

Willie said absently, "What do you think of 'im?"

Tarrant shrugged. "I don't suppose he ever had a mean or vicious thought in his life. But I find his humility and his abstraction a little trying."

"It's not put on."

"I know. His talent makes him a dreamer. It can still be trying, or don't you agree?"

"Me? I couldn't 'ave Luke Fletcher around for long without wanting to go out and do something nasty."

"Exactly so. Lack of vice in another is an unbearable affront." Tarrant studied the paintings again. "He's helpless, he has a crying need to be looked after, and circumstances have set Modesty up for him as a surrogate Bridie. It worries me a little."

Willie's big shoulders lifted. "She loves real talent, and you know what she's likes with a lame dog."

"I recall one or two occasions. But she needs to beware of pity."

"I wouldn't worry too much. She knows you can't solve other people's personality problems. She'll just do what she can."

They fell silent again, looking at the pictures, and after a while Willie said softly, "Amnesia or no amnesia, Luke Fletcher never got 'imself from the Mediterranean to the Tasman Sea under 'is own steam. Blimey, I'd love to know what 'appened to 'im."

6

Today Beauregard Browne was amusing himself by playing Board Meetings. He was seated at the head of the long table in the dining room of the seven-bedroom rented house in Islington. On the table in front of him were several manila files containing sheets of foolscap typescript. These were part of an old engineering report he had found in a bureau drawer.

Clarissa de Courtney-Scott sat on his left, her hair piled in a neat chignon, a shorthand notebook in front of her. Dr. Feng sat beside her, glancing through his coded dossier on Luke Fletcher. The Reverend Uriah Crisp was on Beauregard Browne's right, gazing distantly down at his own big square hands resting on the table. Beside him was a middle-aged, sandy-haired man in a blue suit.

Beauregard Browne rapped on the table with a gavel. He had seen it in a shop in Great Queen Street the day before, and it was this which had inspired him to conduct the present meeting in boardroom style. "I declare this meeting open," he said happily, and smiled round at the assembled company. The gavel banged again. "First item on the agenda." He opened one of his folders and pretended to read from the typescript, which in fact was concerned with the proportions of sand and cement in concrete bridge piers. "To receive a report from Mr. Palmer on his inquiries into the question of gaining unauthorised access to the Royal Academy, Burlington House."

He beamed through his long glistening eyelashes at the man in the blue suit, who looked about him with a touch of unease, then cleared his throat and began, "Well, I've cased it very thorough, guv—"

Beauregard Browne raised a polite hand. "Not guv. Mr. Chairman."

"Oh, sorry. I've cased it very thorough, Mr. Chairman, and you've got scale plans of the whole block. Also the interior, with cutaway of the exterior bit you're interested in." He unrolled a blueprint and turned it to face the head of the table. The others helped to hold it flat.

"Exhibit A," Beauregard Browne announced with delight.

"Er ... that's right, Mr. Chairman. Access to the roof is easy as winking, through these offices in Albany Court Yard. You can get into 'em with not much more than a strip of celluloid."

"Our subcontractors will be rather better prepared than that, one trusts," said Beauregard Browne soberly. "But pray continue, Mr. Palmer."

"Access through door of bulk-head stairs on roof." Mr. Palmer's pencil moved lightly over the blueprint. "Circuit breaking magnetic alarm to be bridged there, and a mortice lock to be jiggered. Same again on fire-doors at bottom of stairs, plus two big interior bolts. Those bolts are really the main problem. But after that, you're in."

"One has arrived at the location of the property scheduled for takeover?"

Mr. Palmer blinked. "Well, I suppose so. You go down these stairs you can see in the cutaway, and through this door. Then you're in the 'all, in the *hall*, where all the good stuff is, including the Jade Queen."

"Quite so. And you have established that the items will be crated on the sixteenth prox?"

Clarissa giggled, and received a disapproving glance.

Mr. Palmer said, "Well, the sixteenth of next month. It's a Tuesday."

"Thank you for clarifying that point, Mr. Palmer. We further understand that the crated properties will be left *in situ* until the morning of the seventeenth prox, when they will be collected for transport to their country of origin."

"Correct, guv. Mr. Chairman."

The Chairman referred to his typescript. "Weight of Jade Queen and crate one hundred and six pounds?"

Mr. Palmer nodded.

"And egress?"

"Beg pardon?"

Clarissa said, "Getting it out, Mr. Palmer," and ran her tongue round her lips when he looked at her.

"Ah. Yes. Well ..." Sid Palmer paused to collect himself. He had worked for this frightening daisy and his weird lot on two previous occasions, and could never make up his mind whether they were mad or joking. Today they had a Chinaman with them. Perhaps that was part of a joke. Sid Palmer did not know whether he was supposed to laugh at Beauregard Browne's present charade or play up to it. On the whole he thought it best to play up. Whether they were joking or crazy, they could pull off a job like nobody's business.

Indicating with the pencil, he said, "The best way out is over 'ere, over *here*. There's this wide service alley on the west side, running the whole length from Piccadilly to Burlington Gardens. Big gates at each end. Half-way along there's a sort of lay-by the size of this room. You lower the crate from a lightweight hoist on the roof, whip it into a van, then you're straight out into Burlington Gardens. Just need to manage the gate at the north end, that's all."

"I'm sure our Traffic Executive, Mr. Crisp, will guarantee

a trouble-free departure," said Beauregard Browne. "Now, for the benefit of this meeting, will you repeat what you have already reported to me concerning security arrangements, Mr. Palmer?"

"Two men patrolling the courtyard in two-hour shifts. Six men locked inside the building, two on patrol at a time, again in two-hour shifts."

"And you have had sight of the duty roster, I believe?"

"Took a bit of doing, that did."

"That is why you are being paid so handsomely, Mr. Palmer." The Chairman looked round the table, violet eyes sparkling with pleasure, and banged the gavel once more. "The Board will be pleased to hear that our Mr. Palmer has selected an inside security guard who is admirably suited for the desired response to a sales approach from our industrial chaplain, the Reverend Uriah Crisp." Beauregard Browne opened another folder and studied a paragraph concerning site preparation. "The name of the prospective client is Albert Ross, of 23 Cheadwell Gardens, Balham. Married, and with a fifteen-year-old daughter. Thank you, Mr. Palmer. We won't keep you from your important duties any longer, but you may be sure that a vote of thanks to you will be recorded in the Minutes. Our Executive for Personnel will show you out. Mr. Crisp, if you please?"

When the door had closed behind the two men Dr. Feng said, "Do you intend that Uriah should in fact execute any personnel during this affair?"

"Ah, a question from our industrial psychologist. Make a note, Clarissa. The answer is no. We want a nice quiet job."

"Uriah is the Hammer of the Lord," Dr. Feng pointed out, "and has a need to function in that capacity, Mr. Chairman."

Beauregard Browne nodded smiling approval. "Well done, doctor. However, he must wait for the propitious occasion, and meantime I shall delegate our Welfare Executive, Miss de Courtney-Scott, to ensure that Uriah has a sufficiency of other healthy exercise to prevent the onset of tension."

"Gosh. Right. Super," Clarissa said, and drew a phallic symbol on her pad, pondering it with dreamy anticipation. It would be necessary, after a time or two, to persuade Uriah that he was doing the Lord's work in submitting to her exacting requirements, but she had been collecting a few suitable texts to that end. Only the most tenuous relevance was required. For Uriah, the drum-roll of the words was all. *"Gird up now thy loins like a man." "I rose up to open to my beloved, and my hands dropped with myrrh." "His left hand is under my head, and his right hand doth embrace me." "Come, let us take our fill of love until the morning."*

The Reverend Uriah Crisp re-entered the room and said benevolently, "Our brother Palmer has truly left this house."

Beauregard Browne said, "Thank you, Uriah. And may we take it that as our spiritual adviser you endorse the action we are now considering?"

"My mind is clear on that, Beauregard," Uriah said grimly, taking his chair. "The Jade Queen is an abomination. I have visited the Royal Academy and sullied my eyes with her presence that I might judge of this." His eyes glittered and his voice began to rise. "Her breasts are bare. Her legs are inadequately swathed. A lecherous man could easily imagine the swell of the thighs, the warmth and roundness—" His voice cracked.

"And as a pagan," said Beauregard Browne, "she lacks the Lord's blessing in the exercise of her sexuality. A blessing not withheld from those of the Elect, of course."

"Quite so," Uriah agreed in a harsh voice.

Clarissa felt an inward shiver of delight. He was in the mood, which meant it would be two or three days before she brought him to the point where he winced at the sight of her. She herded her mind back to the present and said, "May I ask if any decision has been taken as to the local labour to be used for this contract, Mr. Chairman? Bearing in mind the Board's policy of avoiding personal involvement except in an auxiliary capacity?"

"Ah. Now on that point I may say a tentative decision has been taken," Beauregard Browne said judicially, "but with the consent of the Board I should like to leave that till later in the agenda, and move on to item seven: to receive a report on the Luke Fletcher situation. Miss Scott?"

"Me? Oh, right then. Well, we initiated surveillance at Benildon, to get to know the Blaise girl and Garvin man visually—gosh, he's awfully sexy, don't you think? Oh, sorry, Mr. Chairman. Well, Garvin brought Fletcher along, and Sir Gerald Tarrant was present. British Intelligence chief, but present socially on this occasion, we assume. Next morning Tarrant and Garvin drove back to town, but Fletcher remained for several days."

She caught Beauregard Browne's eye, and pretended to look through her note-book before continuing. "Ah, yes. From Fletcher's marked air of delight and content, we conclude that the Blaise girl had taken him to her bed. To avoid making our presence obvious, we then subcontracted surveillance, and it was later reported that Blaise and Fletcher drove to his studio in Cheyne Walk on the fifth."

"The fifth inst., Miss Scott?"

"Oh—er—yes, Mr. Chairman. Well, the studio was in chaos, since Fletcher is incapable of looking after himself. Blaise then arranged for the place to be cleaned and put in order, and took Fletcher to her penthouse overlooking Hyde Park." Clarissa looked up from her note-book. "That concludes the report, Mr. Chairman."

"Not quite. I have received news that she and Fletcher flew out to Malta last night."

Uriah had been sitting with his eyes closed. He spent much of his time withdrawn from the world and in what he believed to be a state of contemplation, though in fact this was simply a device to avoid the constant need to rationalise. Now he opened his eyes and said, "Our fallen sister has a villa in that country, has she not?"

"Yes, indeed, that was in the substantial dossier provided by the good Mr. Palmer."

Clarissa said soberly, "Isn't it a tiny bit worrying, Beau? I mean, Fletcher's a long way away, and if he suddenly started to remember things it could be a bit beastly for us."

Beauregard Browne banged his gavel and smiled benignly upon Dr. Feng. "We will take a report from our Medical Executive. Dr. Feng?"

The Chinese had been mentally compiling notes for writing later in his dossiers of the three who now sat at the table with him, but he was prepared for Beauregard Browne's question and answered smoothly, "The longer the memory blocks hold, the less the risk that they will break down, Mr. Chairman. Under normal circumstances I would say there is not more than a one per cent chance that Fletcher's memory will return." He paused, then went on slowly, "It seems possible that Miss Blaise has taken him to Malta, the location from which he disappeared, in an attempt to stimulate his memory. But there is in fact nothing for Fletcher to remember about Malta, since he was rendered unconscious by a hand-blow to the *medulla oblongata* without sight of his assailant."

"Thank you, doctor," said Beauregard Browne, and surveyed the Board. "Comments?"

Clarissa said, "Well, personally I do think there ought to be some sort of alarm bell. After all, the mind is a jolly funny thing—well, I know mine is, anyway. And if something did trigger things off in poor Mr. Fletcher's head it would be awfully embarrassing. I mean, we do have contact with that frightfully efficient Sicilian lot in Malta, the ones we used for the van Gogh job in Rome, so why not use them for surveillance?"

"The Board will be pleased to learn," said the Chairman modestly, "that I anticipated the Malta possibility on first reading the Blaise dossier provided by the good Mr. Palmer. Instructions were accordingly passed to our subcontractors in Malta, and the main living room and bedroom of the Blaise villa have been expertly bugged in advance of occupation."

Clarissa de Courtney-Scott stared in wide-eyed admiration. "Beau! You clever old stick!"

"Thank you, darling. It seemed a wise precaution. We're rather busy at the moment, but I have a very strong feeling that Our Esteemed Patron might shortly require us to put Blaise and Co. into liquidation, just to make sure they don't jog Fletcher's memory."

Dr. Feng said, "It would surely be simpler and safer to kill Fletcher."

Beauregard Browne threw up his hands. "Our Sublime Patron is a lover of art, my dear sir. Art! Your services were solicited so that we might *avoid* liquidating art people. We shall kill Mr. Fletcher only if absolutely necessary. Now, is there any other business before I declare the meeting closed?"

The Reverend Uriah Crisp opened his eyes again. "The graven image of the great adultress," he said with suppressed fury, "the great green whore who tempts men into the ways of sin—"

"We are speaking of the Jade Queen?" Beauregard Browne interrupted smoothly.

"Yes." Uriah leaned forward, hands clasped on the table.

"Who are to be our brothers in God's work of tearing her down that she may be buried in the caves of earth, away from the sight of men?"

"Ah, we deferred that item, did we not? My dear chap, how good of you to remind me." Beauregard Browne stacked his manila folders neatly in front of him, then looked from one to the other of his companions with a confiding air. "On the question of local labour to be used for the Royal Academy job, I beg to report that your Chairman has every hope of obtaining the very desirable assistance of ..." he paused and looked coyly round the table with a flutter of long eyelashes, "of Miss Modesty Blaise and Mr. William Garvin."

*　　*　　*

She had been awake for several minutes now, giving thought to the morning's task. Luke Fletcher was dozing with his head on her shoulder, an arm across her body. She shook him gently and said, "Here, you. Get up and paint."

He grunted, nuzzled his face into her neck and slid his hand up to cup her breast. "What time is it?"

"Past nine. High time all geniuses were up and on the job."

"M'mmm. Lovely. Here we go." He moved on top of her.

She laughed. "Luke, that's not what I meant."

"It's what I meant. We geniuses have to be inspired, you know."

"I thought I inspired you last night."

"It was this morning, around one o'clock, about an hour after we arrived." His hands and lips began to move over her. "But the inspiration's worn off."

She shifted her hips to receive him. "Are you saying I'm like Chinese food? Only briefly satisfying?"

He settled himself upon her and smoothed a hand over her

112

brow. "Not a bit. But I do find that a few hours later I want you some more. Like now. You don't mind?"

"Any lady who starts minding once a gentleman has got this far is no lady."

He gave a long sigh of contentment. "You're so lovely. So good to me."

"It's nice to be appreciated, but stay cheerful with it, Luke. Making love is much too nice to spoil with the heavy emotion bit."

"All right, I won't get intense. Why are we in a spare bedroom instead of that posh master bedroom you obviously use yourself?"

She laughed again. "You ask the oddest questions at the rummest times."

"Don't do sudden laughs, Modesty, you'll get me all precipitate. In fact you do anyway, that's probably why I asked an odd question, to divert my attention."

"Quite right too. I'm all for prolonged enjoyment. Well, when we arrived, you may remember I wandered around with a funny little gadget in my hand. It's a habit left over from my less innocent days. I always do it when I move in anywhere."

"Yes, but do what?"

"Check for bugs. Listening devices."

"What?" He arched back to gaze at her. "But that's ridiculous!"

"I know. But once or twice it's paid off, and it did last night. There's a bug in my bedroom and one in the living room. Luke dear, I think you'd better move about a bit, or you'll go into reverse."

He was silent for a few moments, then, "Why didn't you just smash them?"

"That would warn whoever's listening, probably from not

far away. I thought I'd look into it a bit first. Please don't worry, Luke, it's nothing very unusual."

"But why would anyone want to listen in on us?"

"I've no idea."

"You said it wasn't unusual."

"I just meant that with my background—which I've told you something about, but which I don't think you register at all—with my background, it's not unusual for things to happen which would be strange if they happened to other people. Now will you please forget it? I only said it to stop you getting all precipitate, and now I'm afraid I've overdone it."

"You ... honestly think it's nothing to worry about?"

"I'm not sure, but I'll find out. You just concentrate on your painting. I mean, after you've concentrated on me for the next half hour. The light here in Malta is marvellous for a painter, but you know that, you've been here before."

"I want to paint *you* some more, Modesty."

"All right, but one thing at a time. Hey, are you going off the boil, Luke? I hope not. Any gentleman who gets this far with a lady and then goes off the boil is no gentleman." She moved her hips smoothly, and he caught his breath.

"No ..." he said shakily with a half laugh. "I'm not going off the boil."

"Good." Her voice was husky and her pupils large as she lifted beneath him. "So now let's improvise a little. No castaway painter is going to have me in the missionary position."

An hour later he was sitting at breakfast in the large sunlit kitchen when she came down from the bathroom in jeans and flat lace-up canvas shoes, buttoning a plain green shirt. Bending to kiss him on the cheek, she said, "Is the breakfast all right."

"Fine, thank you." He held her and kissed her neck. "Eggs just perfect. Are you going to have yours now?"

"I'm going for a walk first, once you let go of my left charlie." She straightened up. "When you've had a bath, go and work on the balcony. You'll find everything you need in that room I showed you last night."

"Your studio?"

"Hardly that." She began carrying some dirty dishes to the sink. "But it's well equipped."

"You said you sometimes paint. Why didn't I see any pictures there?"

She looked over her shoulder at him with a wincing grin. "Not even Willie Garvin sees what I paint. It's genuinely appalling. As soon as I've gone as far as I can bear to go on a picture, I scrape it all off. But I find it restful."

"I could help, you know."

"Thank you, but we'll leave it the way it is."

"Does Willie Garvin know you well?"

"Inside out. No, that could give the wrong impression. We're not bed-mates."

He looked at her wonderingly. "That seems strange."

"It's not strange to us. More coffee?"

"Er—no, thanks."

"I'll see you later, then. Be good."

The villa stood on the high cliffs of the largely unin-habited south-west coast of the island. Here there were places where the ground rose from the sea in broad terraces to eight hundred feet, and other places where the limestone cliffs dropped sheer. The nearest village, Dingli, lay two miles away. Some of the high ground was cultivated, and on the terraces there were a few patchworks of tiny fields separated by drystone walls, but for the most part the ground was of rough stone thrusting through a thin covering of coarse earth and scrub.

Modesty had sighted the car through binoculars immediately before taking her bath. She had looked cautiously from the window of Willie Garvin's bedroom, on the west side of the house. Here the cliff made a great concave curve, swinging out to a point half a mile away. The car, a brown Mercedes, was parked between the narrow metalled road and the cliff edge, in a shallow depression, partly hidden by one of the rough stone hides used by hunters shooting quail in the migration season.

She left the house by way of the garden on the east side, dropping into a broad shallow gulley which curved inland. Fifteen minutes later she had completed a half-circle and was moving up over rutted ground towards the metalled road.

*   *   *

Tasso sprawled at an angle in the car, propped against the door, the earphones on his head, the binoculars resting on his chest. All the car windows were open to prevent a build-up of heat. Beside him was the tape recorder which he would switch on if anything started coming through from the bugs in the villa across the shallow curve of the bay.

He had taken up his position at first light, and so far there had been no conversation to record, only some general background noise which told him that the bugs were working. Tasso was puzzled. He concluded that the man and woman could not have slept in the main bedroom, and had not so far made use of the lounge.

On the rippled blue sea below, a speck that was a motor-boat moved slowly by between the coast and the hump of Filfla island. There was some thin white cloud to the south, and a pleasant south-westerly breeze. Tasso lifted the binoculars and studied the villa. It was twenty minutes since the man had come out on the long balcony and stood gazing out to sea for a while before going in again. Apart from this there had been no movement.

Tasso lowered the glasses, straightened up, and looked about him. Throughout the day an occasional car or van might use this road, but nobody would be suspicious about a car parked on the verge between road and cliff. The position offered a view that invited idle gazing, and in any event the Maltese had a very English lack of curiosity about the behaviour of others. He settled back, stretched his legs, lit a cigarette, and looked at his watch. Only fifteen minutes and Montale would be coming to relieve him. It might be worth suggesting that an extra bug be planted in the kitchen of the villa. It would take no more than half an hour and could be done the first evening that the man and woman went out. There was a big breakfast bar in the kitchen, and—

The car door behind him opened suddenly, and he fell back with a little grunt of alarm. Then his thoughts ceased abruptly. They began to return, in a hazy and chaotic fashion, after a length of time he could not at first assess. The back of his neck hurt, and he felt a little sick. With a sense of unreality he discovered that he was lying on the ground. Lifting his head made it throb. He moved his eyes cautiously and saw a smouldering cigarette, with half its length burned away. Assuming it was the one he had lit, Tasso concluded that he could have been unconscious for only two or three minutes. Turning over painfully on the rough ground he got to his hands and knees, laboriously working out that the door of the car had not been properly latched, and when it opened he had fallen back and struck his head on a stone.

But it was puzzling that he had fallen completely out of the car ...

The car. He froze, and the clouds of dizziness were suddenly dispersed by shock. The car was no longer there. He got to his feet, stared up and down the narrow cliff road, then across to the long road leading inland down the hill. No car. He massaged his aching neck and moved warily to the cliff edge. Again he froze. There was the car, upside down on a rock-strewn, scrub-covered terrace thirty metres below. Slowly Tasso raised his hands and pressed them to his temples. The Mercedes, one of Frezzi's newest cars! *Mio Dio*, but the boss would go mad when he was told! Frezzi had a great passion for cars.

Tasso backed away from the edge and sat down on a hump of rock, resting his aching head in his hands as he tried to work out how it could all have happened. That the door had not been properly latched was unlikely. That he had left the handbrake off was even more so. And surely he had put the automatic gear lever in the Park position? He studied the ground. If anything it sloped very slightly up towards the cliff edge ... or could that be an optical illusion?

He heard the sound of an engine, and stood up to see the Jaguar mounting the hill to the coast road. It turned left, pulled on to the verge between some low outcrops of rock, and Montale got out, staring.

"Where is the car?"

Tasso gestured feebly. "I ... fell out, and it went over the edge."

"What?"

They were speaking in Italian. Montale moved to the edge and looked down. For the next two minutes there was a furious exchange accompanied by large gestures. Montale pointed out the nature of the slope, insisting that Tasso's notion of an optical illusion was ludicrous, and demanding to know how Tasso could have fallen not only out of the car but also out of the headphones he should have been wearing. Several times the name of Frezzi was mentioned, together with eye-rolling speculation as to his reactions and the questions he would ask the unfortunate Tasso.

The flow of animated conversation ceased suddenly when Tasso stopped short, stared, and pointed. Montale turned. A girl in jeans and a green shirt stood some ten paces away, arms loosely folded so that she held her elbows, head a little on one side, watching them thoughtfully. Montale's first impression was that she had appeared from nowhere, then he realised that she had risen from one of the small hollows and gullies which seamed the cliff-top.

Tasso said softly, stupidly, "She is ... you know?"

"Yes. I know." Montale's voice was grim. "And I also know what happened to you and to the car now."

The girl stepped on to the road and came towards them at an unhurried stroll. Her hands were empty, relaxed. She halted two or three paces from the men and said in Italian, "So Frezzi is the one who had the place bugged. Does he still live in that palazzo at Rabat?"

The men gazed at her from wooden faces. She gave a small shrug. "Give him a message from me. Say that I'm very annoyed and I want to know who hired him. He can call and tell me over a drink before dinner this evening. He's invited for the drink only. Seven-thirty."

Tasso edged forward, crouching a little, his dark face ugly with the anger of scalded pride. "Bitch!" he spat. "By God I will hurt you now!" He came at her very fast, feinting as if to punch then leaning sideways to fling a savage, crippling kick at her knee; but she had been poised in an unobtrusive combat stance since she halted, and moved her leg clear without seeming haste.

His kick missed by an inch, then she was balanced on the

ball of one foot, arms spread, free leg swinging horizontally with an almost balletic movement, the foot coming in at him as his flank was presented to her by his own impetus. Her toe hit him precisely on the solar plexus, and his lungs gave out a sound like air-brakes. He dropped as if every sinew in him had been suddenly cut, and lay unmoving on the ground.

Then she was backing away, for Montale had a knife in his hand and was coming at her with the quick wary shuffle of a man who knew what he was about. She moved on to the road, to get even ground under her feet, and her hand vanished momentarily under the green shirt. When it came out she was gripping a small hardwood object, a finger-thick spindle spreading into a mushroom shape at each end where it emerged from her clenched fist.

She said, "Frezzi isn't going to be pleased with you over this. Just take your foolish friend, and give Frezzi my message."

The Sicilian might not have heard her. His face was stony with concentration, lips tight, breathing hard through his nose, and she knew she could not reach him with words now. Twice he came at her, slashing in an upward lunge, and twice she moved directly back with a speed that astonished him. Each time he had either to halt and regain a sound posture, or over-reach himself and give an opening for some form of counter.

Tasso had made the error of assuming she would be easy because she was a woman. Montale had learned instantly from what he had witnessed. His whole being was now focused upon the process of killing her. She had heard them talk, the game was blown, and she knew their boss was Frezzi. Therefore she must die. Frezzi had time and again emphasised that Modesty Blaise must not under any circumstances be allowed to discover the surveillance. To Montale, that left only one course of action now.

It was maddening, frustrating, the way she kept melting away before him. He would not have dreamt that anyone could move backwards at such speed. All the more strange, then, that while she waited for each attack her footwork seemed clumsy, as if she were almost tripping over her own feet. He sprang forward again, shortening his stride so that his timing would be different and he could maintain the attacking posture for an extra two metres. Even as he began the movement her right foot flicked forward from the knee and something hurtled straight at his face.

The shoe. Now he understood that she had been working her heel out of it between his attacks. He deflected the flying shoe with his free hand, but his timing was destroyed and for a moment he was unsighted. In that moment she took him. Something hit his right elbow hard, and a tingling paralysis wiped all strength from his fingers. The knife fell. She was suddenly very close, and a blow he did not see numbed his left arm. She swivelled briskly to avoid his frantic drive upwards with the knee, and struck again to the side of the knee-joint presented to her. A burning pain shot through Montale's leg, and as he put it to the ground it collapsed under him.

He swayed on one knee, arms hanging limply, staring up at her, suddenly terrified, knowing she could pick up the knife and cut pieces from him, yet he could do nothing to resist.

She said in a flat voice, "You tried to kill me. If you ever try it again, you're dead. Ask your boss Frezzi if I mean it. And give him my message when you get back. Seven-thirty this evening, and he's to telephone before he comes." Montale flinched as her hand reached out. A finger and thumb gripped his ear painfully, his head was jerked forward and round, then something hit the back of his neck, and darkness swallowed him.

When his senses returned he was lying just off the road. Somewhere nearby a small bird was singing. He rolled over, propped himself on his elbows, and saw that Tasso was on his knees, hunched forward, massaging his heart. With an effort Montale got to his feet. The Jaguar had gone. Heart sinking, he moved to the edge of the cliff. It had hit the wrecked Mercedes below, bounced off, and ended up another fifty metres lower down.

Tasso wheezed, "The Jaguar?"

Montale nodded. Tasso's groan was almost a whimper. "Frezzi will kill us. Then he will kill her."

Montale shook his head. He did not think Frezzi would kill her, or attempt to. He thought Frezzi would go to have a drink with her at seven-thirty.

Tasso said, "What happened?"

Montale looked out to sea. He did not intend, ever in his life, to tell anybody exactly what had happened in the last few minutes. In that time his concept of the world had been turned upside down, and he was afraid his nerve had been broken.

Tasso said again, "What happened with you and her?"

In the vilest possible terms, Montale told him to mind his own business. Tasso shrugged, and got painfully to his feet. "We had better start to walk," he said. "It is a long way."

When she was a quarter of a mile from the villa, Modesty saw Luke Fletcher coming up the slight hill towards her at a stumbling run. Seeing her, he stopped and waited, leaning against a drystone wall and sucking air into his lungs. She came up to him, gave him a smile, slipped her arm through his, and moved on down the road towards the house. "You're supposed to be painting," she said, "not running up hills.

Did you suddenly remember something? A gleam of light through the amnesia?"

"No." His voice was controlled, but she could feel the effort in him. "I saw, and I was coming to ... to help."

"Help?"

"I saw you with those men. The car. I was on the balcony looking through the glasses, and I saw you talking to those men, and then one of them came at you, and ... and then the other, with the knife, and I just ran."

She pressed his arm. "That was sweet of you, Luke, but I managed."

"I saw you stop that first one who attacked you, but then, oh God, that one with the knife, he was really trying to kill you."

"Yes, I had to be a bit sneaky with him, but it worked out all right. They've gone away now. I'm sorry, I didn't want you to be bothered with all this."

"All this *what*, though? Why, Modesty? What's it all about?" He ran a hand through his hair. "And I don't understand about you. I mean, being able to knock out men with knives and all that sort of thing."

"Luke, darling, I've told you quite a bit about me, but you don't seem to take it in. I'm not a nice kind girl, the way you think of me, I'm more of a lapsed criminal. As for what this is all about, I just don't know. All I know is that this villa was bugged, and the men up there were set to record anything we said within range of the bugs. I found out that they work for a man called Frezzi, a sort of Mafia type I once tangled with in the past, and I've sent a message inviting him to come here this evening and explain what he's doing and why."

They passed into the cool house. Modesty took the little wooden dumbell from under her shirt, put it on the sideboard and said, "You're all hot and bothered. How about some iced tea? I've got some in the fridge."

"In a minute. What's that thing?"

"It's called a kongo, and it's a kind of weapon, if you hit someone in the right places with it. I used it against that knife-man."

He rubbed his face with a harassed gesture. "Do you think it's to do with me, all this business?"

"Yes, Luke. But I can't guess how. I'm hoping for some light from Frezzi."

"You really think a man like that will come to see you after you've done whatever you did to his men?"

She smiled. "Yes, I think so. I didn't just send him a verbal invitation, I sent him a sort of unspoken message, indicating that I didn't like being bugged."

"I don't understand."

"I put about twenty thousand poundsworth of his cars over the cliff. He'll know what I mean."

*   *   *

Frezzi wore a pale grey suit of excellent cut, a maroon shirt with matching bow tie, and a powerful aftershave lotion. He was in his early forties, dark, with a high forehead and large soulful eyes which belied his nature.

Luke Fletcher stood watching the man, trying mentally to put him on canvas. Following Modesty's instructions, he had answered the door to Frezzi a few minutes ago, uttered no word of greeting, indicated that Frezzi was to pass through the hall and into the big lounge, followed him, then indicated further that he was to continue out on to the balcony where Modesty was sitting. There Fletcher had positioned himself at one end of the balcony, still silent, and stood with folded arms regarding the visitor with a penetrating stare. It was, as Modesty had said, a performance which came very naturally to him.

She wore a long skirt and a white blouse with ruffled cuffs and a high collar. Frezzi had not been asked what he would prefer to drink. Like Modesty, he held a glass of chilled white wine. A carafe of it stood on a low table by her chair, together with a dish of olives and nuts. She had greeted him amiably, invited him to sit, poured him a drink, and now sat gazing absently out over a sea that was turning gold with the westerly sun.

Frezzi was not nervous, but uncertainty showed through his pose of smiling relaxation. At last he threw out a hand and said reproachfully, "Signorina, signorina, how could you do such things to me? We are old friends."

She looked at him in mild surprise. "I seem to remember a dispute when you snatched one of my *Network* couriers."

"Ah, but that was a mistake, and was resolved, signorina," Frezzi said hastily. "The girl was released to you quite unharmed."

"So she was. And just as well, or I'd have told Willie Garvin to be even more unpleasant to you."

Frezzi's smile became strained. "Please, let us not speak of Willie Garvin."

"All right. You were saying?"

Frezzi sighed. "My cars. Two nice cars, signorina. It was not necessary to do such a thing."

"The first car was because you were stupid enough to put bugs in my house. The second was because your man tried to kill me. I think you got off very lightly on the second count."

"The man was a fool."

"Keep him away from me, Frezzi."

"He is already on his way back to Sicily."

She nodded, and drank some wine. Frezzi watched her warily. After a little silence he cleared his throat and said with a forthright air, "And I have been a fool also, signorina. They asked me to make close surveillance while you were here in Malta, surveillance with the radio bugs, you understand." He hit his brow gently with the heel of his hand. "And I am a little stupid. I say to myself, Alfredo, it is simply to listen. It is not to *harm* the signorina." He gave a deprecating chuckle at the absurdity of such a notion. "It is simply a matter of business, so I have the little bugs put in, you see, just to listen. A small business operation, signorina, that is all."

"What were you listening for, Frezzi?"

"Oh ... to hear what you and the gentleman say." He shrugged and spread a hand in a gesture of full explanation.

"What in particular were you listening for?"

Frezzi ran a finger round his collar and stared thoughtfully into space. After a little while, in which she did not speak, he came to a decision and said quietly, "It was to hear anything about this gentleman finding his memory."

Modesty looked at Luke Fletcher, and it was obvious to her that he had not taken in those last words. He was still gazing with total absorption at the Sicilian, his whole mind behind his eyes. She said to Frezzi, "Who wants to know about my friend recovering his memory?"

Frezzi put down his glass. "I do not think you will believe me," he said, "but I will tell you the truth anyway. It is this. I do not know who is at the other end of the contract. Once before I have made an operation for this same party, but still I do not know. Their business comes to me through a Maltese lawyer. I have much other business with him, and I know that he also cannot name names, for the other party works

126

through a cut-off. Payment comes through the lawyer, and the price is very good."

Frezzi paused, then turned his head a little to look at her steadily. "I will say this. If I could name a name, I would not do so. Not even to you, signorina. It is possible that you and Willie Garvin can do much to hurt my business, but if I talk I break the only rule, and then the finish of my business is certain."

She studied him for a moment, then gave a nod. When she stood up, he rose with her. She said, "All right, let's leave it there."

He let out a long breath of relief. "It is true I do not know, signorina. I swear."

"I believe you."

"You are very understanding. Very kind."

"I shall be very unkind if you bother me any more while I'm here. What are you going to report to your Maltese lawyer, for him to tell the cut-off man to tell his employer?"

Frezzi fingered his bow tie. "This has been a costly operation for me, signorina," he said plaintively, "and I do not wish to lose the payment for it. I think it reasonable not to refer to your discovery of the bugs, or to this talk we have had. I will simply report that we have heard nothing to indicate that your friend may be finding his memory."

"Good. I was going to suggest that might be the most profitable and least dangerous way out for you."

Two minutes later she stood with Luke Fletcher on the patio at the top of the curving steps, watching the big Fiat move away along the coast road. As it vanished beyond a low crest she took his arm, turned back into the house with him, and said, "What did you think of that, Luke?"

"Well ... not very interesting."

"What?"

127

"I wouldn't mind painting it, but I've seen much more interesting heads."

"Blimey, as Willie would say. I'm not talking about his head, dum-dum. Didn't you hear what he said?"

Fletcher grinned a little sheepishly. "Sorry. Was it important?"

She sighed. "Let's go and eat. I'll tell you on the way."

"Where are we going?"

"A place at St. Paul's Bay where they do fabulous fish." She picked up her handbag and took out the car key. "Luke, I want to get you painting again, because I can't bear wasted talent, but at the same time I'd like you to try very hard to keep at least one foot on the ground."

He smiled and put his hands on her waist, then moved them up to the side-swell of her breasts. "I hardly need to, when you've got both yours so firmly on the ground."

"That's the point. I'm not for ever, Luke. Or anything like for ever."

"No," he said vaguely, "of course not." His gaze had become remote, appraising, and he turned her a little. "I think I would like to do a nude of you, after all."

"Maybe. First show me three landscapes or seascapes and three still lifes, then I'll think about it. And listen. Are you actually listening, Luke? Willie's coming out on a night flight, so don't worry if you hear noises in the early hours."

"Oh." Fletcher looked disappointed. "Why is he coming out?"

She took his arm. "Don't confuse yourself with reasons. And don't sulk. You won't have to stop sharing my bed just because Willie's around."

7

She woke at two, and lay waiting for the sound of the car. At two-thirty she heard it draw up quietly by the garage. Beside her, Luke Fletcher was sound asleep. She pulled on a robe as she went out, closing the bedroom door after her before putting on lights in the hall and lounge.

When she opened the front door she saw Willie coming up the steps, carrying a grip, but he was not alone. As they came into the porch light she saw that his companion was a solidly built man in his late forties, with a wide mouth, a slightly flattened nose, and dark bristly hair cut very short. He moved with a limp, and he was not a stranger. His name was Dick Kingston and he had been in Fleet Street for several years specialising in investigative journalism. Before that he had been an operative in what was then called MI.6. As such he had penetrated *The Network*, his directive being to ascertain the amount and quality of British military and industrial secrets being sold by Modesty Blaise's organisation to the Eastern Bloc.

Her security was good and he had been blown from the beginning, but she had done nothing about it, except to make sure that he had easy access to the information he sought. Since she had long decided that she wished to live in England when she retired, it was her strict policy never to trade in any secrets to the detriment of that country, and she was well pleased for Kingston to discover and report this.

A year or two later, a bullet in his leg on the Greek–Bulgarian border ended his career as an intelligence agent, and he moved to Fleet Street. When Modesty learned of this she made a trip to London from her headquarters in Tangier, sought Kingston out, and established a link which had been useful to both sides.

Willie jerked a thumb at him now and said, "Look what I found, Princess."

Kingston dropped his well-worn case just inside the door, enfolded her in his arms, and kissed her soundly on each cheek. "Mmmm-mph!" he said with emphasis. "Next time round, honeychile, I'm going to be a painter who needs a beautiful girl to inspire him. I mean, sod it, why should other chaps always get the goodies? What's wrong with me?"

"You're perfect, Dick. I just never felt I was worthy of you. Hallo, how are you?"

He gave a hoot of laughter and let her go. "I'm fine. There's nothing like being a gentleman of the press. We're God's gift to the country, if not the world, on that we're all agreed. And nobody shoots you or puts electric shocks through your balls, like they do if you're with Mil Six. I can't imagine why I spent all those years there."

Willie closed the door. "He was on the plane, Princess, coming out to see Luke Fletcher. I thought you might let 'im 'ave the spare room tonight, if he behaves, but I'll run 'im down to the Verdala if it's not convenient."

She gave Willie her hand for his usual greeting of touching her knuckles to his cheek, and said, "No, that's fine, Willie love. I'm not too sure whether we'll let him loose on Luke, though." She looked at Kingston. "Willie will show you where you sleep. When you're settled, I'll be in the lounge. Like some coffee?"

"Please, lady."

Fifteen minutes later Willie said, "D'you reckon Frezzi was lying?"

She gave a small shrug. "He could be, but my hunch is that he doesn't know who's paying him to keep surveillance on Luke. What's interesting is that somebody is very anxious to know if and when Luke starts to remember what happened to him."

"I reckon it's the same party that made those hypodermic punctures in 'is arm. That still leaves who and why and 'ow, and what next, and will they try it again?"

Kingston said thoughtfully, "I'm glad you hit Frezzi hard with those two cars, honeychile. Pussyfoot around with that kind, and they soon start leaning on you. Did you get the name of Frezzi's lawyer here?"

"Oh, come on, Dick. I wasn't talking to him with red-hot pincers at the ready."

"Come on yourself, lady. You know how people can spill something when they're nervous."

"All right. But he didn't."

Kingston sipped his coffee and stretched his legs. "I might just dig that out for you. You could get the whole Maltese legal profession in a bungalow, and they all know one another. Maybe I could find Frezzi's lawyer, and get through him to these anonymous Fletcher-watchers."

"Well, do that thing, Dick. On a fee-and-expenses basis."

"No sale, honeychile. First, I'm following my own line on Fletcher. Second, you want a quick answer and I can't give you one. It could take me weeks to get next to this lawyer, because Frezzi's bound to keep the connection under wraps, and it could take months to get beyond the lawyer, if I manage it at all. I'm not a Mil Six man with a single mission now, I'm a nosey journalist with half a dozen irons in the

131

fire and a living to earn. But if I get anything, I'll pass it on. No charge."

"That's very handsome."

"Bloody stupid, when I could stick you for a grand, but that's Kingston for you, poor old sod. Putty in the hands of a girl like you."

"I expect it's my mind that gets you."

Kingston only half suppressed a guffaw. Willie said, "Dick's got a lovely barmy theory about Luke. Talk about laugh. It's not just the theory, it's the way he tells it."

Kingston snorted. "You're a yokel, Willie. All I want to do is put the notion to Fletcher and see if it triggers any response."

Modesty said, "What notion?"

"Well, I know it sounds a little weird, but we both know that doesn't mean it can't be true." Kingston rubbed his chin and looked somewhat abashed. "As a matter of fact I came across the idea when I was researching that Limbo story, where all those stinking-rich people went missing over a number of years."

Modesty nodded. "I read about it."

"In a pig's eye you read about it. You were there, honey-chile. You were the one who broke it up and got them all out, with a little help from Big Ears here, as usual."

She looked at him, frowning. "What makes you think so?"

"Look, lady. Thirty whispers make one shout." He grinned. "Digging it out is going to be like excavating the Grand Canyon with a teaspoon, but it's going to be worth it."

She said mildly, "Forget it, Dick, if you want us to stay friends."

He looked at her from narrowed eyes for some time, and finally gave an angry shrug. "Willie said he'd break both my arms, but I thought you might be more reasonable. All right,

132

sod it. Limbo's dead. Now where was I? Ah yes, people getting kidnapped. I'll make this short. Before Fletcher, four others of similar stature in the world of art, though not all painters, disappeared in the last two years."

Modesty tucked her feet beneath her on the big settee. "Isn't that about average? Thousands go missing every year."

"No, it bloody well isn't average. It's not average by about a million light years. They weren't the *kind* of people who disappear just like that. Your average missing person isn't really missing at all. He's in another part of the country or another part of the world, with a different name, simply because he couldn't stand his wife or his kids or his job or whatever. But that's not what happened with Fletcher. Or with Robert Soames, or Maria Cavalli, or Jules Baillot, or Gwen Westwood."

There was a silence. Two of the names registered immediately with Modesty. Robert Soames was the American art critic and world authority on the Neapolitan School, a man of strong and controversial views. Maria Cavalli was a phenomenon in that she had first put brush to canvas at the age of forty, with no formal teaching, and within five years had been recognised internationally as a painter of astonishing virtuosity. The name of Jules Baillot rang a fainter bell, but then she remembered his name being in *The Network* files. He was one of the senior curators at The Louvre.

At last she said, "Gwen Westwood?"

"Top art person at Sotheby's. Went on holiday to Greece, didn't come back from a day trip to Sounion. Never seen again."

"Soames got himself lost on a hunting trip in Canada, didn't he? I remember reading about a big search at the time. And the Cavalli story made space in most of the world press. She vanished from her studio. A sort of Marie Celeste mystery, with the half cup of warm coffee and so on. What about Jules Baillot?"

"He was driving from Rouen to Paris, and didn't arrive. His car was found in a lay-by. End of story."

She looked at Kingston curiously. "And you think Luke Fletcher is another in the same series?"

"I think he might be."

"But for heaven's sake, Dick, why? What do the baddies *do* with these people? With Luke and the Cavalli woman it's just possible to imagine making them paint a few masterpieces under duress, but then what? They can hardly start putting them on the market, and anyway it wouldn't apply with the other three. They're experts in art, or objets d'art, but not creative. So why?"

Willie said, "Dick 'asn't worked that bit out yet, Princess."

Kingston laughed. "All right, I know it's all a bit whacky, and I can't get it together to make sense, but I'm playing a hunch. I want to put this to Fletcher. I mean, I want to put to him the whole idea that he was kidnapped *because* he's an artist, and was kept imprisoned and made use of in some way. It just might trigger a reaction."

Modesty sat gazing down into her cup. After watching her for a moment or two Willie said, "If Dick's right, then whoever took 'im before might do it again, unless they already got what they wanted from 'im, whatever that might be. But they didn't hire Frezzi to grab 'im, just to keep surveillance and report any sign of returning memory. If he starts to remember, what do they do? Knock 'im off, I reckon. So it might be a good idea if Luke Fletcher stays the way he is. Seems 'appy enough."

Kingston glared at him indignantly. "You miserable bastard. Where's your natural human urge to find out, to discover, to unravel? Where's your *curiosity*, you dozy bugger?"

"I save all that for girls," Willie explained.

Kingston looked at Modesty. "If Fletcher starts remembering, you'll be the first to know, and we can whip him away to a safe-house until he's spilled all the beans. Then it'll be too late for the baddies to think about knocking him off. They'll have troubles enough of their own. So is it all right with you if I try to trigger him, honeychile?"

She looked up and gave a nod. "Sure, Mr. Bones, I've got no rights over him anyway. And if no reaction?"

"I'd like to hang around for a few days, just to prod it about a bit."

"Staying here in this desirable residence?"

"Of course staying here, mutton-head, unless you're too mean and selfish to put me up and cook and clean and launder for me."

"That's exactly what I am," she said cheerfully. "You can find yourself an hotel tomorrow, Dick."

He grinned. "It was just a try-on, lady. If I'm supposed to be a journalist I have to act like one. How long will you be here?"

"About a couple of weeks. Then I want to get Luke back to his studio."

Willie said, "He'll never stay with a working routine on 'is own, Princess. You've got to figure 'ow long you're ready to look after 'im."

"I know, Willie love. He needs a sympathetic female to organise him and go to bed with him, and I thought I'd see him through for another month after we get home. Then I'll ship him across to John Dall."

Kingston said, "Ah yes, he's one of your millionaires, isn't he? The American tycoon."

"He's my only millionaire, and he's got an organisation big enough to provide just whatever Luke needs, from protection to home comforts." She looked at Willie. "Johnny would love the chance. He's over the moon about that painting I sent him."

Kingston said quickly, "What painting?"

"*Monarch of the Glen*, wasn't it, Willie?"

"Or *Stag At Bay*, I always get 'em muddled up."

Kingston sighed and got to his feet. "I'm going to bed," he said morosely. "Maybe sleep will help me forget life's unfairness for a while. Luke Fletcher gets picked out of the ocean by a very plain but quite wholesome and obliging bird who supplies him with bed, board, and body, together with general cosseting, and *then* arranges for lavish satisfaction of his future spiritual and physical needs to be supplied at the expense of a millionaire. All I can say is, it never happens to poor old bloody Kingston."

*   *   *

Between ten and noon next morning Fletcher painted a small exquisite seascape. While he worked, Dick Kingston talked to him. This was by Fletcher's own arrangement. It was clear that he did not want to start thinking anew about the mystery of his disappearance, but could not bring himself to refuse a friend of Modesty's. Declaring that he was anxious to work, but would be happy for Kingston to talk while he did so, was a way of keeping his participation to a minimum.

Kingston recited his theory twice, very carefully, the first time giving a simple outline, the second time a detailed account with more facts, dates, and background. Fletcher made no comment, and seemed scarcely to have taken in what was said, but that night Modesty had to rouse him from a violent nightmare in which he dreamt of having the top of his head cut off by a Chinaman with no face. She phoned Kingston at his hotel in the morning, and he was at the villa within half an hour. It was Willie who received him and gave him the scanty details.

"A Chinaman?" Kingston said, and rubbed the nape of his neck thoughtfully, leaning back in his lounging chair to look up at the mass of thick bougainvillea which had been trained to provide shade over one half of the balcony.

Willie put a long drink in his hand. "According to the Princess, this Chinaman 'ad something like that gadget you use for cutting the top off a boiled egg, but big enough to fit round your 'ead. He was going to do a trepan job with it on Luke."

"Why according to Modesty? It wasn't her nightmare."

"She woke Luke up from it, and got 'im to babble it all out and get it off 'is chest. By morning it'd faded for 'im, and the only thing Luke remembered was the Chinaman, but the Princess knew what he'd told 'er."

Kingston brooded. "It might have nothing to do with what I was saying to him yesterday," he said at last. "Was there anything else?"

"No. Modesty told you on the phone there was no point in your charging up 'ere. Maybe you triggered something in Luke, maybe not. If so, maybe it'll expand, maybe not. All we can do is wait and see."

Kingston nodded reluctantly. "All the same, I'd like to talk to her now I'm here, Willie. Fletcher too."

"You can't, matey. She's sitting."

"Eh?"

"Posing. Being painted. Luke was suddenly grabbed with the idea of doing a nude, and they're in the kitchen now."

Kingston stared, baffled. "The kitchen?"

Willie grinned. "She's standing at the sink, peeling potatoes."

"Dear God. What's he going to call it, *Nude With Vegetable Knife?*"

"It might be quite a picture." Willie gazed out ruminatively over the hazy sea. "Once she got over the giggles she went into a sort of reverie. If Luke gets the mood on canvas it could make you keep looking for hours. You know?"

"I know." Kingston drained his glass, reflecting that Willie Garvin was the only man he had ever envied. He got to his feet and said, "Tell them hallo from me, and say I'd like you all to come and have dinner with me at the casino Marquis Room tomorrow night. No shop talk, just social."

"Thanks. I'll tell 'er, and give you a ring."

*   *   *

Modesty Blaise closed the menu and said, "I'll have the grilled swordfish with courgettes and sauté potatoes."

"Certainly, madame." The waiter took orders from the three men, and departed.

"It's a curious thing," said Dick Kingston, "when you come to think of it. Those sauté potatoes will be processed into a nice firm bit of girl, a delightful portion of arm or thigh or knocker, perhaps. But if I ate them, they'd be processed into male flab."

"You reckon life's a bit unfair on you?" said Willie.

"That lad has precognition," Kingston declared with a startled look. "There's no other answer. He knew exactly what I was going to say."

"I knew it, too," said Luke Fletcher. "I've heard you say it several times, I think." He spoke vaguely, reaching out to adjust the neckline folds of the white silk jersey dress Modesty wore. "My word, you look absolutely tremendous in that sort of Grecian style."

138

"Thank you, Luke. But don't start re-arranging what any of the other women here are wearing, you could be misunderstood."

"And should an emergency arise," said Kingston, "don't claim artistic licence. Insist that you're a dress designer, and you'll be forgiven any outrage." He looked at Modesty. "Speaking of potatoes, how many bushels did you peel during the painting of the latest Fletcher, or were you only pretending?"

She half smiled. "I'm beginning to feel a little awed about Luke's pictures. About the prospect of being in some of them, I mean." Willie nodded, and she gave him a look of surprise as she said, "You guessed?"

"Sticks out a mile, Princess. Luke's probably already into the immortals, so in a hundred years, or maybe four 'undred, there'll be tourists flying in from colonies on the Alpha Centauri planets to see all the old Earth culture, and there you'll be in the Tate or the National, peeling a spud with nothing on."

She gave a laugh full of delight. "I hadn't thought of it quite like that, but you're so right, Willie love. It's a little creepy to think of people looking at you a few hundred years on."

"Did it come out well?" Kingston asked.

Fletcher said absently, "I was very pleased. I don't think I've done anything better. It won't be for sale, of course."

"I hope," said Kingston, "that an old friend and generous host, one to whom life is so frequently unfair, poor sod, may have the privilege of a viewing." He accepted the wine list from the sommelier and passed it to Modesty. "You choose, honeychile."

Later, when coffee and brandy had been served, Kingston said, "I promised not to talk shop, or in other words to talk

139

about Luke here going mysteriously absent etcetera, but I feel bound to ask if you took note of the customers at the baccarat table as we passed through the casino earlier?"

Modesty glanced inquiringly at Willie, then shook her head. "Was it Frezzi?"

"Someone far less likely. You said John Dall was your only millionaire, but you forgot one. Sam Solon."

"Here?"

"In person, lady. I only glimpsed him through the usual crowd of kibitzers, but it was at pretty close range. I had the impression he also glimpsed us."

Fletcher said, "Good Lord, do you mean that Aussie chap who picked me up in his aeroplane? He was remarkably good, you know. Came to see me in hospital, and made sure I didn't get pestered by hordes of awful newspapermen. Oh, sorry Dick."

"Not at all. Some are indeed awful. I'm different. To know me is to love me. I suspect there was a certain amount of self-interest in Sam Solon's protective attitude. He was keeping you for his own papers."

Modesty said, "Do you know him, Dick?"

"Slightly. He once offered me a job when I was out there on a story. More to the point, I think he knows who the girl in the boat who rescued Luke really was."

"Why do you say that?"

"One of his stringers in London showed me a very good Identikit photoprint of you and asked if I could identify you. I don't doubt the same question was being asked in a lot of places, so evidently Sam Solon wanted to know who you were."

"And what did you say?"

Kingston grinned. "I told him you looked a bit like an aunt of mine, except that your nose was bigger. But Solon has a lot of resources. I'll wager by now he knows you're Modesty Blaise, together with all that implies."

She looked at Willie, then they both looked at Kingston as she said, "Isn't it something of an odd coincidence, Solon being here in Malta just now?"

Kingston smiled. "Nothing sinister, honeychile. I'd be suspicious myself if I didn't know he visits around this time every year. There's a hell of a lot of emigration from Malta to Australia."

"I know. So?"

"So he controls a big construction company in Queensland, and about a third of the labour force is Maltese. I suppose he negotiates numbers with the Minister of whatever here. Sam Solon isn't following you around, lady."

"Good."

Willie said, "Shall we go and take 'im on at baccarat, Princess?"

She smiled and shook her head. "I don't think so. I'm not sure whether he's friend or foe—" She broke off, looking beyond Kingston. "Here he comes."

Sam Solon's brown and weather-worn face held a slightly uneasy expression. He was wearing a fawn cotton suit over a white polo-neck shirt, and gestured quickly for the men to remain seated as he reached the table.

"Excuse me busting in like this." The Australian twang was more pronounced than when Modesty had last heard it. "I reckoned you'd be through to the coffee about now. Your table, I'm told, Mr. Kingston?"

"That's right." Kingston sought Modesty's eye and received the tiniest of nods. "Will you join us for a brandy, Mr. Solon?"

The Australian shifted uncomfortably and ran a work-toughened hand over his head. "Be glad to, but only with the lady's permission." He looked directly at Modesty now. "I was bossy with her a while back, and she set me right. I've been hoping I'd have a chance to apologise next time I was in England, but when I saw Modesty Blaise walk in here this evening I knew this was the day."

She put out her hand. "I was a little brusque myself when we last met, Mr. Solon. Now let me see. You know Luke Fletcher and I understand you've met Dick Kingston before. You evidently know me, so that leaves Willie Garvin, an old friend of mine."

"I've heard a little about him, too, and he looks a bit like a bloke I played poker with a few years back." Sam Solon grinned as he spoke, and looked relieved. There were hand-shakes, and the men moved a little to make room for the extra chair a waiter had already produced.

Kingston said, "Brandy? Liqueur?"

"I'd like a beer, if that's okay."

"Of course."

A few minutes later, after some general pleasantries, Modesty said, "Luke was just telling us that you were very kind to him while he was in hospital, Mr. Solon."

"Sam, please." He turned his hand out in a gesture. "Don't rate that too high, Mr. Fletcher. I was hoping to scoop my rivals and my own editors by finding out just where the hell you'd been." He looked at Kingston. "I bet you're still trying. Right?"

Kingston said, "I'm always trying something, Sam."

"No need to get cagey, son, I'm not out to pinch your story. Tell you what, I'll have a photostat of the Luke Fletcher file sent to you from Sydney. You might find some-thing useful in it." He hesitated. "I don't want to talk busi-ness when you have guests, but if you come and see me tomorrow at the *Dragonara* we could maybe fix a nonreturnable option for the Australian rights of any story you get."

"I'll do that," Kingston said quietly, and glanced round the table. "With the contacts we dispose of between us, we surely ought to be able to dig out exactly what happened. Who did it, and why. The trouble is, Modesty and Willie are only mildly interested, and our boy here, Luke, doesn't seem to give a damn."

Fletcher said, "I'm painting again. All the rest of it seems unreal."

Sam Solon shrugged. "Forget my newspapers, and I'd still like to know." He drank the remaining half of his beer. "If anyone really wants to take a crack at this, give me a call. I'm going to England next week, and I'll be in London for a while, at Claridges." He stood up. "Thanks for the drink."

Kingston began a vague protest, but Sam Solon waved a hand in negation. "Don't get polite, son. I'm intruding, but I've got enough sense to keep it short." He looked at Modesty. "I admire you in a big way, young lady. Any time I can be useful, just pick up a phone." The blue eyes turned to Willie. "The thing I like best about England is the country pubs, and they tell me you've got a real beaut. Okay if I look in for a drink one day?"

Willie lifted a hand in a welcoming gesture. "Any time. I'll leave the address and phone number at the *Dragonara* desk for you tomorrow."

Sam Solon gave a wicked grin. "Don't bother. I know you and Miss Blaise have got maybe a hatful of secrets nobody knows, but I'm an inquisitive bloke, and when it comes to the routine stuff, you could get what I *don't* know about you into a thimble."

8

Beauregard Browne put down the phone. "The whole thing has become quite thrillingly complex since they returned from Malta's sunny clime," he announced, and draped himself languidly on the big settee. "Where is my indispensable secretary, she of the rotating pelvis?"

Dr. Feng said, "Clarissa is at present embracing the Church, in the form of its representative among us."

The violet eyes shone with pleasurable surprise. "You're becoming quite a wit, my merry old medico. Most admirable. I'm sure I could never manage it in Chinese. I think I shall allow Clarissa and Uriah to continue their prayer meeting. There's nothing urgent."

"Blaise and Garvin have not discovered your new system of bugging?"

Beauregard Browne laughed, "Indeed they haven't, it's really quite amusing."

"You do not find Kingston's theory amusing, surely?"

The golden curls bounced as Beauregard Browne gave a shake of his head. "No. He's been rather too perceptive. I've suggested to Our Glorious Patron that we may have to discourage the investigative Kingston with a teeny-weeny killing."

"A suitable case for your Personnel Executive, possibly?"

"Yes, I have Uriah in mind. I'm bound to say, my little mind-bending mandarin, that I'm slightly disappointed with

144

your skills. I mean, it's really not very good that the dreary Fletcher should start having bad dreams about a Chinaman, is it?"

Dr. Feng said quickly, "Has he had more nightmares?"

"On present information, not since the one three days ago, when he again saw this Chinaman, undoubtedly you, but in a different setting. He was strapped beneath an enormous metronome with a blade on the bottom of it, and this was poised to slice off the top of his head as it went back and forth. Pure Edgar Allan Poe."

"I do not understand the reference, but it is clear the nightmare derives from the metronome I used during a number of hypnotic sessions."

"It derives from his *memory* of your metronome, and suggests a hole in his amnesia which may well grow larger. Oddly enough, one gathers that Blaise isn't trying for a break-through, it's the meddlesome Kingston who's set on getting the tedious Fletcher to remember all. Ah, there you are, poppet. I trust there's some of Uriah left?"

"Oh, Uriah's all right," she said. "I left him having a little nap. Did you want to see him, Beau?"

"No hurry, angel. I was just saying to our friend from the east that matters are moving to a conclusion on several fronts."

"Gosh, yes, they are, aren't they?" She sat down and crossed her legs, modestly arranging her skirt to show no length of thigh. "Do you still think you might get Blaise and Garvin for the Jade Queen job?"

"I have every confidence, sweet maid. All we require is the correct key to wind them up, and that is even now being cut, to a great extent by Miss Blaise herself."

"Well, that's super. How about the Fletcher situation?"

"What we've heard through our new and indetectable

bugging system indicates a possibility that he might recollect certain events to our disadvantage, but this could well be made less possible by the removal of the journalistic Mr. Kingston." Beauregard Browne beamed suddenly and sat up. "Oh, yes! Two birds with one stone! I've been reflecting on ways to convince Blaise and Garvin of our sincerity when the time comes, and it's just occurred to me that Kingston would do most excellently."

Clarissa's large white teeth showed in a proud smile. "You always think of something, Beau."

"Yes, I do rather, don't I? And now I want *you* to think of something, my little honeypot. I want some reliable local labour for a nicely judged putting in of the boot. A discouragement operation. Any suggestions?"

Clarissa thought for a moment, absently swinging a well-shaped calf. "Who's to be discouraged, Beau?"

He grinned. "Our Patron has decided that it's time to discourage an uncouth Australian."

She looked puzzled. "That's rather unpatriotic, isn't it?"

"Not really. He only wants him hurt a bit, not crippled."

"But who?"

Beauregard Browne spread his hand. "Darling, I know you're in your après-screw euphoria, but you really must stop thinking with your loins. Who else but the ghastly self-made Antipodean who picked up Fletcher from the yacht, who renewed acquaintance with Blaise and Co. in Malta, and who has maintained contact with them here in London because he's interested in the Fletcher mystery."

She pressed a hand to her head and made an apologetic grimace. "Of course. Sam Solon. That was frightfully slow of me. Mind you, I don't think he'll be easily discouraged."

"Nevertheless, Our Admirable Patron thinks it would be a good idea. It's the thought that counts."

She smiled. "Yes. Actually, I can see his point. I think our best move might be to bring over a little team from Paris or Brussels. If we pick a good location they could be on their way home before P.C. Plod has got his notebook out. It's a nice cut-off."

"Darling, you have a gift for administration. No wonder they made you milk monitor at school."

Clarissa gave a deprecating laugh. "That wasn't actually the reason Mr. Caldwell made me milk monitor. It was so he could have it off with me over the desk when everyone had gone home."

Beauregard Browne smiled happily, got up, and went across to give her a brief kiss. "I know, dear heart. I used that little fact to put the bite on him for a fiver a week during your last term there."

"Beau, you absolute rotter! You didn't give me a penny!"

"It would have made you a professional, poppet, and that would never do." He turned to Dr. Feng, arms spread expansively. "Ah, memories, memories, doctor. Doesn't Clarissa epitomise the enchanting concept of the childhood sweetheart, the girl next door, the English rose? I mean, doesn't she?"

*　　*　　*

Tarrant said, "Have we been able to get any confirmation?"

Fraser looked harassed, and fidgeted with the papers he held. "I took the liberty of sending a man to talk with our French colleagues yesterday, sir."

"With René Vaubois himself?"

"I assumed that would be your wish, sir."

Tarrant nodded. "We're not in opposition on anything

147

just now, and we think they have a source inside Lubyanka, don't we?"

"Quite so, sir. They would not admit it, naturally, but M'sieu Vaubois was good enough to say that he was quite sure our information concerning Ryan was correct." Fraser peered over the top of his spectacles with an obtuse air.

Tarrant held down his irritation. It was stupid to be annoyed with a man for staying in the character he had shown to the world throughout all his working life, but there were times when Fraser's role-playing was irksome, and Tarrant decided that he had had enough for today. The very excellent agent John Ryan, who had been picked up in Sofia and transferred to Lubyanka Prison in Dzerzhinsky Street, Moscow, had not, after all, been sucked dry by his interrogators. Within forty-eight hours, and long before the softening-up process could begin to bite, he had contrived to take his own life.

Tarrant's source had been able to give no details, and he presumed that the same applied to the source Vaubois had inside the prison. It was of little importance, anyway, precisely how John Ryan had killed himself. He was an experienced man, of sound judgment, who had evidently decided that in all the circumstances this was his preferred way out. Having made the decision, he had proved sufficiently ingenious to find a method of implementing it.

Tarrant said, "All right, Jack. Close the file and go through the usual routine."

The use of his first name warned Fraser to drop the bumbling image while they were alone together. He nodded and said, "It's a bastard, losing Ryan. I couldn't stand him myself, with all that easy charm, but he was a good agent." Fraser grinned suddenly, without a shred of humour. "And he outsmarted those KGB pricks in Lubyanka, didn't he? I'll lift a glass to him for that."

Tarrant wrote M B on his desk pad, and said, "I must tell Modesty Blaise. She'd want to know how it came out. Have there been any developments on the Fletcher front that you know of?"

"I had a drink with Dick Kingston the other day, and he seems quite hopeful that Fletcher's starting to get a few cracks in his amnesia. Modesty's still nurse-maiding him, and she got him painting again while they were in Malta. Somebody's still interested in Fletcher, because they had Modesty's place bugged to monitor him, using some Sicilian mob out there."

"Does she know why?"

"Neither why nor who." Fraser made a sour grimace. He would have liked to put a team on the Fletcher mystery, but that was out of the question. Tarrant had told him to keep an eye on it, which was as much as could be justified. The main work of the department was accumulating fragments of information in enormous quantities and trying to make patterns from them. There were areas where crime and intelligence overlapped, and whoever had made those hypodermic punctures in Fletcher was no innocent man-in-the-street, therefore the Fletcher fragment was to be kept in view, with a thousand others, in the hope that several might come together in an unexpected fit. It happened more often than one might suppose.

"There's a new character on the scene," said Fraser. "Sam Solon's over here, and seems to be taking an interest."

Tarrant raised an eyebrow. "I thought Modesty and he had quarrelled when they met in the Tasman Sea."

"Yes, she chucked a couple of his men overboard when he did the superior male bit, but I gather he's reformed. They ran into him in Malta, and Dick Kingston said he's being very useful with Fletcher stuff from Sydney. Hospital reports and so on."

"I'm beginning to wonder if Modesty and Willie really want him opened up. If they did, they'd have been much more active."

"Kingston reckons her only concern is Fletcher's talent."

Tarrant smiled. "It's a very tenable point of view."

*　　*　　*

Willie Garvin said, "Right," and kicked Modesty's feet from beneath her. Before she hit the floor of the long combat room the automatic came into her hand and a shot pierced the head of a man-shaped target at twenty feet.

She got slowly to her feet, eyes thoughtful. "What do you think, Willie?"

"Compared with the thirty-two, I'd say you're either just as fast but not quite so accurate, or just as accurate but not quite so fast."

She weighed the gun in her hand. It was a Star PD .45, made in Spain, and the lightest, most compact weapon of that calibre she had ever handled, smaller and lighter even than the Colt Commander.

"I don't know, Willie. I'm so used to the Colt thirty-two. Or the MAB for an automatic."

"They're only any good if you're dead accurate, which you are, but you've got to be a bit lucky to be dead accurate all the time, because you've got variables in the external conditions and in the cartridge." He nodded at the Star .45 she had slipped into the semi-shoulder holster strapped on the left of her body just below the level of the breast. "That gun fires a forty-five, so a hit anywhere stops 'em. It holds six plus one, which is nice. It's of light alloy, well-made, and easy to conceal. It gives you a quick draw, and it's got adjustable sights, so you can even get some use at long-range with a two-'anded grip."

150

"But it's an automatic, and you've always been worried about automatics jamming."

"With this one, it's a chance no bigger than getting a misfire with a revolver."

They stood in silence for a little while, Modesty resting her hands on her rump, looking at the target, Willie watching her. They both wore dark slacks and shirts, and were sweating, for they had been having a work-out in the dojo section of the long low building earlier. She grinned suddenly and hit his chest with a loosely clenched fist. "So maybe I'll hang up the thirty-two. It's an academic argument anyway. Respectable citizens like us don't need guns."

"Sure." Willie watched her take off the holster. "But we're respectable citizens with an unrespectable past, and it's only a couple of weeks ago that one of Frezzi's boys was trying to gut you with a knife."

"I expect it was really just a cry for help. I provoked him when all he needed was understanding."

Willie laughed. "We're all guilty."

"And sweaty, too." She gave him the holstered gun and turned to move away, peeling off her shirt. "Let's get showered, Willie. Sam's due here for lunch in half an hour."

Fifteen minutes later, as Willie locked the double steel doors of the soundproof and windowless building behind them, one of the barmaids appeared on the brick path which led up to the back of *The Treadmill*. "Just had a phone-call, Mr. Garvin," she called as they approached. "From that gentleman who was here last week, the Australian one."

"Mr. Solon."

"Ah, that's him. I didn't quite get his name over the phone, and I felt silly to keep asking."

"What did he say, Doris?"

"Oh, that he was in Tunbury and his fan-belt had broken, but the garage couldn't put a new one on till the engine cooled down, so he was going to start walking, and would it be any trouble for you to meet him because otherwise he'll be late."

Willie looked at Modesty. "Why start walking?"

"Because he wants his tucker, because he'd rather walk than wait, because the English countryside has enchanted his leathery old soul, because he's Sam Solon."

Willie made a gesture of surrender. "I only asked, Princess."

"We can take the Jensen. It's out in the carpark."

Two and a half miles along the lane which ran through to Tunbury was a bend which brought the little road to within a stone's throw of the river, and here a patch of open grassy ground broke the wooded verge, giving access to the towpath. The car was purring gently round the bend when Willie said sharply, "Jesus! Hold it, Princess, pull off!" As she swung the Jensen off the road she took in the scene. Sam Solon, in a blue shirt and grey slacks. Five other men, all in lightweight track-suits. One held Sam by the throat. The others were spread out in a rough circle.

The Jensen slammed to a halt, and Modesty was out, running, hearing the thud of Willie's feet behind her. She saw a fist swing to Sam Solon's face, and he went staggering back to be seized by the next man, who hit him hard in the stomach. Again he reeled, but recovered his balance and dropped into a wavering crouch, fists lifted as he faced the third man of the circle.

Now heads were turning towards Modesty and Willie. She had dragged her denim skirt up to free her legs, and Willie was level with her. She pointed with two fingers and he swerved away slightly, aiming for the two men she had indicated. With only fractions of a second in which to assess the opposition, he knew they were not amateurs. The eyes, the readiness, and the lack of surprise, all told of experience. Willie went at the first man with fists clenched and body wide open. It was an attack inviting a kick to counter it, and the kick duly came. Willie turned nicely on his toes, hit the inside of the man's knee with one elbow and his solar plexus with stiff fingers of the other hand, then spun and bent to drive a back-heel under the heart of the second man as he came in. Cautiously pleased with the rhythm of his movements, he was regretting, as the heel thumped home, that he had been given no third man for continuity when he heard Modesty saying clearly, "Flat on the ground, Sam. Take the moustache one, half left, Willie."

It was good to feel the whole body respond instantly, so that it used the reaction from the back-heel for a forward roll to gain distance and sight the target, then followed with a sequence of shoulder-spring and drop kick, timed so that the feet shot out above Sam Solon's body as he fell flat in response to Modesty's order. The moustache man left the ground fractionally before collapsing in a huddle. Willie landed in a crouch, straddling Sam Solon, and Modesty said, "All right."

Her shoes lay on the ground a little way off. She stood barefoot, her skirt scrunched up to her thighs as if about to paddle. One man lay at her feet, eyes half open, staring dazedly. Another, on hands and knees, was making strangled whooping sounds as he tried to recover his wind.

She said, "Watch them, Willie," and moved to kneel beside Sam Solon. One eye was swollen, his nose was bleeding, and there was a dark red patch which would soon turn blue on his cheek. Propped on an elbow, free arm clamped across his ribs, he forced a grin and said in a wheezing voice, "I'm bloody glad to see you, sweetheart. Pity you didn't make it a bit sooner."

She pinched his nose hard and said, "What's the damage?"

"I'll be okay. Give me a hand to the car. Christ, I sound like Punch."

"Are your ribs hurt?"

"Yeah. I was going around that circuit for the second time when you got here. The game is, if you fall down you get kicked. So you try to stay on your feet."

"You were doing well." She looked up. "One of us each side, Willie."

Moving carefully they got him to the car. He leaned against it, dragging in air through his mouth, holding a handkerchief to his nose. Willie said, "What about—?" then stopped short. Modesty followed his gaze. One of the men was on one knee now, holding an automatic aimed towards them. Two of the others had moved, one bending over the man Willie had back-heeled, trying to rouse him.

Modesty said, "At fifty yards he's not going to hit anyone except by accident, but if he starts moving in ..."

Willie opened the boot and took out a heavy spanner. "I'll drop 'im at twenty," he said. It was no boast. Willie's ability to throw accurately was stupefying, and not confined to the twin knives he carried on business occasions. "Mind you," he added as they moved round the car, "I don't think they're looking for trouble now. Just want out."

Modesty said, "Get in the car, Sam."

"No bloody fear!" He glared at her over the top of the wadded handkerchief. "Willie, you get hold of one of those bastards for me. I want to know who set 'em on."

Four of them were conscious now, and the whole group was moving slowly towards the towpath and the river bank, two of them carrying the one who was still out. The man with the gun backed after the others, acting as rearguard. Modesty said, "Forget it, Willie. I'm not having you get yourself shot for nothing."

"I was thinking along the same lines meself, Princess."

Sam Solon croaked furiously, "Don't let 'em get away ... goddam pom, you! Yeller bloody pom!"

Willie said mildly, "Too right, cobber." And Modesty added, "Sam, just shut up."

The men were getting into a boat which lay out of sight below the low bank. There came the roar of an engine. Modesty said, "They'll have a car waiting somewhere on the Wixford Road, on the other side. What was it all about, Sam?"

"How the hell do I know?" he said painfully. "They must have followed me from town, and picked this place after they heard me phone from the garage."

"It was a work-over, and that's stupid unless the victim knows why. What did they say?"

"Two words. Every time they hit me, they said, '*Forget Fletcher.*' And they said it with a funny accent. They were foreign."

Later, at *The Treadmill*, after he had refused to have a doctor, Modesty cleaned and dressed his abrasions as he lay on a bed in one of the spare rooms. No ribs were broken, but a raw redness promised extensive bruising and one eye was almost closed. When she had finished, Willie began to pack up the first-aid box and said, "You going to do it, Sam?"

"Do what?" He was sitting on the edge of the bed, buttoning his shirt and glaring resentfully with his good eye. "Don't start telling me to stay in bed a couple of days. I've been hurt a hell of a sight worse than this. Bloody hell, when I was a young feller gouging opal up in Andamooka I was in tougher fights every Saturday night."

Modesty said, "Willie means are you going to forget Fletcher. That's what this was all about."

He regarded her, tight-lipped. "Not me, girl. Up till now I was just curious. From today, I got a better reason." He took his jacket from her. "Funny, but you don't seem too interested in what's behind it all. I reckoned you were a bit more gutsy than that."

She nodded without resentment. "The thing is, Sam, we're trouble-prone and we're trying to break the habit. We've been involved too often, we've ended up hurt too often, so we've decided to give ourselves a break."

Sam Solon shrugged, then winced. "Where does that leave Fletcher?"

She sat beside him on the bed and said, "It leaves Luke with the situation that something weird happened to him, but he can't remember it. Now he's painting again, and he's not particularly interested in remembering."

"Look, somebody *did* something to the poor bastard. Right? Suppose they try it again?"

"If they wanted to, they'd have tried it already. Anyway, he's with me evenings and nights, and when he's at his studio during the day Dick Kingston has a man keeping an eye on him."

Sam Solon sat gazing down at the floor, and she felt a sudden tinge of pity for him. It had nothing to do with his beating-up, but sprang from what she had learned of him during the past two weeks. He had asked her, with uncharacteristic diffidence, if she would spend a little time with him visiting the major art galleries and museums. She had given up two mornings to this, and discovered that he was a man trying late in life to acquire a measure of culture, but was almost totally lacking in taste and perception.

He had constantly asked her to explain *why* a painting, a vase, a sculpture, or a tapestry was good or beautiful, and had listened with growing bafflement to her attempts to define the undefinable. In the end it had not been easy to hide the sorrow she felt for him in his deprivation. Now she was touched by an echo of that sorrow, for again his crude under-standing was defeated, and he could not comprehend why she and Willie should hold back from supporting him in tack-ling the Luke Fletcher mystery.

She slipped an arm through his and said, "Willie has a Mrs. Dawes who cooks for *The Treadmill* and makes the best steak and kidney pudding in the universe. It goes down marvellously with a few cans of Australian beer. I'm only sorry you're much too shaky and upset to have any appetite for lunch."

Sam Solon turned to look at her through the slit of his swollen eye. "Take more than this to put an Aussie off his tucker. Come on, pom girl, let's get at it."

*   *   *

Kingston paid off the taxi, waited for a break in the traffic, and limped across Cheyne Walk. His bad leg was hurting more than usual today. Outside Fletcher's studio he stopped and looked around. A dark, efficient-looking young man got out of a parked car and came towards him.

"Mr. Kingston?"

"Yes?"

"I'm Pimm, from the agency."

"Where's the usual man?"

"Langridge? He phoned in that he's laid low with the runs, so they put me in."

"Right."

Kingston had turned to go through the gate when Pimm said, "He went out for a walk a few minutes ago. He usually does after lunch, according to Langridge's report."

Kingston stopped. "I know that, but why the hell aren't you following him?"

Pimm looked taken aback. "My orders were to make sure he didn't leave the house with anybody against his will, but otherwise to keep in the background."

Kingston said abruptly, "That's about half right. Sod it, does nobody do a proper job these days? Which way did he go?"

"East along the Embankment. I think he usually takes about half an hour." Pimm chewed his lip and gestured towards his car. "Do you want me to go after him, Mr. Kingston?"

"In a car on your own? You can't kerb-crawl with him, and only one of God's angels could find a parking spot along there. No, you'd better drop me off when we spot him, then wait for us back here."

"Right."

They moved to the car, a four-year-old Cortina. Kingston slammed the door irritably after him. He was not particularly worried about Luke Fletcher, and had always believed there was no more than a very small possibility of an attempt being made to snatch him again. But the break-down of protection made him angry. He had been in a business where a slip like that could cost your life, or a dozen lives. It had happened.

Pimm snapped up a chance to join the eastbound traffic and kept to the inner lane. After a few moments Kingston said, "Wouldn't he more likely be walking on the river side?"

"I suppose—ah, there he is!" Pimm swung the wheel sharply, turning left, away from the river. Kingston swayed, braced himself, then looked ahead along the heavily parked road. A hand caught his collar from behind, jerking him hard back against the seat, and something sharp stung his neck. In the three seconds before he slid into unconsciousness he tried to wrench free from the man behind, then tried to lift a foot and smash it through the windscreen, but his strength was draining away. In the last millisecond he wondered if they had killed him, and thought with bitter self-contempt that it was no more than he deserved.

When his senses crept slowly back he had no way of judging how long had passed, but felt in his bones that it was far more than minutes. His stomach churned with nausea, his muscles were stiff, and he was no longer in the Ford but in what appeared to be the interior of a small van travelling at a sustained speed. His wrists were secured behind his back with sticky tape, his ankles bound with something soft. Nylon tights, he guessed, and unbreakable. He was strapped to a stretcher which appeared to be bolted to the floor of the van, and there was a noose of wire round his neck which fitted loosely, until he tried to raise his head, when the wire tightened like a rabbit snare.

The van's speed had not varied, and he surmised that he was now on a motorway or dual carriageway. Methodically he spent ten minutes trying to work his wrists free, then another ten in a careful attempt to extract his head from the wire noose. Achieving either would give him a chance to reach the door with his feet and batter it open. After an hour and several more attempts he was lathered in sweat and still securely held. He lay breathing deeply, relaxing, seeking mental and physical balance for whatever was to come. The van had turned off the main road some time ago. Trying to visualise its journey, he believed it had then passed through a small town and one or two villages. Now it was on a winding road which could only be a country lane.

He was a man used to controlling fear, and was not particularly afraid for himself at this moment, for he had now calculated that whoever had taken him had not done so for the purpose of killing. If they wanted him dead, they could have used a lethal drug in the car. Speculating on their intentions, he had worked out two possible motives. The first, and most likely, was that they proposed to discourage his interest in Luke Fletcher just as they had tried to discourage Sam Solon only a few days ago, down near Willie's pub. Since they were taking him a long way, presumably to some isolated place, it could well turn out to be a far worse beating than Sam had suffered.

The second possibility was that he might be going to get the Fletcher treatment, whatever that had consisted of. If so, it destroyed his rather shapeless theory linking the Fletcher mystery with the disappearance of Maria Cavalli, Jules Baillot, and other art people over the past two years, for he was not in that category himself. He hoped, with a flicker of grim humour, that if he ended up afloat in a dinghy on the other side of the world there might be a Modesty Blaise at hand to pick him up.

The van was moving along a bumpy road now. A track, perhaps. It slowed to a halt, engine still running. A few moments later the doors opened and sunlight fell upon him. Somebody clambered in. Hands slipped the wide noose from his neck. The stretcher was released from the floor, lifted out, and set down on crumbling tarmac. The door of the van slammed, and the engine revs rose as it pulled away

He lay with eyes half closed, waiting for them to adjust to the sunlight. A very wide strip of concrete extended away from him, weeds growing from its cracked surface. The strip narrowed in perspective to be lost eventually in tall grass and scrub. He turned his head and saw the derelict hangar, the nissen huts, the row of decaying offices, some with faint markings still visible on the boards outside them.

An old wartime airfield, empty and long abandoned, except perhaps by ghosts of the past. There were still many such derelict airfields tucked away in remote parts of the country, particularly in East Anglia, runways crumbling, service roads overgrown, buildings neglected and vandalised.

There were hands at his ankles, and he felt the binding fall away, then the strap across his chest was unfastened. He looked up into a bright cherubic face with a halo of golden hair and long-lashed violet eyes, an adult version of the angelic *Bubbles* in the Millais picture, but for the frightening humour in the eyes.

"Upsy-daisy," said the man with a wave of his well-manicured hand. "We're here, Mr. Kingston."

For the last twenty minutes Kingston had been concentrating on loosening his muscles and combating stiffness, but he rolled over slowly and awkwardly now, grunting as he knelt up on the concrete. The airfield was empty but for the two of them. Already the van had disappeared behind a distant line of woodland. Kingston shook his head as if muzzy, and made a show of trying to rise, then sank back on his haunches and stared at the man who stood before him in a frilled shirt and pale green suit. "What the hell do you think you're playing at?" he growled. "Get this sticky stuff off my wrists."

Beauregard Browne flapped a limp hand deprecatingly. "Oh, you are awful, Dickie. May I call you Dickie? It's terribly naughty of you to act all surprised when you know very well you're being a nuisance to us. Well, of course you didn't know it was *us*, if you take my meaning, but you know you've been making yourself a nuisance to somebody. Not that we bear any grudges. Come along, jump up now and we'll have a nice picnic."

"I'll have you for this, you clown," Kingston said belligerently. "You stick a needle in me, drug me, bring me out here, then talk about picnics!"

"Oh, come on, duckie, don't waste time with all this thespian stuff. Are you going to squat there all night?"

"I've got a bad leg. Give me a hand, sod you."

Beauregard Browne beamed at him. "Wicked Dickie! Who's planning one of his nasty old Mil Six tricks, then? A knee in the nuptials and a boot to the head? Our bad leg isn't all that bad, I'm sure." His arm swung. Something lightly touched Kingston's face, then settled about his neck. He saw the length of thin shining wire running from beneath his chin to the elegant hand which held the other end on a wooden toggle. The hand twitched, and again Kingston felt the bite of a wire noose about his throat.

"Up," said the man, and Kingston came quickly to his feet. Together they moved towards the nearest hangar. He noted that the Bubbles character moved with a feminine grace which accorded with his manner and appearance, but Kingston's judgment had been tempered by hard experience and he had no illusions as to his captor's quality. This man was very strong, very fast, and totally confident in his own ability. It was not the misplaced confidence of a fool, and Kingston suddenly found himself fighting against the thrust of fear.

They came through a side door into the hangar. One end was wide open, the great roller doors rusted in position, and though the interior was shaded from the sun there was still ample light. Bubbles, as Kingston now thought of him, waved an arm expansively and said, "I do hope you're going to eat a hearty picnic, sweetie."

A trestle table had been set up near one wall of the hangar. On a fancy paper table-cloth, a picnic had been set out. There were cold meats, salad, coleslaw, rolls and butter, cheese, biscuits, and some bottles of rosé wine. Seated at the table on folding stools were three people. One was a cadaverous priest with the face of a fanatic. Beside him, wearing a quiet grey suit, was a Chinaman, and facing them across the table was a

162

red-haired girl with good strong features and a Junoesque but well-kept body.

Kingston felt reality begin to slip away from him, and pulled himself together with an inward oath. A Chinaman. That tied in with Fletcher's nightmare, and Kingston knew now that he was into the organisation behind whatever had happened to Fletcher. His curiosity was intense, but rising above it was the clamorous warning his instinct was sounding, telling him to get out, to get out fast.

There would be a car somewhere, probably just behind the hangar. They wouldn't have left the keys in it, so who would have them? No solid data, so speculate. Not the priest or the Chinaman, for reasons lurking in the subconscious but probably valid. Bubbles? Possibly. But the girl was more likely. She looked normal and efficient. More likely still, a driver waiting in the car now with the keys in the switch. Yes. Gamble on that, and reckon you need five seconds grace from the moment you reach the car. If you reach it ...

"This is Clarissa," the man with violet eyes was saying, "this is Dr. Feng, and this is the Reverend Uriah Crisp." He laid strong elegant fingers on his own chest. "I am Beauregard Browne. With an 'e'."

Clarissa smiled warmly and said, "Hallo." Dr. Feng, who seemed to be hiding some uneasiness, inclined his head. The Reverend Uriah Crisp stared from red-rimmed eyes and said sorrowfully, "Our brother is a sinner, I fear."

"Quite so, Uriah, but that comes later," Beauregard Browne said soothingly. He indicated a stool beside Clarissa. "Do sit down, Mr. Kingston. I expect you think this is all rather strange, but the fact is we have a monstrously busy schedule, and we have to eat sometime, of course, and I simply can't bear to have everybody gnawing away at sandwiches in a car. It's just too barbaric, isn't it? I mean, isn't it?

163

So I asked Clarissa to make a nice picnic that we could sit down to now, before we get on with the rest of the business."

As he spoke, he had pressed Kingston down on to the stool, ripped away quickly but painfully the plaster securing his wrists, then in some way fastened the toggle at the end of the wire to some part of the stool, so that Kingston could make no move without tightening the noose about his own neck.

Beauregard Browne moved to the head of the table and sat down. Smiling brightly at Clarissa he said, "Come along, poppet, take your hand off the nice gentleman's thigh and put together some cold viands and salad for him. Is that how you pronounce it, I wonder, viands?"

Kingston sat massaging his wrists. Almost as if it were heat, he could feel the urgency radiating from the body of the girl close beside him, but it roused no response in him. For a reason he could not define, this Mad Hatter's Tea Party scared him more than a known and open menace would have done. It was absurd, confusing, and made for difficulty in keeping mental balance. He noted, with remote surprise, that the priest was probably wearing a gun under his jacket. The other three appeared to be unarmed, but he distrusted that appearance. There was nothing within his reach that he could use as a weapon. The plates and cutlery were plastic throwaways. The trestle table itself offered possibilities but would be hard to use while the wire noose held him upright. Still, if he were quick enough . . .

His mind churned on. Vaguely he heard the girl saying, "Is that enough, Mr. Kingston? There's plenty more tongue. Look, I know it's jolly hard for you to manage, but if you just prong it like this . . . here, I'll pop this in for you, shall I?"

Kingston turned his eyes towards her, struggling to look baffled and apprehensive so that she would not see the sudden

164

excitement which had flooded him. *The priest's gun!* He was sure of it now, and it was little more than an arm's length away across the table, under that black jacket, and in a holster angled for a quick draw to judge by the shape of the bulge he had seen as the man leaned forward.

The question was ... when? Not yet, certainly. Wait till the numbness had gone completely from both hands. Gradually edge a foot back, ready to lift the body vertically for a few inches before the lunge forward. That was vital, to prevent the drag of the wire noose. And meanwhile ...?

Kingston put down his fork, picked up his glass of wine, and drank a little. Beauregard Browne broke off in the middle of saying something to Dr. Feng and beamed approval. "Splendid, Mr. Kingston. You're feeling more settled now, I'm sure."

"I wouldn't entirely agree."

"Well, we can only do our best. Look after him, Clarissa dear. After all, it's a rather special din-dins for him, isn't it?" He looked down the table at Dr. Feng. "Now, O dependable diagnostician, you were saying in regard to the Fletcher stroke Modesty Blaise prognosis?"

"I was saying that I have no opinion as to whether or not she will submit to blackmail."

"But you should have. You are employed, O wise man from the East, expressly to have opinions on such matters. We've provided an ample dossier."

"No dossier is sufficiently ample to provide an informed answer to the question you ask. I would require many sessions of tests and analysis in a one-to-one relationship."

"Which you won't get, old prune." The violet eyes sparkled. "But fortunately I am by way of being a rather outstanding guesser in these matters, and I predict sullen compliance. I greatly doubt that we shall need the fall-back plan." Kingston found that he had automatically begun to focus upon what was being said, and was trying to make deductions. Modesty Blaise? Blackmail? He wrenched his mind away and set it to the immediate task of preserving his own existence.

The priest was eating hungrily, his fanatic eyes never leaving Kingston. Beauregard Browne and Dr. Feng were continuing their discussion. Clarissa was eating rather dreamily with the fork in her left hand while gently rubbing her breast with the other. Kingston decided he would never have a better moment. His good leg was now drawn back almost directly beneath him and he had already tested the thrust of it in relation to his centre of gravity. Once he had risen an inch, his other leg would sweep back, kicking the folding stool from beneath him so that he could lunge forward with no more than the weight of the stood pulling the noose tight about his neck. That would not trouble him unduly, and once he had the gun in his hand ...

Positioned as he was, he would have to go for the butt with his left hand, using his right to snap the slide back if the gun was an automatic; unless it was already cocked and with the safety-catch on, in which case he would have to thumb the safety off, using his right hand since the catch would be on the wrong side for left-handed use; or it might be a gun with a grip-safety system. If it was a revolver, there would almost certainly be no safety-catch ...

He turned his head slightly to stare at Beauregard Browne, not listening to his words, but encouraging within himself a swiftly growing rage and hatred towards this supercilious daisy, a fury which released adrenalin into the blood to give him added strength and speed. The moment was now, and his head snapped round towards the priest, leg muscles tightening for the thrust.

Then he froze, fighting to absorb the shock that hit him like a perfectly judged body-blow. Even as his head came round, the right hand of the priest had flickered for a split second. Then it was still, and the Colt Commander automatic it held was pointing at Kingston's face.

The priest said, "Yield not to temptation, brother."

Beauregard Browne laughed. "Uriah perceives the intention to sin almost before the sinner himself has formed it." He stood up. "I think it's time for the Hammer of the Lord to perform his ordained office." Kingston sat trying to maintain his nerve and confidence. Beauregard Browne moved behind him, took the toggle on the end of the wire that noosed his neck, and said, "If you wouldn't mind getting up now?" The priest's gun disappeared. The Chinaman produced a wicker picnic basket from beneath the table, took a plastic sack from it, and in a few seconds swept all the food and debris on the table into the sack, which he then shut in the basket. The table folded in two, and the tubular steel trestles clipped neatly to it.

A car started up somewhere nearby, and a few moments later was driven into the hangar. The girl was at the wheel. Kingston set his teeth. He had not noticed her departure. That was bad. He had to maintain a complete appreciation of the situation if he was to stand any sort of chance. The car was a station wagon. It stopped a few paces away. The girl switched off and got out, leaving the keys in the ignition. She opened the back and helped the Chinaman stow the basket and the folding table and chairs.

Beauregard Browne said, "If you would come this way, Mr. Kingston?" He twitched the wire, pointing, then moved beside Kingston to a spot thirty paces away. "There we are, my jolly old journalist. Now, if you turn right, what do we see? What else but the Hammer of the Lord about to perform the last rites. Let's slip this beastly wire off. There, I'm sure that's more comfy for you. And now, surprise surprise, we are about to place in your right hand this rather duckie firearm, which, as you will observe, is a Colt Cobra thirty-eight Special, one of the models issued as standard to Mil Six operatives and therefore familiar to you. I place one round in this chamber, so, and close the breech. Now it's all yours." Beauregard Browne stood behind Kingston and put the butt in his right hand as it hung at his side. "If you keep it pointed at the floor and pull the trigger twice, you'll have the cartridge in the next chamber to come under the hammer. Right, sweetie-pie? Then go ahead. You may do so without inviting any nastiness from those about you."

Kingston was staring down the hangar towards the priest, between thirty and forty yards away. He could see none of the others, for they were now somewhere behind him. His hands hung by his sides, the .38 in his right hand pointing down. He squeezed the trigger twice, and felt the cylinder turn as the mechanism clicked. The priest stood with something in his left hand, a small open book. His right hand now held a round flat hat.

From behind Kingston and to one side, Beauregard Browne's voice said, "After pronouncing a biblical valediction, which I hope and believe you will find to be not without fervour and sincerity, the Reverend Uriah Crisp, the scourge of sinners and the Hammer of the Lord, will take out his gun and shoot you dead. You, Mr. Kingston, may feel free to prevent this by simply lifting your own gun at any moment you choose, and shooting Mr. Crisp. If the Almighty is on your side, then it is our good brother Uriah who will pass to his well-earned rest, and you of course will be allowed to go your way in peace. Do you understand?"

Kingston did not answer. There were more important

matters to occupy him. The macabre was now being piled on to the bizarre, and he had first to shake off any sense of unreality so that he might think fast and clearly. Two years ago he had spent a few hours at Modesty Blaise's cottage in Benildon, and had watched her practise with a handgun. He had then judged her to be quicker than any man he had ever known in drawing a gun, concealed or on view, and firing an accurate shot. He did not yet know if the man dressed as a priest in this charade was accurate, but certainly he was faster than Modesty Blaise.

Kingston turned his head to look over his shoulder. A few paces away and to his right, Beauregard Browne stood sideways-on to him, a revolver barrel resting in the crook of his left elbow, aimed at Kingston. The man smiled engagingly and said again, "Do you understand, old fruit?"

Again Kingston made no answer but turned slowly back to face the priest. All options open to him would leave him dead. Unless ...

Only the expert could hit a man at thirty yards with a handgun. Make the man a fast-moving target, and it would prove a stiff task for the best of marksmen. The car stood no more than twenty-five paces away, to his right and forward of him. Once he started in that direction, he would be immediately between the priest and Beauregard Browne for a pace or two, inhibiting their fire. After that he would be moving faster, ducking and swerving. He could head round the rear of the car to reach the off-side, and if he made it he would then have some protection. He would also have one shot to use as a deterrent while he got the car started and moving.

It wasn't good, but it wasn't as bad as matching speed with a gun against this lunatic in a dog collar, and at least it had the ingredient of surprise. It was a long time since Dick

Kingston had been in real danger, but as with riding a bicycle, you never forgot how. He drew a deep breath and made his decision.

Perhaps two seconds had passed since Beauregard Browne last spoke. Now he said, "We shall assume that the sinner is mute of malice, Brother Uriah. Pray proceed."

The Reverend Uriah Crisp raised his Prayer Book and cried in a great croaking voice: "*May the words of my mouth and the coordination of my hand and eye be now and ever acceptable in Thy sight, O Lord our strength and Our Redeemer.*"

He took a pace forward, held the book so that his line of sight to Kingston passed just above it, held the hat close to his chest, and began to chant some of the familiar phrases that echoed and churned in his mind as the ecstatic fury welled up within him.

"*The ungodly lie waiting in our way on every side, turning their eyes down to the ground. Up, Lord, and let not man have the upper hand! Let the wicked fall into their own nets. Let them go down into the burning seas of Hell ...*"

Kingston, in his youth, had been a sprinter. Despite his limp he was still fast, and a fit man. Suddenly he was running for the car, eyes fixed on it. Two seconds later Beauregard Browne's gun boomed behind him, and with the sound came the clang of a bullet hitting the far wall of the hangar. He heard the priest cry "*No!*", and from the corner of his eye saw the black spidery figure begin to stalk obliquely forward.

Kingston feinted towards the bonnet of the car, then swerved and ran round the back to come panting up by the offside door, left hand throwing it open as he crouched with the Colt aimed diagonally across the roof at the advancing figure of the priest, who still held Prayer Book and hat in his hands as he marched on with deliberate strides, deepset eyes

blazing with indignation. Fifteen yards, fourteen, twelve ...
Kingston had turned the key and started the engine. Eyes on
the priest, he could not see Beauregard Browne but knew he
must be closing towards the nearside rear of the car. The
Colt held only one shot. If he used it on the priest, that would
leave the evilly cherubic Browne coming up behind as he
slid into the seat. Marginally better to drop Browne and hope
to run the priest down.

Kingston straightened a little and turned his head to sight
Beauregard Browne. It was the last conscious movement he
ever made, for in the same instant the Reverend Uriah Crisp
let the hat fall from his right hand. It had not reached the
ground when the Colt Commander, fired by that same hand,
spat a .45 bullet into Kingston's head.

9

Modesty touched the button and the spindles of the recorder began to turn. First came the soft voice of her Indo-Chinese houseboy, Weng, saying, "Good afternoon, who is calling, please?"

A woman's voice, rather hearty and penetrating. "I'd like to speak to Modesty Blaise."

"Miss Blaise is not here at the moment. Will you leave a message, or a number for her to call?"

"A message, please. Now look, do make sure you get this exactly right, won't you? It's frightfully important."

"You need not be concerned, madame. This conversation is being recorded."

"Ah, jolly good. Well, I just want to say that she'd be awfully silly to go to the police, and that if she really wants to help her protégé she must wait until she hears about Dick Kingston, and then call 493–8181 and ask them to page Mr. Ricketts. That's all." There came a click as the woman hung up.

Modesty stopped the tape. Willie sat in one of the big armchairs near the floor-to-ceiling window of her penthouse drawing room, leaning forward with elbows on knees, heels of his hands pressed to his eyes. After a moment he sat up, shook his head, and said, "I've never 'eard the voice before, Princess."

Modesty nodded and walked to the window, looking out

across the terrace to Hyde Park below. It was lunch-time, and the park was busy with traffic and strollers. She said quietly, "I'm sure they've got Luke. Outside that, I'm totally in the dark."

She wore a silk shirt and jeans, and looked untroubled. Perhaps only Willie Garvin could have perceived the anxiety within her. He looked at the notebook on the arm of his chair and said, "Let's run through it again, Princess. You and Luke 'ad breakfast 'ere this morning, then you drove 'im through to the studio. The agency bloke was on duty outside."

"Not the usual one, Willie. But the same one who was on yesterday evening."

"The phoney, as it turns out. Right. You dropped Luke at the studio to start work, you came back, went for a run in the park for an hour, and when you got 'ome Weng told you about the phone-call and you played the tape. That was about eleven. You rang the studio and got no answer. You rang the agency to 'ave them call their man on the car radio, and they said Dick Kingston 'ad cancelled the protection by phone twenty-four hours ago. You rang me to go to the studio and check it out, then tried to locate Dick. No luck at 'ome or at the office, except that Rogers, the features editor, said Dick failed to keep an important appointment last night, to do with some other story, and this was un'eard of. They'd been trying to find 'im ever since."

Willie paused and glanced up. She stood leaning against the wall by the window, lower lip caught in her teeth, staring absently out across London. He went on, "I checked the studio and Luke wasn't there. No sign of trouble, but you wouldn't expect it with Luke. No sign of the phoney agency man and 'is car, either." He sat back, frowning at the notebook and doodling an arabesque design. "Tarrant's out of

173

town, but Jack Fraser says he'll pass on anything he hears about Dick Kingston. Now we're stuck, waiting for we don't know what. D'you reckon we ought to tell Sam Solon?"

Modesty shook her head. "The fewer people who know, the more we keep our options open, Willie. I didn't offer any explanations even to Fraser when I asked him to listen out for news of Dick. I don't know who took Luke or why, but I think we're a part of it this time. I think some sort of bite is going to be put on us, and I want us to have freedom of action when that happens."

"A money bite?" he hazarded doubtfully.

"I can't imagine so. But I can't imagine what, anyway, so I've stopped trying." She turned her head to look at him. "The woman said, '... *she must wait until she hears about Dick Kingston* ...' About, not from. I hate that bit."

Willie Garvin fully agreed. The phrase had an ominous echo. He drew a rectangle round the telephone number. Fraser had checked it for them, and reported that it was the number of the Ritz Hotel. Willie said, "Want me to slip down to the Ritz and ask for Mr. Ricketts?"

She shook her head. "It's just a timing device, Willie. Whoever's behind the woman on the phone wants to talk to me, but after I've heard something about Dick Kingston, not before. So then I have Mr. Ricketts paged, who doesn't exist, but someone in the lounge is waiting for it and knows it's time for the next move."

"I could prowl around the Ritz, maybe spot someone."

"No. It won't be a principal, just a cut-off." There was an air of remote and troubled prescience about her, as if in some way she had certain knowledge that no line of action had been left open and they could only wait. Willie got up and went to stand by the window with her. After a little silence she said, "It's never been like this before. We've no

174

idea who we're up against, no idea of their objective. It all seems to stem from what happened to Luke, but we don't know what happened to him. We don't seem to know any goddam thing at all from which to make any deductions. All we know is that things keep happening which don't make sense and can't be fitted into a pattern. I've never had such a feeling that the initiative is all with the other side."

She looked at Willie from very dark blue eyes which were suddenly hard with self-condemnation. "I've been criminally stupid, Willie. We had one opening and I failed to take it. We should have found that crook Maltese lawyer who hired Frezzi, taken him out to sea and held his head under till he talked. But I just didn't want to get involved." She gave an angry shrug. "I've yet to find out what I've done to Luke by failing. And to Dick Kingston."

Willie slipped a hand under her arm and began to walk slowly with her down the length of the room, with its picture-hung walls of golden cedar strip, its octagonal floor tiles of dull ivory, and the scattered Isfahan rugs. "You got a lot of faults, Princess," he said reminiscently, "but if I 'ad to pick the worst of 'em it's the way you always grab the credit for anything that goes wrong. You never let anyone else 'ave a share."

She was silent for a few seconds, and when she spoke she had picked up his mood. "Willie, do you mean I'm ... selfish?"

"I'm afraid so. Almost as bad as Anita."

"Who's Anita?"

"American girl I met years ago, when you sent me across to Cappadocia to break the Charif mob. Remember?"

"I remember the Charif brothers emigrated to America when they got better, and you came back with a bit of a thigh wound."

"Ah, well, I didn't mention it at the time, but it wasn't strictly a wound received in the course of duty. It was more an accidental injury acquired when the job was over."

They were moving back down the room for the third time now, and she turned her head to look at him with genuine curiosity. "Is this one of your girl stories, Willie love?"

"One of my what?"

"I used to think you made them up. It was ages before I realised they were all gospel. Go on. What happened with you and Anita?"

"Well, you cabled to say I was to take it easy for a few days before I flew back to Tangier, so I did, and I met this American girl in Ankara. She was with some archeological dig working out from a little village north of Tuz Golu, and 'er name was Anita. She was a very literary girl, and crazy about Ernest Hemingway. Seemed to take a liking to me, so I went back to the village with 'er for a few days. Thought I'd pick up a bit of culture."

"Just culture?"

"Well, no. She was renting a couple of rooms in one of the village 'ouses, and I moved in with 'er. So as well as literary culture and archeological culture, I used to enjoy what she called sexual congress with 'er. She said Graham Greene always called it that in 'is books, sexual congress. I 'ad a job not to laugh. Then there was the Hemingway bit. You know *For Whom the Bell Tolls*, and the way he goes on about it being so terrific for the hero and the gypsy girl that the earth moves when they 'ave sexual congress, only Hemingway doesn't call it that?"

"I thought nobody got the earth-moving bit more than ... was it three times?"

"Something like that. Anita was always trying for it, anyway. Very industrious in bed, she was. Well, about the third night, it 'appened. The earth moved for both of us."

"Amazing!"

"No, honest, Princess. It really 'appened."

They had come to the window again, and now she pulled him round to look up at him with eyes narrowed, head a little on one side. "You mean Hemingway was right?"

"No, not exactly. Next thing was, the roof fell in on us. We'd 'ad an earthquake, and the earth was moving for just about everybody within five miles, whether they were 'aving sexual congress or not."

Laughter gripped her, and she bowed her head against his shoulder as he said, "It was only a bad tremor, an' nobody was killed, but we were pinned down on the bed by a wooden joist, and smothered with plaster. That's 'ow I got a gash in the back of me thigh, from a nail sticking out of this joist."

"You had the joist on top of you and Anita underneath?"

"That's right. And it 'appened at the critical moment. Anita 'ad 'er eyes closed, and she didn't catch on at first, she reckoned it was all 'er fault that the earth moved and the roof fell in, because she was so terrific with the Kama Sutra stuff. She kept 'ollering—" his voice took on a strong, twanging falsetto, " 'Gahd, Willie, I'm sahrry!' "

Modesty stepped back, let out an emphatic breath, then rubbed her eyes with her fingertips. An unhealthy and dangerous tension had been building up within her, but now it was gone. The situation had not changed, but she had changed within it, and for the better. Something bad was coming, and they both sensed it, but at least she had her balance again now. The extraordinary thing was that Willie's story was probably almost entirely true. She knew the thin twisted scar on the back of his thigh, and remembered that he had been very vague about the cause of his limp at the time. How he had managed to keep such a story untold for so long she found hard to imagine, but certainly he had produced it at a grimly propitious moment.

She looked up into his quiet, rather roughly sculpted face and tapped him solemnly on the chest with one finger. "What we need, Willie, is some lunch. Come through to the kitchen and watch me improvise."

*   *   *

An hour and a half later they were sitting at the breakfast bar having a second cup of coffee and mulling over the latest mailing list programme from the National Theatre. They had not spoken again of anything to do with the Luke Fletcher situation.

When the phone on the wall rang, Modesty finished what she was saying as she moved towards it. Then a calm settled on her face as she lifted the instrument and said, "Hallo?"

Jack Fraser's voice said, "I'm sorry, I've got bad news about Dick Kingston."   ,

"Hang on, Jack." She gestured to Willie, and he moved across to take the spare earpiece hooked beneath the instrument. "All right, I was just cutting Willie in. Go ahead."

"Early this morning the Norfolk police had an anonymous phone call from a male, saying there was a dead man at Cawley Fields. That's an abandoned wartime airstrip not far from Penchurch. They investigated and found a body in one of the derelict hangars. Papers in his wallet indicated that he was Richard Charles Kingston, and this has now been confirmed."

Fraser paused, and after a moment Modesty said, "Yes. Go on, Jack."

"They didn't release anything until they were certain of identity. His newspaper knew he was ex Mil Six, so as soon as they got the news they passed it to Chalmers, and as an inter-departmental courtesy he's just passed it on to us."

"Do you have any details?"

"I'll get you the lot in due course, but the preliminary report has it that he was killed some time yesterday by a point four-five bullet in the head, not at close range. Indication of his wrists having been bound with sticky tape. No weapon was found. That's all I've got for now."

"Thank you for calling right away."

"I'm bloody sorry." Fraser's voice was metallic. "Mil Six were never my favourite people, but I once worked with Dick Kingston when he was switched for a special job, and he was good all right."

"Yes. We're sorry, too."

"Look, Modesty, do you know anything that could help nail whoever did it?"

"Nothing, Jack."

"You had to know something or you wouldn't have phoned me in the first place."

"Nothing that helps. If and when I do—"

"If and when you do, for Christ's sake stay with it and put the bastards down yourself, or they'll end up with a two year suspended sentence for being in charge of a firearm while under the influence, or some such bloody nonsense. Given our present masters, the bastards might even get an award for knocking off an ex Mil Six man. And listen, you'd better watch out for Luke Fletcher, hadn't you?"

"We're doing that, Jack."

"Right. I'll keep Tarrant posted when he gets back, but you probably won't hear from him. He'll leave you to run whatever it is your own way. Be careful."

As she hung up the phone Willie said, "You're still not telling 'im they've got Luke?"

"Not till we know where we are." She lifted the phone again and dialled a number. When the operator answered she said, "I want to contact a Mr. Ricketts. Will you have him paged, please?"

*   *   *

When Alice Ross answered the chimes of the doorbell at number 23 Cheadwell Gardens, Balham, she was mildly surprised to find a clergyman standing on the step, a rather comical clergyman to her way of thinking, in old-fashioned trousers thin as drain-pipes, and wearing a round flat hat. This he raised as she opened the door, and said in an anxious, creaking voice, "Does—ah—Mr. Albert Ross live here, please?"

"That's right," she admitted a little warily, "but he's asleep just now."

"You are Mrs. Ross?"

"Yes."

"Forgive this intrusion. My name is Parker. Harold Parker of the Church Missionary Society."

Alice Ross, a plump and pretty woman of forty, had not been inside a church since the christening of her only child fifteen years ago, and felt vaguely embarrassed at having a clergyman actually on her doorstep. She reached for her purse, hoping that a tenpenny piece would speed him on his way, but he said hastily, "No, no dear lady, I am not collecting for the Society. I was asked to call, indeed I might say commanded to call, by a complete stranger only a few minutes ago, and to deliver a message to your husband which I found somewhat cryptic but also possibly alarming."

Mrs. Ross said blankly, "Beg pardon?"

The clergyman rubbed a furrowed brow above red-rimmed eyes. "Is your husband in, Mrs.—ah—Ross?"

"Well, yes, but he's with the Security and he's on nights this week, so he's in bed now."

"Oh, dear. I pray I am not being used for some silly hoax. Tell me, do you know anyone called Caroline?"

"That's our daughter, but she's at her dancing class now. Afterwards she'll be going on to her friend Jane's home, to do their homework together."

The man calling himself Harold Parker shook his head with an air of troubled doubt. "May I please come in, Mrs. Ross? And will you ask your husband to come down and have a word with me?"

"You don't mean something's wrong? I mean, Caroline's all *right*, isn't she?"

"I have no idea, Mrs. Ross, but let us pray that she is, and that my alarm is needless."

Five minutes later Alice and Albert Ross sat side by side on the two-seater settee. His hair was tousled with sleep, and he had pulled on trousers, a sweater, and slippers. Seated in the small fireside chair, and hunched forward so that his shoulders were not far above his bony knees, Harold Parker said in his cracked voice, "I will be brief, sir. I am on leave from Nigeria and lodging with a widowed aunt in this district. Only a few minutes ago I was standing on my own at the Request bus-stop on the corner of Ardmere Road. A car pulled up across the road, and a man alighted from it and came towards me. He spoke in a voice which I believe held a slight Irish accent and asked if I knew 23 Cheadwell Gardens."

Harold Parker spread his large square hands in a gesture. "Naturally I assumed that he was asking to be directed there, and I acknowledged that I knew the whereabouts of this road, though not number 23 in particular. I was about to advise him how to proceed when he said, '*Tell Albert Ross that Caroline is safe for the moment, and she'll be all right as long as he stays by the phone and acts sensible.*' Those were the exact words, for I have been repeating them to myself all the way here."

181

Albert Ross, a stocky man with an abrupt manner, was no longer sleepy. He rubbed a hand across his mouth and said, "What did he look like?"

"I cannot tell you, Mr. Ross. I was not wearing my spectacles, and by the time I found them and put them on, both man and car had disappeared."

Alice Ross had lost a little colour. She said nervously, "Do you think anything's wrong, Bert?"

"That's what we've got to find out." He stood up. "Seems ridiculous to me, some Irish chap giving a message like that to a vicar at a bus-stop. Still, I'll ring that dancing class."

Two minutes later it was known that Caroline had not attended the lesson, which had just ended. With growing alarm, and also with growing caution, Albert Ross telephoned Jane's house to see if Caroline had gone straight there from school instead of to the dancing class first. When he found she had not, he managed to imply that there had been some sort of mix-up, and rang off.

"She's not there, Alice." His face was white now. "Our Carrie's missing." His wife pressed a hand over her mouth and started to cry. He took her in his arms and patted her shoulder.

Harold Parker said gravely, "I think it is time to telephone the police, Mr. Ross. If the affair is a cruel hoax of some kind, so much the better. If not, then no time will have been wasted."

"No, you hang on a minute," said Albert Ross sharply. He had meagre powers of imagination, and as yet the situation was quite unreal to him, but the protective instinct was strong. Somewhere in his mind was a rather shapeless mental image, derived from a score of television plays, of Carrie tied up and terrified in some dingy back bedroom. He had no intention of doing anything which might harm his daughter, or of doing anything at all until he had gathered his wits and knew more about what was happening. He looked at the clergyman over his wife's shoulder and said, "This chap told you I was to stay by the phone?"

"I have given you his exact words, Mr. Ross."

"Right. All right." He nodded, and kept nodding mechanically for several seconds as he spoke. "Yes. All right. Yes. Well, we'll stay off the phone for a bit and see what happens. Now stop crying, Alice, there's a good girl. I know it all sounds a bit nasty, but I don't see how it can be the way it sounds. I mean, it's not like as if one of those bloody sex-maniacs had grabbed her, is it? And why would anyone want to kidnap our Carrie? Christ, we've got no money. Sorry, Vicar. Look, Alice, you go and make a cup of tea, then while we're waiting we'll try and think what to do, but I'm not getting on to the police. Not yet, anyway."

"It ... it couldn't be the IRA could it, Bert? I mean we've never done anything to them."

"No, no, of course it isn't."

"Do you think you ought to phone your cousin Tom? He's with the railway police—"

"Don't talk bloody stupid, Alice! No, I'm sorry. I didn't mean to shout. I'm sorry. But keep away from that phone, see?"

Harold Parker leaned forward in the fireside chair and fell to his knees, hands clasped rigidly beneath his chin, head bowed. "I shall pray," he said. The Rosses stared at the kneeling figure, then at each other, in acute embarrassment. Alice wiped her eyes. Albert gave her a pat on the arm and said in a low voice, "Go on, make a pot of tea, love."

Five minutes later the man from the Church Missionary Society was still kneeling in silent prayer. A tray of tea stood on a low table in front of the settee, and the Rosses sat

183

waiting uneasily, not liking either to talk or pour tea until their visitor had finished. The sound of the telephone brought Albert to his feet and a little scream of shock from his wife. Harold Parker did not stir.

Albert Ross approached the phone warily, lifted it, and said, "Hallo?"

"Mr. Albert Ross?" The man's voice was courteous.

"Speaking."

"Here is your daughter."

He felt the blood draining from his face during the age-long moments of waiting, then came Caroline's voice, high-pitched and wavering. "Dad? Dad? It's me."

"Carrie! You all right? Where are you?"

"I don't know. They've got a blindfold on me and I'm tied up on a bed so I can't move." Her voice broke for a moment, then came again urgently as he started to speak. "No, listen, Dad. They said I haven't got long. They're going to tell you something you've got to do, and if you don't they'll hurt me ever so bad. And they will, Dad, they already did a bit, just to show me." She began to sob. "Please, Dad, please . . ."

Her voice faded abruptly as the phone was taken away, then Albert Ross heard the man's voice again with its slight Irish accent. "Mr. Ross?"

The fear which gripped him was so paralysing that he had to make three attempts before his tongue responded. "Yes."

"It's very simple, Mr. Ross. When you go on the two a.m. shift tonight, you draw the two bolts on the fire doors. And before you go off shift at four, you restore them, using gloves at all times. Do you understand?"

After ten seconds Albert Ross said thickly, "We're in pairs."

"There are four rooms and two corridors to patrol, and you are known to have complained that your colleague, Mr.

Timpson, spends half his time dozing on a bench. Are we to tell your daughter that you can't do it, Mr. Ross?"

"No! No, it's all right, I was only mentioning ..." his voice trailed away.

The man with the Irish accent said, "Good. Just do what we've asked and you'll have Caroline back safe and sound in the morning." There was a click, then the dialling tone. Very slowly Albert Ross put the phone down. Alice was shaking his arm, saying, "What is it, Bert? What's happening? Where's Carrie?" The gawky black figure of the clergyman had not moved. He was still kneeling, head bowed, locked so rigidly in his posture of prayer that it almost seemed he had fallen into a trance.

With a great effort Albert Ross shook off the numbness that gripped him and put his arms round his wife. "She's all right," he whispered, "but we've got to be careful. I'll tell you when we've got rid of him on the floor there. Just keep quiet and say nothing, Alice."

He let her go, moved to the kneeling figure, and said, "Mr. Parker." There was no response. Gingerly he grasped a bony shoulder and shook it gently. "Mr. Parker." There came a long, deep sigh, and slowly the clergyman lifted his head to gaze vaguely about him like a sleeper awakened. A rather dreadful smile spread across Albert Ross's pallid face. "It's all right, Mr. Parker. I've just spoken to Carrie on the phone. She was with some other friends after all." He managed a sound that resembled a chuckle. "Lot of fuss over nothing, I'm afraid."

"Thanks be to God," said Harold Parker fervently, and climbed creakingly to his feet. "But why should that man indulge in such a terrible hoax? It is a shocking thing to have done, and I feel you would be well justified in informing the police."

"No, it's all right," said Albert Ross desperately. "I think I can guess who it was now. A chap at the club. Paddy, we call him, and he's always playing daft jokes. Don't worry, Vicar, I'll have words with him about this. Now if you don't mind, I'm on night duty, so I wouldn't be sorry to get back to sleep."

"Of course, of course, my dear friend. I only regret my intrusion, and the distress I have unwittingly caused you."

"Ah, well, it can't be helped. Goodbye, Mr. Parker, and don't worry. It's all cleared up now, all cleared up nicely."

Ten minutes later, in a dingy three-room flat above an empty shop, Clarissa de Courtney-Scott leaned sideways and picked up the telephone beside the bed. She waited till the chatter of the call-box signal ended with the dropping of the coin, then said, "Hallo? Yes?" She listened for ten seconds, said, "Jolly good," and put the phone back on its cradle.

Beauregard Browne, lying on his back with hands behind his head, said, "Yes?"

Kneeling astride him, Clarissa smiled down and began to move her aching loins again, slowly and luxuriously. "Uriah says it's all right about Mr. Ross. He's going to do exactly as he was told."

"Isn't that nice? And I do hope he liked my touch of Irish, it's a lovely brogue, isn't it?" He reached up to grasp her breasts. "I really think you'd better make it now or postpone the moment, poppet, because we have to be dressed and ready for the Blaise stroke Garvin briefing rather soon."

She tightened her haunches on him and her generous body moved urgently. "No problem, Beau," she said anxiously, "no problem."

*   *   *

The man who sat between Modesty Blaise and Willie Garvin on a bench amid the ever-present throng in Trafalgar Square wore dark glasses and had a strong Scottish accent. Modesty had decided that the accent was as false as the sandy hair, eyebrows, and moustache.

It was half an hour since she had first heard that voice on the telephone : "Miss Blaise? Will you hold on, please?"

Then Luke Fletcher's voice, puzzled rather than alarmed. "Modesty, it's me. I'm afraid something rather weird has happened again."

"Are you all right, Luke?"

"Yes, I'm not hurt. Just feeling a bit sick. But—"

The phone must have been taken away from him then, and the Scottish voice came on again. "Just so you'll know he's still wi' us, unlike the laddie recently deceased at Penchurch. I'd be obliged if you and Mr. Garvin would be feeding the pigeons in Trafalgar Square in twenty minutes." Then the dialling tone as the caller hung up.

They had been in the square for fifteen minutes before the sandy-haired man approached them, a roll of paper tucked under his arm. "Fletcher has a wee bomb strapped to his stomach," he greeted them briskly, standing close so that his voice was lost to anybody else amid the hubbub of the pigeon-feeders, photo-takers, and strollers filling the square. "If I'm picked up, or delayed, or followed, he'll have a hole in him like a Henry Moore statue. Understood?"

Modesty said, "We've arranged no surveillance, no tags."

"Let's sit." He led the way to a bench occupied by three hairy young men in patched jeans who rose at his nod and wandered away. "If you see 'em around later you can question them all you like," said the sandy-haired man. "They're just kids earning a fiver holding the seat for us. No better place to talk business."

Now he was unrolling a blueprint across his knees, at the same time saying dourly, "I'll not be long about this. There's a job we want done tonight, and it's right up your street, the two of you. All planning, timing, and special equipment supplied, your job is just the execution. What it is, we're wanting the Jade Queen from the exhibition at the Royal Academy."

Modesty drew in a long slow breath and made a conscious effort to keep her thoughts focused only on what the man was saying, without letting the implications touch her, keeping at bay the morale-sapping feeling of total helplessness against an enemy who held every advantage.

The Jade Queen. She had seen it only a few days ago with Luke Fletcher. Willie and Janet Gillam had seen it twice during the six weeks since the exhibition had been opened at Burlington House. The Jade Queen was the major exhibit of the treasures unearthed from a huge complex of jungle-smothered temples, discovered five years ago north of Pi Mai in central Thailand. The ancient craftsmen had used gold and silver, ruby and sapphire, copper, jade, and many semi-precious stones. Some of their crude tools had been found, and it was these which had drawn Willie Garvin to a second visit, for it was a marvel that such instruments could produce the jewels and ornaments, the caskets, figurines, armlets, brooches, and bangles, the fluting and fretting, the arabesques and tracery.

Above all there was the Jade Queen, the figure of a young woman carved from a single magnificent piece of jade. She sat cross-legged, naked but for a loin-cloth, in the lotus position. The statuette was about a quarter life-size, measuring twenty-six inches from the base to the top of the plaited hair piled in a coil on her head.

From the other side of the sandy-haired man Willie Garvin

said, "I once cased Burlington 'ouse. It's a roof job, and you'll need a man inside."

"You'll be having whatever's needed, Mr. Garvin." He turned to Modesty. "No, don't worry, lassie. There's someone behind you all right, but she's not going to run an' tell the police. D'ye feel anything?"

"There's something pricking my back," she said slowly.

"It's a sharpened bicycle spoke, wrapped in a bit o' newspaper, and it only needs a wee shove to pop it through your heart, Miss Blaise. Just a precaution in case you or Mr. Garvin get hasty when I tell you the score."

Willie turned his head a little. A big girl with a luscious figure and red hair was standing against the wall behind Modesty, eating an ice-cream cornet. A handbag hung over her arm, and in that hand she held a loosely rolled piece of newspaper which rested against Modesty's back. Red-haired and Junoesque. Willie's memory reached back. That fitted the description Modesty had given him of the woman she had spotted at the Benildon fête. The girl licked her cornet with a long tongue, half smiling, eyes resting on him with idle speculation.

Modesty said, "All right, let's get back to the Royal Academy job. You could be setting us up."

"Aye, we could. But for what? It's a lot more likely that we just want the Jade Queen, and it's a principle wi' us that we use local labour for jobs o' this sort. Now listen and hold still while I tell you two things. First, whether you do what I'm telling you or not, you'll get Luke Fletcher back alive. The only difference is, if you don't go along with us he'll come back wi' no hands. I'm told there's fellers can paint holding a brush in the mouth, so maybe he can learn. It'll just be up to you. Second, we had in mind that you might think we were bluffing, so we took Kingston out to the old airfield near Penchurch an' killed him, just as a sort o' demonstration. For Fletcher's sake I hope it impressed you."

Willie Garvin felt sweat prickling on his brow as he fought the fury that swept him. Beyond the sandy-haired man he could see Modesty's face. It held no expression but was ivory pale under the tan. All about them was the noise of the city and of the hundreds standing or moving about in the square. After what seemed a long time he heard Modesty say, "It was a convincing demonstration."

"Then we'll press on. Will you hold this end o' the blueprint out flat, lassie? Fine, fine. Now, at half an hour after midnight tonight I want you to park in St. James's Square and walk across Piccadilly into Albany Court Yard. You'll have your own instruments to cope wi' breaking into one o' the offices there, dealing with locks an' so forth. In the court you'll find a Post Office Telephone van, or something that looks just like it. That's where we rendezvous." The sandy-haired man smoothed a strong, well-shaped hand across the blueprint. "Now I'll go through the whole operation from start to finish, specifying equipment supplied as we come to it. Then you ask questions. Then we go over it again until you're clear on every move. Right?"

Fifteen minutes later Modesty glanced across at Willie and received a nod of confirmation. She said, "All right. We're clear."

"Good." The sandy-haired man began to roll up the blueprint.

Modesty said, "When we've done it, how do we know you'll let Luke Fletcher go?"

"You don't know, lassie. You just know what happens to him if you don't do it."

"When can we pick him up?"

"Not right away. We have to check the Jade Queen first.

Suppose you were naughty, and took her out o' the crate and put in a couple of fire-buckets o' sand for ballast? Och, no, you'll have to be patient. We'll turn him loose sometime tomorrow afternoon, when we've flown the Jade Queen out o' the country."

"All right." She was reassured by his wariness. It argued that the problem of Luke's release had been thought out.

"Till tonight, then." He stood up briskly. "There's still the bicycle spoke, so bide a wee while." He walked away, moving off to their right. Willie looked round at the red-haired girl. She had finished her ice-cream and stood gazing idly about her, but still with the rolled newspaper casually presented to Modesty's back. Two minutes later she said in a hearty, well-bred voice, "Ah, there we are. I'll pop along now."

Turning, she walked with swinging stride to the western edge of the square some thirty paces away. The sandy-haired man was waiting there on a Honda, wearing a crash helmet. As the girl swung a leg over the pillion she pulled on the helmet he handed her, and two seconds later they had vanished into the mass of traffic crawling round the square.

*   *   *

At five o'clock when the telephone rang in the penthouse Modesty and Willie were playing three simultaneous games of chess. Weng came through from the kitchen where he was preparing a light meal, and said, "It's Mr. Solon, Miss Blaise. He says it is important and he must speak to you."

She hesitated. "All right, Weng." He brought a telephone to her and plugged it into a wall socket, then went back to the kitchen. She said, "Hallo, Sam."

His voice was strident with anger. "They murdered Dick Kingston. I just heard it on the news."

"Yes, I know they did, Sam. I'm very upset."

"Upset? Christ, you English! What are we *doing* about it?"

"For the moment, waiting to know more. The police will be working on it."

"To hell with the police. These bastards beat the shit out of me the other day, now they've killed Kingston. That makes it Us against Them in my book, so let's get to doing something!"

"Yes. And the first thing to do is think, Sam. Think about Luke Fletcher, for starters."

There was a silence, and when he spoke again his voice was more subdued. "Too bloody right, girl. With Kingston gone, they could be set to grab him. We ought to—"

"We've done it, Sam. Willie's standing guard over Luke while I ferret around my contacts for a lead to whoever put Dick away. I'm on my way out now."

"Look, I'll pick you up and come with you."

"Stop acting like a tourist. The kind of people I'll be seeing won't open their mouths if you're there. I'll call you as soon as I have anything, but for the moment just get off my back, will you?"

A humourless chuckle came over the phone. "That's more like it. You sounded like you were sitting on your backside before. You go get 'em, girl, but bring me in for the finish."

"All right, Sam. Goodbye." She put the phone down, looked at Willie and gave a shrug. "We just might tell him later, if and when we get Luke safely back."

Willie studied the middle board of the three, where his king's rook was threatened. "There's nobody else we can tell. It'd put Tarrant or Fraser in a hell of a spot if they knew what we're doing tonight. Anyway, it's not something I'd relish telling."

"No. Giving in to blackmail isn't exactly our style."

"Letting 'em chop Luke's hands off isn't our style either, Princess. But I tell you what is," he added resentfully. "This caper for nicking the Jade Queen, that's our style. It's a lovely smooth job, just the way we'd plan it ourselves."

"Except for the security guard's daughter."

"Yes." He nodded morosely. That had been the one query they had raised on the whole plan—the reliability of the man who was to draw the bolts on the fire-doors. If he had been bought, was it certain he would stay bought? The answer given by the sandy-haired man with the Scottish accent had been blood-chilling, but they no longer had any doubts on the point.

Willie decided on a bishop sacrifice, and made his move. "Local labour," he said with disgust, "that's what he called us." He shook his head bleakly. "Blimey, that would 've made Dick Kingston laugh. Us. Local labour."

10

At forty-five minutes after midnight they were crouched in the back of a van, checking a lightweight alloy hoist which could be assembled and dismantled in five minutes. There was also a low trolley with nylon wheels, an aluminium extending ladder, and the photostat of a loading table which specified the contents of fifty-four crates and gave the code letters painted on the outside of each to identify what it contained. The sandy-haired man, with a silenced pistol, was there to answer questions, but they had none, and barely a word was spoken.

By one-fifteen they had entered the offices of an architect, passed up through three floors and out on to a roof without leaving any trace of their presence. By one-thirty they had assembled the hoist on the western side of the roof of Burlington House, pumping air out of the three suction-pad feet to anchor them solidly. The broad alley which gave access to the storage areas lay below them, with a recess jutting from it large enough for a vehicle to turn round. In this lay-by stood a closed van marked London Security on each side. Both ends of the alley were closed by tall gates.

By one-forty-five they had dealt with the circuit breaker alarm and the mortice lock on the door which led down from the bulkhead stairs. For the next thirty minutes they sat at the foot of the steps outside the heavy fire-door, waiting in silence and without impatience. At twenty-seven minutes past two they heard the sound of the heavy interior bolts being cautiously drawn. They waited five minutes, then bridged the second alarm and picked the mortice lock on the fire-door.

They were dressed in black, and now pulled woollen socks over their plimsolled feet, black stocking-masks over their heads. The lay-out of the exhibition rooms was clear in their minds as they moved down two short flights of stairs and along a broad corridor. The next ten minutes were spent in reconnaissance. One of the two guards was dozing on a bench in the room where the crate containing the Jade Queen stood with a dozen others. The second guard was standing at the end of the short second corridor, resolutely looking out of a window into darkness.

Modesty slid along the floor, under the bench, and held a chloroform-soaked pad gradually closer to the sleeping guard's nose. When his breathing grew heavy, she slipped out, put the pad away in the small bag strapped to her belt, and beckoned Willie. He came forward carrying the trolley. Two minutes later they had located the crate and were lifting it on to the low trolley by its rope handles. The nylon wheels made no sound as Modesty ran the crate smoothly out of the room and along the corridor to the stairs. Willie followed, using his woollen foot-covers to polish away any tracks left by the wheels.

Between them they carried the crate up past the fire door, set it down, relocked the mortice, and removed the magnetic alarm bridge. It was possible to use the trolley to cross most of the roof, but one gable had to be negotiated by the extending aluminium ladder they had set in place earlier, and here Willie bore the whole weight alone, with the crate in a leather harness on his back.

At fifteen minutes past three the jib of the hoist had been

swung out over the lay-by and the crate was being slowly lowered. A trap in the top of the security van was open now, and the crate passed through. A few seconds later the nylon rope went slack, then came two sharp tugs on it. They wound the rope up and began to dismantle the hoist. There came the slight sound of the van being started, but they could barely hear its carefully tuned engine as it moved away up the service alley to the gate at the Burlington Gardens end. There was a long pause, presumably to await a look-out's signal, then the gate opened, the van turned out, and the gate closed again.

Dismantling the legs of the hoist, Willie Garvin felt almost sick with humiliation. In the past they had known enjoyment and artistic pleasure from the planning and performance of such a caper, but there was no joy for them in tonight's work, for they had been no more than puppets. Modesty hit him sharply on the arm and lifted a warning finger. He knew that even though she was unable to see his face behind the stocking-mask she had sensed his momentary loss of concentration. He nodded, touched a hand to his heart and dipped his head in apology, then thrust everything from his mind except the immediate essentials of the situation.

In the hallway of the architect's offices they removed their masks and over-socks. The hoist, trolley, and extending ladder were now packed in a medium-sized suitcase. From a plastic bag Modesty took a silk caftan, some evening sandals, and a long blonde wig. Willie unfolded a blue nylon mack wrapped round a pair of shoes, and a dark wig. Two minutes later they stepped out into Albany Court Yard and closed the door after them. The caftan covered her from neck to ankles, and hid the bag of instruments, masks, and plimsolls she carried. Willie wore a bib beneath his mack, which gave the impression that he was wearing a frilled white shirt and mauve bow tie. He was smoking a cigar now.

The figure in the driving seat of the Post Office Telephones van said softly, "All clear." Willie opened the back of the van, dumped the suitcase inside, and closed the doors. As they strolled past the van, arms linked, heading out into Piccadilly, the figure in the driving seat said, "I'll call you at three. Don't try to trace the call, I'll not be on long enough."

In silence they crossed Piccadilly, walked down Duke Street and turned towards St. James's Square. As Willie threw away his cigar and unlocked the car he said, "We couldn't get the police to tap the line anyway, not without explaining that we've just nicked the Jade Queen."

"Yes. And the same thing applies to that guard who let us in. If he gets his daughter back safely, he's going to keep his mouth shut."

Willie held the door for her. "But maybe not otherwise, so that's a good sign for the kid."

"Let's hope so."

He moved round the car and got in. "All right if I stay with you till it's over, Princess?"

"I was counting on it, Willie. Your room's ready."

"Let's get 'ome, then. You sound a bit tired."

"I'm a bit flattened. I suppose apart from worrying about Luke, my vanity's hurt. I'm not used to being manipulated like a pig with a ring through its nose. It's bad for the ego."

He was driving along King Street now. She took off her own blonde wig and his dark one. As he cut round beside the Ritz he said, "What about when we've got Luke back?"

She slid an arm through his and leaned her head against his shoulder. After a little silence she said, "We'll think about it then, Willie."

*   *   *

197

At six-thirty that morning the car in which Caroline Ross was riding drew to a halt. A hand helped her out and guided her across the pavement. A female voice said, "Mind the step." Then there was an odd silence, as if some sort of solid barrier enclosed her. Warily she reached out. Her hand touched something smooth. A glass-panelled wall. Then another at right-angles to the first.

Nervously she began to pick at one of the two thin strips of plaster which closed her eyes. Nobody stopped her, nobody spoke. When the plaster had peeled painfully away and her eye adjusted to the pre-dawn light, she found she was in a telephone booth. She began to sob with relief, pulling the other plaster away regardless of the pain. It was not until she pushed open the door that she realised this was the telephone booth outside the library only two streets away from her home.

A postman cycled by on his bicycle. Along the road she could make out a boy delivering newspapers. Remembering the warning spoken by the other voice, the man's voice that frightened her so, she held back her tears and began to walk quickly, but after a few moments she broke into a run and did not stop until she reached 23 Cheadwell Gardens.

*　　　*　　　*

The midday editions of the evening papers carried the first news of the theft, which was discovered only when the two big trucks with their security and police escort arrived to transport the Pi Mai exhibits to Heathrow. Half an hour later, the Foreign Office announced that profound apologies had been sent to the Thai government, and that no stone would be left unturned to recover the missing Jade Queen.

At two o'clock Sir Gerald Tarrant called Fraser into his

office and said, "I've just spoken to Brook at the Yard. So far they haven't an inkling as to how it was done, or when. It's not our pigeon, of course, but have you had any thoughts on it?"

Fraser blinked at him over the top of wire-rimmed spectacles. "I really would not wish to venture an opinion, sir."

"It doesn't rouse echoes in the memory?"

Fraser cringed slightly. "Not what I would actually call echoes, Sir Gerald. Do you have anything specific in mind?"

Tarrant sat back. "Yes I do, Jack. This bit of magic brings Modesty Blaise and Willie Garvin instantly to my mind."

Fraser exhaled audibly, and nodded. "That's right. I just didn't want to say it first." He took off his spectacles and began to polish them, looking sour. "Where's the bloody sense in it, though?"

"We're probably guessing wrong."

"I told her I hoped she'd croak whoever did for Dick Kingston, so I wouldn't have been surprised if a few unaccounted-for stiffs had shown up sooner or later, but this R A thing doesn't fit. Has she been in touch?"

"Not for a few days."

Fraser put his spectacles on. "Are you going to ask her about this?"

Tarrant shook his head. "Not yet. Later perhaps, after my retirement date. For the moment I'd rather not know."

Fraser grinned evilly. "She wouldn't nick the thing for herself, and even if she did, I wouldn't give a monkey's. Not when you count up all we owe her. So if you find out, let me know. I'll lose no sleep over it."

Soon after three, Modesty Blaise answered the telephone to hear a voice with a heavy sing-song Welsh accent. "Miss Blaise, is it? Chust to say there is a message of good cheer awaiting you at 21a Broadway. Good afternoon, Miss Blaise."

Beauregard Browne put the telephone down with a giggle of delight. "I was minded to use my Pakistani accent that time, but then thought I'd save it for a possibly more loquacious occasion." He looked round Luke Fletcher's studio. "What a lot of pictures he's painted in a short time."

Clarissa de Courtney-Scott said, "He's still nice and dopey from the shot we gave him before leaving that rather frightful dump over the shop. I've just left him dozing on the bed. Perhaps I ought to go and loosen his clothing and all that sort of thing."

Beauregard Browne took her arm in a grip that hurt, though she was careful not to show it. "Neither his nor your clothing is to be loosened just now, angel," he said with a bright smile. "You mustn't allow your hormones to make you neglect your work, you know."

"Golly, no. Sorry, Beau. I suppose we ought to be getting along, now you've made the phone call."

"No hurry, sweetie." He gazed at the clutter of pictures stacked along one wall of the studio, most of them on hardboard and unframed. "The fact is that when you look up Broadway, and the *The* Broadway, in the A to Z, you find there are about sixteen of them spread all over London, so Blaise and Garvin, and possibly the Unspeakable Antipodean if they co-opt him, will be hurtling around for a couple of hours before they get far enough out to find our obliging greengrocer, the one with whom we left the message to be handed to anyone inquiring for a Mr. Fletcher. Then they'll head hot-foot for this desirable residence, to find the lost sheep safely returned to the fold and in his very own pen."

He began to pull out one or two of the pictures, head bent to look at them. "By which time we shall be airborne out of Heathrow, where even now the trusty airplane awaits only our arrival to take wing."

Clarissa said, "I must say it's gone jolly well, Beau."

200

"Not least due to your splendid staff-work in administering a complex operation, *ma chère*. You shall be rewarded. When we're back on Dragon's Claw you shall be rewarded with a day in Paradise."

"Oh, Beau!" She closed her eyes and shuddered ecstatically at the thought. Only once before had she spent a whole day in the place where Beau pursued his passion for growing orchids. Paradise was cradled in the peak at the western end of the island. There were two acres of grassland, with half the perimeter consisting of a curving barrier of rock pierced by a narrow gulley, and the rest being cliff edge where the ground fell away to leave a sheer drop of over nine hundred feet to the sea. For most of the year the place was sheltered from the prevailing winds, yet in summer's heat there was always a gentle breeze.

On an occasion when he had been especially pleased with Clarissa, and in a particularly benevolent mood, he had orchestrated what he called a day in the Garden of Eden for her, a day in which he had run wild and naked with her in the high pleasaunce under a warm sun, indulging her in every orgiastic whim, his astonishing control enabling him to satiate even her clamorous demands by the day's end. The thought of another such day made Clarissa feel hot with dreamy anticipation.

Beauregard Browne broke in on her reverie, and she opened her eyes. "I must say," he declared, pulling out another picture with his gloved hand, "that our inscrutable oriental colleague has also done astonishingly well with his mind-bending party trick. Not that I propose to extend him the same reward, poppet. But consider Fletcher's recent reaction. When the dreary dauber came to his senses and set eyes first upon you and then upon me, he looked vaguely as if he were trying to remember what day it was, but recognition came there none."

"It really does look as if Dr. Feng's mind blocks have worked out all right," Clarissa agreed. She was looking carefully about her to make sure they had left no sign of their visit. "Mind you, I think it was just as well not to let Fletcher see him. After all, he'd been having one or two nightmares about a Chinaman."

"Even as she spoke ..." said her companion, and held up a painting in which only two colours had been used, black and green, to produce a startling, distorted, yet easily recognisable portrait of Dr. Feng. "I don't think it matters particularly," Beauregard Browne went on, riffling along the next two or three pictures. "Obviously you and I aren't here. But oh, I say, look at this, my treasure."

There was no distortion, no strangeness of style in the picture he held now. The heavy features of Condori stared at her from the hardboard.

"Now isn't that odd?" mused Beauregard Browne. "Why should the face of the efficient Condori hang in the dark reaches of remembrance? Clearly the gormless Fletcher doesn't associate the face with its background. It's simply a face, and I suppose artists are interested in faces. Perhaps it's a rather good face, somewhat powerful would you think? It's certainly Condori to a T, as they say. Perhaps we should take it back for him." His eyes focused beyond Clarissa, and widened a little. "Well, well. Whom have we here? It's sleepy-headed Luke, I do declare. Another little beddy-byes shot is called for, I fancy."

Luke Fletcher stood in the doorway, not quite steady on his feet, eyes heavy with the residual effects of sedation. His brow was furrowed, he was staring at the picture and breathing deeply with deliberate effort, as if trying to clear his head.

"Condori," he said slowly. "Yes, you're right. That was his name. I remember now. But ... who was he? Where ...?"

He shook his head and took a pace or two forward, tugging at his chin, eyes half closed. "Wait a minute. Condori. Oh God, yes! He was in charge of all those men. The guards. That was the name the Chinaman used to call, when he'd finished talking to me. Talking, always talking. He'd call Condori to come and unlock the door. That's right. I remember ... yes!"

He stood with hands pressed to cheekbones, long fingers clamped to his skull, eyes wide and blank now as he stared down the tunnel of the past. "There were the paintings, and all the other things in that place where ... he kept boasting ... in that house where we had dinner, and afterwards ... boasting ... what was his name?"

Luke Fletcher's eyes focused suddenly. He stared for long seconds at Clarissa. "That's where I saw you! You were there." His gaze turned to Beauregard Browne. "And you. God, yes, I remember *you* now! And then the guard was drunk that night, and when he checked the door he left it unbarred, and after he'd gone to sleep I got out, and down to the bay, and there was the rubber dinghy and I paddled for ages before I started the engine, so nobody would hear,"— Fletcher was sweating now, words tumbling from him uncontrollably—"and there was so little water, and no food. I was frightened. Day after day, and the sun burning. I tried to make a sail with my shirt and it blew away, and I tried to catch fish but I didn't know how, and it went on and on ..." He drew in a long, shaking breath. "And then Modesty found me."

There was a silence in the studio. Fletcher stood with arms hanging limply, drained by the terror he had just re-lived. Clarissa looked at him thoughtfully, lips pursed. At last she said, "Oh, dear."

Beauregard Browne put the painting of Condori back

among the rest without haste. "As you say, poppet. Oh, dear. Our wily oriental friend seems to have done less well than we thought." He moved towards Luke Fletcher, smiling brightly, violet eyes dancing with amusement, right hand toying with the corner of white silk protruding from his left sleeve. "A hairline crack in the mind blocks is one thing, old prune, but now you've brought the whole damn lot tumbling down, and we simply can't have that, can we? I mean, can we? I'm afraid you've just done yourself no good at all, Luke, sweetie."

The golden hair, cherubic face, and violet eyes were very close now. Fear, sharp as a knife-blade, struck suddenly through the muzziness clouding Fletcher's mind, and his nerves snapped taut with the message ordering his body to turn and run. But he had made only a clumsy half turn when the long strip of silk flew out, its weighted end curving smoothly about his neck.

*   *   *

Weng was acting as their link for communications. At five o'clock, in Hanwell, Willie Garvin phoned in for the fourth time to report that he had drawn blank. Weng said, "Miss Blaise has found the correct Broadway, Mr. Garvin, but Mr. Fletcher was not there. It is the address of a greengrocer. He had been paid to tell anyone inquiring for Mr. Fletcher that he was now to be found at his studio, so Miss Blaise is on her way there now."

"How long since she called, Weng?"

"Six and a half minutes, sir. She was then in Penge."

"I'm on my way. Did you ring the studio?"

"Just once, sir, but there was no answer. I did not try again, as I wished to leave this line open for you."

"Right. Thanks, Weng." Willie pushed open the door of

the phone booth and made for his car. You could always rely on Weng, he thought. The things Weng knew, and kept hidden behind those bland intelligent eyes, would have made his fortune, but he was not interested. His connection with Modesty Blaise went back to his early youth, and was such that disloyalty was not a possible concept for him. In the past she had often urged him to do something with his life, but her urgings had found no response, perhaps to her secret relief, for Weng was unquestionably a treasure. Always correct but never deferential, he was a raging snob and enjoyed the very good life he led, so much so that he preferred his situation to any other he could imagine.

Willie glanced at his watch as he slid behind the wheel. She had a lead of seven minutes, but was the wrong side of the river. With average traffic they would reach the studio at about the same time. Odd, and a little disturbing, that Weng's call to the studio had not been answered, but perhaps Luke Fletcher was doped. With a mental shrug he decided that making guesses was fruitless, and settled down to concentrate on driving.

Half an hour later, as he sought a space to park, he saw Modesty from a hundred yards away, a dark-haired figure in brown slacks and a yellow shirt, hurrying up the steps to the front door. Less than two minutes later he was on the stairs, calling as he reached the landing. "Princess?"

"In here, Willie." The door of the studio stood ajar. Her voice sounded quiet, almost gentle, yet there was something in it which made the muscles of his stomach tauten suddenly. He pushed open the door and went in.

Luke Fletcher lay on his back on the floor beside a big table cluttered with his paints, jars, and brushes. He was wearing his old corduroy trousers and a cotton shirt with a thin pullover on top. Modesty was kneeling on the floor beside him, one hand resting on his shoulder, the other limp in her lap, as still as he. Willie moved forward, then stopped. Luke Fletcher's head was twisted to one side, his neck at an impossible angle.

Willie breathed, "Oh, Jesus ..." then turned and went methodically through all the other rooms. When he came back, Modesty was in the same position as before. He said quietly, "There's nobody 'ere, Princess."

She drew in a slow breath, then leaned forward and straightened the dead man's head. When she looked up at Willie her eyes were dry, her mouth tight as if from pain, her eyes very dark. She said, "It wasn't the greatest love affair ever ... but he did need me, and I was happy I could help. He had such talent. And he was a good man, too ... he could never hurt anybody, even with a word. Whoever killed him was dirt compared with Luke."

"I know, Princess." A little silence, then, "What do we do now?"

"We?"

"I'm in."

"Thanks, Willie. Well ... first we'll have to report it, leaving out the kidnap bit. That doesn't matter now, and it raises too many awkward questions. Then we'll have to go through the inquest and all the rest of it."

"Sure. And then?"

She rested a hand on Luke's cheek for a moment, then got slowly to her feet. "First Dick Kingston, now Luke, both in the coldest of cold blood. I know Luke wouldn't want me to do anything about it, even now, but I can't go along with that any more. There comes a time when you have to stop people." She looked at Willie. "So when all the due process is over, we'll set out to look for them, Willie. And we'll find them. And then we'll kill them."

*   *   *

On a cool grey day of drizzling rain, Sam Solon drove through the village of Benildon and a few minutes later turned off the road on to the long track which wound down to the cottage called *Ashlea*. By the time he had parked his car alongside Willie's Porsche and gathered up the bunch of flowers he had bought in the village, Modesty was standing in the open doorway of the cottage.

She wore a black skirt and a white jumper, and he noticed that her face was unshadowed by sorrow. She said, "Hallo, Sam. We thought you'd gone back to Australia."

"No, I've been busy here and there. And keeping off your back, like you said. These are for you. First flowers I ever bought a girl."

"Well don't look so sour about it, and thank you." She put a hand on his shoulder and kissed his cheek. "We've just had lunch, but I can fix you something if you haven't eaten."

"No, I stopped on the way down, thanks."

"All right. Go and talk to Willie while I find a vase."

Willie Garvin was in the dining room. A blanket had been spread over the table, and on it lay a variety of objects, only some of which could be easily recognised. There were three handguns, two varieties of holster, several knives, a twin sheath fitted to a harness, two short ebony clubs, and a leather sling. There were also four objects which looked like detached boot-heels, a telescopic steel tube tapering at both ends, a lump of something like plasticine, two or three small flat boxes, an open box of ampoules, and a dozen other items whose functions varied from the conjectural to the unfathomable. Willie was tightening a thin screw in one of the boot heels. He gave an amiable nod and said, " 'Allo, Sam. How's your luck?"

"Not bad." Sam Solon sat down. "I reckoned it'd take three weeks for the story to die, unless something fresh came up."

Willie put down the heel and screwdriver. "Three weeks today since the inquest on Luke, and I 'aven't seen even a small paragraph on an inside page in today's papers. There's just the art boys in the posh weeklies still doing their double-talk. You guessed about right, Sam."

"I run newspapers, I ought to guess right. Has Modesty had a lot of aggravation from journalists trying to dig out a background story?"

"Not too much. We worked out a technique for boring 'em stupid. The Princess kept going for forty minutes once, explaining 'ow she taught Luke the standard defence to the king's gambit and queen's gambit while he was 'aving a painter's block."

"And did she?"

"Blimey, no. Luke would 've found Snakes and Ladders a bit baffling."

Modesty came into the room with the flowers arranged in a vase, and placed them on the window ledge. "They're beautiful, Sam. Thank you again."

"My pleasure. I kept out of the way because I reckoned there was no way I could help, but I haven't given up, and I haven't been wasting my time. Can we talk?"

She hesitated. "Sam, we don't want to involve you in what we're going to do."

"I'm entitled to be involved, girl. You let me decide what chances I want to take. Now look, here's a question. The way I see it, something's got scrambled somewhere along the line. Dick Kingston was killed late one afternoon. We heard it next day, and you said you were covering Luke. But the day *after* that, Luke's alone in his studio and someone kills him. So where were you and Willie?"

She gave him a wry look. "They already had Luke when I told you we were covering him. They put the squeeze on us to do that Jade Queen job for them at Burlington House. If we didn't, they said they'd cut Luke's hands off. They killed Dick simply to show us they weren't bluffing. We couldn't tell you, Sam."

Staring, he let out a long whistling breath and said, "Bloody hell, girl! Holy bloody cow!"

They waited, saying nothing, allowing him to work it all out. At last he ran a hand through his tight grey curls and said, "So you did what they wanted? And they killed him after all?"

"Yes."

There was another silence. He eyed the collection of objects on the table and said, "So now you're going after 'em, whoever they are?"

"Yes, Sam."

"Got any ideas for finding out who they are?"

"We have one lead. The Maltese lawyer Frezzi spoke of. That's where we start. We're going to Malta next week to put a name to that lawyer."

"How? You said Frezzi wouldn't talk."

"The lawyer must have links with Frezzi, and we have some good contacts in Malta."

Willie said, "We'll finger 'im within a week, Sam."

The Australian nodded. "Okay. And then what?"

Modesty said, "We snatch him and set him up. We work a variation on a theme we've used before. He's going to think he's been snatched by a Mafia family in rivalry with whoever he works for, and he'll sing like a bird without us having to lay a finger on him. We'll find out *who* hired him to hire Frezzi, and get him to spill it in the middle of a lot of other stuff we don't want anyway. He won't even realise what he's told us."

"You sound pretty certain, sweetheart."

209

"We've done it before, Sam. Carl Zappi used to run the Rome sector of *The Network* for me, and he'll supply the actors."

Sam Solon gingerly picked up one of the beautifully made throwing knives on the table and weighed it thoughtfully in his hand. A hard grin stole slowly over his face. "Sounds good," he said. "I almost hate to spoil it."

She eyed him speculatively. "Spoil it?"

"I said I'd been busy. This lawyer, his name's Mocca. Office in Old Bakery Street, Valletta. Private residence in Marsaxlokk."

Modesty looked at Willie, then shrugged and laughed. "I'll be damned."

Willie said, "So that's where you've been, you crafty old Aussie."

Sam Solon was grinning broadly now, enjoying his moment. "You poms aren't the only ones who can think."

"How did you finger 'im?"

"I'm just a crude Colonial. I got hold of a man called Montale." Solon looked at Modesty. "He's the one Frezzi sent back to Sicily for trying to knife you on Dingli cliffs. I paid him twenty thousand sterling and a passage to anywhere he wanted. Don't worry, he hasn't tipped of Mocca."

Modesty said, "How do you know that, Sam? Have you done anything about Mocca?"

He shook his head. "Not yet. I wasn't too sure how to handle the next bit, and I reckoned it was maybe more in your line. Anyway, I know Mocca isn't alerted because he's not in Malta. He left for Melbourne ten days ago, and he's not expected back for another three weeks."

"Melbourne." Modesty nodded slowly. "Yes, that figures. It's all tied up with what happened to Luke before I picked him up in *The Wasp*, so it's centred out your way some-where, Sam."

"Too right it is. Mocca's travelling around Australia on business, but the man he's really going to see is a bloke called Roper. Wasn't too hard finding that out from the other end. You heard of C. J. Roper?"

Modesty lifted an eyebrow at Willie, and both shook their heads. Sam Solon went on, "He's what you poms call an eccentric. What we call a nut case. Made a fortune in sheep fifty years ago and built himself a castle in Tasmania, on Lake Edgar. It's staffed by immigrants from southern Europe. He doesn't have any friends locally, and he's a recluse, but every now and then he has visitors from Europe or the States, and they're usually people like Mocca, who are in the kind of business they wouldn't want anyone to look into too closely." Sam Solon put down the knife he had been holding. "I can't give you any more detail off the cuff, but I've told my people in Sydney to get it all together."

Modesty said, "What do you think it adds up to?"

"Hell, I don't know. We never *have* known any answers since this whole goddam Fletcher business started. But it's a racing cert that Mocca knows something, so let's start with him and then go on to C. J. Roper. Right?"

She looked at Willie. "We could adapt the Mafia scenario to con Mocca into singing, wherever we pick him up."

"Sure, Princess."

She thought quietly for a few moments. "How long do you need to finish checking our stuff and packing it?"

"A day. If we need any 'eavy equipment, like scuba gear, we can hire it out there."

She stood up. "All right, Sam, we're off. And thanks for saving us a lot of time. When are you flying back? Maybe we could get on the same flight."

"I'm flying back just whenever I choose to walk aboard and say 'Go.' What the hell's the point of being a millionaire if you're going to act the same as if you weren't? I've got a private jet, Modesty girl."

She smiled. "Here?"

"At Heathrow. And it's a bloody sight better than flying public, so if you want to fly out with me just say the word. She sleeps six passengers in comfort, the way I've had her modified."

Willie laughed and began to dismantle one of the handguns. "I bet you vote socialist," he said.

"Too right, boy. What else?"

Modesty put a hand on the Australian's shoulder and said, "Listen. We'll be glad to have you backing us, but when we get to the action phase you're out of it, Sam."

His eyes narrowed. "I can still handle myself."

"No. I want a promise now. Otherwise you go ahead your way and we go ahead ours."

He scowled, then slowly the scowl faded into a wry grin. "You're pretty near as bossy as me. Okay. It's a promise."

*   *   *

The interior of the executive jet was more than comfortable. It had been adapted to take the problems out of long-distance travel and reduce jet-lag to a minimum. There was a small but pleasant dining compartment, a crew of three, and a cabin staff of one steward and one stewardess. A wide selection of films and music was available, and there were compact facilities for physical exercise. The aircraft could cruise economically at over five hundred m.p.h. with a range of almost four thousand miles.

On the first night, over the Adriatic, after an excellent

dinner and a two-hour poker session with Sam Solon, Willie tapped on the frame of Modesty's cubicle and said softly, "Princess."

She pulled back the curtain, and reflected his grin when he saw that she was wearing a pretty cotton nightdress. "Well, I had to bring something to wear in bed, Willie. You never know how public a private plane's going to be."

"I bought meself some pyjamas." He glanced along the narrow passage. "You signalled you wanted a word."

"Yes. Is anyone about?"

"No. Sam's in the bathroom."

"It's just this. I rang Tarrant to say we were going to Australia with Sam Solon. He didn't ask any questions, but he knows what we're trying to do. He called at the penthouse for ten minutes this morning, to give me an emergency contact. Larry Houston, head of Australian Security. He's more or less Tarrant's opposite number out there, and they're good friends. Tarrant was in contact with him yesterday about us."

Willie scratched the lobe of his ear. "We don't want anyone official on our backs."

"No. But I've been given a frequency and a code prefix. In an emergency, any message we send on that frequency and with that prefix will get to Houston personally."

"Blimey. I can't see us sending any messages, but it's certainly the red carpet treatment."

"I gather Houston owes Tarrant a biggish favour, and he's a man who pays his debts. We've hidden nothing else from Sam, but I couldn't say this in front of him. It's not our secret."

"Sure. Go ahead, Princess."

Very quietly she gave him the frequency and the code prefix. He nodded, without making any apparent effort of memory. "Right. Transmit in clear?"

"At discretion. Alternatively, use a keyed columnar transposition cipher with 'magnitude' as your key word."

Again he nodded. "It's nice to 'ave friends, but this ought to be a pretty straightforward caper now we've got the initiative."

"Yes. But not one to enjoy. I'll be glad when it's behind us."

"Me too." He looked down at her soberly for a moment, then shrugged. "I'll go and put me posh pyjamas on."

She touched a hand to his cheek. "Goodnight, Willie. Sleep well."

Karachi. Calcutta. Singapore. To Sam Solon's disgruntlement. Modesty Blaise and Willie Garvin proved poor company. They seemed to have both the inclination and ability to spend most of the time asleep, except for exercise and meal breaks. Between Singapore and Perth he prevailed upon them to show him the weapons and explain the gadgetry they had brought with them. His interest and enthusiasm were in marked contrast to the reluctance with which they answered his eager questions.

At eight that evening they took off from Perth, and dinner was served as they climbed to cruising height. At nine Modesty announced that she was going to bed, and Willie declared that this was his intention also. Sam Solon looked from one to the other of them with disgust. "Bed? We'll be landing in Sydney soon after midnight. What's the point?"

"The point is," said Modesty, "that we can get in two or three hours of sleep, and the more you sleep on a trip like this, the quicker your biological clock adjusts itself. I'm not saying that's scientific, I just say it works."

"Hell, I thought we'd have a poker session."

"Not tonight, Sam. You're winning, so stay that way."

"Okay, but have a brandy."

"Not for me, thanks."

"Bloody hell, girl, you're worse than a Sunday School teacher."

She smiled. "Not always. But we're on business."

"A brandy won't hurt you, for God's sake. It's something special, a cognac I picked up in Rochefort, and I've only got three bottles left. You going to let me drink alone?"

"All right, I'll stay for a brandy. And thanks."

Sam Solon looked balefully at Willie. "You?"

"Well, I was going to ask for Ovaltine, but just this once, then. Like you said, what's the point of being a millionaire if you're going to live like common people?"

Sam Solon grinned crookedly and signalled to the attentive steward. "That's right, Willie boy. And if you poms hadn't forgotten a few simple truths like that, your country wouldn't be going around with its arse hanging out of its trousers."

Two minutes later he lifted a balloon glass and eyed the splendid amber liquid. "What's the toast? Rough justice? Success? The winners?"

Modesty shook her head. "Let's just drink the brandy, Sam."

He eyed her curiously for a moment, then his brown face crinkled in a smile. "Maybe you're right," he said. "We'll wait and see how it comes out."

11

The first thing she registered was that there was no aircraft noise. That should have been impossible, for her inner monitor would have roused her with any substantial change of altitude, let alone with the disturbance of landing. Her head ached, and there was a sour taste in her mouth. The air about her smelt different. The bed in which she lay felt different.

Warily she opened her eyes. She was facing a wall of natural rock, flat and vertical, but showing toolmarks. Above her the slightly curving ceiling was also of rock. Light came from a fluorescent tube recessed into the ceiling, a soft light. The single bed was wide, with a sprung mattress and fresh linen. Beside it was a table and chair, both with tubular legs. On the far side of the small room—the cave? the chamber? the vault?—was a limed oak dressing table and a wardrobe. Her own toiletry had been set out on the dressing table.

She sat up, feeling sick, knowing she had been drugged, and with the impression that many hours had passed while she slept. She was still wearing the nightdress she had put on to go to bed in the aircraft. To her right was a doorless arch in the wall, and beyond she could see another room. The composition floor felt neither warm nor cold to her bare feet. The other room was larger, and furnished as a living room with two easy chairs, a gate-legged table, and a sideboard bearing a record player, a rack of discs, a shelf of coffee-table books, and a pile of quality magazines.

Here the light was natural, for in one wall of rock was set a long picture-window looking out from what appeared to be a height of fifty or sixty feet over an expanse of sea. When she looked closely at the glass, she judged it to be a laminate some twenty millimetres thick and built to withstand any assault.

In the wall opposite the window was a door. It had a small square peep-hole, again of laminated glass, at present masked from the outside. There was no handle, latch, or keyhole. The door was of teak, and since no hinges were visible she knew it must open outwards. A small grid was set in the wall beside the door, and there were two larger ones, presumably for ventilation, set high up in the two inner corners of the room.

She tested the door gently, found it unyielding, then went back into the smaller room and found another door beside the wardrobe. This opened on to a lavatory with a shower and hand-basin. Inside the wardrobe were hung some of the clothes from her luggage, two dresses and the black shirt and slacks she favoured when operational. Three pairs of shoes rested on the shoe-rack, and on the shelves her tights and underwear had been neatly stacked.

She moved about the two rooms, arms crossed, holding her elbows, no longer observing, simply moving about to hasten the passing of post-sedation nausea while her mind fitted together the pieces of the puzzle. The main area of it had been plain to her within thirty seconds of waking, and now other smaller pieces were dropping into place.

It was difficult, but she knew very necessary, to hold down emotion and keep careful control, for what had happened was enough to destroy every shred of confidence if she allowed it to do so. Twice she was beset by a surge of anger and contempt at having delivered Willie and herself into a trap which might have been detected. Twice she had to prevent herself speculating uselessly on the motives of the opposition; this was an area of the puzzle still unknown and unguessable.

At the end of ten minutes she had recovered her balance, and the impulse to anger had passed. The trap was certainly detectable with hindsight, but there had been nothing to trigger suspicion that the enemy had planted himself within their counsels long ago. She might have used her own sources to double-check on the existence, whereabouts, and activities of the Maltese lawyer, Mocca, and of his supposed employer, C. J. Roper, but it would have seemed an intolerable waste of time, and there had been every reason to accept the information provided.

She looked unseeingly out of the picture-window and thought about Sam Solon. He had made no mistakes. He had even hired professionals to give him a genuine but carefully calculated beating that day by the river, timing it so that she and Willie would arrive on the scene. It was a move which had completely averted any suspicion. A tough, painful move, but typical. All the moves had been beautifully managed; the encounter with Solon in Malta after Frezzi's failure to bug the villa, his involvement in Dick Kingston's investigations, and the frequent contact with Luke Fletcher, both of which had kept Solon well informed on the crucial matter of whether or not Luke was regaining his memory.

Somewhere, she knew, there were others behind Solon, and a link with the theft of the Jade Queen, but this was the blank area of the puzzle, and would remain so until somebody filled it in for her. She thought that might be soon now.

Solon had figured in whatever Luke Fletcher had forgotten. That was why, when the Australian flew out from Sydney to *The Wasp*, his first question had been, "Did you tell Sydney we've found you?" A negative answer would probably have meant death for Luke and herself. There would have been a killing in any event if the sight of Solon had triggered Luke's memory. It had been a clever move, showing himself to the sick, dazed man right from the start, for this made it less likely that Luke would later recall his face from the eclipsed area of memory. The association would be with *The Wasp*, the flight to Sydney, and the hospital visits. She wondered briefly why Solon had later held back for so long from having Luke killed, since it was clear that killing did not trouble him. Again this was a question where speculation was a waste of mental energy, and she put it aside.

Still standing by the window she studied the sea, the swell, the sky on the horizon; she allowed her mind to encompass the voyage of *The Wasp*, the point where she had picked up Luke, and a strangely non-visual concept of the geographical area for a thousand miles around that point. Then she closed her eyes and let her inexplicable gift act upon the known data, sensing the earth turning beneath her and the unseen stars wheeling above her as she sought to know where she stood on the planet's grid.

After a few moments she opened her eyes and crossed through the bedroom to the shower. Ten minutes later she dried herself, put on bra and pants from the wardrobe, then carefully examined every item of her clothing and luggage which had been placed in the room.

Her combat boots, with the hollow soles and the detachable heels which could be primed to make miniature grenades, were not there. She had registered this with her first check of the room. Now she found that the kongo was no longer in its pouch in her black slacks, nor were the lockpicks in the seam. The flat strip of lead had been removed from the cuff of her shirt, the piece of celluloid and stiff wire from the collar. The steel comb had been removed from her toilet case and replaced by one of plastic. The lipstick holder which fired a jet of tear-gas no longer held the capsule of gas. Every item which might be used as a weapon or for escape had been found and removed.

She was bleakly certain that the same thing had happened to Willie Garvin's personal gadgetry. He had probably spent the last half-hour going through much the same process as she had herself. There was not, she thought, any immediate cause to be anxious about Willie. That they were both scheduled to die eventually she had no doubt, but she knew in her bones that more was to happen first. The whole shape and nature of the operation promised it.

She put on the shirt and slacks, a pair of socks and some moccasin style lace-up shoes, then turned to the dressing table and began to brush her hair. A small piece of ribbon from the nightdress served to tie it back in a short pony-tail, and she had just completed this when a voice sounded in the larger room. "Mis Blaise. Will you have the goodness to step this way, Miss Blaise?" It was the false Scottish voice of the man who had sat briefing them in Trafalgar Square on the theft of the Jade Queen.

She walked through the arch and saw that the cover of the peep-hole had been swung back. An eye was staring through the thick square of glass. From the grid beside the door the voice said, "Be good enough to sit down, lassie, where I can see you. Otherwise we'll pump in some tear-gas till you feel more obliging."

She moved to one of the armchairs and sat down. After a moment the door opened and a man swept dramatically into the room, halting in an exaggerated pose of open-armed welcome. Golden hair, violet eyes, enormous lashes, cherubic smile. A lean, broad-shouldered, graceful body. He wore a frilled ice-blue silk shirt with no jacket, and lemon-coloured trousers with open sandals on which diamanté sparkled. His toe-nails were lacquered to match the trousers. Behind him came a man with gingery hair and fanatical eyes, all in black; a cleric, fitting the description of the man who had been watching Willie Garvin at Barnwell on the day of the fête.

The second man moved to one side and stood with his back to the wall, hands loosely clasped in front of his chest. The cherubic man said, "Hoots, och aye, and ye'll tak' the low road. Did you like the Scottish accent, sweetie? Yes, yes, it was I and none other who sat betwixt you and the gorgeous Garvin in Trafalgar Square that day. Beauregard Browne, with an 'e'. Master of disguise and mimicry. May I sit down? Oh, now look. Watch the Reverend Uriah Crisp for a tiny moment, will you? Uriah, please." The priest's hand twitched and there was a gun in it. If she had not controlled all reaction her eyes would have widened, for she had never seen anything as fast. She looked away from the priest without apparent interest as the other man said, "Thank you, Uriah." From the corner of her eye she saw the gun vanish.

Beauregard Browne came forward, moving dancingly on his feet, and sat down facing her, his smile brilliant. "Welcome to Dragon's Claw, dear lady."

She had the look of one trying to hide a measure of boredom as she inclined her head and said, "An island in the Tasman Sea, somewhere between thirty-five and forty degrees south, and around one-sixty east."

The violet eyes froze for a moment. Then: "That was rather clever. May one ask how you knew?"

She gave a shrug. "I was discussing probabilities with Willie Garvin before we left England. With Willie and others."

His eyes sparkled. "I think you're trying to disconcert me, Miss Blaise. How very naughty. Never mind. I popped in to see that you were comfortable and to explain one or two things you might be wondering about. Our Esteemed Patron insists on his guests being made as comfortable as possible during their visits. Incidentally, this is the first time we've had *two* guests to entertain and speed on their way. Garvin is in the next block. Segregation for security. Since the ridiculous Fletcher did his escape trick, Our Beloved Patron has been very security minded."

"You mean Solon?"

"Indeed I do. Our indetectable human bugging system, as you've no doubt guessed. The Unspeakable Antipodean himself, though you mustn't quote me on that, he's *the* most sensitive man. But really. He's not here at the moment, by the way, because he got off at Sydney with Modesty Blaise and Willie Garvin—or rather with his steward and stewardess dressed up in wigs and suchlike so that they could pass as the two of you. And they had your passports, of course. They'll be at one of Mr. Solon's hotels for a day, closeted in their rooms, and then they'll pop off to Tasmania, but not in search of the non-existent Mr. C. J. Roper. They'll just take off their wigs and things, and become themselves, and one fine day someone somewhere will say, I wonder whatever happened to that nice Modesty Blaise and Willie Garvin? And you'll be simply nowhere to be found, will you? I mean, will you?"

She indicated Uriah Crisp with a slight movement of her head and said, "That was a Colt Combat Commander, wasn't it? A forty-five?"

The carefully shaped golden eyebrows rose. "So I believe, duckie, so I believe, but you must try not to be irrelevant when we're having a nice chat. Now what was I going to say next? Ah, yes. As mentioned above, Our Adored Patron, the distinguished New South Welshman, remained in Sydney to make sure that the Blaise stroke Garvin substitutes went

through their bit nicely, but he'll be flying out early tomorrow, and then all will be made known to you, as they
say. The following morning is your departure time, when
even more will be made known to you, according to
scriptural authority, isn't that so, Uriah?"

The priest looked at her with burning eyes and said in a
quivering voice, "In the life to come there shall be no
mysteries."

"So you see, sweetie? Isn't it all exciting?" Beauregard
Browne stood up. "As for today's programme, I shall now
pop along to have a word with dishy Willie Garvin, to brief
him, as it were. Then we'll all have a nice lunch up at
Dragon's Heart, that's the house where we live. I'm sure you
must be madly hungry, you've been asleep for simply ages,
you know. And after lunch I'll take you on a splendid tour
of Dragon's Claw island. Captain Cook discovered it, actually, and you may well feel he should have left it at that instead of going on to find Australia, but anyway, the story is
that one of his jolly Jack Tars picked up a shark's tooth on
the shore here and vowed it was a dragon's claw. Of course
they had maps with '*Here be Dragons*' marked on them in
those days, didn't they? However, the semi-circumnavigatory
Cook thought it was rather enchanting, I suppose, and he
duly called it Dragon's Claw. It's not a frightfully large
island, and nobody comes here because it's privately owned
by Our Prosperous Patron, and hardly anybody has heard of
it anyway, but there's lots to see, and I simply must show
you my orchids. I actually have a dragon's-mouth orchid in
splendid condition, isn't that apt? Now is there anything you
want? The tap water is pure as a maiden's heart, should you
be thirsty, but if you'd like a drinkie sort of drinkie, do tell
me now and I'll arrange it."

She looked thoughtfully at the corner of white silk which
protruded from the slit of a fob pocket below the waistband

223

of his slacks, and said, "A forty-five Colt. Did your clerical friend here kill Dick Kingston?"

Beauregard Browne looked down at her with dignified reproach. "Uriah acted as the Hammer of the Lord in sending a sinner to judgment," he said stiffly.

She was still considering the little triangle of white silk. "And was it you who killed Luke Fletcher? Thug-style, with the *rumal*?"

He gazed at her with enormous interest, head a little on one side. "Well, bless my soul," he said at last, "you really are rather quick, duckie. Yes, you can put the ludicrous Luke down to me. We'd just popped him back in the studio when something he'd painted triggered off a fatal attack of memory. So dispatch was necessary." He smiled sweetly. "Not that the reason interests you, I imagine?"

"That's right. The reason doesn't interest me." There was no threat, either in her voice or her expression, as she sat looking through Beauregard Browne with midnight blue eyes, but somewhere there was a tiny black flame in those eyes, and for the first time in many years he felt a curious *frisson* which he only later realised had been a stab of genuine fright.

He was at the door, looking back at her with a small frown of perplexity, when she leaned forward, eyes suddenly glinting with anger, voice harsh, and said, "If you're seeing that stupid bastard Garvin, you can remind him that this is *his* fault. I told him to check the Roper story, and he didn't bloody well bother."

Beauregard Browne ran a finger along one eyebrow and giggled, his equanimity restored. "Yes, of course I'll remind him, darling. I simply adore people bickering and squabbling. It's so enthrallingly entertaining, isn't it? I mean, isn't it?"

* * *

224

An hour later, when her inner clock and her estimate of the sun's position told her it was noon, a deep foreign voice from the grid by the door ordered her to sit in view of the peep-hole. When the door opened a man in drab green shirt and slacks entered, a strongly built man with a dark face and a beak of a nose. He wore a belt with a holster which was empty at this moment. The gun in his hand was a Star PD .45. Beyond the doorway stood two men in similar garb, one holding an automatic rifle.

The first man said briskly, "I am Condori, in charge of security here on Dragon's Claw. You are now to be taken to the house. I am instructed that you are a dangerous person and must be restrained while in transit. You will please turn round and place hands behind back."

She obeyed with neither haste nor delay. A time for action would come, would have to be seized or contrived if she and Willie were to live, but this was not the time. Condori said, "Fouad." A moment later she felt hands on her elbows, drawing them back, then a broad soft strap securing them. It was done so quickly that she was sure the strap must have a few inches of Velcro fastening, easy to fix or peel off, but impossible to break by a lateral pull.

Condori said, "We go now." When she turned, she saw that it was the third man, probably Arab, who had secured her. They were clearly taking no chances. She passed out through the doorway and half turned as if awaiting directions. There was no lock to the door, only a handle for pulling it open and an iron bar, two inches wide and almost half an inch thick, which slid across the door and into heavy iron brackets grouted into the rock wall. She judged that the fit was snug, for there had been no movement or rattle when she had carefully tested the door earlier.

She was now in a rectangular space somewhat larger than

the room she had just left. In one corner, positioned to face the cell door, a guard sat at a table smoking. To her left, a broad corridor ran for a few metres then turned at right-angles. To her right she could see a narrow passage with a steel-grille door a few paces along it. Through the door the passage seemed to continue into another open space similar to where she now stood, and she guessed that somewhere beyond the grille Willie Garvin was held in a cell much like her own.

Condori pointed and said, "This way." She turned to her left, following the unarmed guard along a corridor which turned twice before debouching through a doorless opening on to a short stretch of tarmac road. Across the road stood a jeep and a Land-Rover. Behind her Condori said, "Wait."

She stood still, looking about her. A mild sun was half veiled by hazy cloud. Behind her was a low cliff which housed the complex she had just left. A hundred yards along it, to her right, she saw another opening in the cliff. Willie Garvin, in black shirt and slacks, came strolling out followed by two guards. His arms were fastened behind him. The big fair-haired figure, moving with indolent unconcern, was a heart-strengthening sight to her, but she gave no sign of it and looked away. Within a stone's throw the sea lapped against a rocky beach where a jetty had been built. There were several boats tied up, two sailing dinghies, an inflatable, a motor sailer, an Alaskan 53 off-shore motor yacht, and a big powerboat, an Arrowbolt 21. Three men were working on different boats, stripped to the waist. Another, wearing an aqualung and mask, and carrying a long spanner, was emerging from the water.

The beach formed the end of a narrow quarter-mile inlet which widened steadily towards its mouth and was hemmed on each side by low cliffs. To her left, the tarmac surface shortly gave way to rock, and the road curved out of sight

226

inland, rising at a good incline. When she lifted her gaze above the line of the bluff behind her she saw the high point of the island, perhaps a mile away, a flattened peak rising sharply to eight or nine hundred feet.

There came the sound of an engine, and a jeep appeared at the turn of the road. A guard was driving, and in the back sat Beauregard Browne and the strapping red-haired girl she had seen once at the Benildon fête and again in Trafalgar Square. Beauregard Browne sprang out as the jeep halted, but the girl remained.

"Ah, there you are, sweetie," he cried, advancing upon Modesty, "and here comes that thrillingly rough fellow Garvin, to join us all for lunch. I do hope you have an appetite. Oh, and I've been so *mean*, darling, I actually forgot to say what a truly marvellous job the two of you did with the Jade Queen. I meant to say it before anything else, but you looked so fresh and beautiful and thoroughly edible when I came in this morning, I was completely swept off my feet. I'm really awfully susceptible to lovely ladies, aren't I, Clarissa? Oh, this is Clarissa. You've met before of course."

Clarissa smiled and said, "Hallo again."

Modesty studied her for a moment, remembering the sharp touch of the bicycle spoke at her back as she sat in Trafalgar Square, then said, "You were in on Dick Kingston's killing? And Luke Fletcher's?"

Clarissa's smile became frosty. "As it happens, I attended both events." Her voice held the lofty admonition of the Head Prefect. "But if you don't mind my saying so, you're not actually in a position to get tooty about anything."

Modesty said, "I like to know these things." She turned her head to look at Willie as he arrived with his escort. His mouth was set hard and he was eyeing her with cold anger. She knew Beauregard Browne had passed on her message and that it had been understood. A convincing enmity was a worthwhile deception which had paid off before. As Willie halted he said, "You made a right bleeding cock-up of it, didn't you!"

"*Me?*" There was fury in her voice.

"You! I was the one who wanted Roper and Mocca checked before we let that bloody Aussie rush us off—" He stopped and gave a contemptuous shrug. "Ah, forget it."

Beauregard Browne gave a crow of delight. "A rift in the lute! Now isn't that simply delicious? I mean, isn't it? But you must squabble some more for us later, it's time for our buppies now. Willie dear, will you be an angel and hop in with Clarissa? She's been dying to have you all to herself. And I shall escort the lovely but presently somewhat sulky Miss Blaise." He took her arm and guided her to the other jeep.

She stumbled as she mounted, falling back against him so that he had to catch her. It was a move made to test his strength, and he was even stronger than she had suspected, lifting her bodily into the seat with a laugh. As he climbed in beside her she said savagely, as if to herself, "That smart-arse Garvin's got too big for his boots."

Beauregard Browne grinned. "He was saying to me earlier that he's getting rather sick of being ordered around by a snooty bitch." A limp-wristed hand flicked the air. "But I said to him what I say to you, poppet. Don't worry. Simply don't worry. I mean, it won't be for long, will it?"

*   *   *

In the cool dining room Dr. Feng sipped his glass of white wine poured by one of the three Indonesian house staff, and studied Modesty Blaise. She and the man Garvin sat on the

228

other side of the table. The Reverend Uriah Crisp was beside Dr. Feng, a matter which brought the doctor a sense of relief. The two opposite were highly dangerous, he believed, and it was good to have the paranoid priest, with his gun, in a position to act quickly now that the restraining straps had been removed. It was also good to have the two armed guards standing directly behind Modesty Blaise and Willie Garvin, and only two paces away.

Clarissa sat at one end of the table with the man Garvin on her right, Beauregard Browne at the other end with the Blaise girl on his left. It was a satisfactory arrangement, Dr. Feng decided, and allowed himself to relax so that he could give his whole attention to studying the two prisoners with a view to deciphering the animosity that hung between them. Both appeared to be brooding inwardly. They had asked no questions and had barely responded when addressed.

This had not in the least dampened Beauregard Browne's spirits. Since they sat down he had been holding forth effortlessly, mainly to Clarissa, and pretending to be oblivious to any lack of interest from the unwilling guests. He had demonstrated his Scottish, Welsh, Irish, and Pakistani accents; he had gone into a chuckling do-you-remember dialogue, with Clarissa merely feeding him, in which he had made quite clear first how Kingston had died, then Fletcher; now he was saying happily, "I do think, though, I really do think that Uriah's dispatch of the sinning policeman in Amsterdam was his most outstanding performance. That was the day we took the Hsuan-te chair from the Bor Museum, if you remember. A nice diversion."

The priest's long jaw stopped champing for a moment and he said, "The end of a sinner is not a diversion, Beauregard. Let us beware the wrath of the Most High. He will not be mocked."

"Heaven forbid!" exclaimed Beauregard Browne. "You wrong me, dear brother, and it is indeed a sad thing to be wronged by the Hammer of the Lord. I was referring to *our* operation with the Hsuan-te chair as the diversion, permitting the exercise of *your* duty in dispatching the sinner. Which our foolish man-made laws might otherwise have thwarted."

Uriah Crisp nodded. "I ask your pardon for my misunderstanding," he said.

Dr. Feng leaned forward a little. "Miss Blaise, I observed a slight reaction when my colleague spoke of the affair in Amsterdam."

She glanced at him, then went on boning the fish on her plate as she said, "The cowboy thing, when the patrolman was killed. It was in the papers." Her head lifted and her very dark blue eyes hit him suddenly so that his nerves twitched for a moment. She said, "Did you have a hand in the kill'ng of Dick Kingston and Luke Fletcher?"

Dr. Feng was trying to compose a reply when Beauregard Browne said brightly, "I feel sure, my almond-eyed medico, that our Miss Blaise is planning to mete out justice to those of us she deems to have been naughty, and we really must include you in, mustn't we?" He looked at Modesty with huge delight. "Yes, duckie, put Dr. Feng on your list. But you'll have to be rather quick, I'm afraid, because it so happens that you are on Uriah's list. His list of sinners."

In a choking voice the Reverend Uriah Crisp said slowly, "She is an abomination in the eyes of the Lord. There is lechery in her mouth, and in her breasts there is lewdness. Her loins move men to debauchery, and her limbs invite fornication." He rose, pale face flushed, and strode from the room on long spidery legs.

Clarissa said, "Golly, he never says nice things like that about me."

"You're not a sinner, darling. You're a helpmeet and a comforter." The smiling violet eyes turned to Modesty and Willie. "When you've made a tour of the island, you can watch our Uriah give a demonstration of his skill as the Destroyer of Sinners, the Hammer of God, etcetera. And may I assure you that when you come to face him in Execution Square, you really will have a chance, because Uriah insists that the Lord Almighty must decide the issue. So you'll have just one bullet for the Lord to work with."

Willie Garvin finished the last of his fish, jerked his head towards Beauregard Browne, looked round the table, and said, "Anyone know what Shirley Temple's talking about?"

There was a silence, then Clarissa said, "Honestly, Beau, it was a bit cryptic for anyone not knowing the drill."

"Sorry, poppet. Sorry, Willie dear. Sorry, adorable Miss Blaise." He drank some wine and leaned forward, his eyes suddenly cold. "Now listen and I'll tell you exactly how it works."

When he finished speaking two minutes later there was another silence. A long one. Modesty fidgeted nervously, tapping a finger, touching an ear-lobe, running a finger across her lip. At last she said, "Which gun do I get?"

"Your Colt thirty-two, from the little armoury you brought. With the hip holster."

"I want the Star. The heavy calibre." She was still fidgeting.

"If the thirty-two proves inadequate you must complain to the Lord, duckie. It'll be his fault."

Modesty sat looking down at the table. After a while she said slowly, "Count me out. I can kill him all right in this shoot-out charade of yours ... but then I get signed off by you, don't I? Oh, no. I'm not playing cowboy games for you."

"Ah, but you're wrong, little honeypot," said Beauregard Browne quickly. "You can actually play to win, though I'm

231

personally sure you have no chance. But if, I say *if* you managed to send our Uriah to higher service in the Great Hereafter, then we should urgently need a replacement of like calibre, and you would immediately be offered a lucrative position in our little community, subject to certain safeguards. You and the husky Garvin both."

She knew he was lying, but shrugged and said, "That's different. I'll play if there's something to play for."

Willie Garvin had been looking at her with stony eyes, reading her signals. Now he said angrily, "Never mind about 'er. Suppose she gets knocked off, what about me?"

"Don't worry, you gruff old thing. The same conditions will apply."

"I can take 'im, easy. But not with a gun. I never use 'andguns."

"So we understand." Beauregard Browne smiled upon him sunnily. "And in your case, Uriah has proposed that you actually be permitted to use your knives for the moment of judgment. Isn't he a sweetie? I mean, really. Isn't he?"

*　　*　　*

Ninety minutes later, a cigar gripped between his teeth, Condori brought the jeep to a halt by the shooting range. Willie Garvin sat beside him, a guard in the back with a levelled carbine. Modesty was in another jeep, driven by Beauregard Browne. Behind her sat Clarissa de Courtney-Scott with a sharpened spoke set in a short wooden handle. Both captives were shackled by one wrist to the frame of the seat.

For an hour Beauregard Browne had been exuberantly conducting a tour of Dragon's Claw. They had seen the airstrip, with the two-seater Schweizer Teal amphibian in the open hangar; the little harbour, the lavishly equipped complex where Condori's men lived, the swimming pool, gymnasium, and cinema. Beauregard Browne had pointed out the radar aerial on the hill west of the airstrip, and had spent some time at the place he called Execution Square, extolling the combination of scenic and functional qualities to be found in the site.

Now, on the southern coast of the island, the off-duty men were gathering along a flat stretch of ground which ended in a low bluff banked with sandbags. A deep trench had been dug in front of this to provide for the operation of targets. Beauregard Browne braked to a halt beside the first jeep and stepped out languidly. "Now you'll simply love this," he said. "It's the sort of demonstration our Uriah used to give when he worked on a dude ranch, before he was called to higher duties, of course. He'll be here any minute. Are you nice and comfy? Do feel free to hop out, but we're not going to unlock the wretched handcuffs, because with guns and suchlike around you might be tempted into a bit of naughtiness."

Both prisoners got out of their seats and stood looking about them with torpid lack of interest. Clarissa moved to stand behind Willie, then edged closer, with seeming unawareness, until her breast pressed against the arm shackled to the jeep. After a moment or two he looked round at her speculatively and with new alertness.

"Ah," said Beauregard Browne, "here he comes." One of the Land-Rovers was moving along the track to the butts. It stopped, and the Reverend Uriah Crisp climbed down from the passenger seat. He was wearing a black stetson, check shirt, narrow cowboy pants, and high-heeled boots with small spurs. From twin gunbelts two revolvers hung at his hips in traditional holsters.

He might have appeared a laughable figure, but none of Condori's guards showed amusement. They watched with respect as he walked forward on to the range. Surprisingly, his gait in the high heels was less awkward than his normal stalking carriage. He gave Modesty and Willie a long admonitory stare as he passed, then strode on to halt ten yards from the butts. As he halted, a man-shaped target slid up into view, black except for head and heart.

For a moment he stood with arms hanging limply, then suddenly, smoothly, the guns were in his hands, spinning on their trigger guards. One left his hand, whirling in the air, and in the same moment the other fired, drilling a black hole in the white head. As the first gun dropped into his hand he shot a hole in the heart while the second gun spun in the air. Six shots from alternate guns. Two close groups of three. For the next few minutes the Colt .45 six-guns flashed and roared as the Reverend Uriah Crisp displayed his skill in jugglery and marksmanship. He made trick shots, he demonstrated the border shift, he hit different targets firing with both guns simultaneously, he reloaded one gun by thumbing cartridges into the cylinder from his belt while at the same time planting six shots from the other gun into a target.

At last he paused, re-loaded, and holstered both guns, then stood with his hands at his sides, waiting. Beauregard Browne said, "One does sometimes wonder if Uriah didn't miss his vocation when he took Holy Orders. Now do watch this, Modesty poppet, and you, Willie, because this is rather like the last thing you'll ever see."

The man-shaped target had gone. In its place was a slender pole some eight-feet high with a white clay disc at the top. Uriah Crisp called benignly, "A preliminary test, please, brother." The white disc dropped, flashing down the pole under its own weight to vanish into the trench. "Thank you."

The pole swung down, and reappeared a few moments later with a white disc again at the top. The guards became very quiet. Every eye was either on Uriah Crisp or the target. Nobody moved except Clarissa, who swayed to press herself harder against Willie's arm. He did not register it. From where he and Modesty stood, behind and slightly to the priest's right, they were perfectly placed to watch his right hand while at the same time keeping the white disc in peripheral view. Willie had seen the man draw a gun from a shoulder holster in the cell earlier, but he had not been ready for it. Now he wanted to see it with his senses fully tuned. He had no doubt that Modesty was in the same situation, though her expression as she stood watching was one of amused condescension.

Five seconds passed. Ten. Twelve. The disc dropped like a stone, and a bullet from the Reverend Uriah Crisp's right-hand gun shattered it when it was three feet above the trench. Willie felt his stomach muscles tauten. What he had seen in the cell had been no freak. The man was unbelievably a tenth of a second faster than Modesty. He would be able to kill her while her gun was coming to the aim, and she knew it.

The guards applauded politely. The Reverend Uriah Crisp put away his gun, took off his hat, lifted his face to the sky, and cried passionately, "O Lord, let me be an instrument worthy of Thee." He turned, and walked to the Land-Rover. When he had settled himself in the passenger seat again it pulled away.

Modesty watched his departure with the same air of casual condescension. Willie Garvin was grinning a little as if at some private joke. She looked at Beauregard Browne and said, "Yes, he's pretty good for a vicar. Who gets first crack at him?"

235

Golden head on one side, he studied her mischievously. "Oh, ladies first, naturally."

"Good. He's dead. You could start briefing us on our new job."

Beauregard Browne laughed joyously. "All in good time, sweetie. Our Uriah isn't *quite* dead yet, you know. And I rather think that you and the stalwart Garvin are putting on a teensy weensy bluff." He moved to his jeep. "Well, that was the penultimate treat for today, and now we come to the ultimate. Places please, everybody. Come along Clarissa, stop rubbing your luscious titty against him. Off we go to Paradise."

Five minutes later the two jeeps stopped a few hundred yards from Execution Square, at the big chair-lift cabin where the cables ran up to the high peak at the western end of the island. Condori went inside and pressed the switch to set the endless cable moving. Twin chairs were suspended from it at intervals of thirty yards. They were brought into the cabin on the down-cable, moved slowly round the machinery in the centre, allowing ample time for passengers to seat themselves, then travelled on with the up-cable on their way to a similar cabin on the peak, a five-minute journey over a rugged slope which finally swept up over the last hundred yards to become sheer.

Beauregard Browne said, "Right, now. Forward the Peewit Patrol. The order of ascent will be as follows. Since Scout Garvin and Scout Blaise are on probation I shan't trust them to behave with any of us in the same chair, so Second-in-Command Condori goes first, with Guard Fuzuli, watching our probationers who will be in the next chair, handcuffed to it and to each other. Cub Mistress de Courtney-Scott and I will bring up the rear. Good? Good. Now where's my own little gun? Ah, here we are. I'll point it at Modesty's delightful belly while you see to the cuffs, Clarissa."

Condori and Fuzuli moved off. The machinery was stopped for Modesty and Willie to be secured to the next chair, then restarted. As Beauregard Browne waited with Clarissa she said softly, "Oh golly, Beau, I'd simply adore to have that Willie Garvin for a few hours before he goes. It seems such a frightful waste."

He giggled and held her arm as they took the next chair. "Sweetie, you fairly radiate it. Look, I hate to be mean, but after all, once he's got hold of you he could threaten to break your pretty neck if we don't provide a watertight way out."

"I don't think so, Beau. I mean, he knows very well you wouldn't play."

"True. And he can guess I'd crucify him if he screwed the said pretty neck instead of more suitable parts. All the same ..."

"He'll try to subvert me. I think it should be rather fun, really, Beau. I'll allow myself to be carried away, and I'll keep promising to drug the guard or whatever, so we can flee to freedom and live happily ever after. It might even help to worm out of him any little plot he's got in mind."

Beauregard Browne squeezed her thigh. "Clarissa, angel, it's simply splendid. Tonight you shall have fresh meat, my little rabbit."

In the instant that the chair bearing Modesty and Willie left the cabin and they could whisper without being heard, they looked away from each other and spoke in a verbal shorthand through barely parted lips, very rapidly, wasting no words as they exchanged their appreciation of the situation.

Willie said, "Location?"

"Thirty-five to forty south, one-sixty east. Air?"

"Not without the Gulfstream pilot."

"Teal too short-range?"

"Yes. And boats are out. They radar fix and gun us from the Teal."

"Message?"

"Possible. I can get out tonight."

Her heart lifted. O rare Willie Garvin. She said, "But?"

"Noisy. Bang and run. Can't reach you."

"No matter. Help to blow lights?"

"Yes. Allow seven seconds."

"All right. Wait."

She stared blankly up the cable towards Condori and Fuzuli in the next chair, their heads turned to watch, and a dozen threads of thought flowed swiftly through her mind, interweaving in a constantly changing pattern. Willie could break out but there was nowhere to go. Neither boat nor seaplane offered an escape route. The plane had a limited range and would run out of fuel somewhere over open seas. Any boat would be located by radar long before it was out of range, and sunk by small-arms fire from the Teal. Sam Solon's twin-jet Gulfstream was the only way of escape from Dragon's Claw, and neither she nor Willie had flown such an aircraft. Presumably it would arrive with Solon tomorrow, but it would be closely guarded. Every sensitive point on the island would be closely guarded.

She did not wonder or ask how Willie could break out. That he had said so was enough. But with no way off the island he would be recaptured sooner or later. Like a flywheel gathering speed her mind raced faster and faster, no longer following a logical progression in permuting various possibilities step by step, but taking great intuitive leaps to embrace entire and intricate concepts. There were known and unknown areas in the situation, there were facts and numbers and personalities to be taken into account. There were machines and terrain and physical conditions. There were original intentions and present intentions to be reassessed.

They had been gliding steadily up in the chair for not quite three minutes when she began to speak rapidly and very concisely, still barely moving her lips as she stared out over a steadily widening panorama of the island. "Willie, the only time we're going to be together and in with a chance is when it's time for us to be killed in Execution Square. We get surprise advantage when I take the vicar. Then we can break one of two ways. When you get out tonight, you cover them both. Like this . . ."

Willie was mentally recording every word. When she finished, twenty seconds before they reached the upper cabin of the chair-lift, he sat looking dourly at the ground, now far below, inwardly wondering at the way she had used every element of the situation to wring advantage from disadvantage, yet without restricting his initiative and flexibility.

He felt his blood stir, his pulse quicken. Until now they had been fighting in the dark. No, not even fighting, for there had been nobody to get to grips with. But now the enemy was known, and this meant that the remaining mysteries no longer mattered, for in essence the issue was simple. Win or die; a good mind-cleansing simplicity. Even the huge odds against, and the seeming inevitability of the conclusion, could not destroy the feeling of relief that suddenly uplifted him. Very softly, as the chair passed across the edge of the drop and moved on towards the cabin some twenty yards away, he said, "Right, Princess."

The guard stopped the machinery and covered the captives while Condori released them from the chair and linked them wrist-to-wrist with a single pair of cuffs. At his command

239

they stood in the doorway while the next chair was brought up. Beauregard Browne threw off the safety-bar, helped Clarissa to alight, then clapped his hands and said, "Pixie Patrol will now fall in for a tour of Paradise Peak." He moved forward into a short gulley, and Modesty registered a new eagerness in him, a genuine and unaffected excitement. She had sensed it in him once before, she recalled, in the cell when he had spoken of showing her his orchids.

The gulley opened on to the grassy top of the peak, which was slightly sunken and in the shape of a rough half-circle. Two hundred yards of cliff edge formed the straight section of the perimeter. On the landward side the peak was hemmed by a low curving ridge, pierced by the gulley which gave access to the chair-lift. This configuration served to shelter the hollow, for the air was warm and still here. Against the centre of the ridge stood a hut like a miniature Swiss chalet, the door hooked back to reveal a tiny front room with a table, two chairs, and a Calor gas-stove. Beyond was a larger room with part of a bed on view.

A little way past the chalet, but also against the ridge, were two long glass-houses and a smaller one, each with a north side of brick, the roof and the other three sides of glass set in a thin metal framework. Roller blinds could be seen drawn partly across each sloping roof. A complex of pipes ran from the glass-houses to a large prefabricated concrete structure with double doors. There was some garden furniture set out nearer to the cliff, together with a bamboo awning and a large sun umbrella.

Beauregard Browne spread his arms and said, "Paradise Peak. The pinnacle of happiness. You won't be allowed *into* the glass-houses, of course, but I can show you some of my little friends from the outside." He beckoned Modesty and Willie forward almost confidingly, and now the last shreds of

240

affectation fell away. There was passion in the violet eyes, a kind of fanaticism comparable to that of the Reverend Uriah Crisp.

Inside the first of the two large glass-houses there seemed to be every imaginable colour, and no two of the plants bore flowers which looked alike. Most were in pots of different sizes, some in suspended teakwood baskets. Willie let his gaze touch Modesty, and saw from her eyes that she had switched ninety per cent of her attention from Beauregard Browne in order to absorb and store for later consideration all the data offered by Paradise Peak. Willie followed suit, and the enthusiastic voice faded into the background.

". . . and here's the little friend called dragon's-mouth. You see? There, the reddish-pink one with the three erect sepals and the purple-blotched lip. Isn't she pretty? Under natural conditions she grows only in North American bogs and swamps, so it's rather good to have her here, isn't it? Lots of acid in the compost, of course, and she needs to be kept moist and cool. I don't say that absolutely all of these are rare, but I do have some really rather special little friends among them. Now over here, you see? *Paphiopedilum Stonei*, awfully special, from Borneo. Don't you love those blackish-crimson streaks? Oh, and here's a frightfully unusual *Dendrobium* species from Java. Some of my little friends aren't actually terribly difficult to grow, but others really are a teeny bit demanding. Hallo, sweeties! Are we all being good little flowers? Pleased to see Daddy, eh? That's splendid. Now over here I have something really rather lovely . . ."

Beauregard Browne talked for fifteen minutes, his words and phrasing as precious as ever, but his face, eyes, and manner intense and serious. He stopped at last, gazed raptly for a while at the display in the second of the large glass-houses, then took out a lavender-coloured handkerchief and dabbed his face and brow. The old manner returned abruptly and he said with a giggle, "Isn't it all fascinating? And now I really must let you admire the view. This way, please. There, isn't that somewhat lovely? You can look right across the curve of the island to the harbour. So pretty with all the boats tucked away at the bottom of the inlet. What are you doing, Condori?"

The big Mexican had an unlit cigar in his mouth and was slapping the pockets of the loose bush-jacket he had worn during the tour of the island. "Excuse me, señor," he said, "I had some matches." Modesty remembered seeing them when Condori lit a cigar down by the swimming pool, a big box of red-headed matches. The man's eyes narrowed suddenly and he moved towards Willie Garvin. Very carefully and thoroughly he felt all over his arms, legs, and body.

Clarissa laughed and said, "Golly, did you think you had your pocket picked? You might at least have asked *me* to search him, Condori."

Beauregard Browne tapped his white teeth thoughtfully with a finger nail. "It's not exactly alarming," he mused, "but it's a nice excuse for me to grope Miss Blaise, though one can hardly imagine where she might conceal those great flares you use, Condori. However, hands well up please, duckie. Thank you. I must say you feel very pleasant. Oooh, there's a nice squidgy bit. No. No, I'm afraid she hasn't got them, Condori. We need fear no arson. I expect you left them down in the recreation complex. Now, is there anything else for our visitors to see? I think not, so let's return in reverse order. Follow me, Pelican Patrol."

As they entered the chair-lift cabin, Willie stumbled and lurched sideways, dragging Modesty off-balance. She caught at the manacles, gave him a hostile glare and said, "That bloody hurt my wrist."

He shrugged sourly. "All right, it 'urt mine, too. Is that all we got to worry about?"

Fastening the bar across Clarissa and himself, Beauregard Browne said, "Now children, no squabbling."

Two minutes later, hanging beneath the steel cable with Willie beside her, Modesty said softly, "Matches?"

He gave a barely perceptible nod. "I dipped 'em in the jeep and 'id them on that ledge beside the door before we went out on the peak."

And he had picked them up again when pretending to stumble, she knew. It had been very well done. A box of matches, and a particularly large one, was not the easiest thing to manipulate without noise, even for a card mechanic as skilled as Willie Garvin. She did not know how or even if he would use them, but that was his concern. She said, "Clarissa's a nympho and she's seething for you. You'll have her to cope with tonight, if Browne allows it."

Willie Garvin looked away. After a moment or two he spoke, and she heard a slender thread of amusement in his whispered words. "Thanks, Princess. She might come in useful."

12

Half an hour before midnight, turning slowly on the bed in the dimmed light of the cell, Clarissa said breathily, "Oh God, you're too good to waste, Willie."

He cupped a hand about one fine full breast and whispered in her ear. "You don't 'ave to convince me, you little raver. Can you fix anything to get me off the 'ook?"

A long throaty sigh escaped her. "Yes. Yes, like that, Willie. Ahhh, good ..."

"Listen. Listen, will you? I'm useful. I got years of experience and lots of contacts. Ask your bloke Browne about me joining up with your lot. Or is it Solon who's got the say-so? What sort of influence 'ave you got with 'em, Clarissa?"

"I ... I have quite a lot ... uhh!" She threw her head back and clung to him, panting. "Once more, Willie. Please. Once more now. Then I ... then I can think for a while before it's time again. Like that. Yes ... go on, Willie, go *on*!"

She had come to the cell at seven-thirty, followed by two guards bearing food and wine. It was obvious that she wore nothing beneath her thin cotton dress, and the situation was made plain to Willie within the first few minutes. He had accepted it warily at first, then with apparently increasing hope and enthusiasm. They had eaten a leisurely dinner and lingered over the wine, Clarissa enjoying the exquisite torment of deliberate delay. At last she had called the guards to remove the remains of the meal. When they had barred the door after them, Clarissa had taken Willie by the hand, led him into the bedroom, pulled down her shoulder straps and let her dress fall to the floor. It was then nine o'clock.

Five minutes later, by the light filtering through from the outer room, Willie had brought her to her first stormy climax. And now, two hours later, when she slumped beside him with long sighs of satisfaction, he felt deeply thankful that her requirements throughout had been entirely selfish and did not include any desire to be of reciprocal service.

Quite gently he turned her over to lie face down, then lifted himself and knelt astride her, massaging her shoulders. She gave a drowsy laugh and was starting to say something when his fingers slipped about her neck and tightened with precise pressure on the carotid arteries. For a moment her body went rigid, then she tried to heave him off, to reach back and claw him with her hands, but the sudden clamping of his knees against her ribs drove the breath from her, and in three seconds her body went limp beneath him.

When consciousness crept back she still lay prone on the bed, but now her wrists were securely bound behind her with strips torn from a sheet. Her ankles were similarly bound, and a makeshift gag was wadded in her mouth, held in position by a wide strip of sheet. When she turned her head muzzily and was able to focus her eyes, she saw Willie Garvin in slacks and shoes, about to put on his black shirt, watching her.

He took a pace forward and bent to turn her on her side. She lay breathing deeply through her nose, gathering her wits as she watched him slip the shirt on and start to button it. She pushed against the gag with her tongue. It prevented a cry, but it did not prevent some sort of noise which might be loud enough to attract the night guard in the hall outside. She drew in a breath and tightened her stomach muscles.

"MMMM—!"

He was very quick. In less than half a second his hand was at her throat, choking off the rising sound. She glared at him, then her anger turned to panic as he kept her from breathing until her vision darkened. When he let her go, and she had recovered a little, he pointed a finger at her face, then moved it to indicate the small table by the bed. As she watched, he picked up the table, laid it on its side, then struck down suddenly with the edge of his hand at one of the adjustable tubular legs. There was barely any sound, but she saw that the leg had bent to a sixty degree angle. He turned, hooked a hand under her neck and pulled her to a sitting position. A spurt of terror froze her as he took her by the hair, jerked her head back, and swung the other hand at her throat, so fast she heard the swish of air. The hand-edge stopped dead at the flesh, without impact, yet the touch sent a shock-wave through her body. He let her fall back, and his cold blue eyes held her gaze from behind a warning finger pointed straight at her face. After a moment she swallowed hard and nodded her understanding of his message.

He finished buttoning his shirt, then went down on one knee and began to work on the upper part of the table leg, flexing it backwards and forwards at the point where he had first bent it. The tubular metal became flat at the angle, and at last broke off to leave a chisel edge at the point of fracture. Willie Garvin stood up and slowly drew the inner section of the extending leg from within the outer section, then pushed it back again, watching the sliding movement closely. The fit was snug. The outer tube was about eight inches long, with one end completely closed by the fracture. The section sliding within it was twice that length and of solid metal with a plastic ferrule on the foot.

Setting the table upside down on the floor, he went through to the washroom and returned after a few seconds with a big box of matches. He squatted by the table, put one of the magazines on it, tipped out the matches from an almost full box, then began very carefully to use the short, chisel-edged piece of tube to scrape the red head of each match on to the magazine.

Clarissa lay on her side, watching. She was a little frightened now, but not of Willie Garvin, for she believed that as long as she heeded his warning he would not kill her. But if he broke out, Beau might punish her and that could be unpleasant. Not that it would do Willie Garvin much good to break out. There was no transport on the island which could take him to safety, or even beyond radar range. As the little pile of match-head chippings grew, a memory came back to her. She and Beau, in his father's garage, when she had just reached her teens, in the days when their pleasures had come from frottage rather than coupling. A boy at school had shown Beau the key-and-nail trick, and now Beau was showing her, and she was trying to look enthusiastic though longing for him to take her into the woods.

He had an old key, the type with a hollow barrel, and a nail which fitted loosely into the key. He had just scraped the heads off three matches with his penknife and tipped the scrapings into the barrel of the key. Now he tied one end of a short piece of string to the handle of the key, the other end to the nail, and slid the nail into the barrel of the key. Holding the two carefully by the loop of string, he walked to the door, bent over the concrete step, and swung the contraption so that the head of the nail struck the vertical face of the step, driving it hard into the barrel of the key.

There was a fierce, sharp *crack*! A whisp of smoke. Beau straightened up, gazing with delight at the key dangling on the string. "That was a hell of a good bang, wasn't it, Clarrie! I say, look, it's blown a hole in the barrel!"

"Golly! So it has."

247

He took up the nail and slid the end back and forth in the key barrel with wondering satisfaction. Sudden heat flooded her loins as she watched, and she pressed closer to him. "Let's go for a walk, Beau. In the woods."

He had laughed and tossed the nail and key away. "You're going to grow up into a nympho, you are. But who's complaining? Come on."

Now, watching the little pile of crushed match-heads grow, she knew vaguely what Willie Garvin planned, knew that he must have had it in mind when he contrived to steal the box of matches from Condori. When the last match had been scraped clean he picked up the magazine carefully and carried it through to the outer room, together with the short piece of tube and the solid leg. In seconds he was back, lifting her from the bed and carrying her through to sit her down in a chair where he could see her.

For a moment he stood close to the door, the edge of one hand resting across his chest just below one of the shirt buttons, and she realised that he had previously registered the height of the bar on the outside of the door against his own height. He scratched a mark on the door two inches from the outer edge, then began to use the piece of tube with the chisel end like an auger, twisting it against the solid timber.

After ten minutes he had cut a recess a few milimetres deep. He paused, flexing his cramped fingers, then went back into the bedroom and returned with the small table. Working in silence he flexed another leg till it broke off, and doubled one end back on itself to form a T. Now he had a crude auger considerably longer than the first, and with a handle to give purchase. Setting the chisel end in the recess, he began to turn the instrument carefully, making no discernible noise.

After an hour Clarissa fell into a doze. She woke some time later to see him tipping his pile of crushed match-heads into the short piece of tube, using a page torn from the magazine as a funnel. He tamped the powder down into the chisel-edged base of the tube, using the solid length of table leg, then inserted a small wad of paper. When he moved to the door and slid the tube base-first into the hole, she saw that it went in for about an inch and and a half, and knew that he must have drilled almost through the door. He removed the tube, wrapped a half-page from the magazine round it to make a tight fit, then spent several minutes working the tube fully into the hole again.

The wrist-watch she had taken off when going to bed now lay on the larger table they had used for dining. Beside it was the solid length of metal leg and two objects she could not at first place. Then she realised that they were two lengths of thick lead piping, part of the waste pipe from the wash-basin, which he must have prised from the wall earlier or while she slept. One was over two feet long, the other about eight inches.

He looked at the watch, wound it, slipped it into his pocket, then crouched to unfasten Clarissa's ankles. A finger under her nose warned her again as he straightened up. Taking the solid metal leg, he slid the end into the tube protruding from the door and pushed it gently home till it rested firmly on the wad and powder. He picked up the eight-inch piece of lead in his left hand, gripped Clarissa by the arm and urged her briskly to her feet, then guided her to stand with her back to the wall a little to one side of the door. Her mouth was dry and musty from the gag, and she wanted to cough, but restrained the impulse. Instinct told her that Willie Garvin's unspoken threats were no bluff.

Now he took up the two-foot length of lead in his right

hand, stood with his left shoulder pointing towards the door, and measured his distance, the flattened end of the lead resting against the metal plunger of his home-made explosive device. His arm moved back, then brought the lead club swinging down and round in a hissing curve to smash squarely on the end of the plunger, driving it home on to the confined powder with tremendous force.

The noise of the explosion was louder than she had expected, even though almost all the energy was vented against the bar on the far side of the door. Willie took a step back, then smashed a foot flat against the timber close to the charred hole. The door swung open as the fractured bar which held it fell in two pieces. Next moment Clarissa found herself grabbed by an iron hand, spun round, and hustled in front of her captor through the door and across the anteroom to where the startled guard in the corner was just getting his feet down from the table. He was reaching for the rifle which lay before him, and she was trying to shriek *"Don't shoot!"* through the gag, when the short piece of lead hurtled past her ear and hit the guard with bone-crushing impact on the temple. He fell sideways and lay still.

From behind the grille in the narrow passage separating the two wings of the prison came a sharp questioning shout, and next moment alarm bells were ringing. Willie gave the naked girl a push which sent her staggering towards the grille, and again she struggled to scream a warning to the man guarding the other wing as he came along the passage with submachine-gun ready.

Willie caught up the rifle on the table, a spurt of delight coursing through him as he saw that it was not one of the Ingram M-10's most of the guards carried, but the Goff laser-sight automatic rifle from the equipment he and Modesty had brought from England. As he turned for the broad corridor leading out, the guard on the section where Modesty's cell lay appeared at the grille door separating the two wings, but Clarissa's naked body blocked his view as she ended her stumbling run against the bars. He was staring at her with dazed bewilderment when the lights went out.

At the moment of the explosion Modesty had started counting to herself. She was in her nightdress, perched on top of the head of her bed, which was propped at an angle against the wall near the junction box which fed the lighting. The plastic cap of the junction box had been unscrewed and removed. In her hand she held a plastic beaker full of water. On the count of seven she sloshed the water into the junction box. There was a satisfying fizzle as the circuit was shorted and darkness fell upon the room. Carefully she climbed down, listening to the sound of the alarm bells. It took several minutes of heaving and groping to restore her bed to its natural state. Then she got in, lay on her back, and waited.

Ten minutes later, the blown fuse restored, Beauregard Browne stood eyeing the charred hole in the door of Willie's cell and the broken bar. He had obviously dressed in haste, and for once his camp affectations were muted. There was a dangerous rigidity about his face and his artificial smile. In the white house he had given instructions brusquely, telling Dr. Feng and the Reverend Uriah Crisp to remain where they were and on the alert.

Now he said to Condori, "You've given clear orders?"

"Yes, señor. No attempt to seek Garvin in the dark. All sensitive points to be diligently guarded—the harbour, aircraft, armoury, white house, radar."

The violet eyes glinted. "And Paradise Peak. I don't want the bastard doing any damage up there."

"I have two men guarding the chair-lift, señor."

"Good." He ran a finger round the charred hole, then dusted his hands. "Clever. Your matches?"

"I fear so, señor," Condori said stolidly.

"Why did Rocco have their new laser rifle here with him?"

"To examine it during his shift." Condori glanced at the dead man. "He was our armourer."

Beauregard Browne looked at Clarissa. She had put her dress on and stood a little to one side with an embarrassed air. "I thought Garvin was going to try to win you over while he was screwing you, darling. And you were going to have fun pretending to be persuaded."

"Well, he did seem to be trying, Beau," she said apologetically. "It was all going frightfully well, really, until he suddenly put me out with a sleeper hold."

"Our Beloved Patron isn't going to be too joyous about this. I think I may have to sentence you to a spell of celibacy, sweetie."

She looked down at her hands. "Don't be rotten, Beau. I mean, there's no permanent harm done, is there? He can't get away, and we'll catch him easily enough tomorrow, using the Teal for spotting."

"I don't like mistakes," he said sharply. "It spoils one's reputation. At this moment we have a very able fellow loose on the island with a very efficient rifle. I don't doubt the situation can be contained, but it's still not good. He could knock off half our strength before dawn if we played the hand badly."

Condori said, "It will not be played badly, señor. The men know they are to remain in pairs, and that they are to select suitable points for observation. Once in position they will not move unless they sight Garvin."

Beauregard Browne nodded grudgingly. "It's somewhat of

252

a relief to find that the man's soft," he said, and looked at at Clarissa. "Only a fool would fail to reduce the odds when the chance was there."

Clarissa sighed, still subdued. "Yes, if he was going to escape it was jolly stupid of him not to kill me. I could hardly believe it at first, but he definitely didn't *want* to kill me, Beau. He went to quite a lot of trouble not to, actually. It might be because I'm a girl and he'd just screwed me." She gave an awkward laugh. "There are some funny people about."

Beauregard Browne said, "You and I will sleep the rest of the night in Garvin's cell. I'm not making the trip back to *Dragon's Heart* till it's light, not with Garvin lurking somewhere out there. And when I say you and I will sleep here, I mean I shall sleep on the bed and you in an armchair, Clarissa. I'm extremely annoyed with you." He turned away. "But first a word with Blaise. Come with me, Condori."

When Modesty Blaise failed to appear in peep-hole view on orders spoken through the speaker-grid, Condori went in first, very warily, gun in hand. It was not until he switched the light on in the smaller room that he saw her. She was lying in bed, but not pretending to be asleep. When Beauregard Browne came in she glanced round without moving her head and ran a thumb under the shoulder strap of her nightdress to adjust it. He said, "As you may have guessed, poppet, your friend Garvin has temporarily left us."

"Why bother me with it?"

He smiled to hide his bafflement. Her question was one he found hard to answer, even for himself. Possibly he had simply wished to observe her reaction, but there was virtually no reaction to observe, which was highly disconcerting. He was distantly aware of a small but growing uneasiness that stemmed from a sense of having lost some measure of initiative. It was a feeling new to him, and absurd, for she was his captive and helpless.

He said brightly, "I'm tempted to spend the rest of the night here and give you a rather bad time, duckie."

She looked at him levelly from dark blue eyes and said, "All right."

"On second thoughts, you'll keep."

She said with a kind of irritable contempt, "You want to stop bluffing, Browne, you're not very good at it."

"I beg your pardon?"

"Willie's been a fool. He can't get away. But the fact is that Sam Solon wants us both alive and kicking tomorrow. I don't know what for, but I know damn well that's what he wants. And he's your boss. Yes, sir. So you won't do anything to Willie when you catch him tomorrow, and you won't try giving me a bad time tonight, because if you did, Solon would have your guts for garters. Now piss off and let me get some sleep."

She settled her head on the pillow and closed her eyes. Beauregard Browne stood gazing down at her, his pupils like pinpoints, one hand opening and closing, his face strangely pale. At last he turned and walked away without a word. Condori, the Star PD .45 still in his hand, followed slowly, a look of troubled uncertainty in his eyes.

Two hundred yards away, Willie Garvin drew himself silently on to the deck of the motor yacht. He had long since located the position of the two men watching the harbour, and had been careful to keep himself screened as he made his way from boat to boat. It was not easy, working in fitful moonlight, and he did not find what he was seeking on the boats, but an hour later, in one of the boat-houses on the west side of the harbour, his search was rewarded. Soon he was in the water again, occupied with the slow task of towing the equipment out to where he wanted it.

When he had finished he rested for a few minutes, reflecting philosophically that all he had done so far might well be wasted if they had to fall back on the alternative plan. The thought did not depress him. Modesty Blaise had launched him on the first moves of a counterstrike, and that was a stimulus of immeasurable potency.

In a hollow on a rocky slope, half a mile from the harbour, he wrung the remaining water from his shirt and trousers, put them on again damp, then sat down to check the Goff 180 rifle. Modesty had managed to secure it from America through John Dall only a few months ago. It was a .22 automatic rifle with a disc magazine fitting on top and a rate of fire of thirty rounds per second. Not that this mattered. The important thing was the laser sight. It threw a red dot which showed up plainly on the target. Where the red dot showed, that was where the bullet went with deadly accuracy, single shot or automatic burst. It was, as Modesty said, like playing golf with a homing golf-ball. A cheat. An affront to marksmanship. But it was a very good weapon if what you wanted to do was win.

Twenty minutes later Willie Garvin was on his stomach, reconnoitring Execution Square. When he had carried out his mission there he returned to the little hollow. His clothes had dried now, and he settled down cross-legged, hands resting on his knees, eyes closed. His breathing became very slow. In his mind a picture formed, a long rectangle divided into many small squares, nine in a horizontal row. Above the top row he mentally inscribed the word MAGNITUDE, and beneath each letter he visualised a number derived from the order in which the nine letters appeared in the alphabet.

Now, like the laser sight, his concentration narrowed to a fine point as he filled the squares with his message and etched the finished image firmly on his mind. This kind of ability was one of several he had learned under a very old man called Sivaji who lived in the Thar Desert and had been Modesty's friend and mentor long ago. It was she who had sent Willie to spend many weeks with him after Willie had become her right-hand man in *The Network*. That time had been for him an experience which might truly be described as out of this world.

At last he stood up, checked the time from Clarissa's watch, and began to move with all the caution of the expert poacher he was on the next part of his exacting night's work. He was no longer thinking of messages or letters or numbers, but the image of the enciphering was tucked away in his mind like a card in a card-index, available at a few seconds' notice.

*　　*　　*

At six a.m. the Gulfstream swept along the fifteen hundred metre runway built on the tail of Dragon's Claw and slowed to a halt. Sam Solon was the only passenger. He came down the steps with his wide-brimmed felt hat tilted back on his head. The eyes in his weatherbeaten face grew sharp as he saw that there were four waiting to greet him, Beauregard Browne and the girl, Dr. Feng and the gun-crazy priest. He noticed also that there were several of Condori's guards with guns spread about the top end of the airstrip by the hangar.

He said, "What's wrong, Beau?"

"Hardly a thing, dear old sport." The smile was easy and mischievous again. "In fact we have a slight additional morsel of excitement in having mislaid the preposterous Garvin."

"You what?"

Beauregard Browne sketched the situation with amusement. "I was a tiny bit worried during the night, and in fact we're missing three men this morning, and after strict orders

256

to remain in pairs, too. So it really is time they were shaken up and taught a sharp lesson, wouldn't you say? Anyway, wherever Garvin is at the moment, he's not within shooting distance. I took the Teal up to look for him just before you came through for landing, and he's nowhere on this section. Or anywhere covering the road up to *Dragon's Heart*."

Sam Solon stared at him without expression for several seconds, then took a strip of chewing gum from his pocket, tore the paper from it, and put it in his mouth. "Let's all get up to the house," he said. "We'll talk there."

On the way up in the jeep he was silent, but once in the long cool living room he tossed his hat on the table and said abruptly, "You bitched it up, Beau. You made a right bloody mess of this one."

Beauregard Browne raised elegantly shaped eyebrows. "Now come on, dear old sport," he said protestingly. "We've had a small contretemps, that's true, but over the last few months I've run a fabulously complex and interlocking operation for you without putting a foot wrong. We've cleared the Fletcher affair, we've stopped Kingston, we've secured the Hsuan-te chair and the Jade Queen, and we've brought you two absolutely splendid candidates for your particular pleasure."

Sam Solon stared out of the window. "They're not art people."

"You mean they're not specialists, dear old sport, which is to say they don't know everything about very little. But they do know quite a lot about quite a lot, which should make them rather more satisfying, I would say."

Dr. Feng cleared his throat. "May I make a suggestion?"

Sam Solon looked at him. "Go ahead."

"In the matter of securing Garvin quickly. He and Blaise have presented themselves as having fallen out, each blaming the other with some bitterness for their capture. My study of them leads me to believe that this is an act, a pretence. If so, then we can readily use Blaise to compel Garvin's surrender."

Sam Solon ran a hand impatiently through his hair. "An act? Christ, of course it's an act. I don't need to shrink heads to know that. They'd cut an arm off for each other, the bloody idiots."

Beauregard Browne smoothed an eyebrow and said, "The aggravating Garvin is tucked away in hiding at the moment, somewhere in the rough. He can't move without being seen, as we have spotters placed to cover the island. I think if Clarissa toured in a jeep with a loud-hailer he couldn't fail to get the message."

Solon nodded curtly. "Do it that way. I'm bringing the programme forward, and I want 'em ready for me at ten o'clock. We'll do the tour, then lunch, then that Jesus freak of yours can knock 'em off afterwards."

Beauregard Browne looked surprised. "It's usually dinner, followed by execution in the a.m., old sport."

"Sooner we get these two wrapped up the better. When they didn't know what the hell was happening we could string 'em along. Now they're dangerous. You give 'em long enough, they'll beat you."

Beauregard Browne spread a limp-wristed hand and gave a giggle of amusement. "But my dear old Esteemed Patron, they've lost, and they have no way back. You may safely leave everything to me."

Sam Solon pointed a finger at him. "You do it the way I said, Beau. I want this finished today. And listen. Up to the Luke Fletcher job you did okay, you and the rest here. But by the bloody right, you've been paid for it. What did that chair-lift cost me, so you could grow your daisies up there? Seventy thousand? Fine. But Fletcher walked out, and now

Garvin's bust out. That's two slips. You make one more cock-up, Beau, and I'll find some other bloke to take your place. Right?"

There was a silence in the room. The golden head tilted back and the violet eyes studied the ceiling pensively. At last: "I hear you, dear old sport."

"Good. I'm going to get some sleep. Is my suite ready?"

"As ever, Most Excellent Patron. Shall Clarissa join you?"

"I said sleep." He glanced at her and relaxed a little. "Be around for tonight, eh? And Beau, you wake me at ten with Blaise and Garvin all ready for me." He turned and walked away, out of the long room and down the broad corridor which led to his own suite.

After a moment Beauregard Browne said softly, "I feel unappreciated. Hurt. A tiny bit vicious, perhaps."

The Reverend Uriah Crisp had been gazing blankly out of the window. "The man lacks respect," he said, turning. "God will not allow His servant to be mocked."

"Indeed not, Uriah. We must pray for guidance." There was an ugly twist to Beauregard Browne's mouth. "But first let us deal with our sinners-in-waiting."

Half a mile away, in the radio hut which stood on a small peak between the airstrip and the harbour, Kerenyi was waiting to be relieved. Kerenyi had been on the night-shift, and was feeling troubled. At some time in the early hours he had been sitting before the radio, listening out on the usual frequency, and reading a girlie magazine. Then he had fallen asleep. At least, he thought that was the case, though in fact there was a curious gap in his memory. All he knew for certain was that he had woken up to find his head resting on his folded arms as he sat at the radio table. His neck felt stiff and his head ached.

For a moment he had felt panic, thinking that the escaped

259

Englishman had attacked him, but everything was in order. His M-10 submachine-gun was there in its rack beside the table, the set was still tuned to the same frequency. He went out to find the guard Condori had sent up to keep watch on the radio hut when news of the break-out first came through. It was Regan, and he was dozing in the grassy hollow he had chosen for his position, leaning back against a boulder. It had been difficult to rouse him, and then he had been very bad-tempered and confused.

Kerenyi was a little perturbed by all this, but he had no intention of reporting that both he and Regan had fallen asleep while on duty, however briefly. That would be madness. In any event, it was probable that nothing out of the way had happened. If it had, there was no sign of it, and certainly no harm had been done.

The telephone rang, and Condori's voice told him that when he was relieved he would be required at once for search or guard duties until the Englishman had been recaptured. Kerenyi thought, "What about my breakfast?" but he did not speak the question aloud. Condori would have considered it frivolous, and deserving of a painful answer.

*   *   *

Willie Garvin lay in a broad rut near the edge of the low cliff south of Execution Square. He had carried out his tasks for the night and even managed to get in two hours' sleep. He had heard the Gulfstream land at first light, and take off again half an hour later. Evidently Sam Solon was staying for a while. Soon after the take-off, searching guards had passed less than a stone's throw from Willie's hidey-hole without seeing him. Now he was listening to Clarissa's voice, made metallic by the loud-hailer. He had heard the same warning three times before from different distances as she moved about the island, and he was thinking that Modesty would be pleased if she could hear the message.

"Willie Garvin. Attention Willie Garvin. If you fail to surrender, Modesty Blaise will be taken to Execution Square at nine o'clock for punishment which will begin with a flogging."

Very nice. It saved him having to contrive his own discovery and capture. Another good point was that it had rained during the night, which provided an excellent excuse for the stained and crumpled state of his clothes. Absently he ran a hand along the length of copper tube he had found in the boat store. A short piece of wood and a big disc of insulating tape were now wired to it. Very nice.

All in all, these small advantages were not much to set against the mountainous odds stacked on the side of Sam Solon, but they were encouraging. It was a pity the Gulf-stream and its crew had gone, but that was sound security and you couldn't expect too much all at once. Long ago he had learnt from Modesty by observation that when you seized the initiative, no matter how hopeless the situation, the thing called luck would start edging your way, and Willie was confident that this had now begun. He looked at Clarissa's watch and saw that it was eight-thirty. Putting it away, he decided that Modesty would want him to wait until the last moment. Her policy was to anger Beauregard Browne, to shake him, to disconcert him and pressure him in every possible way, for then his thinking and anticipation would lack edge. So it would be good to keep him sweating for a little longer.

Willie Garvin closed his eyes and allowed himself to doze.

At ten minutes to nine they brought Modesty from her cell, well guarded, and walked her up the long road to

Execution Square. She had showered, her hair was tied back in a pony-tail, and she wore the same black shirt and slacks as before. Her face and eyes were without make-up. In the square, a rough triangle of six-by-three timbers had been set up. Beauregard Browne was there with Clarissa and Dr. Feng. Four guards were spread out well beyond the square to watch for any sign of attack by the missing prisoner, though Dr. Feng had insisted that this could not happen since it might bring immediate death to Modesty Blaise.

Condori stood holding a short piece of piping with six feet of insulated cable secured to one end. A makeshift whip. When her guards brought her along the path above the excavation on the east side of the square, Beauregard Browne said, "Our eloquent Dr. Feng has told you what is to happen, I understand?"

She nodded absently. "Yes, he was very graphic. First the whip and then some rape."

"Isn't it exciting, poppet? I'm so looking forward to the occasion."

"Yes, I'm sure you would be, Bubbles. I expect you suffered from poor potty training as a baby. What do you think, doctor?"

Beauregard Browne's smile was too bright and his laugh too casual. Before he could speak she said with a sudden grin, "I heard Solon come in this morning, and I bet he wasn't too pleased with what his golden-haired lad had to tell him."

After a moment he said thinly, "They're going to strip you and tie you to the triangle now. Get on with it, Condori." He turned and looked slowly about him, shading his eyes. Clarissa was also looking beyond the perimeter of guards, biting her lip. As Condori signalled two men to move upon her, Modesty lifted a hand and said, "I don't need any help." Without haste she unbuttoned her shirt, took it off, and tossed it to one of the men. She was stepping up to the triangle when there came the distant sound of a shrill whistle. Every head turned. Three hundred yards away, near the edge of the low cliff, they saw a black-clad figure rise seemingly from the bare rock, both hands lifted high, the right hand waving the Goff rifle. Clarissa made a faint but audible sound of relief. Beauregard Browne said, "Watch him. He's got that damn rifle."

"He is holding it by the barrel, señor," said Condori.

In the distance, Willie Garvin slowly lowered his hands, took a firm grip, then spun like a hammer-thrower. They saw sunlight glint on metal as the weapon soared up and away from him.

Condori said, "He has thrown the rifle into the sea."

Beauregard Browne nodded. "It doesn't amuse me. I very much wanted that."

Empty hands raised high, the figure of Willie Garvin began to move towards them. Modesty Blaise turned casually away from the triangle, twitched her shirt from the hands of the man who held it, and began to put it on. Dr. Feng eyed her for a moment, then switched his gaze to Beauregard Browne, who stood examining his nails. The man was perturbed, thought Dr. Feng. The eyes were a little too narrow, the pose a little too rigid. It was not difficult to guess what was in his mind. Blaise and Garvin were playing some game under his nose and he couldn't see it. Something was wrong, and he didn't know what it was or what to do about it. He was like a chess player, a queen and two rooks up, yet with a creepy feeling that his opponent was in some impossible way dictating the game.

The Patron was right, thought Dr. Feng. The sooner this woman and this man were executed, the better.

263

13

Sam Solon was waiting sprawled in an armchair by the window of the big living room when they were brought to him, their arms secured behind them with the Velcro straps. Modesty Blaise looked fresh and rested. Willie Garvin's chin was bristly, his clothes dusty and creased with damp, but he looked bright-eyed and in no way fatigued. Condori and Uriah Crisp were guarding them.

Solon threw aside the paper he was reading and stood up, blue eyes hostile in the square brown face. "You read the book?" he said.

They regarded him without interest. After a moment he stepped up to Modesty and slapped her hard across the face. "Don't keep acting tooty, girl. You been giving me the snob condescending bit right from when I told you to get off that sloop, but it's finished now."

She said without anger, "Almost everyone gives you the snob condescending bit, because you can't see it any other way. Ask Dr. Feng. That's what this is all about."

They had read the book he spoke of during the past twenty minutes in another room, with Clarissa turning the pages. It was a leather-bound scrap book with a dozen pages of cuttings spanning twenty years. They were not news reports or articles about Sam Solon's life, or his climb from a penniless opal digger to a multi-millionaire. They were primarily gossip-column items.

Because this book was clearly significant, Modesty and Willie had given it their attention, but at first without comprehension. Towards the end there were two typical sneers from consecutive issues of *Private Eye*. One referred to Solon as the Unspeakable Antipodean, and described a gaffe he had made at a Sotheby's auction. The other declared that a sycophantic article about him, published in an Australian women's magazine and illustrated with colour photographs, made clear that the design and décor of his home in Hobart cried out for the creation of a Nobel Prize for Bad Taste.

Willie had said softly, "Blimey, I believe it's a Hate Book." He looked at Clarissa. "Turn back, will you?"

As with all gossip-column material, there were condescending barbs, patronising turns of phrase, and the usual assumption of sophistication and cultural superiority in the writers. The edges grew harder and sharper with the passing of the years, but there was nothing here that went beyond what any public figure in any field might suffer at the hands of the press.

Clarissa said, "That's a jolly good name for it, actually. A Hate Book. Being a rough diamond, he has rather been put down by people right from the beginning, and it's sort of eaten into him, you see. This is only just a selection of stuff, of course."

Sam Solon. A man with a worm in his gut. Modesty sat back against her bound arms, eyes gazing through Clarissa, trying to assess the man, to understand his pattern of reaction so that she might anticipate his moves. Willie, too, had stopped reading and was gazing speculatively into space.

It was then that Clarissa closed the book and said, "All right, Condori. Take them in."

Now, standing before Solon, her face stinging from the blow of his rough hand, Modesty looked for the light of

265

obsession in his eyes and found nothing. She knew then that the worm that ate into him was not in his gut but in his soul, and so well hidden as to be indetectable.

The face beneath the curly grey hair creased in a sudden malicious grin as he said, "They all do it, even the blokes who write in my own papers. You just have to read between the lines. Ignorant bloody Aussie, wouldn't know the Mona Lisa from the Chinese Girl, or Mark Twain from Micky Spillane. That's the image. But you know something? My old man came from Greece. Right? I got three thousand years of culture in my blood. My people were building the Parthenon when you poms were running round in woad and the only folk in Australia were abo's." A vein in his neck was pulsing visibly. "And there's something else. Greek blood doesn't forget. You stick two fingers up to a Greek, and he'll wait twenty years to kick your arse off. But me, I'm waiting more than twenty. I'm waiting till I'm dead or dying. Then they'll eat their bloody words all right. Them and you and all your kind."

He turned, jerking his head at Condori. "Okay, bring 'em along."

Condori gestured with his gun, and they moved after Solon. At the end of a long passage was a spacious lift, big enough to carry a dozen. They were made to stand facing the door. Behind them stood Condori and the Reverend Uriah Crisp. A window was set in the door, a vertical oblong. As the lift sank down, Modesty saw steel mesh outer gates at ground level, but the lift continued to descend. Another mesh door, and a glimpse of generators, a muted sound of humming, then down again for perhaps fifty or sixty feet before the lift came gently to a halt. The inner doors slid open, then the mesh doors beyond. They were in a large square room with walls and ceiling of textured plaster. To their left the light was bright.

Sam Solon led the way. As they passed out of the square room and into the great hall which lay beyond they saw that the brightness was not artificial. Daylight poured through a series of great arched windows along one side of the hall, and beyond the windows lay the sea, a hundred feet below. The hall was lofty and had been excavated from solid rock so that the windows looked out from half-way up the cliff face. Whatever great steel beams or ties held the roof were invisible behind a Venetian ceiling from which hung two great seventeenth-century Bohemian crystal chandeliers. The walls were panelled in light oak, with Greek Doric half-columns at intervals. The marble floor was divided into sections by heavy silk ropes looped between ornamental posts, but all sections were to some extent visible from the entrance, since the wall opposite the tall windows was gently concave. At the far end, on a high tapering dais, was the Jade Queen.

Sam Solon said, "No secret about me owning Dragon's Claw. I bought it from the government fifteen years back, then hired labour from Taiwan to fix it up the way I wanted." He picked up something from a Corradini table. "Right. I got the latest catalogue here. It gives the usual run-down on every item, but then we go on to say where it was stolen from, the date and time, the method, everything. You'll figure in the next printing, when we put the Jade Queen in." He chuckled suddenly, and his eyes shone with puckish glee. "Just wait till I kick off and leave Dragon's Claw to the nation. They'll have plenty to say about Sam Solon then, all over the world, but they won't bloody well patronise him any more!" He opened a beautifully printed booklet with a silver and gold cover. "Right. This is the guided tour."

The picture section held seventeen paintings, many of them easily identifiable without Solon's commentary. A Parmigianino, two Stubbs, and two Picassos, a van Gogh, a

Brueghel, and a Raphael. There was also one which rang a bell for Modesty as a possible Flauve Vlaminck, and a group of five Russian modernist paintings among which she recognised a Chagall and a Kandinsky.

Beyond the pictures a dozen small animal figures in jade were set out below a Qajar portrait from Persia and a group of Cosway miniatures. In another section a collection of Fabergé was displayed on black velvet, a jewelled clock, a figure group, an imperial Easter egg, and a spray of flowers in enamelled gold with diamonds, rubies, and emeralds. Elsewhere a carved red-lacquer chair stood beside a seventeenth-century cabinet decorated with marquetry of pewter and tortoise shell on a palisander ground. Beyond, the oriental theme recurred with an early Chou bronze, a Honan ribbed black-glazed jar, and a Ch'ang-an silver stem cup with acanthus scroll motifs, all backed by a huge Gobelin tapestry; and in another section stood a monumental Louis XIV long-case clock backed by a Kashan carpet from the Shah Abbas group.

It was a breath-taking collection, and priceless, yet still it was a hotch-potch, a magpie assortment selected by a man with neither style nor taste. For over an hour the two prisoners moved slowly round with Sam Solon as he read every word about every item, both the cultural and the criminal provenance set down in the catalogue. He had begun briskly, but soon he was revelling in his treasures, crooning over them like a lover, inviting admiration of them, angry when it was not forthcoming. And throughout, Condori and the Reverend Uriah Crisp kept a precise distance from the two bound captives, the distance which made a surprise attack impossible but was close enough to ensure the accurate placing of a bullet.

Solon closed the catalogue at last and turned to look at Modesty and Willie. "And it goes on," he said triumphantly.

"That Beau, he's the best ever. Gets sort of cocky and needs chopping down to size, but that's natural with a bright kid. Him and his team, they just go out and get anything I tell 'em. So it goes on from here. Right? Jesus Christ, when they come along and find all this *and* the rest in maybe twenty, thirty years, they're going to know old Sam Solon was no roughneck after all. He was just taking the piss out of 'em all this time!"

Modesty looked at the Jade Queen. "But you have to show it all to somebody *now*," she said slowly. "That's often the problem for gloaters, Sam, for the people who maybe buy a stolen picture. They daren't show anybody, and that spoils it for them. But it's different for you, isn't it?"

He chuckled again. "No problem. Sure I have to show a few people, or there's no taste in it, but I do this whole thing big, and I fetch big people here to see what I've got. Art people, who understand what it all means."

"Like Robert Soames? And Maria Cavalli? And—"

"Like that. Dick Kingston had it right."

"So you killed him."

Solon glanced at the Reverend Uriah Crisp, a twinkle in his eyes. "He was a sinner, girl."

"And the others, the people you bring here to see your treasures, you classify them as sinners, too?"

He shrugged. "What else? I'd have to be crazy to let them go back and talk. I did reckon we might try brain-washing, and that's where the Chinese head-shrinker came in. He spent quite a while putting a block on Luke Fletcher's memory, but then the silly bastard went walk-about, and it didn't quite hold. I'm not risking it again." He looked at his watch. "Time for lunch. Then we'll see you two off. Watching 'em go isn't my usual kick. I never stayed around for it before, because it always looked like being pretty bloody pathetic, especially with the women." He stared at her with distaste. "But I don't mind waiting around to see Uriah knock off a couple of stuck-up poms who fancy their chances."

*　　*　　*

Lunch was served in the dining room at half past one. Sam Solon sat at the head of the table in a reverie of release that was akin to sated gluttony or lust. Beauregard Browne carried most of the conversation, with a flow of malicious reminiscence about "the late and lamentable Fletcher's sojourn among us". This was designed to anger Modesty Blaise, and by a few small changes of expression she contrived to give the impression that he was succeeding.

Clarissa watched with a hint of anxiety, and said little. Uriah Crisp ate wolfishly and ignored everybody. Dr. Feng smiled placidly, fed Beauregard Browne a line or two when it seemed appropriate, and hoped his worry was not showing. He had come to the conclusion that there would be no more brain-washing experiments, and wondered about his future position in the Dragon's Claw set-up.

At three o'clock Sam Solon roused himself and said, "Let's get on with it."

Beauregard Browne sat up straight. "We hear and obey, old sport. Condori, you've got the Garvin knives and the Blaise thirty-two?"

"Yes, señor."

"Right. Call Fuzuli in and take them both down. Blaise to be judged first." He glanced at the Reverend Uriah Crisp. "If the Lord favours His faithful servant, Uriah, as He usually does, and Blaise falls, then you put the knives on Garvin for him to be judged. But keep him strapped till then, and on the sidelines. No more than five of your men to watch

270

the show—or shall we say, to witness the will of the Lord being done. That leaves eight, and they're to remain on duty until the event is over. We're short-handed, what with Garvin caving in Rocco's skull with that hunk of lead and three going missing overnight. What happened to them, Willie?"

Willie Garvin looked vaguely surprised. "Two of 'em lit a fag," he said. "Then they sort of fell in the sea. The other one was walking down the road on 'is own. Last I saw, he was under a bush a little way off the road. I expect he'll make 'is presence known in a day or two. You should lay in some Airwick."

Beauregard Browne glanced at Solon and said easily, "Oh, we're glad to have a weed-out of incompetents. But what did you hope to achieve, Willie?"

Willie looked about him, then leaned forward with a confiding air. "I'll tell you some other time," he said.

"Oh, please. Now."

Modesty said quietly, "I'll tell you. I'll tell you several things of interest, given a clear run."

Beauregard Browne looked down the table, received a nod from Solon, and said, "The floor is yours, my little treasure."

She sat back and looked slowly round, her gaze serene and untroubled. "What did Willie hope to achieve? That's easy. We're on your ground and up against your kind, so we're playing for keeps. Willie's reduced the odds by four, and that's a good start. Next point. Let nobody here imagine they can put their hands up, now or at any time, and expect to walk out of this. Some of you could well pass for crazy, but you're not. The turbulent priest there knows exactly what he's doing, and pretends to himself that he doesn't. He likes killing people with a gun, and the Hammer of God bit is pure phoney."

She looked at Beauregard Browne. "Then we come to Bubbles. A lot of earnest people these days believe that anyone who goes around doing evil things must be insane. But you're not insane, Bubbles. You know what you're doing, and you do it because you enjoy it, and it pays." Her eyes turned to the other end of the table. "No excuses, either, for our Euro-Aussie with the blood that never forgets. Your only problem, Solon, is that you've got a chip the size of the Sydney Opera House on your shoulder, and enough money to cosset it. Even to the extent of kidnapping people to feed your ego and killing them afterwards because they're inconvenient."

Sam Solon blinked like a lizard and stirred in his chair, but did not speak. She went on, "Clarissa's tied to Beauregard Browne, I'm not quite sure how, but it's probably a novice/adept connection. He initiated her into his bizarre pleasures and now she's an addict." She looked a query at the Chinese. "That wasn't very technical, I suppose? I'm sure you have a good psychiatric excuse for each one of them, doctor, but I like my reading best. As for yourself, I'd say you're one of those experts who'd happily put anyone's brains through a mincer to see the effect, providing you were being well paid."

She turned to look again at Beauregard Browne. "You said yesterday that Willie and I were aiming to mete out justice. You were sending us up, of course, but you were also wrong. We didn't come after you to mete out justice. We don't have that kind of arrogance. We don't have the stomach to give people like you what you deserve." She looked slowly round the table again. "We came to kill you, that's all."

With a leisurely movement she stood up and nodded towards the Reverend Uriah Crisp. "And if you've decided he's to be first, let's get started."

The gun had appeared in the priest's hand with her first

movement, and behind her there was a rustle of sound from Condori and the guard who had now joined him. Nobody spoke. The effrontery of her words had been stupefying, all the more so in that it was impossible to believe her confidence was forced. She stood relaxed, yet about her there hung an almost tangible aura of power.

Suddenly Beauregard Browne gave a high-pitched laugh of astonishment. "How to win friends and influence people! I rather think you've just let yourself in for a rather bad time, duckie. Isn't that so, Uriah? I mean, isn't it?"

Above the clerical collar the lean face was bone-white with rage, the red-rimmed eyes flaring. "Whore!" breathed the Reverend Uriah Crisp in a terrible whisper. "I will show unto you the judgment! And it shall be slow as the grinding of the mills of God!"

*   *   *

She stood in the middle of Execution Square, an empty holster hanging at her thigh. Behind her lay the narrow road which wound down to the harbour. To her right the square was bounded by a path of coarse grass where four guards stood with Willie Garvin, his arms strapped behind him. Beyond the strip of grass was the excavation for a sunken garden Beauregard Browne planned to establish there. Before her the green hill sloped away, gently at first, then rising more sharply to the white house. There were four figures on the long balcony, one of them a little apart from the rest. That would be Solon. She caught a glint of sun on glass beneath bright gold hair, and saw that Beauregard Browne was using field glasses to watch.

When she turned her head she saw Condori standing behind her and to her left, four paces away, his hand resting on the walnut grips of the Star PD at his hip, watching her. Over his left shoulder hung the slender leather harness with twin sheaths bearing Willie Garvin's knives. Behind and to her right, on the verge of the road, was a motorcycle with a long trailer attached. A guard sat hitched on the end of the trailer. Condori had addressed him as Regan, and she knew that it was his task to take the bodies away after the execution.

Of the guards in charge of Willie, all wore revolvers and two carried M-10's slung. They were of mixed nationalities, using corrupt English as their lingua franca. The Reverend Uriah Crisp's angry intentions had travelled the grapevine, and one of the men was laying bets on how long it would take her to die. Against the chance that it would take more than an hour he was offering short odds of only two-to-one on.

Every detail of the scene, in the round, was imprinted on her mind now, and she was relaxing, breathing deeply but without effort, watching the flights of steps which zig-zagged up the hill, estimating distances and calculating times. Condori spoke, and one of the men with Willie came forward carrying her Colt .32. Holding it up in front of her he swung the cylinder out, inserted a cartridge in the chamber which would be next to come under the hammer, displayed the cylinder to her, clicked it back in position, then moved to her side and slid the revolver into her holster before turning to walk back to the grassy path.

Something moved, high on the hill, and the guards fell suddenly silent as the spidery black figure of the Reverend Uriah Crisp began his descent of the first flight of steps below *Dragon's Heart*. The brim of the flat round hat shadowed his face. The Prayer Book, invisible at this distance, was held out in his extended left hand. In a high-pitched voice he began to cry his clamorous diatribe against sinners. Willie Garvin set his eyes to register the scene, then emptied his mind and be-

274

came totally still, withdrawing his inward self from the group about him so that they might cease to be aware of him.

He did not know what Modesty would do during the next minute, and wasted no energy on speculation. She could have made no fixed plan herself until the scene was set and every detail of the situation known, but he knew her resource and her power to improvise. And when the break came, he knew precisely what she expected him to do, for it was inherent in the situation.

Slowly the chanting of the wild-eyed priest grew louder as he made his way down the steps. "*I will shew unto thee judgment of the great whore, for she is as Babylon the great, the mother of harlots and abomination of the earth.*"

Seventy paces away now.

"*The smoke of her torment shall ascend up for ever and ever; she shall have no rest day or night ...*"

The voice brayed on. When he was starting down one of the oblique flights of steps a full fifty paces from the square, Modesty turned her head unhurriedly as if to speak to Condori, then her body followed, swivelling, and the Colt was in her hand, speaking, and Condori was beginning to topple, his own gun half lifted, as her bullet pierced his heart and she lunged towards him, dropping the .32.

In that instant Willie Garvin swung his right leg high in a scything kick to the larynx of the big Cuban on his left. The man was dying even as he fell back over the eight foot drop into the sunken garden area, and the other three guards had barely begun to react. Willie glimpsed her as he spun to kick at the guard on his right. She had reached Condori before he hit the ground, catching the Star PD .45 as it fell from his hand, turning, still crouched, to fire under her left arm at Regan, by the motorcycle trailer. The shock of the heavy bullet brought a reaction from his nervous system which made it seem that he had been hurled back across the trailer by a hammerblow, limbs flung wide like a puppet with cut strings.

Willie's kick had missed the death-point he aimed for, but took the second man high on the chest and knocked him back over the drop. The third guard, out of Willie's range, was snatching for his gun when the Star .45 barked a second time. The man dropped with a shattered head, and as Willie turned the last man leapt down in panic to find shelter below. No more than three seconds had passed since she used the single cartridge in her Colt to kill Condori. Willie ran forward a few paces, then dropped to one knee and froze to avoid distracting her. He had registered the sound of one shot from the priest's pistol, then had come a second, almost coinciding with the shot from Modesty which had dropped the third of the guards. But she was untouched.

A surge of exultance swept Willie Garvin as he glanced up the hill. The Reverend Uriah Crisp had dropped his Prayer Book and his hat had fallen off, presumably as he ran down the diagonal flight of steps he had been descending when she made her astonishing move. He must have realised that he could not fire on the run with any chance of hitting her, could not even keep her in sight while moving fast down the steps, and he had halted to fire half-way down the flight, at a range of a little over forty yards.

And this was still too much for him. She had assessed him dead right, thought Willie. In the cowboy demonstration he had displayed his skills—all of them. And they did not include accuracy at long range with a handgun. He was, in Hollywood terms, a fast gun; superfast, perhaps. But accurate only in a confrontation at ten yards maximum. Now he was shrieking as he aimed the Colt Commander one-handed. *"Blasphemer! Mocker of God! You commit sacrilege! Die, daughter of Satan! Die!"*

Modesty stood with legs apart, knees a little bent, the Star gripped in both hands. She had taken one precious second to adjust the backsight before dropping into the Weaver stance and taking aim. A third shot from the hill passed fifteen inches to her right as she squeezed the trigger.

The Reverend Uriah Crisp dropped bonelessly when the bullet ripped through his chest. Limbs jerking, he rolled down three steps before coming to a halt. He still clutched the gun, and his head was lifted as if trying to sight her when she fired again. His body shuddered to the shock, then he was still.

Seven seconds of action.

By the time Willie reached her she had scooped the harness from the body of Condori and was sliding one of the knives from its graphite-lubricated sheath to slash the strap binding his arms. He took the knife and harness from her and ran on across the narrow road. She moved to the motorcycle and straddled it, never taking her eyes from the path which edged the sunken garden.

Willie Garvin crouched, reaching down into one of the crevices in the volcanic rock beside the road. He stood up with the Goff laser-sight rifle he had cached there some twelve hours ago. Even as he cocked it and swung to look up the hill towards the white house there came a shrill cry which carried clearly from the long balcony. *"Down! Everyone down!"*

The distant half-figures vanished below the balustrade before he could bring the weapon to bear. He grimaced, and trotted across to push Regan's body off the trailer with his foot and mount it himself. Modesty thumbed on the safety-catch of her gun, rammed it into the holster she still wore, and kicked the engine to life. There was one man, possibly two, capable of action in the sunken garden, but Willie was watching for them now.

Even as the motorcycle began to move, she saw from the corner of her eye a figure in drab green come into view, holding an M-10, backing warily across the excavation to gain a line of sight over the lip of the path. The man was raising his submachine-gun when the red dot of the laser rested for an instant on his chest before vanishing as the bullet drilled into that precise spot. Next moment the motorcycle and trailer were accelerating away down the winding road which led to the harbour.

On the balcony of the white house, Beauregard Browne rose to one knee and peered over the balustrade. He was breathing with a faint whinnying sound, his face shone with sweat, and the pupils of the violet eyes had shrunk to tiny black specks. "Get inside!" he said in a voice that cracked, and lunged for the open window. By the time Sam Solon, Clarissa, and Dr. Feng had followed him he was at the telephone.

Solon's teeth were bared, and a mottling of small veins showed on his cheeks as he swore foully and said, "You blew it to hell and gone, Beau! Garvin could've *killed* me with that laser thing!"

"Or any of us. If *I* hadn't spotted it in time and got everybody down." Beauregard Browne's tone was vicious, and he rattled the cradle of the phone angrily.

"It must have been a sort of dummy rifle we saw him throw into the sea this morning," Clarissa said numbly. "But ... but that means they had it all planned."

"Rubbish!" Beauregard Browne was pulling himself together with a huge effort. "Don't talk like a silly bitch, poppet. They're extremely smart and they've been extremely lucky, but let's not get awestruck—" He broke off to speak into the phone. "Cooper? Listen. I want the harbour post and the airstrip post in that order. And *hurry*!"

Two minutes later Modesty brought the motorcycle to a halt between low rock walls where the road debouched on to the harbour approach. Willie dropped from the trailer, moved forward, and peered warily round the rough corner of the wall, jerking back a second or two later as a spray of bullets chipped the rock above his head. He padded back to Modesty, frowning a little. "No chance of reaching the boats, Princess. They're firing from good cover. Looks like Bubbles wasn't too shaken to think straight."

"We'll have to play it the other way, then."

In the big living room of *Dragon's Heart* there was an ugly tension in the air. Sam Solon stood with hands in pockets, jaws moving as he champed a piece of gum, eyes on Beauregard Browne, who now lounged at one end of the settee with the phone to his ear. Clarissa sat at the other end, hands clasped between her thighs, trying to subdue the urgency roused in her by the enormous excitement of the last few minutes. Dr. Feng stood a little to one side of the window, looking out. He could see the body of the Reverend Uriah Crisp lying where it had fallen. Four guards had died last night, Dr. Feng was thinking, and in Execution Square there were now five more probably dead. He had seen only one man emerge from the sunken garden, and that one clearly had injuries to shoulder and leg, sustained when Willie Garvin had kicked him over the edge of the excavation. Dr. Feng was not moved by sympathy for the dead and injured, but he was moved deeply by the realisation that in less than twenty-four hours the two prisoners had somehow destroyed not only the paranoid killer-priest but also the formidable Condori and half the strength of the guards on Dragon's Claw.

Beauregard Browne said into the phone: "Yes? All right, I know they tried the harbour and had to turn back, but I want to know where they went then, sweetie-pie. What? Ah, well I'm very *glad* you're just coming to that, Cooper. Say on, my informative Oklahoman."

He listened for several seconds, then: "The chair-lift? They must be mad. Have you—? Yes. Good."

He put down the phone and smiled brightly at Sam Solon. "When they couldn't get to a boat, they didn't try for the Teal amphibian, as we thought they might. The dusky Li Gomm spotted them starting up on the chair-lift for Paradise Peak. He was guarding the radio hut, and phoned Cooper, who sent three men speeding off in a jeep to stop the machinery. He said they'd have ample time, so when we arrive on the spot we should find Blaise and Garvin suspended 'twixt heaven and earth as sitting ducks."

Clarissa looked up. "Except they have that beastly rifle, Beau," she said diffidently.

*　　*　　*

They were half-way to the top, kneeling in a twin chair to face downhill, when the jeep appeared below. Bracing himself with an elbow on Modesty's shoulder, Willie placed the red dot of the laser on the chest of the driver two hundred yards away, and squeezed off a single shot. The jeep swerved and cannoned into the rough rock at the side of the road, where it stalled. Two men jumped down. One flung himself flat behind the low ridge bordering the road, the other began to run, crouching, towards the chair-lift cabin. Willie picked him off when he was twenty paces from his goal, then swung the rifle back to the man who had taken cover.

Modesty said, "He hasn't moved. I fancy he won't try getting to the machinery, and he's even thinking hard about whether he can risk showing an eye to fire a burst at us."

280

"I don't blame 'im," Willie said soberly, and ran a hand gently down the butt of the Goff. "This gun's enough to make a marksman sick, but it isn't 'alf impressive. Nobody's going to take liberties with it."

Five minutes later the Land-Rover driven by Beauregard Browne was halted short of the chair-lift cabin by Tan Sin. The Malayan had crawled a hundred yards down the road on his belly, hugging the ridge for cover, till a low bluff jutting into the curve of the road gave him protection.

Sam Solon, in the passenger seat, looked at the man's sweating face and said, "What happened?"

"They on chai'-lif' when we come, boss. *Bang!* They shoot Riza dead an' the jeep crash. We jumpin' out an' Orozco he run to stop the motor for chai'-lif' an' *bang!* He is dead too. Then I go on belly to come away. That gun, you show one finger they shoot him off!"

Solon hawked and spat. "Christ, so they just knocked off another two. You have everyone stay out of sight till we've had time to think, Beau."

Beauregard Browne said, "Have they reached the top, Tan Sin?"

"I t'ing so, boss. I hear motor stop jus' when you coming."

Clarissa, in the back seat, said hesitantly, "At least they're bottled up now, Mr. Solon. I mean, it won't take long to get the chair-lift covered so they can't come down, and there's no other way off the peak. Well, I suppose it's possible to climb down on this side, but not in the dark, and by day it would take ages anyway, I mean, like two or three hours, so we'd have lots of time to shoot them."

"How about the cliff side?"

Beauregard Browne leaned on the steering wheel and said curtly, "No chance. Those cliffs drop nearly a thousand feet into the sea, and they're not just sheer, they lean out. Nobody's going to come down there after dark, not even with boots, ropes, and pitons. You'd have to be crazy to try it any time."

Solon said, "Just the same. Get a man around there in a small boat. He can sit out of range and watch till sundown."

"We're getting a teeny bit short of men, dear old sport," said Beauregard Browne, "but it shall be done. The problem then reduces itself to how we get at that bitch and her tame gorilla without making a siege of it. I must give thought to that one."

"No problem. I've got some military stuff tucked away illegally in a warehouse in Sydney. Got it from the same dealer who supplied the M-10's."

Beauregard Browne ran a well-manicured thumbnail along his teeth and eyed the Australian warily. "What sort of military stuff, sport?"

"Like hand grenade sort of stuff. Explosive grenades and white phosphorous incendiaries. They fry you worse than napalm. I'll get a cipher off to Charlie in Sydney and he'll send out the stuff in the Gulfstream. We'll have it first thing in the morning, and we use the Teal for dropping it."

The long lashes fluttered and the violet eyes widened in shock. "But my dear old Revered Patron, you simply can't *destroy* Paradise Peak. I have my orchids up there."

Sam Solon raised a thick, work-worn finger an inch or two from Beauregard Browne's face. "You listen to me, son. We got a pair of tigers by the tail. I'm not blaming you any more than me. I brought 'em here. But now I'm telling you it's top priority to wipe them bastards out, and if we lose your bloody daffodils while we're doing it, that's too bad. Right? We made a mistake with Blaise and Garvin. Oh sure, we licked 'em all along the line while they didn't know who and what they were up against, so we got cocky. But now the deck's face up, and that's different. Starting from no chance at all, by Christ they're beating *us*. Right? So you forget the fancy stuff, Beau. You play this straight and hard to a finish, and bugger your daffodils, or you're out. Right?"

Beauregard Browne smiled. It was a very bright smile, almost feverish. "You couldn't have put it any plainer, old sport. And if we're going to put first things first, let's rig some sort of shield to get two men into the chair-lift cabin so they can watch this side of the peak. Then we'll send for your grenades etcetera."

"Now you got it."

Beauregard Browne nodded and began to turn the Land-Rover in the narrow road. As he did so, Clarissa saw the look which flared briefly in his eyes. She knew then that only by a very small margin had Sam Solon escaped the soft grip of the silken *rumal*, the sudden wrench that snapped the neck. She knew, too, that Beau had managed to check himself only because the guards were basically Solon's men, chosen by him and paid by him, and it would be madness to have civil war on Dragon's Claw while Modesty Blaise and Willie Garvin still lived.

14

Willie Garvin sat on a bench in the chair-lift cabin, looking down and across the valley through the small hole he had cut in the timbers. Two hours before, when Modesty was on watch here, she had seen a jeep, shielded by a teak door lashed in front of it, creep slowly up to the lower end of the chair-lift and deliver one or perhaps two men to the cabin there. They had been very careful not to expose any part of themselves to the accuracy of the Goff rifle. An hour later the Teal had made two passes over the peak at a safe height, beyond the range of the rifle. Since then all had been quiet.

Willie turned his head and glanced through the window at the sky. In half an hour it would be dusk. Whatever Solon and Beauregard Browne were planning, there would be no immediate assault on Paradise Peak. The machinery of the chair-lift was jammed with a crowbar, and there was not enough daylight left for Sam Solon's men to cross the valley and make a two-hour cliff climb, even if they could be driven to such a suicidal attack.

Keeping low, Willie moved out of the door at the rear of the cabin and on through the short pass which led out into the wide basin of Paradise Peak. He had spent an hour here earlier, while Modesty kept watch. During that time, after filling one or two containers with water against the chance that it would be cut off from below, he had prowled about the peak, examining the small chalet, the glass-houses, and the prefabricated structure which proved to be a combination of boiler house, workshop, and store room. The peak was supplied with electricity, and Willie surmised that this might not be cut off, since it was used for the heating system, and Beauregard Browne's little friends, the orchids, were presumably dependent on this for their lives. He was still glad to find a Tilley lamp and a supply of paraffin in the workshop.

He had spent some time moving about the peak, noting the terrain and studying the cliff face which dropped to the sea far below. Finally he had rejoined Modesty in the chair-lift cabin and taken over while she made her own study of the situation.

Now, as he came out on to the peak again, he saw her lying prone with her head over the cliff edge. He moved to a grassy spot ten paces from the edge, put the rifle down carefully, then extended himself on his back and closed his eyes. When he woke refreshed from a cat-nap ten minutes later she was lying on her back beside him, chewing a piece of grass.

She heard him stir, and reached out to rest a hand on his arm. "Better than this time yesterday, Willie love."

"Lot better." He yawned and stretched. "That was a lovely smooth stroke you pulled, down in the square."

"High time I made some contribution. And you were right about the Star forty-five, Willie. When you hit them with that, they stay hit." She paused. "Do you know who flies the Teal?"

"Bubbles." He grinned at the sky. "Bubbles. I liked that, Princess, it narked 'im no end. Yes, he flies the Teal. I got that out of Clarissa last night during a short break."

She half smiled. "Last night? It seems longer ago than that. How did you get those three guards?"

"With sling-shot. I'd already made the sling from the underside of a leather armchair cushion in the cell, and I used big steel bearings from the boat store for shot. Real skull-crackers, they are." He spoke roughly, as if touched by anger.

She said, "You were right to whittle them down while the chance was there."

"Oh, I'm not bleeding for 'em, Princess. I was just remembering the way they laid bets on 'ow long it'd take you to die from being gut-shot by that parson."

"They're not nice people." She rolled over and lay propped on her elbows, frowning. "I wish we could get down from here, Willie."

"Me too. I don't like relying on that message to Aussie Security. Even if it gets to this bloke Larry Houston, there's no guarantee 'ow fast he'll move."

"Tarrant said he's a good man, but it's a message that's going to sound pretty weird."

"Funny thing, Princess. When I'd finished, I gave the frequency their radio was set to before I changed it, the frequency they transmit on from 'ere. But I don't know why I did it."

After a little thought she said, "I'm glad you did, but I don't know why, either."

"Ah, well." He rubbed his bristly chin with distaste. "Just before I dozed off I asked meself what they'll try next, and my 'orrible little mind came up with the notion that they've got plenty of fuel. Petrol, oil, paraffin. So it wouldn't be too difficult to rig up a few fire bombs to drop on us. If the Teal came in fast from the landward side, 'opping over the ridge, it'd be 'ere and gone before we could get a shot at it, and we've only got what's in the magazine anyway." He looked about him. "If I was in their shoes I could turn this 'ole place into a bonfire without much trouble. There's tar and paint in the boat store. You could rig up some giant molotov cocktails—"

"I doubt if they have your gift for improvisation, Willie. All the same, some sort of air attack is a possibility. They could easily bring stuff in for it." She glanced up at the sky. "If they send messages they'll be in cipher, but with any luck Aussie Security will be listening in, and they ought to crack it pretty fast. It's not likely to be a tough one, and these are computer days."

Willie lifted his head to look at her in surprise. "Hey, is that why I did it, then? Sent their transmission frequency, I mean, so Aussie Security might pick up a bit of confirmation?"

"It smacks of the infallible Garvin instinct to me."

He lay back, screwing up his eyes. "It might mean someone coming to 'ave a look at Dragon's Claw sooner or later, but it's not much 'elp at the moment. Pity we couldn't get to the 'arbour and work your first-choice caper, Princess. I don't relish sitting 'ere waiting for the cavalry to rescue us. 'Specially when it might not arrive in time."

She nodded, frowning. "And even if it does, we won't have signed off Browne and Solon, which is the main job." She blew the chewed blade of grass from her lips and looked about her. "I don't much like any of this fall-back plan, but it was the best I could come up with at the time."

Willie wagged his head sorrowfully. "You'll just 'ave to try 'arder, Princess." He got to his feet and moved to kneel at the cliff edge, studying the face. Something caught his eye, and he saw the motor sailer hove to a mile off-shore.

Behind him Modesty said, "There's no climbing down that way, Willie, even if you could fix us up with makeshift pitons. But could we get down the other side on one of the cables after dark? I mean, rig a sling and slide down from chair to chair."

He shook his head, and they both moved back out of sight of the boat. "I was thinking about that while I was on watch,

Princess, but you couldn't do it without getting movement on the cable. The guards in the 'ut below are bound to twig, then we're sitting targets."

She stood holding her elbows, staring down at the ground. "You didn't find anything to help while you were looking around earlier?"

"Like what, Princess?"

She shrugged and pulled a face. "I don't know. Go and check the valley, Willie. I'll have another prowl around before it gets dark."

"Sure."

There was no movement to be seen from the chair-lift cabin. Willie estimated that Beauregard Browne had somewhere between six and ten men left, ignoring the three Indonesian house staff who were probably non-combatant. There was one guard in the look-out boat, one or two in the lower chair-lift cabin, and there would be one on radio duty. There was also a lot of clearing up to be done by any spare hands, for morale would not be uplifted by leaving bodies around. The opposition would strike tomorrow, Willie decided. Whichever way they chose, it would be tomorrow.

When he returned to the peak Modesty called to him from the small chalet. She had found some provisions in the kitchen and made two mugs of coffee. For a while they sat in silence on the step, sipping the hot liquid, then she said, "I know this won't work, but it's a thought-starter."

"Go on, Princess."

"Well, there are some big sheets of polythene in the store here, the sort that's sometimes used for glass-houses instead of ordinary glazing. There's also quite a lot of flex and cable. Is there any way we could rig a couple of parachutes? If we can get down safely to the sea we shouldn't have too much trouble swimming round to a place where we can get ashore.

And God knows the polythene's tough enough. I always have to use my teeth even to open a packet of peanuts."

Willie shook his head slowly. "You need shape for a parachute. And besides—"

"Could we cut out panels to get the shape? There's one of those gadgets that heat-seal polythene, and they've left the electricity on."

"There's no way it could work, Princess, and a dozen reason's why it wouldn't. You've got to attach the lines some'ow, and I doubt if we'd even get as far as that. Then there's the jump. I know the cliff's got a bit of an overhang, but you'd 'ave to jump with the 'chute bundled up in your arms, and you'd most likely get throttled by one of the lines. If not, you'd be into the cliff face as soon as the 'chute started to open."

She looked out into the dusk. "No way at all?"

"Sorry, Princess."

She nodded. "That's the second lousy idea I've had this evening. Let's see if I can make it three—" She broke off as she felt him freeze suddenly beside her. For a moment she thought he had seen or heard some sign of danger, and she was reaching for the Star .45 when he said softly, "Polythene. I could rig a wing."

"What?"

"When they first started experimenting with hang-gliders they used polythene for the wings. If we could put together a wing big enough to carry both of us, and if it worked all right, we could land pretty well anywhere on the island."

"A wing?" She peered through the gathering darkness towards the sun awning. "Is there enough bamboo there to make a frame?"

"I didn't think of the bamboo." He considered for a moment, then shook his head. "We'll need two-forty square feet of wing area for the two of us, and there's not nearly enough bamboo for that. But those glass-'ouses 'ave got a framework of angle-metal. Some sort of light alloy. Won't be as strong as the usual alloy tube, but—no, 'old on! We can rivet two lengths together for each member, and make square tube instead of round."

She laughed, excitement bubbling within her. "Can you really do it, Willie?"

"I don't see why not. She's only got to fly once, and that's a big 'elp. I checked the workshop earlier, and there's more tools than I'll ever need. I can 'acksaw the cross-members of the framework off, and drill 'oles for joining. I don't remember seeing any nuts and bolts, but there's one or two thin rods of mild steel, so we can cut bits off to use as cold rivets." He sipped from his mug, eyes half closed as he visualised the stages of the work. "Main thing is to keep it nice and simple, so we'll go for a delta wing. Square tube for the frame, and there's plenty of wire around for the rigging. Won't need a kingpost and top rigging anyway, not for a once-only job. Won't need a harness or seat, either. I can make a control frame big enough for us to stand in, say a six foot base, and we operate it with body movement. No problem."

She sat listening, sensing the exhilaration that sparkled within him, feeling it flare within herself. Today, for the first time, the first time since that moment when she had dragged Luke Fletcher from the sea, they had clawed the initiative from the opposition, and it was as if they had suddenly emerged from sour-smelling confinement into fresh air.

It was odd, she thought, how Willie Garvin held the fixed belief that when it came to improvising with externals she was supreme; in fact this was one of his own fields of excellence, and she regarded him as having no equal in it. Alone, he would have devised the idea without prompting. Together, he tended to rely on her, and therefore needed to be prodded with suggestions, no matter how unworkable.

He was still shaping the idea aloud, anticipating problems, finding the answer. "We can heat-seal the polythene, double thickness, like a big envelope covering the frame. Sharp edges, though. But we'll cut strips from the bedding in the back room 'ere, and bind any nasty corners. You could be cutting some rivets while I sort out the members for the frame ..."

When he had finished she drained her mug of coffee and said, "It's a long way down, Willie. What are our chances?"

He turned to look at her and she saw his grin in the gloom. "That's the beauty of it, Princess. We don't 'ave to find out the 'ard way." He pointed to the far rim of the ridge which embraced the hollow of Paradise Peak. "That's a good slope for a take-off. We can do a nice little twenty-yard run and get a seventy-yard glide to the other side."

"A practice flight? We're being spoiled."

"About time. And if she flies, that's it. She flies."

*   *   *

In the white house, soon after midnight, Clarissa de Courtney-Scott said, "I'm sure it's going to be all right, Beau. You were marvellous this evening." She was entwined with Beauregard Browne on his big bed in the soft pink light from a bedside lamp. He was passive, lost in his own thoughts, and for once she was not urgent in her needs.

"I know it was beastly, losing Uriah and Condori and lots of the guards, and I thought Solon was absolutely rotten to you, but you really jollied him round marvellously this

291

evening." She moved slowly, voluptuously about him as she spoke. "You were so enthusiastic, talking about how we'd really get everything together once we'd settled Blaise and Garvin, and about it being time for recruiting fresh blood to the guards, and then telling Solon to pick any three pictures or objets d'art in the world and you'd guarantee to have them for him within a year. It was all so forward looking and up-beat, you fairly swept Solon off his feet in the end. He'd completely lost that sour look."

Beauregard Browne roused himself to take her by the nape of the neck and shake her gently. "Yes, poppet. But I note that Our Esteemed Patron didn't require your services tonight. I rather think he's dissembling slightly, and doesn't trust us."

"Well, that's not very nice. Ohhh ... I mean, what *he* did wasn't very nice, not what you're doing. That's lovely."

"But his mistrust is justified, Clarissa, my angel. Because I rather think the time has come for us to stop being unselfish. I feel we may have to ride on into the future and start a new life, you and I. After settling everything here first, of course."

"Golly. Everything?"

"Perhaps. We'll see what the morrow brings. Ah, now that's very ingenious of you."

"Is it? Good. Beau, we really will finish those two up on the peak tomorrow, won't we? I'm ... well, I'm just a tiny bit jumpy about them."

"And rightly, my luscious nibbler. They're devastatingly good. But tomorrow we shall cremate them. They're bottled on Paradise Peak, and there's no way down except by the cables or climbing down into the valley. We have every available man on watch there, and two spotlights from the yacht to scan the cliff below the upper chair-lift cabin at random intervals." His teeth showed in the soft pink light.

"And our people won't go to sleep on the job. They've seen half their colleagues wiped out, plus Condori and the Hammer of God himself. And that sort of thing tends to concentrate the mind wonderfully, doesn't it? I mean, doesn't it?"

She laughed deep in her throat, and relaxed. "Good old Beau. You always bring us out ahead in the end. You always have. I bet you'll think up something pretty good for us when we move on. I'm dreadfully sorry about your orchids, though. I really am."

"Thank you, treasure. But no more chatter now from that adorable and capable mouth. You have better things to do."

*   *   *

At two hours after midnight, on Paradise Peak, the sailwing rested on the grass outside the workshop, in the light which shone through the wide-open doors. Modesty had just returned from the chalet, and they stood surveying the wing as they sipped fresh hot coffee. Willie was stripped to the waist, and sweat glinted on his body. He had measured and cut the main spar, keel, and leading edge booms with infinite care. Then had come the task of drilling, riveting, fixing braces, and rigging wires, with Modesty acting as his second pair of hands.

She was almost telepathic, Willie thought, always knowing what you wanted next. Strange how she had laid all credit for the idea on him, smiling and punching him gently on the shoulder as they moved to begin work. Yet it was basically her conception, born through him under the thrust of her relentless quest for an answer.

When the frame was complete she had bound any sharp corners and edges with strips of sheet, and while she did so he had cut out the polythene for the wing, two matching shapes which had been positioned to envelope the frame and then heat-sealed round the edges.

She said, "What do you think, Willie?"

"I'm pretty confident, Princess. The frame's a bit 'eavier than tube alloy, but there's only a few pounds in it, and I've compensated with a bigger wing area." He turned his cheek to the gentle breeze. "It's a decent night with not too much wind, and that's blowing in nice an' steady off the sea, so we're lucky there. I reckon we ought to get a glide ratio of about four point five at eighteen knots, and that'll take us well over a thousand yards."

"It should get us round the corner and almost as far as the harbour, surely?"

"About that."

"Let's try it for size."

"Right."

Five minutes later, with the big A-frame held in front of them, the wing spread above, they began a steady trot down the grassy slope from half-way up the ridge. Lift-off came after a few paces. They hitched themselves in unison on to the horizontal bar, standing with outer hands gripping the sides of the triangle, inner arms across each other's back, trying to hold the wing in a shallow glide. It veered, dipped, and they touched down, running, struggling to hold the wing so that the frame would not strike the ground.

A little breathlessly, Modesty said, "Is she out of balance?"

"I don't think so, Princess. I reckon it was weight distribution. I need to stand with the outside foot a few inches in, instead of right in the corner."

"Let's try it that way."

The second attempt was more stable. After it, Willie shifted the strip of rag he had tied to the base bar as a marker, moving it another two inches away from the corner of the triangle. They carried the wing up the slope for a third take-off, and this time it glided under good control for over seventy yards to a smooth touch-down. Carefully they set the wing on the ground and looked at each other.

"That's about it, Princess."

"All right. We'll go in five minutes." She hooked an arm round his neck, pulled his head down a little, and pressed her cheek hard against his for a moment. "I'll be glad to forget this caper, Willie love. All of it except for this particular bit —at least there's some real satisfaction in that. After all the rest of this bloody mess, I'm looking forward to flying off those cliffs with you. Win or lose."

She turned and went into the light of the workshop to wrap up the Goff rifle and tie the Star .45 securely in the holster. Willie strapped his knife harness in position so that the Gerber Armorhide hafts protruding from the sheaths lay in echelon across his left breast. He put on his shirt, then made his way out through the pass to the chair-lift. There he removed the crowbar set to jam the machinery, and pressed the button which set the motor working below. With a squeaking and groaning the thick steel cable began to pass round the great wheel, carrying the chairs.

Willie Garvin grinned, imagining the alarm and specula-tion going on below. Certainly all attention would be focused there in the valley for a while. It had been Modesty's idea, and he liked it.

She was waiting for him when he returned, the rifle now wrapped watertight in polythene and slung across her back. Together they carried the glider to the top of the ridge and prepared for take-off. The breeze was a little stronger now, and they had chosen a different position on the perimeter to give them a heading straight out over the cliff. The moon was thin, and they could not see the cliff edge from where they stood.

"All set, Princess?"

"Ready."

Holding the big control frame, they began to run down the slope. The wing lifted them and they stepped up on to the A-frame base, hanging ten feet in the air, then twenty, thirty, as the ground fell away, losing a fraction of that height across the level ground, and sailing on and out over the edge, with the black sea ruffling the base of the cliffs with white lace far, far below. The wing dived a little sharply, but not unexpectedly, as it struck the colder air over the sea. They eased the control frame forward, levelling out, then leaned gently to one side to put the port wing-tip down, aiming for the long curving glide which would bring them round the headland and on a course for the low ridge which formed the eastern jaw of the harbour.

The wind sighed past their ears, rippling the wing above them to make a steady rustling sound. A monstrous bird, the glider slid easily through the air, two hundred yards out from the descending line of the cliff. Like brandy in the stomach, happiness warmed her as she stood beside Willie Garvin in the slender metal frame and they rode the blue darkness of the night together, high above the sea.

"She's a beauty, Willie." Her voice was a whisper. "A real beauty."

"She's very well be'aved. This is the life, eh?"

For perhaps sixty seconds they were in another world, revelling in a simple gladness compounded of many strands; relief, pure sensation, the exhilaration of unpowered flight, the brief freedom from having to do anything but fly, and the honeyed pleasure of achievement.

Then Willie gave a faint sigh and murmured, "We've got a nice high glide ratio, Princess. I reckon we could make it to be'ind that rise near the chair-lift. They'll all be there, and looking the other way."

She was silent for several moments, and when she spoke there was a hint of tiredness in her whispered voice. "No, Willie. No pitched battles. I don't want to shoot any more of their mercenaries. We'll play it the way we planned, except that we can use the Goff as a lure now."

Ninety seconds. Now they could see the long jaws of the harbour, and still they had a height of two hundred feet. They slipped across the ridge with fifty feet to spare, then turned to come down the long inlet of the harbour to the boats at the jetty. They were a hundred yards away when their feet skimmed the water and they let go, dropping back together. The A-frame snagged the surface, tipping the wing forward so that the leading edges drove under the water, yet even then the polythene did not rip.

Treading water, they had to slit the envelope, releasing the air to hasten its sinking, and when it was gone they began to swim slowly and without splashing towards the boats.

*   *   *

Sam Solon and Beauregard Browne, both hastily dressed, were in the cabin at the lower end of the chair-lift when the sound came faintly from the harbour. They had arrived a few minutes before, and given orders for the machinery to be stopped. In the silence, as the guards exchanged uneasy glances and the air grew heavy with doubt and speculation, the distant sound of a powerful engine came clearly through the night.

Sam Solon, eyes like thin blue gashes, jaw muscles knotted,

said, "What the bloody hell? Everyone's here or accounted for, aren't they?"

Clarissa came into the big hut in slacks and a thin sweater. "It sounds awfully like the powerboat, Beau," she said. She looked pinched, as if with cold, but there was perspiration on her brow. The telephone in the cabin rang, and Solon picked it up. Cooper, controlling the remnants of the guards from the switchboard, said, "It's Kerenyi in the radio room, boss. He just saw the powerboat pull out of the harbour. It's moving west, so you'll see it soon."

"Right." Solon put the phone down slowly and went out, unwrapping a piece of chewing gum. The others followed. Two minutes later they saw the white wake of the Arrowbolt 21 come into view from their left, a mile off-shore, heading away at an angle.

Sam Solon said laconically, "That's Blaise and Garvin. There's nobody else it could be. Any guesses how they did it?"

There was a silence. Beauregard Browne went back into the cabin. They heard him say, "Cooper? Get through to Chater and have him watch that boat on radar. It seems Blaise and Garvin are on board. I shall want to know where to find them in a couple of hours' time, at first light." He came out of the hut and said to Solon, "From now on we know precisely where they are, and we can catch up with them in half an hour, using the Teal."

"We knew where they were on Paradise Peak. We had them bottled up there, remember?"

"Yes. But if they leave the boat, they'll eventually drown. They can't actually *go* anywhere in it."

"Why take the powerboat?"

"It was stupid. Fast, but limited range because of heavy fuel consumption."

"They weren't stupid getting off the peak."

"Indeed not, old sport. I'll pop up and see what's to be seen. Let's have your gun, Tan Sin, just in case. Clarissa, you may join me, poppet."

In the twin chair going up through the darkness she said, "They can't get away, can they, Beau?"

"Not now. Not unless they have a way of making fuel from sea water. But listen, sweetie. The Unspeakable Antipodean has taken against us. I can smell it. So we must prepare to wander off hand-in-hand into the sunset together, you and I. Which means that while I'm away with Solon, dispatching that bitch and her performing ape, you will be having a busy little time here on the island."

"All right, Beau. Tell me what you want me to do."

Twenty-five minutes later, when they came into the white house, Sam Solon was waiting for them in the living room, a drink in his hand, his manner brisk but not unfriendly.

"Did you figure it out?"

"Not at first." Beau lounged on the arm of the settee, swinging a sandalled foot with pale orange toenails. "They'd wrecked one of the glass-houses. One assumed for a purpose rather than for malice." He smiled a bright artificial smile. "Bits of the frame had been cut up, and we found pieces of polythene and various etceteras that all seemed rather baffling. But then our ever-useful Clarissa recalled seeing Garvin do that hang-gliding exhibition at the Benildon fête, and it seems probable that they actually contrived a workable thingy on which to glide down from the peak."

Sam Solon looked down into his drink. After a while he said, "Not bad."

"Rather good, in fact. One even recognises a trace of genius, though it's flawed by a lack of thinking the situation through. The powerboat wasn't a good notion at all."

299

"Maybe not. But they haven't had too many bad notions lately." He looked grey and tired. "I'll say it again. The sooner we kill 'em the better. I'm going down to my museum for an hour or so. You call me when it's time, Beau."

"Will do. And don't worry, dear old sport. They've put themselves in an impossible spot this time, in one small boat with nowhere to run. In fact they'll be out of fuel and a nice easy target."

"They've still got that rifle."

"I hadn't forgotten, and a very valuable item it is. But we have a Bren in the armoury and plenty of magazines, so you can sit in the doorway and spray them from above while we make passes out of their range. I've told Cooper to have a safety harness rigged for you—unless you'd rather I took somebody else?"

Solon looked up sharply, a glitter in his eyes. "No bloody fear. This time I'll do it myself, then I'll know it's done right."

       *   *   *

The blip on the radar screen had stopped moving long before the Teal took off. Now, with the sun creeping up over the horizon, the powerboat rested on a calm sea two thousand feet below. Beauregard Browne brought the amphibian round in a wide circle and spoke into the microphone. "All right. We've found them. Over and out."

In the radio hut Kerenyi glanced round at the red-haired girl beside him. She was big and meaty, and she smelt good. Desire stirred in him as he felt the heat of her closeness. He looked away and said, "Now it is finished."

"Yes. You'd better switch back to the usual frequency."

"Of course, hanim effendi."

He reached for the dial, and as he leaned forward she

drove the sharpened wire spoke up under his shoulder blade and into his heart.

Sam Solon focused the field glasses on the white boat below as the Teal banked round to port. "Christ!" he said harshly. "It's empty!"

"What?"

"There's nobody in the boat."

"Let us not be deceived, old sport."

"I'm bloody telling you!"

"I'll go down a bit. They'd have spotted us before we saw them, so they're probably huddled under the foredeck. Or perhaps they've hopped over the side and are lurking under the bow."

Three minutes later Solon said, "I still can't see 'em. Make a low run from aft, so I can get a look under the foredeck. Nobody's going to shoot us down."

The Teal banked more steeply, dropped, straightened, then flashed low over the boat, banking again to give Solon a view. As the nose came up he lowered the glasses, dragged a hand across his mouth and said brusquely, "There's nobody. Anywhere in or around the boat, nobody. No sharks, no people, no corpses. Nothing. But the wheel's lashed, and I saw that laser rifle lying on the seat."

"*What?*"

"Unless it's a dummy, like when we thought he chucked it over the cliff."

Beauregard Browne's mouth was tightly pursed, and there was a ring of pallor round it. He said, "I'll go in at fifty feet this time. Get a good look."

Sitting at the switchboard, Cooper said, "I've kept them all standing to, lady, except the domestic staff. They're still up at the house. Right now I got Chater and Tan Sin at air

301

control, Ludz at the harbour, Li Gomm at look-out on the point, and Kerenyi at the radio."

"Jolly good." She pondered, gently tapping the rolled up newspaper she held on the palm of her hand. "Ring Kerenyi, will you? I want a word with him."

"Sure." Cooper turned his back on her to push in the plug, and she leaned towards him.

Sam Solon lowered the glasses. "There's only the boat," he said with quiet savagery. "No Blaise. No Garvin. The wheel's lashed. The laser rifle's lying on the seat, and it's the real thing. Right? Now listen. Suppose what they did last night was to take the boat out of the harbour while we were all at the chair-lift. Then they laid her on course, lashed the wheel, and opened her up as they slipped over the side. Suppose they're back on Dragon's Claw now, knocking off what's left of us?"

Some moments later, his face very white, Beauregard Browne gave an odd laugh and said, "I don't believe it. Why put the rifle in the boat? It doesn't make sense. But I'll tell you what does make sense, regardless of anything else." He eased the nose of the amphibian down, heading in a wide circle to come towards the boat again. "We'd be out of our minds if we went back without the laser when it's there for the taking. Whoever holds that rifle has got the edge."

Ludz did not quite know what he was supposed to be doing, on duty at the harbour, but Cooper was in charge now, and he had given the order. Ludz felt uneasy, and wished he had company. It was not pleasant to be alone just now. What had happened in the last thirty-six hours was enough to make anyone nervous. It was as if a plague had swept through the island. He heard a sound, and was pleased to see the English girl arriving in a jeep. She was very good to look at, very sexy, but out of bounds, of course. Still, it was nice to look

at her breasts and at those exciting buttocks. As he moved
towards her she waved a rolled-up newspaper she was carry-
ing in friendly greeting.

The Teal rested on the water fifty yards from the powerboat. Solon sat in the open doorway on the starboard side,
his feet resting on the threshold, a cocked submachine-gun in
his hands. Beauregard Browne pushed the small inflatable
clear of the plane and picked up the paddle. The Colt automatic which had belonged to the Reverend Uriah Crisp was
stuck in his waist-band. He knew that such a precaution was
unnecessary, and was sure Solon knew the M-10 was unnecessary too, but neither man had mocked the other.
Modesty Blaise and Willie Garvin were either on Dragon's
Claw island now or mysteriously dead by drowning. Yet it
was a comfort to have the gun at his waist, to have Solon
covering him ...

Carefully he began to paddle towards the Arrowbolt 21.
Unless he concentrated, he found that his mind kept going
blank for a moment or two. It was very disconcerting. Keeping a tight hold on his thoughts, he told himself that Clarissa
would be all right. Even if Blaise and Garvin took her by surprise, they would not kill her. There was a dangerous soft
spot in them both. She would be all right. She might even
manage to take care of them more successfully than the
guards had done. She was a uniquely able girl ...

Solon watched the dinghy. It had travelled no more than
twenty yards when a hand gripped his ankle with shocking
strength and he was jerked forward. The M-10 smashed
against his chest as he hit the water flat, then it was gone.
The hand took him by the nape of the neck, lifting and turning his head. He glimpsed a half-naked torso in a wet black
shirt, a leather harness on the chest bearing two sheaths but
only one knife; above it, the head of Willie Garvin, scuba

303

mask pushed up on his brow, an aqualung strapped to his back, the mouthpiece hanging free, one hand raised to grip the threshold of the plane, bright blue eyes pitiless and bitter.

It was the last sight Solon was ever to know. Willie said with quiet but ferocious contempt. "She was a friend. She'd 've gone through fire for you." He flung Solon face down on the water again. In the same instant he released his hold on the threshold of the Teal and brought that arm scything down like a felling axe, the hand striking with the force of a great blunt blade to the back of Solon's neck.

Beauregard Browne had heard the first heavy splash. As his head jerked round, the dinghy lurched suddenly sideways and great bubbles began to gurgle from the air chamber. Next moment he was in the water, clutching in sudden terror at the high density nylon of the dinghy where some buoyancy still remained. A scuba-masked head broke the surface a few yards away. He saw the shimmering of her black-clad body below the water, and when she lifted her hands to push the mask up and take out her mouthpiece, he saw that she held one of Willie Garvin's knives, and knew she had used it to slice open the dinghy from below.

Beauregard Browne made the greatest effort of his life and smiled at her from a face white and stiff as plaster. "So *there* you are, sweetie. Where on earth did you get the aqualungs?"

She trod water, watching him sombrely. "Willie found them in the boat store when he broke out the night before last. He put them aboard ready for us."

Hatred ate into him like acid. "Oh, come now, poppet, don't try to tell me you had this all planned."

"I'm not trying to tell you anything."

The crumpled dinghy was slowly sinking. With an arm hooked over the dwindling bulge of air he tried to heave himself up a little as he said in a voice suddenly shrill, "It's lovely talking to you, darling, but actually I have a slight problem. I don't swim, you see, and I'll be going under in a second or two if you don't lend a hand rather soon."

She looked at him from remote, dark blue eyes. "That saves me a nasty job, because leaving you to die a long death isn't our style."

Like a gash in the white face, his mouth opened in a scream, head tilted back, long lashes curling up from violet eyes now bulging as terror shattered his pretence of calm. His free hand came up from beneath the surface, holding the Colt automatic. He shook water from the barrel, then lowered the gun to aim with downward angled wrist at her submerged body.

Reluctantly she said, "Willie." From twenty feet the knife took him in the side of the neck, driving home almost to the hilt. His hand fell limply with the gun, and as it did so the last of the air escaped in one small bubble, turning him sideways. The bright golden head went down and the body rolled. A sandalled foot with pale orange toenails showed briefly. Then nothing.

Modesty had already slipped off her aqualung and weight-belt, letting them sink, and was swimming towards the Arrowbolt. Less than a minute later Willie reached down to take the Goff rifle and their shoes from her, then lifted her easily into the Teal. "There may not be a shark for twenty miles," he said, relieved, "but now there's blood in the water I'm glad you were quick, Princess."

She sat squeezing water from her clothes and said, "Yes. They scare me."

Later, when the Teal had taken off, Willie checked the instruments before turning to look at her as he said, "What about Clarissa and Dr. Feng?"

She smoothed her wet hair back and shook her head with a little grimace. "Only if we have to, Willie. I know that's what I said, but I've had enough."

*　　*　　*

Clarissa de Courtney-Scott watched the amphibian touch down and roll along the landing strip. To her surprise it continued to the small hangar and through the doors. That was odd. Beau always left it to be towed in.

She climbed into the jeep and drove towards the hangar, feeling very well content. Beau would be jolly pleased with her. She had taken care of everybody left on Dragon's Claw, including the house staff. Everybody except Dr. Feng. She had not yet found him, and knew that he must have become suspicious. Never mind. She and Beau would find him, and then it was just a question of waiting for the Gulfstream to arrive in an hour or so from Sydney. The crew were Sam Solon's men, but they were in no position to rush off and talk to the police. They'd have to do whatever Beau told them to. He was good at making people do that.

She brought the jeep to a halt by the corner of the hangar, and as she did so Willie Garvin stepped out. He held the laser rifle at waist height, the deadly red dot from it showing on her chest. Beside him, Modesty Blaise said, "Get out."

She stared with total incomprehension, her mind blank, and said at last, "Where's Beau?"

"I said get out. You're going to use the loud-hailer to tell the guards that Browne's dead and Solon's dead. It's all finished here. The only thing left for them is to get rid of their guns before the Australian Security men arrive, and try to pretend they were just maintenance staff here. We'll back up those who do."

"Dead? Beau can't be dead."

"He is."

"Not Beau." The wide green eyes were glazed, and the voice was growing tighter, shriller with every word. "Not Beau. I mean, that's not possible. Beau always makes things come out right. He can't actually be dead ..."

She began to make an eerie mewing noise, in time with her exhalations. It grew louder and became an intermittent scream. Willie lowered the rifle, moved to the jeep, leaned over, and slapped her sharply across the face twice. She stopped screaming and slumped over the wheel with head bowed, saying in a querulous voice through chattering teeth, "Not Beau. You can't have killed Beau. It's one of his tricks, I expect ..."

Willie turned to look at Modesty. "She's not going to be any 'elp, Princess. It's a bit weird, with no sign of anyone around."

"We'll talk to them over the loud-hailer, Willie—"

The shot came from very close, and the sound was of a heavy calibre handgun. Willie was spinning, dropping to one knee, and the Star automatic was in Modesty's hand as Dr. Feng emerged from behind the corner of the hangar, lifting both hands high and with a smoking revolver in one.

"I was trying to decide how to present myself to you without being shot," he said. "And then ..." His gaze was on the jeep. Clarissa de Courtney-Scott lay sprawled face down across the wing in an uncompleted lunge. Her right hand still gripped the wooden handle in which the long, needle-pointed bicycle spoke was set. On the white shirt she wore there was now a black, red-rimmed hole between her shoulder blades.

Dr. Feng said, "I do not claim to have saved your life, Mr.

Garvin. You are very quick, and she was not able to choose her position, but it is possible I have prevented an unpleasant injury." The black eyes moved to Modesty. "Under the circumstances I am hoping you will reconsider your promise to destroy all who sat at table with you yesterday."

Willie moved forward and took the revolver from him. A single bead of sweat trickled down Dr. Feng's brow and into the corner of his eye, but he did not blink. Modesty holstered the automatic and said, "You're off the hook. Put your hands down, Feng. Where's everybody?"

Dr. Feng looked at the splendid body sprawled across the jeep. "You will not need a loud-hailer," he said. "In the past hour she has murdered the remaining guards, one by one, using that very effective weapon. She has also wiped out the three Indonesian domestic staff with a submachine-gun, and for the last ten minutes before you arrived she was trying to find and dispose of me. I have no doubt that Beauregard Browne had instructed her, and that he intended to kill Mr. Solon before returning here in the amphibian—after disposing of you, of course. I hid myself here in the hope that I might . . ." he gestured diffidently, "might have the advantage of him when he arrived."

Modesty said softly, "God Almighty, what a bunch." She rubbed her eyes hard, and for a moment Willie saw the sick tiredness in her. Then it was gone. He allowed no sympathy or concern to touch him. It was not time yet, and any sign of it would have angered her. She put hands on her hips and looked at Dr. Feng. "Keep out of our way, and make up your own story," she said, then turned away from him. "All right, Willie love. Let's get ready for the last bit."

*   *   *

It was an hour before noon when the Gulfstream, its radio calls unanswered, came down from a blue and white sky to sweep along the runway. As it touched down, a jeep pulled out and followed a hundred yards behind, closing up on the port side as the aircraft came to a halt.

The howl of the twin Rolls-Royce Spey engines died, and at once a Cockney voice speaking through a loud-hailer came clearly to all in the plane. "Attention, Gulfstream crew! Do not, repeat NOT open doors until instructed. Watch the ground fifty yards dead ahead."

Something dark and cylindrical soared through the air, turning end over end; a bottle, with a flame curving from something tied about its neck. When it hit the ground there was an explosive gout of fire which settled to a pool of flame. The loud metallic voice said, "That was one molotov cocktail. We've got a dozen ready 'ere, plus small arms. Now you can open the door, and we want to see the man in charge, with his hands up, and nobody else. Right. Now do it."

Thirty seconds later the integral airstair door opened. A man in his fifties stood there, hands at shoulder height. He wore a suit of fine brown check and had thick black hair streaked with grey above a strong face with a massive square chin.

After the whine of the engines and the squawking of the loud-hailer it was very quiet on the airstrip of Dragon's Claw. The newcomer, from his position in the doorway, looked down upon a man and woman in damp sea-stained clothes standing ten paces away behind a jeep. The woman held a submachine-gun aimed. The man held a bottle with a short wick of rope tied to the neck in one hand, a home-made paraffin torch alight in the other. Several more molotov cocktails were ranged on the bonnet of the jeep in front of him.

The man in the doorway said, "We got your message. I'm Larry Houston. Internal Security."

Bright blue eyes and midnight blue eyes surveyed him without goodwill. Then the dark-haired girl with the long lovely neck and smudges under her eyes said, "We've had a lot of trouble lately from trusting people. Say a little more."

The man said patiently, "We got a message the night before last on the frequency Tarrant gave you. Reception was bad, and parts of the message came out corrupt when deciphered. But we got a frequency for listening out, and we picked up another message on that frequency yesterday. It took our cryptologists a while to crack the cipher. The message was from Sam Solon, telling his agent in Sydney to send a supply of grenades and other military stores out here to Dragon's Claw island this morning. It tied up with the parts that weren't corrupt in the message you sent earlier. We went to talk to Solon's chief pilot, and found the plane being loaded. He tried to run when we started looking in the crates." Houston pointed a thumb behind him. "So I'm here with a sergeant and ten soldiers from an infantry regiment."

The girl put down the gun on the bonnet of the jeep. The big fair man was treading out the wick and the torch under his heel. Houston lowered his hands and said, "I've assumed you're Modesty Blaise and Willie Garvin."

The girl said, "That's right. By all means have your men disembark now, Mr. Houston, but there's not much soldiering to do. Sam Solon and his friends got into a hassle and killed each other off. We're all that's left. Oh, and a Chinaman, Dr. Feng. We don't know where he fits in. Maybe he was a prisoner, like us."

Thirty minutes later Larry Houston stood with Willie Garvin in the lofty underground museum where tall arched windows looked out upon the sea. For some time they had been moving slowly and in silence round the exhibits, with the Australian trying to keep dazed incredulity from showing in his face. At last he said, "All right, Willie, I've seen it. Now what's the story?"

Willie Garvin lifted a shoulder. "All we know is what they told us, Mr. Houston. Solon 'ad a gang that nicked all this stuff for 'im. He needed to show it to someone, so he picked on people like Luke Fletcher and Maria Cavalli and one or two others. He got 'is 'eavy mob to snatch 'em, and enjoyed a nice gloat showing 'em 'is treasures. But he couldn't send 'em back, so he gave 'em to a barmy parson for target practice."

Houston stared moodily at the Fabergé collection. "Maybe Dr. Feng can fill in the picture. He says he's been held here under duress for a long time, though he doesn't seem to know why. Where's Modesty?"

"Gone to 'ave a bath."

"We had you both tagged as being in Hobart."

"Yes, Solon 'ad ringers for us walk off the plane at Sydney. They must've gone on to Hobart."

Houston moved on to look at the Gobelin tapestry. "You two were pretty lucky not to end up as targets for the barmy parson. Or for that nice girl with the bicycle spoke."

"Certainly were," Willie agreed warmly.

"But you did break out the night before last?"

"That's right, and I managed to get that message off to you before they caught me. After that we were locked up in a cell, and that's when Solon and Browne fell out, I suppose. Some of the guards on one side, some on the other."

Larry Houston nodded. "Quite a quarrel. Not a single survivor."

"They must 've gone at it 'ammer and tongs all right."

There came the sound of the lift doors, and a moment later Modesty walked through from the ante-room. She had evidently found her belongings, for she had changed into a skirt and a cotton polo top. She looked scrubbed from her bath, with no make-up. Her hair had been brushed and was tied loosely back. She said, "Do you think we can leave here today, Mr. Houston?"

He studied her with profound interest. "I'll be staying here myself until someone comes out to take over." He looked about him. "There's going to be a lot of coming and going here for a while. But I'll send you and Willie back to Sydney today, and I'll join you very shortly. We'll see the media don't get this until we've decided how to handle it. Maybe we can keep you out of it altogether."

"We'd be very grateful."

There was a haunted look about her eyes, he thought. Aloud he said, "You've had a pretty rough time."

"No. We didn't get hurt, and it wasn't really bad for us." She looked at Willie. "Let's wait on the balcony until it's time to go. You could catch up with some sleep there, Willie. You haven't had much lately."

"Sounds fine, Princess." He smiled and took her arm, knowing what oppressed her. It was not what had happened to her in the past two days. Throughout the whole of her remembered life, fear had been a regular companion, and this she could handle. But now that the time of danger was past she was plagued by her imaginings, by the mental picture of those who had died in Execution Square and who were unlike herself, in that they were not armoured and equipped against such horror.

Take a woman like Gwen Westwood or Maria Cavalli. Put her through the shock of kidnap, of imprisonment, through the torment of being in the hands of Beauregard Browne and his followers. And finally, put a gun in her hand and stand her in the square to watch the wild-eyed, ranting figure of the Reverend Uriah Crisp coming steadily down the steps to kill her. To the ordinary man or woman, unschooled in violence, defenceless, hopeless, alone, it would be terrifying beyond description.

Willie Garvin knew what Modesty would do now. She would sit on the balcony while he slept, and look down at the square, conjuring up those hideous scenes in her mind until the horror was fully realised. Then, if they were alone, perhaps she would turn to him when he woke, and weep silently on his shoulder for a little while. She would dry her tears, close her eyes, and sink into a coma-like sleep for an hour or more. Then it would be over for her. Finished. The ghosts laid, the haunting ended, the past expelled.

As they reached the lift Larry Houston said from behind them, "Did Browne and Solon get killed in this civil war? The soldiers haven't reported finding either of them yet."

They stopped and turned. Willie screwed up his eyes in thought. Modesty pinched her lower lip. They looked at each other, then Modesty said, "It was all over by the time we broke out, but Willie has a hunch that they both took off together in one of the boats."

"Patched up their differences?"

"That's hard to say."

"You reckon it's worth looking for them?"

She shook her head slowly. "I wouldn't bother, Mr. Houston. I'm sure you won't find them."

The trap-like mouth above the big chin spread suddenly in a grin. "Nice going," said Houston. "Tarrant said you were dependable."

15

"If there's one thing I cannot stand," said Judith Rigby, "it's these ghastly carol-singing rehearsals in this freezing hall."

"It's only for an hour, darling," her husband said consolingly. "You should have put something warmer on."

"Thank you, George. I shall remember that for next year." She glanced across the hall. "I note that we're honoured by the presence of visiting gentry."

"That's because John Cranwell invited them. We needed a few more voices."

The vicar turned from his consultation with the pianist and said, "Could we try *Hark! the Herald Angels Sing* just once more, ladies and gentlemen? Then we'll take a break for coffee."

The thirty-odd men and women grouped in a rough half-moon before the low platform lifted their duplicated sheets, the pianist played an introduction, and the carol was sung. Among the voices in the village hall were the very good baritone of Sir Gerald Tarrant and the excellent contralto of Lady Janet Gillam.

"Thank you, ladies and gentlemen, that was very nice," said the vicar. "We'll try *Wenceslas* and *While Shepherds Watched* after the coffee."

The carol singers relaxed and there was a buzz of conversation. The vicar made his way to one end of the half-moon and spoke to a dark-haired girl in a leather coat. She was with a group of four, and as she turned to him her eyes were full of laughter at something the girl with short chestnut hair had just finished saying.

"Good evening, Miss Blaise. I just wanted to say how pleased we are to see you here with your guests."

She smiled. "I bludgeoned them into it, Mr. Cranwell, just as you bludgeoned me when you called the other day."

"Oh, come now. You were very easily persuaded, I'm glad to say."

"That's because I was counting on my friends. The truth is, I can't reach either the high or the low notes, so I just have to mime all the time. So does Mr. Garvin."

"You're joking, surely. There was some splendid singing from this direction."

"All from our friends." She indicated the older man the vicar knew to be Sir Gerald Tarrant, and the tall girl with a limp who was whispered to be Lady Janet Something.

"I'm sorry you can't actually participate, but do please continue." The vicar clicked his fingers. "I have an idea. Will you excuse me for a moment?"

He moved off briskly. Three ladies appeared with trays of coffee. Willie Garvin slipped a flask from the pocket of his fur-lined jacket and said, "It'll need tweaking up a bit to keep the cold out."

Janet said, "Lovely. I'm enjoying this. People seem to groan at the prospect of Christmas these days, but I love it. I've a childish liking for all the trappings and traditions."

Modesty laughed. "I was too cowardly to say it first, but I feel exactly the same. I get really excited, especially if the weather's right. I'm longing for it to snow, so that when we go out carol singing on Christmas Eve everything will be white, with big snow-flakes falling. I've got Weng busy fixing up lanterns on sticks, just like the pictures on Christmas cards, and I've bought a white fur hood to wear. Willie, I was wondering if we could push a portable coke brazier round with us somehow. Think how lovely it would look."

Tarrant said, "And you claim you were bludgeoned into this?"

Modesty shook her head, holding out her cup of coffee for Willie to lace with brandy. "I was lying. I did say no at first, but then I remembered you and Janet would be here. I knew from Willie that Janet had a real voice, and Fraser once told me that you'd sung in amateur opera when young, so then I jumped at the chance to join in. Anyway, he's a nice sort of vicar." She half smiled, a little absently. "Much better than the last one."

Janet said, "But I understand this one has been here ten years."

"Oh, I didn't mean the previous vicar here. I meant the one I—" She stopped, and gave a dismissing shrug. "I had a brush with a clerical gent recently, that's all."

"Some of them can be rather irritating," said Tarrant easily.

The vicar reappeared and said, "Excuse me, but if you won't actually be singing on Christmas Eve, would you and Mr. Garvin help with the collecting? Just a matter of knocking on doors and persuading people to part with as much money as possible."

"I'm sure they'll be marvellously good at it," Lady Janet said soberly, and flickered an eyelid at Tarrant.

"Splendid. May I carry them off just for a moment to introduce them to Mrs. Rigby? She's in charge of the collecting, you see."

When Modesty and Willie had been ushered away, Tarrant said, "She's relishing the mundane, isn't she?" He looked about him and went on softly, "Has Willie told you anything about what happened on Dragon's Claw?"

"Very little." She moved closer. There were bonds between herself and Tarrant, for both had come very near to death at the hands of the same ruthless men. She said, "I think they hated it all so much they don't want to speak of it, apart from something to do with building a hang-glider. Willie told me of that. As for the rest, I wouldn't ask direct, but I just pick up wee bits that emerge now and then, and I try to fit them in with what I've read in the papers. That man Solon, the one they made friends with, he tricked them, didn't he? So I think it must have been an awful close thing, and I know it was all mixed up with that poor man Luke Fletcher being murdered. Have you found out much from Modesty?"

"Not a great deal, apart from the thing with the hang-glider and some remarkable break-out feat of Willie's. She almost started to say something about a vicar just now, and that ties in with an extraordinary thing my contact in Australia passed on to me. I'll tell you as soon as there's a chance. The rest is guesses. I'm quite sure they destroyed the people who murdered Luke Fletcher—and another friend of theirs, Dick Kingston. But under what circumstances, and what happened during those two days on Dragon's Claw, I've yet to discover."

"Let's make a project of it over Christmas," said Lady Janet. "We're not the only guests, they have the Colliers arriving tomorrow, and they'll help. Do you know them?"

"Very well. Steve has the nerve to demand a complete report from Modesty, and I think Dinah might coax something out of Willie."

"Aye, he has a big soft spot for her. And then we'll have a secret get-together and pool our findings." She gave a little laugh, as if at herself. "The reason I want to know what happened is that I'm disgustingly inquisitive. What's your reason, Sir Gerald?"

"The same, my dear. The same."

"Oh, I was thinking it might be official. But you're retired now, of course."

"Not exactly. My successor elect had a heart attack last week, and the Minister has asked me to remain for six months while they find somebody else."

"Don't. Och, that was very impudent. I'm sorry."

"Not at all. We're old friends." He finished his coffee and brandy. "I must say both Modesty and Willie look well and happy, whatever may have happened to them on that island."

"Yes. They have an enviable knack of starting to live the rest of their lives from the present moment, whenever that may be. And here they come, so what we've been talking about is singing descants on the third verse."

Willie was grinning. As they came up Modesty said, "He told Mrs. Rigby we'd probably do better if we wore stockings over our heads and carried guns."

"It would be more in character," Tarrant acknowledged.

"Mrs. Rigby wasn't amused."

The vicar clapped his hands. The buzz of conversation died, except for a female voice somewhere trailing into silence with, "If there's one thing I cannot stand ..."

"Off we go, ladies and gentlemen," said the vicar, and raised a hand ready to beat time as the pianist began his introduction.

Modesty Blaise and Willie Garvin watched him with great attention and prepared to mouth the words. Sir Gerald Tarrant glanced sideways at Lady Janet Gillam, and they exchanged a conspiratorial smile. Then, as the vicar's hand came down, they launched themselves enthusiastically into the singing of *Good King Wenceslas*.